NEVER BEEN IN THE SAND

Part I

A Tomas O'Malley Story

KENNETH S. KAPPELMANN

Black Rose Writing | Texas

ISBN: 978-1-68433-629-6
PUBLISHED BY BLACK ROSE WRITING
www.blackrosewriting.com

Printed in the United States of America
Suggested Retail Price (SRP) $19.95

Never Been in the Sand is printed in Garamond Premier Pro

*As a planet-friendly publisher, Black Rose Writing does its best to eliminate unnecessary waste to reduce paper usage and energy costs, while never compromising the reading experience. As a result, the final word count vs. page count may not meet common expectations.

This book is dedicated to the
2020 Superbowl Champion, Kansas City Chiefs

NEVER BEEN IN THE SAND

Part I

1 The man slammed his hand down on the large mahogany desk. "What the hell do you mean, you're not sure? Either he has our back or he doesn't. There's no *maybe* when it comes to the actions we've taken."

"Hey, just a minute, sir," the other man replied. "We all agreed going into this. We never asked for his buy-in. We all talked and agreed he was too much of a Boy Scout. Had we brought him into the loop, this process would have never gotten past first base. We are circling third now, and there is no way to go back to second or first. Either we go for home or we go to jail."

"Well, there's no goddamn way I am going to jail. Do you know what that would do to our stock and our shareholders? They would bring a class action lawsuit against the company and all of us. We would be ruined and the company would take a billion dollar hit. I need to understand the options."

The two other men in the large and immaculate office paced around a few steps and then stared at each other, evaluating who was going to respond. The one who had just spoken walked over to the bar and poured himself a whiskey on the rocks and instantly swallowed it hard. He turned back to the other two. "What do you think?" he asked, passing the buck to his counterpart.

The other man pressed his lips together tight, annoyed that he was now put on the spot. He turned and walked toward the bar as well, but did not pour a drink. He used the chance he had turned away to mouth the words, *fuck you*, to his partner. He turned back to the man still sitting with his hands pressed against his desk staring back to him. "I think we only have two options: We kill him, or we get his buy-in."

"No shit," replied his boss. "My question is, *can* you get his buy-in? I have worked with this man my entire career. We came up through the ranks together. We built this company to what it is today with my business acumen and his science. We are friends. If you're telling me I have to kill my friend, I want to be damn sure there are no other options."

They looked at each other and could tell that no answer would be received well. The first man poured himself another drink and stepped back up to the front of the desk. "Here it is, straight up. We can talk to him and risk having him go to the police, the SEC, the FDA, or a variety of other government entities, which will result in everyone in this room going to jail and the stock price in the toilet. Or I can talk to the same man who handled our previous issue and this can all go away."

There was a long silence in the room before the man behind the desk spoke again. "Nothing makes everything go away. You eliminate my longtime friend and there will be an investigation. He has ties to the medical community and the Chicago Police Department. He goes down, and it will be like killing one of their own."

"Yes, there is risk," the man replied. "But my guy is a professional. Remember the Polino and Moretti case last year? He was their guy and walked away untouched. This guy cleans up messes. He comes with a steep price, but you get what you pay for."

"There is no price I wouldn't pay to make this problem disappear. In a handful of months we stand to make so many millions on the trial results, and from that point on, the success of the drug is immaterial." His response was said with some inflection that indicated he was in deliberation with himself. The two men knew what he was comparing—killing his longtime friend to protect himself, or risking bringing him into the loop on something so illegal it crossed every line, including murder.

The man with the now empty glass in his hand broke the silence. "So, are you asking me to make this go away, or do you want me to call him into your office for a private discussion?"

The man behind the desk now stood and walked slowly over to the bar. He pulled out a bottle of Crown Black and poured some on a couple pieces of ice. He took a small drink and turned back to four eyes locked on his every move. He took a deep breath and stared back toward the man with the empty glass. "Make the problem go away." He finished his drink.

* * * * *

"So, are you going to tell your spouse that we're together?"

"Are you going to tell yours?" the man asked in return.

"You have more to lose financially. I'll be fine with a divorce. Once you take your action, I will take mine." She walked over to him, her naked body pressing up against his causing him to feel things start to move. "Do you want to be together?" she said in her sultry voice.

"Of course I do. You know that."

She smiled. "Then there's nothing stopping us. Just two divorces, some fights with lawyers, a few real estate transactions, and we're there." She squeezed him tight pushing all air out between their bodies. They were like one.

"Okay. After this weekend, I'll talk to her." They kissed and fell back into the bed.

•　　•　　•　　•　　•

The Day of the Party—Saturday

I pulled into the circular drive in the Barrington Hills home of Doctor Elise Gerstenberger and Doctor Alan Grove. It was easily going to be the largest house I had ever been inside. When she sent me the address, I went ahead and Googled it and found on Zillow that it was currently valued at 14.7 million dollars. Now, a typical medical examiner would never have that kind of money, but when you consider she also operated a private practice where she owned the building and acted simply as president with her team of doctors performing the daily medical duties, that got her more into this high-end neighborhood. However, it was her husband who, although also a medical doctor, went the pharmaceutical route and was near the top of the food chain at one of the largest companies in the country, Abbunex Labs, which really solidified their financial mark. Together they eclipsed what anyone else I knew made, but when it came to my good friend Elise, she would just as soon have an Old Style tall boy at a Cub's game than pour from a $500 bottle of wine.

I was fairly close with Doc G, as everyone called her, mainly because I had worked with her for more than twenty years. She was the only Chief Chicago Medical Examiner I had ever known. Yes, I worked with other M.E.'s at different times, but just as most of the larger homicide cases seemed to come my way, they did to her as well. In all those years, we had been out for a few drinks, we had shared a few hard times involving colleagues' deaths or cases gone south, even hit a ball game or two, but never had I been to her house. Until one week ago, while leaving a crime scene in downtown Chicago, she asked the very innocent question in passing: *"Hey, Tommy, we're having a dinner party next Saturday. Any chance you want to come? It's going to* be all my husband's cronies and I need someone I can kick back a beer with when nobody is looking. By all means, bring Tammi if she's in town."

I was caught so much off guard I instantly replied that I would be there. Now, as I drove up the long private drive and then glanced down at the suit I was wearing compared to the tuxedo-clad valet (yes, they hired a valet service to park cars), I realized I was out of my element. I then glanced to the empty passenger seat of my 1974 shit-brown Camaro and knew it was going to be a long night.

I exited the car and the young man, probably about twenty years old, came up to me. "You alone tonight, sir?"

Way to put salt on the wound. "Yep, just me tonight."

"Three-fifty small block?" he asked.

I turned, surprised at the engine reference. "Exactly," I replied.

"Is it all original?" he asked.

This was getting a little weird, I thought. My father was the original owner of this car. It was bought in 1974 directly from Chevrolet. He gave it to me when I graduated from college. Now I had a kid in front of a million dollar house, parking cars valued at greater than seventy-five to a hundred thousand dollars asking specifics about my old Camaro that I might be able to get two thousand for from the right person. "My father bought it new. Neither he nor I have done anything to it that would make it special. The engine was rebuilt two years ago, but all stock. You must like cars."

He smiled and took the keys. "I would much rather work on this car than go anywhere near any of these others." He panned his hand across the driveway where I saw multiple BMWs, Mercedes, and even a Ferrari.

"I see what you're saying," I replied, stepping aside.

"I'm working through mechanics school. I want to open my own shop someday. Right now, I make some money at Jiffy Lube and then use this valet job to make sure I can pay my bills."

"Well, feel free to take her for a spin, but once you sit behind the wheel, you will never want to leave."

We both smiled and he plopped himself into the front seat and immediately hit the gas with the car still in park. The engine fired loud and actually sounded pretty damn good. "If the car is not here when you come out, can I consider it my tip?"

I reached in my pocket and pulled out my badge. "If you think that's a good choice, absolutely."

He held his smile and stuttered just a bit. "I guess there's a good chance it will be here." He pulled out without another word. I turned back when I heard the engine shut down immediately. I shook my head. The kid had parked it diagonally in the very front spot. Every person attending this party would be looking at my Camaro and wondering why the hell that car was parked there. I loved it.

I glanced at my phone and saw that I had successfully just killed three minutes. If I could just do that another sixty times, I could get out of here somewhat unscathed. I walked up toward the front door where another tuxedo-clad man, this one much older and who looked like a black-and-white tree, was there to greet me.

"Invitation, sir?" Tree said in a voice that sounded exactly like the male version of my British GPS voice.

I am sure I looked surprised. "I actually don't have an invitation. Elise Gerstenberger invited me personally at work."

Tree did not look pleased with this response and he went out of his way to show it. He leaned over to a second person who was standing just inside the doorway, whispered something then turned back to me. "Your name please, sir."

I always thrived for that question, but never in a situation quite so perfect. Like my not-so-good friend and district attorney, James Esson, who always used the James Bond response, I followed suit. "O'Malley, Tomas O'Malley."

Again Tree seemed put off but he did not speak further. The other man disappeared inside and Tree shut the door behind him leaving me and him alone on the front entry staring at my car and my valet, who had been joined by a second valet during this exchange. They were pointing at my beast of a vehicle and I actually believe the kid was bragging that he parked it.

I looked up to Tree. "That's my ride," I said pointing.

I believe he issued some sort of grunt or moan, but nothing in the form of an actual word. I am sure it was because he was so impressed that he was speechless.

It was only a few seconds later when the door opened and out popped Doctor Elise Gerstenberger. "Tommy, I can't believe you came," she said reaching out her arms. "I have been in there hoping someone I could hang with would get here. Fiiinnnaaalllyyy you arrived."

Her initial comment made me feel like I had no business being here, but after that, it sounded pretty damn good, like I would not be hiding in a corner all night. "No problem. Your man here just did not want to let me in without an invitation— probably thought I was overdressed."

"Oh, shoot. My fault, Holden," she said turning to Tree. "Mr. Tomas O'Malley is definitely with me."

I am not sure if Tree, or Holden as I now heard, was pleased or upset. I think he was looking to throw me out which would have been an interesting sight. His lips pinched together before releasing with a smile. "No problem, Doctor Gerstenberger. I just wanted to verify."

She smiled and placed her hand on his arm as she passed, leading me inside. I accidently brushed by the same arm making more contact than I probably had intended but not saying "excuse me" or "sorry" either. Tree was just doing his job, but nobody was trying to break into this party. It was not like it was the Academy Awards or anything with red carpet rolled out, and if someone was going to try to infiltrate the house, doing it in a 1974 shit-brown Camaro would not be part of the plan.

When I broke the plane of the doorway, I just about shit my pants. That is a completely unprofessional thing to say, so by just thinking it instead of saying it, I felt I was very proper. This house and this party were just like what you would see in the movies. Everyone was dressed as if they were receiving Oscars later that night. There were individuals delivering champagne and hors d'oeuvres on trays. Most of the food items were things I would never even consider ordering at a restaurant, which basically meant the food stunk. There were people all through the entryway, or *foyer*, as she called it. However, this foyer was larger than my entire apartment. There were people talking, laughing louder than they should be to draw attention to themselves, and basically trying to be seen. It was clear I knew nobody in this place except Doc G and her husband, and it was also clear my Men's Warehouse suit was not going to cut the mustard in the best-dressed contest. No wonder Tree looked down on me.

"Come with me, Tommy, I want to show you the ballroom. My husband flew in the house band from the Majestic Steak House in Kansas City." She turned and smiled. "You are from Kansas, right? Do you know the restaurant?"

"No, I'm afraid not. Kansas City was not my home and by the sound of it, the Majestic was not my normal stomping ground."

"Well, Alan went there for a pharmaceutical conference and it was right by his hotel. I guess the basement of the restaurant is an old jazz club from the early 1900s and he loved the band so much that he wanted them to play at this party, and you know my husband, what Alan wants he can usually get. You have to hear this band. They're amazing."

We were standing at the far end of the foyer that led to a large staircase that split halfway up to curve into two directions. Behind the staircase, below a huge chandelier, were two sets of double doors. It appeared like we were walking toward an auditorium to watch a Broadway play or something. However, when we got to the doors, they opened to a large ballroom. On the far side was a stage where, as expected, a jazz band was playing with a mix of couples watching and dancing on the floor in front. The acoustics were incredible, and to be honest, I could not have been more out of place. Doc G took my arm and wrapped it through hers to give the impression I was leading her in. It was pathetic that I could not take the lead in any fashion, but I was a fish out of water, and she knew it.

"I don't show this at work, do I?" she asked.

"Doc," I replied, "you don't show this at all. We have kicked back with cheap beers in every seedy bar in downtown Chicago, not to mention at a baseball game on occasion. I had no idea you could've *bought* the team."

She smiled as I had started speaking but then it turned to more of a frown of embarrassment. "Please keep it a secret for me?" She looked at me and I saw something in her eyes that I liked. It was trust. She invited me because she could trust me.

"Your secret is safe with me," I replied. "But I have to be honest. You didn't have to invite me. I would be more comfortable at a prostate exam."

She laughed but did not acknowledge the last comment and focused on the one before. "The reason I brought you here was not just for the band." She kept walking toward the far side. "This bar over here has both Wild Turkey and McNaughton's. When we met after Clark died, you seemed to like the Canadian brand so I keep it stocked now. It's been a hit with almost everyone."

Instantly I softened. "It's about time. I can't believe I've already walked this far without a drink in hand."

We made our way to the bar with half a dozen people greeting Elise on the way and sizing me up in the process. I am sure *Who the hell is the creepy guy in the cheap suit?* came to several of their minds, but to her credit, Doc G did not care. It was at the bar when her husband, Dr. Alan Grove, made his way over, a band of three well-dressed men by his side.

He leaned in and kissed his wife on her cheek. "You look fabulous, honey." He turned to me. "Tommy, we're so glad you could make it. Have you tried the McNaughton's?"

I lifted my glass with one hand and shook hands with the other. "Trying it now, and thank you very much for including me." I paused, then remembered one of the conversation starters I had tried to think of on my way north. "You know, Dr. Grove, I met your father." I had met his father, the Minneapolis Chief Medical Examiner, on a case that took me to Lakeville, Minnesota, a few months ago.

Alan smiled. "Yes, both Elise and my dad told me about your paths crossing—one of those small world things."

He stopped right there and said nothing more. So much for my conversation starter.

Elise felt the break and quickly interjected. "Gentlemen, this is Detective Tomas O'Malley, a close friend and colleague of mine."

"Yes," Alan took over quickly. "And please excuse my rudeness for not introducing everyone. Detective O'Malley is probably the most well-known and successful Chicago homicide detective since Jack Muller." The group seemed instantly impressed, though I was sure not one of them knew who Jack Muller was. I barely knew the obscure reference to the man best known for writing parking tickets to every famous person in Chicago. An alleged 15,000 tickets written over his career and to the best of my knowledge not ever in homicide, so the reference was not only obscure, it was wrong. Alan introduced everyone in the group, and each shook my hand as he went. "Doctor Reed Anderson, President of R&D, Julian T. Stover, Chief Financial Officer, and this is Doctor Darryn Hermann, CEO."

"It's a pleasure to meet you all," I replied politely.

"I'll bet you have some stories," Darryn stated.

I was a little caught off guard but Elise was not going to let this crew put me anywhere she did not think I wanted to be. "Come on, boys, Tommy just got here. This is his first drink. The stories will get so much better in an hour or so. Give me a chance to show him around."

"Very well," Alan replied. "But Tommy, have Elise bring you by the study around ten. I just got some cigars that I think you will die for."

I smiled and gave the impression I would be all over that, however, Elise knew I strongly was against smoking, especially cigars. My father had smoked for the better part of forty years and my mother had recently died from complications related to emphysema. Smoking was not on my top ten list, to say the least. That being said, I would like to see the study. Other than playing a game of *Clue*, I had no idea what a study actually was. I think I may have been in a study in Naperville on a case once, but that may also have been a den. Bottom line, I wanted to go. Someday when I had a study, I would absolutely keep a lead pipe or candlestick in it just in case.

Elise used the next forty-five minutes to give me a walking tour of the place. The party was basically restricted to the first floor, excluding the kitchen and a wing to the east which she said led to the indoor pool and patio area. It was too cold outside to use the patio area. She told me about another party they had where the pool became a negative, so they have closed that area off, except for an occasional pool party in the summer.

I was truly impressed with the house. I did not actually believe people lived this way and I certainly did not think anyone I knew lived this way. "You hide it well, Doc," I stated as we walked.

She smiled. "I'm not hiding it. I simply don't want to be judged by it." She paused and took another drink of the beer she had grabbed when nobody was looking. She kept a glass of champagne to the side, but made it clear to me she would be much happier with a Henry Weinhart's Blue Boar. "Alan and I met in school. As an undergrad he was in business. However, when I was going to med school, he decided he would too. Can you believe it? Who changes majors to med school? We took our first residency together. We have lived in California, Kansas, and now Chicago. We have worked very hard to get where we are today, and I don't want anything to jeopardize that."

I returned the smile. "Then do you mind if I ask you a fairly pointed question?"

She looked slightly uncomfortable. "Go ahead."

"Why the hell am I here? We're close, but not cocktail party close. You have always shown me great respect, and I hope I have done the same in return. However, my car, my suit, and me for that matter, don't fit in here, and the detective in me believes there's something more you wanted me here for?"

There was pause. Not a long pause but long enough for me to see I was right. "Maybe I want to leave my husband and start a life with you."

I had just taken a small drink of my whiskey and instantly coughed causing some to end up in my hand and down my Men's Warehouse special. "Sorry, but now I know you're not serious."

She smiled. "No, but I do have several friends I would love you to meet. You are a very good man, Tommy. If things don't work out with Tammi, I would love to connect you." She paused again and looked away. It appeared she wanted me to say something. I knew the information was coming, but it needed to come on her timeline, so I let the silence sit. She looked back to me. "Tommy, you're a great detective. I have worked with you almost my entire career in Chicago. I trust you."

"And I trust you," I replied.

"What I am about to tell you is off the record. By that, I mean I want your advice but unless I ask you to investigate, I don't want you looking into it, even though it may be illegal. Can you do that?"

Now it was my turn to pause. I had over the course of my career come across several friends or acquaintances that had been involved in misdealings. Just because they were friends, I could not look the other way. However, in those cases, my investigations had led me to them. This was different. I had no investigation. I was being asked for direction. I needed to choose my words carefully. I stood and paced around the hallway. I could still hear the music and party noise in the distance, but we were alone now. I turned back to Elise. "Doc, I can't ignore a crime. I'm sorry, but I can't. However, if you're asking me for feedback on a hypothetical situation, then I would have nothing to investigate."

I could tell by her expression that she understood. "Tommy, I have a hypothetical question for you. Let's pretend you and Tammi were married and you found out Tammi was possibly involved with something that might be illegal. What would you do?"

I thought a moment. The hallway we were in ran along the outside of her house. It was not a normal hallway. The outside wall was completely done in glass and looked out over a beautiful lighted garden and walking trail. The inside, where we were standing, had a roughly twenty-inch wall a few feet from the house, which was filled with its own flowers and plants. As you stood, you felt as if you were standing in an arboretum. I took a step closer to the interior plant retaining wall and sat on the ledge. She sat down next to me and appeared to be trembling. Obviously she had used the word "hypothetical" but I knew who she was talking about.

I looked straight into her eyes. "Completely off the record and I will not follow up without your direction—is Alan in trouble?"

A tear began to form. "I don't know, but something is not right and he won't tell me."

"Are you sure it's illegal?"

"I don't know. He doesn't know."

I thought a minute on that. "Are you saying he came to you, or you just suspect something?"

"He came to me, but swore me to secrecy. He would be furious if he knew I even implied anything to you." She wiped away a tear. "I can't believe I am crying."

"Crying should be the least of your concerns," I replied. "As you said, I've known you a long time. Never in my career have I ever met a more thorough investigator. You don't make snap judgements so if you are telling me this, you have a gut feeling that something is not right. If Alan is involved, it must also be at a level that is extremely serious. My advice is this. If Alan feels something is wrong, he needs to go to the police."

She shook her head. "He can't do that. You know the company he works for. There are stockholders, thousands of employees, factors involved I could never even begin to understand or describe."

"Elise, what you just described takes things to millions of dollars. When you start talking about that level of money, the people involved will stop at nothing to prevent the information from coming out. If Alan found something or saw something he shouldn't have, then he is in danger. At some point you have to weigh what is most important to you—making the tough call or being made to permanently keep quiet."

She looked at me surprised. "I think you're jumping to conclusions now, Tommy."

"Maybe I am," I replied. "I don't have any facts about a hypothetical situation. You asked for my advice and I am giving it to you. If he asks for an investigation and there is nothing there, then nobody is harmed. If there is something there, maybe the investigation prevents the issue from escalating. There are no guarantees when it comes to crime."

She stood, wiped the final tear from her eyes, and then saw her husband walking toward them. "Alan, what are you doing down here? I'm sure the party needs you."

"Well, it seems my wife had vanished and several of her friends were wondering where she might have gone. I knew you were giving Tommy a tour and..." He stopped when he got close enough to see her face. "Have you been crying?"

She could not speak so I interjected. "Sorry, Dr. Grove, I stole some time from your wife. I'm still having trouble with Clark's loss. I think my story got to her." I let it sit a bit before continuing. "I want to thank you both for including me in this. You have an amazing home. I should probably be going."

"No," they both said at the same time.

"Please stay," Elise continued on her own.

"Yes," broke in Alan. "We haven't tried those cigars yet."

I shook my head. "No, thank you. I need to be getting home anyway. It's a long drive back down to the city."

They were going to protest again but both let it drop. The three of us walked back. I tried to determine if Alan bought my story referencing Tom Clark, the vice detective who was killed about five months ago. He had attended the funeral with his wife. It was the last time I had seen Alan, and although I was not broken down into tears, he had seen the pain I was in. He also knew I was close with Clark's ex-wife and her pain was also weighing on me. I thought the story was sound and Elise would not feel the brunt of twenty questions from her husband.

We came to the mouth of the hallway which emptied back into the foyer. The majority of people attending had moved into the giant ballroom. The band was going strong and the rumor mill of flying in a jazz band from an old time Kansas City club had only ignited the excitement further. A younger man, probably in his mid-forties, approached us as we emerged.

"Alan and the beautiful Doctor Gerstenberger, I have been wandering around for an hour and never been able to connect." He looked at me and appeared to be displeased at what he saw. "And I don't believe we have met."

I started to introduce myself but was cut off by Alan. "Dr. Randy Thompson, this is Tomas O'Malley, Detective Tomas O'Malley. Randy runs our laboratories at Abbunex."

He reached out his hand, then paused just for a second when he heard the word "detective." It is my job to notice these things. It was not a sure *tell*, but my immediate impression was this man wanted to know why a detective was in the house. I shook his hand.

"I hope you're not here on official business?" he said to me smiling as if it were a joke but definitely wanting to know the answer. He had turned from me and directed his question more to Alan.

"No," Alan replied smiling. "He's good friends with us. Elise and Tomas work together in the city."

I nodded. "And please, call me Tommy."

Immediately Dr. Thompson seemed to relax. "Well, good. I was afraid you had been robbed or something. I am glad to hear this is an unofficial visit, and Tommy, please call me Randy."

"Well, it is good to meet you, Randy," I said in return, "and I'm glad this is not official business either, as I am a homicide detective." Randy Thompson was about 6'3", he had a full head of hair which I thought was fake, and he carried himself as if his shit did not stink. I did not like this guy, but I had no reason not to. Sometimes you just get a feeling about someone. However, my issue with Randy was that he was at least ten years younger than me and I was sure he lived in a house just like this one. He was rich, smug, and a born-again asshole. I could just tell.

"Tommy," broke in Elise. "Are you sure you have to leave? Do you not have time for at least one more McNaughton's?"

"McNaughton's," stated Randy. "Did Alan introduce that to you as well? I love it. I keep it stocked in both my wet bars ever since I had it here."

"Same here," I replied smiling. I turned to Elise. "Maybe I do have time for one more. It will take the valet a little bit to bring my car up anyway."

"Oh," replied Randy. "Unlucky for you. I threw an extra twenty his way to keep my Beamer close. I'm the fifth or sixth spot away from the house."

"Well, I saw Tommy's car..." Elise started but stopped when I raised my hand.

"One more McNaughton's sounds just fine." I was going to add, *you pompous ass*, but I kept that part of the phrase to myself. I was sure by her smile that Elise could read my mind.

2 The Day Before the Party

"Hey, Joseph," Randy Thompson said, "you have a minute?"

Joseph Reingold was the Vice President of Testing and Quality for Abbunex Labs. He had been with the company his entire career starting out as a quality control analyst just out of school. He had worked nights while attending Northwestern and completed his PhD in 1994 in Microbiology. To say he had worked through the ranks was an understatement. Everyone at the North Chicago site knew him, and he worked closely at every level, all the way up to the CEO.

Dr. Reingold smiled at his direct report. "Have I ever not had a minute for you?"

"I was looking through the samples and found something odd. These tissue samples are all the same."

Dr. Reingold smiled. "Well, of course they're the same. They have to meet a certain requirement to even be accepted for the test. Then we infect them, confirm the infections, and then treat them."

Dr. Thompson frowned. He also had his PhD and had been working at Abbunex for more than ten years. He was not some first-year lab student. He oversaw the Research and Development group that did all the testing for every pharmaceutical product developed in Chicago. No drug was produced that did not go through his labs. "Joe, with all due respect, I'm not saying they are from the same sample group and all match in factors for the testing. I am saying they are all from the same person. Every factor matches exactly."

He appeared concerned, but only mildly. "Randy, I'm sure that's not true, but even if it is, we need multiple positive or negative cases so if we repeat tests on the same tissue, it's not the end of the world. But we should verify where the error occurred, if in fact it did."

Thompson did not like the nonchalant attitude from his boss, but the feedback did make sense. "You know, I don't have time today, but I will hold off on putting anything else through until Monday and do a full retrace on all the samples we have in the workup now."

"That sounds fine," replied Reingold. "I'll be leaving shortly as well and then I have a dinner party tomorrow. Let's just circle back on Monday."

It was not what Thompson had wanted before he decided to speak to his boss, but it at least got the issue on the table. He had plans this weekend with his family, plus he intended to take his wife to the same dinner party, so delaying everything until next week actually saved him. Tracking back the hundred plus samples would take almost two full days due to the number of places they had to get samples from. He also would need the help of a colleague who set all the sampling up, and Monday was always easier than Friday to make that happen. "Okay, boss," he stated as he rose and turned to leave. "I'll get back to you on Monday with our game plan."

"Sounds perfect, Randy, thank you." He raised his hand as if to say good-bye and then added, "Say, Randy?"

"Yes," Thompson said, turning back as he reached the door.

"Good work, but until we know for sure what's going on, let's keep this between us. We don't want any rumors getting out so close to our earnings call and the update on the project."

"Thank you, sir, and don't worry, I understand and completely agree." Randy nodded as he turned to leave.

"Say, can you pull the door shut on your way out?" he added with a smile and wave.

He did so. After he heard the door latch shut, Reingold picked up his phone and texted: *I think we may have a problem on the IGB100 Emplex project.*

•   •   •   •   •

It was Sunday. I rolled out of bed and had to get my bearings. I had not had too much to drink by any standard at the party. In fact, I had three drinks the entire night. However, I decided on my way home that I should park at my apartment building and then Uber to Flap Jaws to make sure the place did not close early. Fortunately, my old partner Franky was there and we stayed past 2:30 AM. He was one of the few in my life who knew it was the eve of my 55th birthday. I did not tell him about Doc G's house or the conversation that had taken place. At this point, there was nothing to tell about her concerns, and her wealth was something she wanted kept a secret. Who was I to change that?

Roy Pura, my friend and late-night Flap Jaws bartender and owner, was the only other person who knew it was my birthday, probably because he had celebrated the last six with me. He even spotted me a full bottle of McNaughton's. The damn distributor should have spotted me more than that for all the bottles I had placed on shelves across Chicagoland. That supercool dude, Doctor Randy Thompson, had two bottles of his very own in his two wet bars. *Jackass*, I thought. Last call was at 1:00 AM, but Roy, Franky, and I told stories until after 2:00. That was the last thing I remembered.

I turned on the TV in my bedroom hoping to see the NFL pregame, and then remembered it was April and football was done. I smelled something. I recognized the smell but could not place it for sure. It smelled like pizza but it wasn't quite right. I swung my feet to the side of my bed and felt the rush go directly to my head. "Shit, this is going to be a long day." When I said the words, I knew nobody was there to hear them, but I wanted to make sure I could still speak. My throat was so dry that my voice hardly sounded like its own.

I got up and instantly realized I had to use the bathroom, before I checked out the smell. I was still wearing my suit from last night. I don't remember Franky asking about it, but he probably had. I would have to think hard about what I might have told him. I could hear the question now: "Why the hell are you wearing that nice suit?" My natural response would have been the truth, but if I had told him I had been invited to Doc G's, he then would have immediately asked what her place was like. I would have to really think about what I might have told him.

"Shit, I don't have any idea, and I absolutely have to pee." I always talked to myself. I don't know if all guys do, all cops do, or if I am just weird, but I do. I guess I don't worry about it until I start answering my comments back or start using multiple voices. For now, I'm going with the idea that I'm normal. And by the way, the pee was incredible.

I made my way into the kitchen to find my oven on 400 degrees and a Red Baron pepperoni pizza scorched black inside. I tossed it and in the process gave myself credit for not burning the place down. I grabbed a bottled water from my refrigerator and half stumbled my way to the living room. When my body hit the couch, I actually think I sighed.

My doorbell rang. "Shit!"

I knew it was Franky. He was probably coming to check that I was alive. I did not want to get up but I could see from where I sat, the door was locked. Franky had a key, so I would just wait this one out. My voice was so blown I could not even yell to tell him to just use his key and come in. However, I knew when I did not answer he would do that anyway so I opted to just sit.

Again, the doorbell rang, this time twice. "Goddamn it, Franky!" I stammered. "Come on in."

There was no response. Then, instead of a doorbell, I heard a knock and a voice that I was sure was not Franky.

I climbed to my feet and made my way over to the door. "I'm coming," I said as loud as possible, but my voice was still slurred and I sounded as if I was still drunk. It was after 10:00 AM so most of the liquor should have worn off.

I undid the lock and slowly pulled open the door ready to bitch at whoever was there.

"Hi, Daddy, happy birthday."

"Hi, Pop. Happy fifty-fifth. You don't look a day older than sixty."

"Mallory? Alex? Oh my God, what are you guys doing here?" Usually I can temper any emotion in my speech even when I'm caught off guard. I could not hide the excitement of seeing my kids, since I had not seen them in several months. They live with their mom and her new husband in the western suburbs, while they're going to college. They saw the look in my eyes causing Mallory to fall into my arms with a large hug.

"Happy birthday, Daddy," she whispered again. There is something magical about being called *Daddy* by your daughter.

"Come on in, kids. I can't believe you're here." I was truly at a loss.

"Mom is here too, Pop," Alex said. "She's parking the car."

"You look like crap, Daddy," added Mallory. "Are you feeling okay?"

I smiled. "Just waking up," I replied. "Leave the door open so your mom can just walk in. Come on in and sit down. Can I get you guys something?"

"We have things for you, Dad. It is your birthday and all," Mallory said in her normal lighthearted tone.

Mallory was the typical daughter, tough as nails and beautiful. She rarely said a negative thing about anyone or anything and when she did, it was along the lines of, "that person is a big meanie." Alex, on the other hand, was tough as nails and did not mix words. He would describe the same person the way I would, full of expletives, and he would not leave any area of interpretation to his feelings. Most people saw Alex as an asshole. I saw him like I was looking in the mirror. What was that saying about me?

They all sat, and in a few moments in walked Stephanie Bascom. She always looked incredible, but boy, did I hate her for not sticking out our marriage. I didn't blame her. I was hardly home, and when I was, I brought everything home with me. I had nightmares, I drank too much, and I was basically like my tell-it-like-it-is son, an asshole. She carried with her a box with some wrapped gifts in it. To be honest, I was moved.

"Hello, Jo." My ex-wife's name was Stephanie Jo Bascom, but only Franky called her Stephanie. I did not know why he did, and I did not know why she did not push him to change it, but he always had. To me, she would always be Jo. "How are you doing?" I said, a touch of caring in my voice.

"Better than you, it looks like," she replied smiling. "Rough night?"

"Believe it or not, I attended a party at the largest house I've ever been to in Barrington Hills. I felt so out of place that when I finally was able to sneak out, I was feeling sorry for myself and thought I would swing by Flap Jaws. Franky thought I deserved a birthday drink or two after midnight."

She smiled. "How is Franky? I miss him. How is he doing since Kathy died?"

I shrugged. "He never talks about it, but he also never dates or even pretends he wants to. He has his two-hundred pound dog named Vader, and I believe they may actually tie the knot soon."

"Well, Dad," Mallory broke in. "We brought you breakfast and presents. What do you want first?"

I already knew what the breakfast was because I could smell it. "The Dagwood will get cold so we should start with that, but the presents look pretty damn good also."

Alex smiled and grabbed the brown Mr. J's bag. "Thank God, I'm starving." He proceeded to tear into the sack. He did not pass around the burgers for anyone else but simply ripped into his. Like I said—asshole—but a normal young man, and guess what, he was me thirty years ago and I loved him.

We all finished our greasy breakfast burgers with Mallory and Jo actually sharing one, since both were still on their constant diet. I glanced at my ex-wife and mouthed the words, *thank you*. She smiled in return.

"So," I started as I wiped my mouth. "Don't misunderstand this question, but you've never done this before. I can't tell you how wonderful it is, but why now?"

Jo stood and paced toward the door and then back to face us on the couch. "Well, you can blame your daughter for that. She wanted to surprise you for your birthday and called the Chop House to speak with Tammi about setting it up. She learned that Tammi had moved to California and she realized you were most likely alone."

Mallory now took over the conversation. "We got to talking and realized that we never make an effort for you. Our whole lives you came to our soccer games, our basketball games..."

Alex interjected. "Hell, you even went on that awful camping trip when I wanted to be in Cub Scouts."

I shook my head remembering the trip from hell that not only ended Alex's run at scouting but confirmed my permanent placement to the title of "resort guy."

"Well," Jo now continued, "the three of us decided to make sure you were not alone on your birthday, and a night at Flap Jaws with Franky is not being with someone."

"Your husband okay with this? I mean, the last thing I want..."

"Shut up, Tommy. John is good with anything we want to do for you. He has nothing but incredible things to say about how you've handled our mixed family."

I nodded agreement. John was a good guy. In some ways a lucky guy, but he always treated me with respect and most importantly, he treated my kids equal to his own. "So, what's the plan?"

Mallory jumped over and snuggled next to me. She always was a daddy's girl, no matter how infrequently we saw each other. "It's time for your presents, Daddy." She reached over to the box of gifts and grabbed a long one. She handed it to me. "Here's mine."

I took the box and began to open it. It was light and in the ever-so-familiar Amazon box. I peeked inside and smiled. "You shouldn't have..."

"They're Darth Vader slippers made for size thirteen." She was so happy. She was 19 years old but was acting like a 6-year-old. "And look inside them..."

I reached inside and pulled out a folded piece of paper. "Tickets?"

"Yes, tickets to opening night of the new *Star Wars* movie on the Monster Screen in Naperville. Will you go with me and Alex?"

I smiled so broadly my face hurt. "I wouldn't miss it for the world."

Alex now threw a huge present on my lap. It too was very light but it was probably two square feet around the outside. I knew what it felt like but it couldn't be. I tore through the paper to find it really was.

"A twenty-eight pack of toilet paper? Do you think I have a bowel problem?"

"Dad, we are O'Malley males. We absolutely have bowel problems."

I nodded but then started to look closer at the paper. "*Word of the Day* toilet paper?"

"Yeah, it's really cool. You always say you have a terrible vocabulary and you sound like a dork when you talk. This is perfect. Every ten squares is a new word. You wipe, learn the word, and use it that day. Every day you learn a new word."

"Or in your case, two or three words every day," Mallory added laughing.

"Believe it or not," I said smiling, "this is perfect." I paused, looked at the outside wrapping of the package of toilet paper and added, "I mean, this is superlative."

"There you go," Alex said. "Superlative. I'll use that today as well."

Jo added, "And don't worry, Tommy, Alex bought a pack for our house as well. John wouldn't let him put it in the main bathroom though, only the upstairs."

"This is great, guys, thank you very much."

"There is one more, Daddy," stated Mallory. "Mom has one for you as well."

I looked toward her. "Jo, you didn't have to..."

"Relax, Tommy, I'm not trying to lose my bitch status." Mallory giggled and Alex was about to add something but let it slide when he saw his mom's immediate glare to hold his tongue. She handed me a large, tan envelope.

I opened it up and found a check. It was made out to me and had quite a few zeros on it. "What is this?" I asked.

"Whether I was married or not, I was with John for the most part from the day we separated. I may have tried to hide it in the beginning, but you and I both know the truth, and so do the kids. Every dollar you ever paid me for child support and any other cost, other than those that went directly to teams or direct costs, John and I put in a separate account. When the kids were both in school, we said we were going to split it evenly between us. I divided it by four and each of us got an equal cut. The kids can use the money when they go out on their own, and you and I can use it for whatever we want. It's my way of saying I was sorry for giving up on us and thank you for all your support since it happened."

I was moved. I pride myself on not showing emotions, and I always do a good job, but it is much more difficult when situations are thrust upon me. This one caught me. "You did not have to do this."

"I know, and so does John, but we thought it was a good idea. We thought about it a long time ago and just stuck to it."

"I also know you did not give up on us," I answered, my tone still carrying my surprise. "I didn't give you a choice."

She smiled. "Nobody is blaming anyone, Tommy. We are all way past that. Mallory brought it up and got us talking. We're a great family, whether you and I are married or not is immaterial, and that is a testament to how you've been. You never made money or anything else an issue. You simply were there every time you were needed without question."

I looked down to both my kids who were staring back at me and then back to my ex-wife. "Unfortunately, I think your bitch status is in jeopardy."

"No, it's not, Dad," stated Alex. "She is absolutely a superlative bitch...still."

"Nice," I replied, giving him five. Just then my phone rang. I wasn't going to answer it because nobody calls me on Sunday other than work calls, and because I wasn't next in line for a weekend case, no work issue should be coming my way. However, I thought maybe my dad would be calling so I opted to pick up. I glanced at my phone and was surprised when I saw who it was. "O'Malley," I said.

"Tommy," issued a somewhat frail woman's voice.

"Yeah, this is Tommy. What is it, Elise?"

"I'm downtown, near the White Sox stadium. There's a case. There's another detective working it but I want you. Can you take it?"

"I don't know, Doc. It is my birthday and I'm with my kids. Also, just like you don't switch..."

"Tommy, please," she was pleading.

In all honesty, detectives don't jump in on other detectives' cases. It leads to bad mojo in the department. "Doc, I can't. We just don't..."

"I know him, Tommy. I know who was killed, and you met him last night."

3 Guaranteed Rate field, which I still feel is the worst name in history for a ballpark but they make too much money with naming rights to keep calling it Comiskey Park, is located on the south side of Chicago. As I think about it, even US Cellular was a better name, but I guess since everyone has Apple or Samsung now, the *Cell* quickly went the wrong direction. When Doc G said she was near where the White Sox played, I did not realize she was under a bridge about three hundred yards from the entrance. She was standing to the side, well outside of the crime scene tape.

I had placed a call to Carter regarding the request from Elise. He was not on board with making a change but agreed to have me join the scene. Then, I could speak with the assigned detective about how he wanted to proceed. Carter was concerned, not only because he didn't want to switch detectives for personal reasons as it obviously led to conflicts of interest, but he also didn't want to upset the current smooth-running department. Recent cases had thrown some questions on Carter's ability to handle the downtown Chicago homicide department and he needed all noise to go away. That being said, he had also worked with Doctor Elise Gerstenberger for almost his entire career and her needs were a factor in any decision. My partner, Patti Halterman, had left town for the weekend to visit her kids because we were not on call. She was due back today and I called to let her know what I was doing. She was in Gibson City, Illinois, when she got my call and would not be on the scene before it was cleaned up. Regardless of what I felt, she said to get the case if I could. "Anything to help Doc G," were her exact words.

The detectives on the case were Hannifin and Parker, and yes, everyone in the department did recognize that there was a technology company called Parker-Hannifin, and they were very tired of the comparison. Parker was only about two years in, but I had worked with Hannifin for more than ten. He was a straight shooter. We were not friends by any means, but there was respect there. I liked that he understood how things really worked. That meant he would not take it personal if he gave up this case. I would make it up to him another time, or I wouldn't, and either result would be fine. Carter had already prepped him by the time I arrived, so it really was going to boil down to whether I was too close to this case or not. Since I had met the deceased less than twelve hours earlier, that answer could very easily be yes.

I saw Elise on the far side of the crime scene on the outside of the tape. In any case that involves friends or any level of acquaintance, any cop, detective, medical examiner, or even lab tech is required to disclose that relationship immediately upon recognizing it. I assume she came to the scene to work the case, began her investigation, and upon seeing the body, was instantly forced to remove herself from the workup. I also saw Parker and Hannifin. Hannifin waved to me to come over. I acknowledged his wave and then pointed to Doc G. He followed my point, nodded, and understood. I headed over to the woman I spent most of the early evening with just a day earlier.

"How are you holding up, Elise?"

"Damn it, Tommy. I told you something wasn't right. I called Alan and he was shocked. I asked him point blank what was going on and he didn't know a thing, so he says."

I raised my hand to her. "Hold on now, Doc. Let's not jump to any conclusions. There's a lot of work to do before we go accusing people of withholding information."

She turned and locked her eyes on me in what could be called a nasty stare only a woman can give to a man. She was speaking with great force but in a whisper so only I could hear. "I told you something was up. I was right. I know my husband is involved and he won't tell me. So don't you tell me to hold on."

"Listen, Elise," I said softly. "This is not my case, but I have requested it be turned over to me. I believe both Sargent Carter and Detective Hannifin are on board with handing the case to me and Halterman, but I have to let you know now that if your husband is involved, there's nothing I can do to protect him. You understand that, right? Furthermore, I may have to remove myself as well, but most importantly, there are no more off-the-record conversations."

She looked at me and then looked away but did not answer.

"Elise?"

"I know, Tommy," she finally said after another brief silence. "Just get the case. I'm not looking for favors, but I do trust you will find the truth and not settle for whatever is easiest."

I took that to mean she understood my requirements and respected my work. "Now, can you tell me who this is?"

"Randy Thompson," she replied. "You met him when we first walked out of the hall after we were joined by Alan."

"Yep, I remember. He had something to do with the lab testing, or something like that."

"Yes," she replied. "He is, or was, the lab director. He ran the labs which handled all the new product testing, patent testing, results, and so forth."

"If we go by your theory that it's related to Abbunex, do you have any knowledge as to why someone in that position would be targeted?"

She shook her head. "No. In the big scheme of things, he has a pretty low position, though he liked to think he was a big deal, as you heard last night."

I nodded. "Okay. I'll speak with Carter and Hannifin and see what everyone thinks. I'm going to disclose how I know him and everything that transpired last night. You asked me to keep your finances a secret, and I will, as long as they don't interfere with solving the case. Do you understand?"

"I do," she replied flatly.

"Okay, sit tight here and I'll be back with an update on what is decided."

Elise stared at me, but now her stare held a clear message that I needed to take this case. Normally I would not push for a case. It just wasn't done in our department. That being said, Doc G had saved my ass numerous times and if could help her, I would. My immediate fear was that she may not like the answers I found.

I turned and walked over to where my counterparts were standing. Carter nodded and Detective Hannifin reached his hand out. "You want this one, Tommy?"

"I don't know that I want it, but I'm already slightly involved in it. That is what I need to talk to you guys about." I turned and pointed to Elise who was staring our direction. "Doc G and her husband invited me over to their place last night. They had a party and Doc wanted to talk to me about a feeling she was having about her husband's work. Nothing on the record and to be honest, I didn't think anything of it because she had no evidence. She just had a gut feeling, and during that party, I met and had a short discussion with the Director of Lab Testing. His name was Randy Thompson. He worked with Doc's husband at Abbunex Labs up north but was much lower on the totem pole. That Randy Thompson I met last night is lying about ten feet over there with the plastic over his head."

"Does that make you too close to this one, Tommy?" asked Carter.

"If I really knew the man or had any relationship with him, that would be one thing," I replied. "But to be honest, he's no different than anyone I walked by yesterday on the street."

"Why is Doctor Gerstenberger requesting you then?" Carter added onto his last thought. "Does she think you will protect the company or her husband?"

"I don't think so," I replied, then paused, thinking about the situation. "You know, it may be just the opposite. She may be asking simply because she trusts me. Keep in mind, I have worked with her in some capacity for over twenty years. I think she trusts that if her husband is not involved, I will work hard to prove it."

"And if he *is* involved?" Carter added.

"Then she will trust the information I find and not believe he was targeted or railroaded."

Carter seemed to chew on that for a while and then turned to Hannifin. "Hannifin, this is your case. However, if you're good turning it over to O'Malley, you can. I won't prevent it."

Hannifin shrugged. "I'm not going to stand in the way of Tommy if he wants the case. We haven't even started on the scene or the witnesses. If you and Halterman want it, then let us know if we can help. I would much rather watch basketball today anyway."

I reached out to shake Hannifin's hand. "You and me both," I replied, then added, "and Jim, thanks."

"No problem, Tommy. Stay safe and I'll see ya tomorrow." He turned toward his partner and hollered. "Ollie, O'Malley is going to take this one. Let's go."

Oliver Parker walked over. "I'm already here, Tommy. You want some help gathering evidence?"

I smiled at the younger detective. "I'm not stupid. If you want to help, I'll take it. Halterman won't be here for a while anyway so you can definitely help get this one cleaned up."

"Sounds good," he replied. "I have a group of potential witnesses over there. I'll start with their statements." He pointed to a girl sitting on a chair by a black-and-white police cruiser. "She's the one who found the body."

I nodded. "Why don't I take her and you work the rest of the area? I'm going to have a brief discussion with Elise and then get to it."

"Okay, Tommy. We can regroup in an hour or so."

I walked back over to Elise. I would say she was patiently waiting, but I would be lying. "Hey, Doc," I began.

She stepped forward. "So, what is the decision?"

"They agreed to hand it over to me and Halterman. With Patti being gone now, Parker agreed to work this scene until she arrives or until we can clear it. I will take lead and then we'll go from there."

"Thank you, Tommy," she replied, catching me off guard when she moved and hugged me tightly. "I know you'll find out what's really going on."

I pushed her shoulders back and held her at a distance equal to my outstretched arms. "Elise, I need you to understand one hundred percent that you may not like what I find, and if that happens, there's no gray area for me. Do you understand what I'm saying?"

"I understand completely," she replied. "I would not expect anything less."

At that point I left Elise standing in the cold. I did not look back to her as I walked toward my first interview, the woman who found the body. I glanced to the team working on the body of Randy Thompson. It was the Assistant Medical Examiner, Denise Bitty. She, like Doc G, was a lifer with the Chicago coroner's office. She, not like Doc G, was single, but similar to my long-term friend, she was hot. She was 50 years old, I would guess, but looked 25. I always tried to flirt but got nowhere. I had worked with her a great deal. There was only a slight drop-off from one to the other in ability, but I had never worked with Denise when she did not have Doc G as a source of reference or support. Because of Elise's relationship with the deceased, she could have no contact in this case.

I approached the woman who found the body. She was sitting in a folding chair, legs crossed, then uncrossed, then crossed again. She was clearly jumpy, uncomfortable, or both. My guess was drugs, most likely amphetamines, but I would want to talk to her before building my final theory. Regardless, I did not hold much hope for this witness's information.

"How are you doing?" I asked.

The woman did not lift her head, but her eyes did angle up toward me. Her hair was curly and tangled and lay over most of her forehead making it difficult to see her expression. She was dressed in clothes that had not been washed in some time. I could not detect any smell, but I assumed she would prefer to have a cigarette in hand based on the stained color of her nails. Her voice cracked and it sounded like her throat was incredibly dry.

"Fine. What's it to you?" she answered.

I thought I would go a different direction than to immediately asking questions about what she saw. I needed her to join the world right now, and to do that, I needed to bridge the wall she had built. "Would you like a smoke?" Now she actually raised her head to look directly to me. She heard that, and I even think her lips turned up just a bit.

She coughed lightly. "Do you have one?"

I did not answer but had noticed a uniformed officer smoking as I walked up. It bothered me because smoke and ash had the ability to contaminate a scene. You should never smoke at a crime scene but these young guys did not know shit about real police work. "Hey you!" I hollered toward that officer. "I need to bum a smoke."

For a moment, his expression seemed to say, "What the hell, man. No way." Then there seemed to be short pause while he had some conversation with himself deciding what he should do. Reluctantly he reached into his pocket and removed a pack of cigarettes. He bumped them the way the cool guys do and one cigarette poked out from the top.

I reached out and took it. "Thanks, Mack, now how about a light?"

"It's Smith, Detective. Officer Rob Smith." I acknowledged his name with a nod, but did not reply. He held out his lighter and struck it so the flame emitted.

Reaching my hand out, I took the lighter from him causing it to extinguish as I made contact. I smiled and put the lighter in my pocket. "Thanks, Mack." I walked away. I'm not sure, but I think I heard him whisper, "Asshole" to himself as I left.

I handed the smoke to the woman and then removed the lighter from my pocket and struck it to flame. The woman put the cigarette in her mouth and leaned toward me. She sucked in deep and released a ball of smoke to the side. "Oh God, it's better than sex." Her voice was clear now. It was ironic. If I put a cigarette in my mouth and lit it, I would cough and be incoherent. She does it, her voice clears up, and she appears completely dialed in.

"Thank you, Kojak. I needed this," she replied.

She was still jumpy, but at least I didn't feel like I was talking to a ticking time bomb. "Can you tell me your name?"

She paused, thought for a minute, and then said softly, "Mandy."

There was no chance her name was Mandy. "Well, Mandy, can you tell me what you saw today?"

"What do you mean, what I saw today? I saw a dead guy on the ground right where he's sitting now."

"How about we take a few steps back?" I said softly. "What were you doing over here? Walking? Working? Scoring drugs?"

She frowned. "Oh, that's how this is gonna go. You're just trying to arrest me. Well, this is bullshit and—"

I cut her off with my hand. "Just hang on, Mandy. I have no personal interest in anything you were doing and why. I'm just trying to determine what time you were here, who was around, was it daylight? Were you meeting someone? Anything you can give me may help us determine who killed that man. If we can determine who did it, maybe we can get him off the streets. If we get him off the streets, you can be safe to do whatever you need to do."

It was clear I spoke way too long. She had lost focus and interest. She took another deep suck on her smoke and stared glassy-eyed at me. "What did you ask me?"

I took a deep breath. "When you walked up, was this man already lying on the ground dead?"

"Yes, he was lying exactly where he is now." Her voice cracked but she seemed somewhat engaged all of the sudden.

"Did you see anyone else in the area?" I asked.

"Nope," she said flatly. She then paused, tilted her head, and rubbed her hand across her face as if wiping her nose. "Other than Jimmy, that is."

Intrigued. "Jimmy? Who's Jimmy?" She immediately cowered slightly, looking down to the ground. I knew the answer. I softened my voice. "Mandy, I'm not interested in whether you were here for less than legal reasons. I'm only interested in what you saw." I paused and noticed her slowly peeking her eyes upward. "Is Jimmy your dealer?"

She shook her head. Her voice was weak, as if she was now scared to say anything. "No, he's my..."

"Your?" I added after a pause, trying to get her to finish.

"My matchmaker."

Now I understood. Mandy was a professional and Jimmy was what we used to call her pimp, and now with the Internet and technology, they tried to claim they were a dating service. Mandy was simply a hooker, nothing more. My voice was light, and I even came across as pleased. A hooker meant it was easy to provide immunity for information for her and Jimmy. "Hey, Mandy, no problem. I have no problem if Jimmy is arranging dates for you all night. What I really need to know is if you think Jimmy might have seen anything?"

She shook her head again, but appeared slightly calmer since I was okay with her profession. "I don't know. I was late, so I assume Jimmy was here before me. If I had been on time, we would have met here thirty minutes earlier."

I was confused with the statement, but I think what she was saying was that she was thirty minutes late so if he arrived at the time they were supposed to meet, he would have thirty minutes on her. "Hey, Mandy, wait here. I want to check with the investigators on something."

I walked over to where the assistant medical examiner was actually finishing up on the body. "Dr. Bitty, I don't want to disturb you, but any chance you can tell me the approximate time of death?"

Dr. Bitty glanced up to me. "Hello, Detective O'Malley. It's been a while."

"Yes, it has," I replied, adding to the small talk but not really interested in it. I cut my response short and even I thought it sounded contrite.

"Well, to answer your question, to be honest, I believe we must have gotten the call moments after the victim was killed. Based on the body temperature, combined with the outside temp right now, I would say this man was killed less than sixty to seventy-five minutes ago."

I did some quick math in my head. The original call came in about that time, and I had arrived on the scene at least thirty minutes later. The end result was that if Jimmy did not kill this man, he was most likely here when it happened or immediately after. I had been looking into the air as if doing math on an imaginary chalkboard and quickly turned back to Dr. Bitty. "I can assume you're sure he was killed here, and not dumped."

She smiled, almost as if she knew I needed her and she would never provide me information on her own. It was clear that I would have to drag it out of her. What is it about medical examiners?

"Yes, he was definitely killed here. The blood spatter from the gunshot wounds is unmistakable. He was most likely shot while sitting or lying on the ground. It appears he was shot three times but we found seven shell casings so I will confirm the actual number of shots in the lab."

"Seven shell casings? Jesus, it would have sounded like a war," I replied. Professional hits did not use seven shots. Professional hits did not use more than one shot, for two reasons. First, a professional only needed one shot. Second, the more shots, the more sound. The more sound, the more attention. The more attention, the more chance for an unforeseen witness. "A witness," I said mostly to myself. "I need to find Jimmy."

"One more thing," she added looking directly toward me and holding up a clear plastic evidence bag. "This was on the body."

"What the hell is that?" I asked. "It looks furry."

"Put it this way," she replied. "It did not bring this guy any luck."

"A rabbit's foot?" I asked.

"Yes. An artificial rabbit's foot. I don't know what it means, but because of the lack of blood on the fur, it was placed there postmortem."

I walked back over to Mandy who was now drinking some bottled water. "Mandy, I need to talk to Jimmy."

She shrugged. "Well, there's no way in hell I'm going to tell you where to find him. That wouldn't go well for me."

I understood, but unfortunately I needed to speak to him. "Let's back up again, Mandy. Are you sure Jimmy is all right? Did you talk to him when you arrived?"

"Yeah, I talked to him," she said. "I told you I got here late, but he was here. He told me my appointment got jumpy and took off, but he was pleased that the reason I was late was because my previous appointment went long but was..."—she thought about what she was going to say then continued—"appreciative that I stayed, which worked out well for both me and Jimmy."

I nodded. "For the ease of conversation, you got a bonus for staying late and that bonus offset having your new date leave before the date started."

She smiled. "Yes, a bonus, Detective. That's what it was exactly."

"Where did Jimmy go after you told him about the bonus?" I asked.

She coughed a bit as she sucked in deep on her cigarette, blowing smoke in about five directions including across my face. "Sorry about that. Sometimes it goes down the wrong pipe."

I repeated my question. "About Jimmy. Where did he go?"

"I assume he just went back to the clu—" she stopped in mid-sentence.

"What club?" I asked.

She did not answer and looked away. I reached down and turned her chin back to face me. "Listen, Mandy, I am not after you. I don't want to throw you in jail and take all the money in your pockets right now as evidence. I am not going to arrest Jimmy. He didn't do anything wrong." I had no idea if this was the case or not. For all I knew, he killed this man and then fled. "All I need to know is if he saw the man who killed this victim. That's all. I will ask him that question and then leave him alone, forever."

She seemed to be toying with answering. She was almost having a discussion with herself on whether she could trust me. I needed to continue to push.

"Mandy, the options are clear. You tell me the name of the club and you leave without any further questions, or you head downtown with me now and who knows when you get back home. You have anyone waiting for you? Because it might be forty-eight hours before you're back."

That got an instant response. "No," she said flatly. "I have to go home. My son is home and..."—she paused and seemed to fight for words before finishing—"and I only have a sitter until this afternoon."

I didn't miss a beat. "Then, if you don't want your son taken into protective custody, you need to tell me two simple things: where is Jimmy and what is his last name?"

"*Two* things? A minute ago it was just one."

"Things change, Mandy. Pray I don't change them again. Every time I have to repeat myself, I add some information. Tell me now and it's only those two things." I had her on the run now.

"Teague," she said defensively. "Jimmy Teague." Her voice trailed off.

"And where can I find him?" I asked.

"Most likely the Door, but I don't know if he's there. It's not like he told me where he was going, but he wanted to leave in a hurry. I didn't even see the body until he had left."

I knew what she meant when she said the Door. The Green Door was a tavern on Orleans. There were worse bars in the area, but not by much. However, I had heard this one was going through a revitalization. Within the next three months, the Jimmys of the world would not be allowed in. The whole area was cleaning itself up. I actually liked the Green Door. It was no Flap Jaws, but still a nice spot by itself. Part of me wondered if she was lying.

"Thank you, Mandy, now I'm going to have this officer drive you home." I waved to a uniformed officer about fifteen feet away.

She immediately reacted. "That's not necessary, Detective. I will walk."

"Actually, Mandy, no, you will not." The female officer arrived by our sides. I had seen her before but I didn't know her. She was a large officer who looked more like a prison guard than a police officer. I looked at her name badge. "Hello, Officer Duncan. I need you to take Mandy home. I need you to walk her in and verify her son is okay. If all looks good, you can leave her there with no follow-up. Just shoot me her address, please, when you leave." This served two purposes. I did not like having kids left at home, and I had no idea if she was paying for a sitter. I wanted to know that her son was okay. Secondly, I needed her address, and I had already limited my questions to her and did not want to go back on that. If Jimmy was not at the Door, I needed a second shot at finding him and my only option would be Mandy.

Again, Mandy was about to protest but Officer Duncan would not have it. She was African American and spoke like someone you just knew was not going to put up with any shit. Mandy barely had her mouth open when Duncan interrupted. "All right, let's not ruin this with a bunch of talk. Just shake a leg over to my car there,"— she pointed to a black-and-white sedan just on the other side of the crime scene tape—"and make sure that cigarette is out before we're within fifteen feet of my car. Take a bunch of breaths also because I don't want that smell lingering. Do you understand me, Ms..." She drew her last words off waiting for the woman to respond with her name.

When she just rolled her eyes and blew smoke toward the officer, I interjected in an attempt to keep Officer Duncan from ripping her lips and cigarette out permanently. "Officer Duncan, this is Mandy and she is helping us with our case, so let's keep that in mind and make sure we are clear and understanding."

She glared at me just for a moment, then smiled. "No problem, Detective. I'll make sure she gets home safely." She turned back to the woman. "Mandy, I want to make sure the goals here are clear to all parties. You are going to ride with me to your apartment. You are going to do that by walking over to my car and getting into the back seat. Prior to arriving at my car, you are going to extinguish that cigarette such that you have plenty of time to clear any lingering smoke out of your lungs to ensure nothing makes it back into my car. If I feel some *does* make it into my car, then on the way to your apartment, we are going to stop at the Duds and Suds Car Wash and you are going to hand-clean my seats and carpet. Once we arrive at your apartment, you are going to take me inside to meet your son. Assuming everything is acceptable at your house and with your son, our relationship will come to an end. Any diversion from that plan will bring you downtown and Social Services to your home to get your son. Do you understand?" She paused and then turned to me with a *fuck you, asshole* smile. "Was I clear enough to be understood that time?"

I have to admit, I didn't know Officer Duncan, but I liked her. "Perfectly clear to me," I replied. "Mandy?"

Mandy removed her cigarette and tossed it on the ground using her shoe to extinguish it. Her voice was raspy now, as if the smoke had instantly tarnished it. Speaking to me, she said, "Don't tell Jimmy I told you where he was." Turning to

Duncan. "Listen here, Officer Bitch. Not one word in the car or not only will I light up in the back, I will put my next cigarette out on your head cushion."

I actually thought Duncan was going to tear her in half, but to her credit, she rolled her arm out in an *after you, head this way* pose, guiding the woman to her car. Duncan swung her head back to me and gave me a slight wink. I had no idea what it meant but I was too scared to ask. I did, however, need the address. "Can I give you my cell number so you can text me the address?"

"I have your number already, O'Malley, but thanks."

How the hell did this woman have my number? Shit, I needed a new phone.

• • • • •

Oliver Parker tapped me on the shoulder causing me to jump. "Damn, Tommy, you may not believe this, but nobody saw anything."

I smiled. Franky and I used that line all the time so it was nice to hear it getting carried over to the younger guys. "Big surprise, huh. I've got a lead on someone who might have been present during the shooting. You up for a run to the Green Door?"

"Like I told you before, I'm already out here. If Halterman is not going to be back, I would be happy to swing by with you."

I knew Hannifin much better than Parker, but what I knew of Ollie was good. He had spent his whole career in Chicago and had worked his way up through the ranks. Further, without Halterman, I wasn't allowed to follow up with witnesses on my own. The department had rotated to team investigations, which is why I had Patricia Halterman as a partner in the first place. They wanted the younger detectives partnered with the older detectives and that is why, for the first time in as long as I could remember, Frank Sullivan and I were not working our cases together. Our unique setup led to too much solo work which in turn led to weaker cases and higher risk, two things the department did not want. However, if Parker would join me, all was good. I could fill in Patti when she got back into town and start breaking down the evidence I gained if I could find Jimmy and anything the ME obtained from the autopsy. I nodded to Ollie. "Let me have a brief word with Doc G and then we can head that way."

"No problem," he replied. "I'll follow up on anything the crew found with the body or the scene."

I raised my eyebrow wondering what the impact of that would be. If I tried to do that with Doc G when she was on a case, she would rip me a new one. "Good luck on that one," I said. Without waiting for another response, I headed back to where Doc G had been standing previously and to her credit, she had not moved.

"What did you find out, Tommy?" she asked.

I shook my head. "Now, Elise, you know I can't talk to you about the case. For all we know your husband is involved, or conversely, it could be completely unrelated to Abbunex at all. I came over here to tell you to go home. The case is mine and I will let you know if something happens that you should be aware of. I will probably set up a time to speak with your husband tomorrow. However, I do have a lead or two to follow up on tonight so we'll see where the leads take me."

"Was he murdered?" she asked.

"Go home, Elise. Clear your head. Let your husband know his lab director is dead and share with me anything your husband tells you that might help us on the case. I will most likely see you tomorrow."

She did not like my answer, and it was ironic because normally she was the one with all the information and I was asking for conclusions before she could draw them. I wasn't sure if I liked it reversed. However, I was sure *she* didn't.

Surprisingly, however, Elise reached out her arms and pulled me into a tight hug. "Thank you for taking this case. I know you will find the truth." With that, she released me, turned, and headed toward her car.

4 The Green Door was one of the only wooden structures to survive the Chicago fire. Why I knew that, I was not sure, but I did. A few hours ago my son had given me *Word of the Day* toilet paper where every ten squares was a new word. Since that time, I had already learned five new words. Knowing a fact like that about the Green Door Tavern made me feel equally as smart as using the word "abecedarian," which as everyone knows means being arranged alphabetically. I just needed someone to share it with and I did not think Detective Parker was that person. I would have to wait until I told Halterman where we had gone to use that fact with her. She would appreciate it.

We had driven separate cars to the original crime scene and it made no sense to leave a car in that area unattended. The drive to the Green Door was only about five minutes. Jimmy Teague could have walked it, but my guess is he drove also. I had never met Jimmy Teague or even heard of him so my initial thought was he was still pretty small time. That being said, he could simply be good at keeping himself clean, or in this case, good at avoiding getting caught. Regardless, on my way to the tavern I called into the station to see if they had any information on the man, especially a picture. I would have been incredibly surprised if this guy had not been picked up before, and as expected, he was in the system.

Jimmy Austin Teague, originally from Gibson City, Illinois, which was odd, because that is the small town Patti said she was driving through on her way back from seeing her kids. I was not sure where Gibson City was, but I would guess it never came up in anyone's conversation twice in the same day. I thought it was near Springfield. Out of curiosity, I would check later. For now, however, after arriving at the tavern and with Parker right by my side, we were headed inside with a picture texted to each of our phones of the man of the hour.

"He's not a good-looking guy, that's for sure," Parker stated as he opened up the message.

"Nope," I replied. "Not very many in that line of work are. At least, that's what my experience has taught me."

"Which line of work are you talking about?" he asked. "Crime in general, or something more specific?"

"Crime in general, but running women more specifically." I turned to him as we pushed through the large green door. "Pimps basically are not good-looking, but they don't need to be, I suppose."

He motioned to the front. "At the least the name of the place matches its entry." I'm not sure why he commented on the color of the door, other than I guess he was done talking about ugly pimps.

"During Prohibition, doors were painted green if they had a speakeasy in the back. They have kept it since then." Right after saying it I had to wonder why the hell I had.

"Were you alive during Prohibition?" he asked.

"Fuck you, Parker." Now we were getting along better. I would much prefer to bullshit with people than pretend I'm smarter than I am.

We had killed enough time with the small talk. It was a nice enough bar. I had been there in the past but it did not look like this. It had already gotten a very nice face-lift. In fact, I instantly thought that Ms. Mandy had led me astray. There was no way Jimmy Austin Teague was going...

"There he is," stated Parker, motioning with his head but not pointing.

I fanned my eyes the same direction and saw the man nestled at a corner table. Unfortunately, our eyes met and I knew two things. First, he knew I was a cop. Second, he was going to run. There was no use pretending or trying to be subtle. "Stop right there, Jimmy. We need to talk."

The man knocked over his beer as he bolted from the table and headed to the back.

"Shit!" exclaimed Parker. "You follow him and I'll run around the back and see if I can catch him coming back this way."

I did not answer as I was already after him on foot. I did believe I was too old for chasing down suspects but because of my constant training to maintain my black belt level, I could run with almost anyone and I rarely ran out of gas. I wasn't the sprinter, but I was good on distance. Some may be faster, but I would eventually catch them if I could keep them in my sight.

"Stop!" I yelled again as I reached the kitchen. I saw the man darting down the line between the fryer and grill area and the hot lamp where they place the food before it's delivered to the table. All eyes turned toward my voice.

"Just what do you think you are doing in my kit…" yelled a voice from who I believed was the kitchen manager.

"*Get down*!" I hollered back as the first shot rang my direction. This created a huge stir among the five or six employees in the area. My quick calculation came up with three or four kitchen employees and one to two wait staff. They all dove. Several screamed. And one clearly yelled profanity. "*Get down*!" I yelled again, drawing my gun toward the man running. "Stop right there. Police. Drop your gun and get down on the floor."

The man stopped and ducked behind what looked to be the corner of a walk-in cooler. "No, you put your gun down, Officer. I'm going to walk out of here now, before anyone gets hurt."

My gun was affixed right on the corner. I knew for sure where he was, but unless he poked his head around, I could not see him. But the odds were even. Unless he poked his head around, he also could not see *me*. "It's too late for that, Jimmy." I replied. "One of your shots took down an employee. If they die, that's a murder charge. Don't make it worse and make it a capital charge. That would come with the death penalty." Yeah, I was bluffing. Nobody was hit that I saw and there was no death penalty in Illinois anymore since about 2011. Most serious criminals knew that, but for the small-time guys, it still made them stop and think.

"What? I hit someone?"

"Yes, Jimmy, my partner just pulled him out. It doesn't look good." My voice was soft. I was trying to give the impression I cared, even though I didn't.

"Shit, shit, shit!" he yelled. "Goddamn it."

"Relax, Jimmy. We can still keep this from getting worse. If the man you hit lives, then you have a huge bargaining chip with what you saw today over by Comiskey, but you need to come out now with your hands up. Set your gun on the ground, walk two steps out from behind the cooler, and then lay down face-first with your hands behind your head." I paused and let that sink in. "It's the only way to not spend the rest of your life in prison, Jimmy."

"I didn't see nothin', cop, so I got nothin' to bargain with."

Oops, I thought to myself. *How do I save this?* "Hey, Jimmy, how do you know what you saw or didn't see? And even if you didn't see anything, the options are still clear. Come with me now or start the rest of your life on the run. We know who you are. It took me less than thirty minutes to find you. I will find you again."

I knew he was at least thinking about it because the silence that ensued was deafening. There were still at least five employees in the kitchen. I needed to rethink my priorities. "Hey, Jimmy."

"What?"

"It looks like there are some other small injuries. Not related to your gunfire directly, but caused by those diving out of the way. I'm going to get them out of here so nobody else gets hurt. All right?"

There was again a long pause, and I didn't think he was going to answer so I answered for him.

"Great, great. Thank you, as we don't want anyone else to get hurt. I'll start moving them out now."

"Hey, man, I didn't agree to anything," he stated immediately.

"Good," I replied. "We're talking again." But I was not going to wait. I knew he could not see what I was doing unless he stuck his head out, and I had my gun affixed right on the corner he was hidden behind. So if he stuck his head out, I was going to take the shot. My first priority, however, was to get these people out.

I kept my eyes focused on the wall. Then, a quick glance down to a man on the ground and the process was in motion. I signaled him to get the others and begin moving back into the main bar area. To my surprise, he understood and followed suit without delay. I brought my attention back to Jimmy Teague. "Jimmy, it will mean a lot to the D.A. that you let these people go with no more bloodshed. I know you didn't mean to shoot anyone. What I need you to do is to come out. Let's stop this right now before it gets worse." Right at that time I saw a door in the back of the kitchen that had a small window in it. The window probably served no purpose other than to allow those going through it to see if there was anyone on the other side. In that window, I saw Parker. From his angle, I was certain he had a clear view of Jimmy Teague.

I glanced down to see the last of the kitchen and wait staff making their way out through the door into the bar. With the shots fired, I assumed the bar area was empty and the police were on their way. However, in this part of the city, you just never knew for sure until they actually arrived. "Jimmy," I hollered. "I'm going to step out and put my gun away." I could still see Parker. He had his gun pulled and pointed directly toward where I believed Teague was. He was, however, going to shoot through a window which always provided some level of inaccuracy. "The time to end this is now. There is nobody here but me, and all exits are blocked. You are not going to leave so my suggestion is you step out and drop the weapon and lie face down on the ground with your hands behind your head."

There was no response, but I could hear his breathing. I had stepped out from behind the counter where I had found security when the shots were fired. However, I was still close enough to leap back that direction should this go south. I glanced toward Parker and saw him signal. I didn't know for sure what the signal meant, but because I heard some movement from Jimmy's direction, I think it meant he was moving.

"All right," he stated. "All right. I'm coming out. Don't shoot."

The man I had only seen briefly when he burst up from the table, slowly came out. His gun was still in his hand but his hands were in the air. Parker moved through the back door and I removed my gun and locked it on Teague. "Jimmy, I said drop the gun."

"No, sir," he replied.

"Jimmy," I said again, "don't do this."

Parker was now about fifteen feet from him and said, "Jimmy Teague, any movement with that gun and I will take you down."

The voice from the side startled Jimmy just a bit as he obviously had not seen him. "No, sir," he repeated again. "I want to get out of here and you guys are going to help me."

"We can't do that, Jimmy," I replied. "You opened fire on police officers. Trust me when I say you need to come in now. If you hit the streets, the Chicago PD will be shooting first and asking questions later. You need me to bring you in right now."

He put both his hands, even the one holding the gun, to his eyes as if he was trying to subdue a headache. "Damn it!" he yelled, not directing the comment toward either Parker or me, just shouting it in general. He dropped his hands to his side but didn't release the gun. The movement caused both me and Parker to tighten our grip on the trigger but not fire. "It's not going to be that way, sir."

"No, Jimmy, don't do it." I could see where this was going.

He lifted his hand holding the gun toward me.

Parker and I both fired before his gun drew in line.

"Jesus, I leave for one weekend and you end up in a shooting?" That was my partner, very sympathetic to my needs.

"Yes, Patti. That is exactly what I did. I searched for any case I could get my hands on even though we were not up. I found one and muscled my way into it. I identified one lead and one lead only, and followed that lead to a bar where I proceeded to fuck up so much I killed the only witness I had." I may not have handled the response correctly, but I had just sat through a two-hour interview with my union rep as Internal Affairs grilled me on why I was even on the case in the first place.

She could hear the tension in my voice which was not typical for me, even at times of stress. She often said I hid my emotions as well as anyone, so for me to bite her head off now told her more than just the words were saying. She quickly changed the direction of the conversation. "Carter already filled me in on the case while you and Parker were getting your asses handed to you." She paused. "You okay?"

I nodded but did not answer. She read the message perfectly. *No, bitch, I am not okay*. She raised her hand.

"Okay, partner, I get it. Do you want to talk about it now, or hold off till the morning?" Her voice had dropped about ten decibels and carried a much higher level of empathy than the previous sarcasm.

I shrugged. "Yeah, we can talk. Is Parker out?"

"I haven't talked to him but I saw him emerge about ten minutes before you."

I grabbed my phone and clicked on his number but still replied to Halterman as the phone rang. "Let's go into the Royals Room. I'll get Parker and see if Carter wants to join as well."

"You okay?" rang a voice through the receiver.

"Yeah, Parker, how about you?" I asked in return.

"Fucking I.A. assholes. Where do they get off basically telling me I shot a man without probable cause? I wanted to shoot those I.A. fuckers right there in that room."

"And had you done that, I would have backed you that you had probable cause. Those guys are always assholes." I have been through numerous officer-involved shootings. I have fired my gun at criminals more times than I care to mention and am responsible for more than twenty deaths. Together with Frank Sullivan, we are known for closing more homicide cases than any others in the department. However,

Franky has done it without all the blood on his hands. Therefore, that always brings up questions. By association with me, Parker now was in that mix. "Don't sweat Internal Affairs, Ollie. They're just doing their job. It's just that their job sucks." I didn't believe the comment, but it seemed like the right thing to say.

"Whatever," he replied. "What did you need?"

"Will you join me and Halterman in the Royals Room? Carter may come too. I just want to run through everything with my partner so I can cut you loose from the case."

"I'll be right up. I needed to grab some air. Give me ten minutes and I'll meet you guys there."

Parker's voice seemed tired. I imagined he was. To my knowledge, this was his first shooting with deadly force, since becoming a detective. I made a mental note to talk to him sometime soon after work. I was much older than Parker. The first time you kill someone in the line of duty affects everyone differently. If he needed support, I wanted him to know I was there and had experience. We had both fired, so there is no saying whose bullet did the trick. Neither were going to give Jimmy Teague the option of having a death on his belt. That much was certain.

A hand on my shoulder caused me to jump. "You okay, buddy? I heard about the shooting."

"Jesus!" I exclaimed as my eyes met my old partner's. "Did everyone come in today? It's Sunday afternoon, for Christ's sake."

Franky smiled slightly. "It may be Sunday afternoon, but two of our own were involved in a shooting. Where else should we be?"

I shook my head and then I smelled it. "You're shitting me?"

"Yep," Franky replied. "It's on your desk."

I glanced over and saw the foil-wrapped burrito. I would know the smell of El Famous anywhere. "Bean and cheese only?" I asked.

"Would I get you anything else?" He paused and tilted his head slightly asking again if I was okay without verbally saying a word. When again I did not reply, he added, "I felt it was more of a burrito day than a Dagwood, but you can correct me if I was wrong."

"No, partner, a burrito is perfect, and..."—I paused and lifted the football-sized beast to my mouth—"considering I shot a man today, I'm as fine as I can be."

"That shitty, huh?" he asked.

I nodded as I bit into my burrito.

"Well, if you don't mind, I'll join you in the discussion as an extra set of ears."

Whether I told him it was necessary or not would make no difference. Franky was most likely going to be the first one in the Royals Room and would take over writing on the whiteboard as we talked. "No problem, buddy. Join us in five."

◆   ◆   ◆

Over the next hour, we ran through the case. I included everything I knew from the party the night before and everything that I learned at the scene. I also did not hold back about Doctor Elise Gerstenberger, her house, her party, and her wealth. Although I told her I would do what I could to keep it a secret, I had learned a long time ago that secrets in an investigation served no purpose when those you were working with were kept in the dark. I explained her desire to not let her wealth become an issue at our respective jobs, and asked everyone involved to treat it with respect, but if they were going to be part of this investigation, they needed to know what I knew. I would circle back with Doc G later and let her know what I had shared and with whom. I hoped she would understand. I was pretty sure she would, but with everything going on, I really had no reason to be certain of anything. Regardless, I assumed I would not be invited to any future cocktail parties at her home.

"What's your next step?" asked Carter as he bit through some beef jerky he had brought with him.

In the room was Detective Oliver Parker, my partner Patti Halterman, Franky, and Carter. All eyes turned to me and for that instance, I wished I could fart on demand. We needed the icebreaker that only the remnants of an El Famous Burrito could bring. Alas, nothing happened and I almost shit my pants trying. Enough said on that. I turned to the board that Franky had filled with some extensive drawings. It included everything from a box flowchart of events to the people whose names we knew who could be knowledgeable on the events or involved in the murder. Halterman was actually pulling online pictures and printing them to go with the names.

I pointed. "I need to speak to both Elise and Dr. Alan Grove, her husband, as part of a formal interview. We also then need to follow up on Randy Thompson and retrace his steps from Saturday night until his murder more than thirty miles away Sunday morning. We need to know who he talked to and what he did in the last twelve hours of his life and perhaps the month or so prior." I paused and tilted my head without meaning to as I thought through the events. "You know, we need to learn everything we can about Thompson's life. We're all assuming this is related to his work or the pharma company in some way, but who says it's even related for sure?"

Franky shook his head. "I know you don't like to assume things, but I don't see how we can argue that his death and the concerns from Doc G aren't related."

Halterman seemed to agree with the comment but then added, "Jimmy Teague is probably a dead end. However, maybe he talked to someone at the bar or on his way there."

"And maybe he talked to the hooker," added Franky. "I know how they think. He was her protection. She would have called him to let him know you were coming. Maybe he said something to her."

Carter nodded. "Okay, let's start there. Ollie, you guys were officially next up. You want to speak for Hannifin and want to stay on this one with O'Malley and Halterman, or hand it off to Franky and Huston?"

Parker glanced over to Franky and then back to Carter. Parker may be newer to the department, but he knew how long Franky and I had worked together. "Hannifin and I will ride the bench this time, Sergeant. Until another case comes in, we will work the office for Tommy and Franky and help with some of the background and support. If nothing comes in for a week or so, you will have all of us working the case. Does that sound like a plan?"

To be honest, it was perfect. Carter wanted us both on the case. The three of us—Carter, Franky, and me—had worked with Doc G for more than twenty years. If she was in trouble or needed anything, he wanted the three of us working it. Parker's answer did exactly what Carter wanted. It allowed him to save face with the case order program he had initiated that removed favoritism from the department, but also put the teams on the case he wanted. "That sounds good with me," Carter answered. "Franky? Tommy? You both good?"

We both nodded as did Halterman. Franky then answered. "I will bring Huston up to speed tomorrow morning. We will hit it first thing."

I looked to Patti and then back to Carter. "I may blow a call into Doc G this afternoon and run back out there tonight. I need her and her husband to let me know what the hell is going on, and then I want some time to digest anything I learn." Turning back to my partner, I said, "Patti, I know you just got in. If you don't have time, because of who this is, I would be fine doing the interview on my own."

"I was going to suggest heading there tonight myself," she replied without hesitation.

"So be it," Carter replied. "But if they're not available, go ahead and put it off until tomorrow. Tread lightly on the doc and her family, but be thorough."

"Understood, Sargent," I replied, though he already knew I did.

With that, our meeting broke. I again thanked Detective Parker for his assistance and Franky for coming in on a Sunday. I pulled out my phone and spun through my speed dials to Doc G and hit the call button.

5 Detective Halterman and I arrived at Doctor Elise Gerstenberger and Dr. Alan Grove's house about an hour later. It was going on 7:00 PM and it had been approximately twenty-four hours since the first time I visited this house. I never thought I'd be back the next day for any reason, much less a murder. I could tell by her gaze that Patricia Halterman was amazed by the appearance of the home, or should I say, *estate*.

"You came to a party here?" she stated, more as a question than a statement. "Talk about being out of place."

"What the hell does that mean?" I asked in return.

Shaking her head, she said, "I mean no disrespect. In fact, I would rather you be someone out of place here than someone who was at home. But I couldn't afford the driveway, much less the whole property."

"It pays to be a doctor," I replied. "Now, put that prejudgment behind you and focus on the job at hand."

She got the message and quickly turned her tone back to the reason they were there. "I know Doc G is a friend of yours, Franky's, and Carter's for that matter. Do we handle the interview any differently because of that?"

"Not on your life," I replied. "We are interviewing persons of interest on the case. Nothing more, nothing less."

"You sure about that, Tommy?" she asked.

I stopped then grabbed her arm and turned her to face me. "I am sure."

My attempt at being more serious and forceful came across as trying to overstate something. I actually think I sounded less sure than if I had just answered normally. In truth, maybe I *was* less sure. Maybe I didn't want Elise's husband to be involved. I shrugged and turned back toward the front door. "Let's go."

As we approached the house, we heard the latch click and the door swing open before we were even within range of ringing the bell. Standing in the entryway was

Dr. Elise Gerstenberger and her husband, Dr. Alan Grove. They were dressed casually and although Alan reached his hand out to shake mine and Patti's, it was clear he was uncomfortable. I had called Elise prior to coming over. For starters, I wanted to make sure she was there, as it was a long drive out to the northern suburbs; moreover, I wanted to see what she did in response. Was she going to have prepared statements and answers? I told her I would like to speak to Alan as well and the warning gave him the opportunity to not be available. It's a little trick I use early in investigations to see if anyone has something to hide. The good news was that both Alan and Elise were here. Now came the tricky part. How do I get them to talk?

"Tommy," stated Elise first, breaking the momentary silence. "Thank you again for taking this case."

She reached out her arms in more of a hug than a handshake. To say it was awkward would be an understatement. I broke from shaking Alan's hand and then worked my way through to give Doc G a polite, quick, welcoming hug. I was sure she recognized I was uncomfortable. "So," I began and then was cut off.

"I'm so sorry, Tommy," she interrupted. "I didn't mean to..."

I now raised my hand. "No problem, Doc, but I do think we should go inside. Detective Halterman and I have some questions we need to ask both of you about this case."

"Of course," she replied. "And please, Patti, come in and make yourself comfortable." She motioned to the side. "I think it will be most comfortable in the study. Don't you agree, Alan?"

I think he was caught off guard as he stumbled over his response. "Uh...sure, the study would be fine." He began walking behind his wife before continuing. "Can I get either of you anything? Coffee, soda, Perrier?" He then stopped and turned to me. "A McNaughton's?"

I believe he meant it as a joke, but I really was in no mood, and my initial impression of my "friend," Dr. Alan Grove, was not good. If I didn't know him and this was a normal interview, I would believe he was uncomfortable and did not want me here. He was basically giving me the impression he had something to hide. He was jittery and awkward and in short, he did not like having two detectives in his house for reasons other than a friendly visit. I gave a slight laugh but did not answer. He turned and continued his walk to the study.

I watched Patti's eyes as we entered. "So this is the study?" she stated.

Elise replied, "It's really just an office,"

Patti looked on in disbelief. "An office that you could park two full-sized SUVs in and still have plenty of room to sit in front of the fireplace and grab a drink at the bar."

Patti had a way with words.

"Perhaps we should all sit at the table?" Elise was clearly trying to change the subject. She was definitely not comfortable with the conversation. "I did not hear if anyone would like a drink. McNaughton's aside, that is," she added with a slight tone directed toward her husband.

"I think we're fine," I replied. "I really don't want to take up too much of your time. We really just want to talk about the murder of one of your coworkers,"—I motioned toward Alan as I spoke—"as well as the concerns you discussed with me last night that suddenly seem more important now that someone has been killed."

"You had concerns, hon?" Alan asked toward Elise.

That was an interesting start to this, I immediately thought. I could see the instant hesitation and surprise in her response. I wondered if Halterman saw it as well. When I glanced at her, I was certain she had.

Elise stumbled just for a second and then replied, "Well, Alan, something simply didn't seem right. In the course of a conversation with Tommy, I must have alluded to that."

Alan didn't respond to the comment but turned back toward me. Although noticeably angry about that exchange, it showed only in his facial expression, not in his tone. "So tell me, Tommy, what do you need to know?"

I took the lead. "For starters, the easy question is, tell me about last night. After I left, did anything out of the ordinary happen? More specifically, did anything out of the ordinary happen with Dr. Randy Thompson?"

I had directed the question toward Dr. Grove, but Elise immediately responded, "No, nothing I was informed of. When you left, I did the tour around the house— shaking hands, making small talk, saying hello—you know, all the host's duties."

I nodded and turned to Alan. "But as I remember it, you were going to bring the group in here to talk and have some cigars. Did you end up doing that?" Again, Elise went to answer and I held up my hand. "I really need to hear from your husband on this one. He was closer to the situation and clearly spent more time with Dr. Thompson."

Alan twisted a little in his chair as if he had been sitting so long that he had started to feel pain from the position. He did not speak immediately and appeared as if he was trying hard to remember. He appeared to be poised like Rodin's statue, *The*

Thinker. This had to be for show, and it was not changing my initial impression of him today.

He finally broke the silence. "I don't remember anything unusual." Then it went back to silence. Uncomfortable, long silence.

I don't remember anything unusual? I thought. That's all you have for me. So I sat in silence and stared at him. I did not reply nor did I break my stare. His eyes were locked on mine in return. I actually didn't know what the hell was going on here. I was becoming nervous and uncomfortable so I knew Elise must be coming out of her skin.

"Alan, you have to give Tommy more than that," she stated, breaking the monotonous silence. "What did you guys talk about? How long were you together?"

"Even how much did you drink and smoke?" Halterman added. "We need to know about Dr. Thompson's last night alive. We can ask these questions here or we can do it at the station tomorrow. It's one hundred percent your call. You should realize, though, the latter would give the impression you have something to hide."

Wow, I thought. Good cop-bad cop. I did not expect it and I never got to play good cop, but because of my relationship with them, it worked. I glanced toward my partner; she recognized my look and knew I liked her direction.

"Just a minute," stated Alan, now a bit defensive. "I don't have anything to hide. Tommy asked me a question and I answered it. You didn't ask me about specifics, just if anything out of the ordinary happened, and it didn't."

I smiled slightly and responded in a soft tone, almost speaking like a teacher to a student. "Actually, you did not answer it originally. You said you didn't remember. Not remembering is a trademark answer for someone who is hiding something. It's a way to answer a question and not say anything that can be used against them in a court of law, because later, under oath, they can say they didn't remember at the time, but they do now. What you just said—that nothing out of the ordinary happened— are not the words of a guilty person. It's a statement about the evening. Now, to steal some questions from your wife, let's talk about what took place after I left. When I was introduced to your small group, you all had drinks. How much did you drink?"

"What does that have to do with anything?" Alan asked, with a touch of tone still present.

"I'm trying to determine if Dr. Thompson left your house under the influence. He was found nearly forty miles away. We need to know what state he was in to determine if he drove or was taken there. However, if you don't mind and in the interest of time, I would appreciate it if you let me ask the questions and you focus on answering them."

He didn't react to what I just said and actually went straight into a description of the evening. "After you left, we all came to this very room. We had several discussions about Abbunex. We had several drinks from the bar, and yes, we each had a cigar. For us, the evening ended for the most part right here."

"Did you talk about anything other than Abbunex?" asked Patti.

Back came *The Thinker*. Jesus, this guy.

After several moments, he answered. "Several of us have kids in college or even older. Randy was the only one with younger kids. We talked about them a bit. His boy plays hockey and Randy hates the team because it's so political. His daughter dances and he complained about how much dance costs. Other than that, no, we didn't talk about anything other than Abbunex."

"What about Abbunex did you discuss?" I asked.

"Mostly the IGB100 Emplex Project," he answered.

My ears perked up as that sounded important. "What is the IGB100 Emplex Project?"

He stood and began to pace a bit. It was not completely out of what I would call normal behavior, and could simply have been that he thinks better when he walks, or it could have been a delay tactic as he thought about what to say. In other words, it could be nothing, or it could be something. He turned back to Patti and me. "I can only speak to what is public knowledge. Because of SEC rules and such, when a pharmaceutical company has new products in trials, only the information that has been released may be openly discussed."

Patti interrupted him. "SEC rules?"

Alan pressed his lips together making an, *are you serious?* face. "The Securities and Exchange Commission. The governing body over publicly traded companies and designed to protect investors." He paused and then directed a question toward my partner, "Do you not know anything about public companies, trading stocks, and so forth?"

"My portfolio is a little low right now," she responded snidely. "Just go on with..."—she paused and added a touch of sarcastic inflection—"the information you are *able* to share because it's public knowledge."

Alan rolled his eyes and continued to pace. During that pause, I felt I could use the opportunity to interject my position. "Listen, Alan. I mean no disrespect, but neither of us are going to use any of this information for the purpose of stock trading.

We could pool our disposable income and not purchase one share of Abbunex stock. We are investigating a murder. A murder in which the last people to see the victim alive very possibly are standing in front of us. I would suggest for your own future, you cut the crap and tell us what the hell you know about Randy Thompson. I need to know everything that took place last night up until the last moment you saw him. Who did he talk to? Who did he leave with? Did he use the bathroom? Was he gone for any period of time? Did he take a phone call or receive a text message that upset him? Did he appear agitated? I need that information immediately. Regarding whatever that Emplex thing is, yes, I need to know what your discussion was about it, but I only care if it caused any issues or you sensed anything special about it. I need to know why someone wanted Randy Thompson dead, because I find it hard to believe the person who wanted him dead was not in your house last night."

I thought Elise was going to interject something but I shot her a glance and she held her response. I really didn't think Alan was guilty of anything, but I also thought he was not telling me everything. While I was speaking, Alan stopped his pacing and turned back toward me. His stare was hard and locked directly on me. His demeanor changed. He no longer gave any appearance of nervousness. It was as if my small push on him took him to some different level. He started acting like an unemotional executive. Instantly, I was reminded why the guys with the brass have the brass, and the guys like me don't.

"Well, Detective, it really doesn't matter if you're the President of the United States or a homeless man on the street, the law is very clear on what I can or cannot say about Emplex. The answer, therefore, is I cannot speak about the conversation my team had last night on the subject."

I did not interrupt him but I was surprised he called me by title rather than my name. After all, I had known him for more than twenty years. Yes, his demeanor had changed.

"Regarding Dr. Thompson," he began.

Again so formal, I thought. This is a man he worked with, he had at his house last night, and he had clearly known for years. Why not call him Randy?

Alan continued, "He was a great guy, liked by all at Abbunex. In fact, the only thing I ever heard him complain about was his kid's hockey games, specifically the politics around it."

I really wasn't concerned about his kid's sports, but I could tell Alan was separating from me and I wanted to show interest. "Tell me about that. How do you know about the hockey stuff?" Patti swung her eyes to me in a, *what the hell are you asking that for?* glance.

Alan seemed to soften. "Well, he even talked about it last night. He was the head coach and one of the other parents very openly didn't like his coaching, didn't like how he split up playing time, and basically made his discontent well known to everyone."

"How did he do that?" I asked.

He tilted his head. "I don't know for sure. I think he said things, complained to the league, and talked to other parents...you know, things like that."

"I see," I replied, now pretending to take notes. "Do you happen to know the parent's name that had the issue?"

Alan now smiled. "You know, I do, but only because Ryan made such a joke about it." He paused and for a second I wasn't sure he was going to actually answer the question. Then he continued, "His name is Ryan Larson, but his wife's maiden name is Beamer and she kept it as her middle name. Because of that, he said everyone called him Beamer." He laughed as he said it. "He kept saying Beamer was always complaining to me about my coaching."

I wasn't sure why it was a joke, so my interest was raised. "Why was that funny?" I asked.

Alan was still smiling. "Because he had the perfect nickname to drive a BMW, but instead he drove a Mercedes." Neither Patti nor I reacted correctly because Alan felt he had to take it further. "It would be like being named Tesla but driving a Ford. Don't you get it?"

"Oh, yeah," Patti answered. "We get it."

"Okay," I stated, breaking into the conversation. "Beamer doesn't like Dr. Thompson." I felt powerful using his title now that Alan had converted back to his first name. "But do you really think from what you heard about this story that he's a suspect?"

Alan now sat down in a chair next to us. "You know, he would be as good as any suspect because there's nobody at Abbunex Labs that would have anything negative to say about Randy."

"Fair enough," I replied. "Why don't you tell me about Abbunex Labs?"

"What is there to tell you? We are one of the largest and most successful pharmaceutical companies in the world. We're too big to ever be bought and we are the ones buying up other companies. We have numerous products in our pipeline and business is good."

"So why, then, did someone on your senior leadership team end up dead last night?"

Elise now broke in. "You know my theory, check out the family."

Fascinating, I thought. Doctor Elise Gerstenberger would never offer a statement like that during one of her investigations. She was all about the facts. What the hell did she mean by that? I knew her well enough to ask. "Doc G, are you throwing out a theory without any facts?"

"On the contrary, Tommy. I'm listening to my husband tell you he has no idea who would want Dr. Randy Thompson dead, and you are pursuing hockey parents and fellow workers."

That was a far cry from the woman who twenty-four hours ago swore that there was something fishy going on at Abbunex and her husband was involved with it.

"Is that true, Alan, that you have no idea who would want Dr. Randy Thompson dead?" Patti asked.

He nodded. "That is absolutely true. The man was well liked, end of discussion."

I glared at Elise but she didn't care. I think she sensed the same thing I did—that her husband was indeed hiding something—or if nothing else, acting strange about this discussion. His tone had changed too much, and he was not trying to help the investigation. He was trying to answer questions quickly and with as little information as possible.

"Back to Abbunex Labs," I stated turning back to Alan. "Who is on the senior leadership team?" He pressed his lips together and acted like he didn't want to answer. I did not give him a chance and shot back immediately. "Goddamn it, Alan, get off your bullshit. I can go online and find out every name. You're acting like you're hiding something and these are not even hard questions. Just help me out here."

That seemed to strike a nerve. He glanced toward his wife then back to me. I thought he was going to protest or be defensive, but to my surprise, he simply answered. His voice again was hard and flat, with no inflection or nerve showing. "Besides me, there is Dr. Darryn Hermann, CEO; Doctor Reed Anderson, President of R&D; Julian Stover, CFO; and Dr. Joseph Reingold, SVP Quality." He paused then added, "And then there's Dr. Dennis Child who is the head pharmacist."

"You didn't mention Dr. Thompson?" I asked.

"That's because he is below Joe in Quality," he replied.

"So Dr. Thompson was not on the senior executive team?"

"I believe I just answered that," Alan replied.

Ignoring the tone, I proceeded with my next question. "And if you don't mind," I asked, "what is your title?"

"I'm the President of Manufacturing."

"Nice," I replied. "You have obviously worked hard to get where you are."

"So who is below Dr. Randy Thompson on the organization chart?" Patti asked.

Alan turned to her and rolled his eyes. "What, you think someone killed him for a promotion?"

"Did they?" she answered with a question of her own.

"No, they didn't," he stated flatly.

"Then there's no harm in telling me who will be moving up on Monday."

He shrugged. "You will have to ask Joe. Quality is not my department."

Yep, I thought, he's definitely hiding something. I knew it, Patti knew it, and Doctor Elise Gerstenberger knew it.

"Do you have any other questions?" Elise asked.

"I have a shitload of questions, Doc, but I think they will wait." I turned back to face Dr. Grove. "Alan, you really seem to be hiding something. I'm not sure what it is, and I'm going to give you the benefit of the doubt today because you lost your friend and are probably in 'circle the wagon' mode because you don't know how this will affect the company, but I will be back with more questions and you will need to figure out your answers when I return."

"I don't know what to tell you, Tommy, I have told you all that I know."

First names now, interesting. "I hope so," I replied, turning my comment more to Elise than Alan. "I'm sure your wife can tell you how critical it is to deal with facts in these situations, and how the longer we wait, the less chance there is of solving a case."

Just then Alan's phone rang. He looked at the screen and made a face. "I apologize, Detectives, but I need to take this." He stood and walked a few steps toward the door. "This is Alan," he stated into the phone, but his voice dropped significantly, and I was confident I wouldn't hear any more of the conversation.

As if on cue, my phone rang. I looked at the number and it was Carter. "What's up, Sergeant?" I answered.

His voice was direct and to the point. "They have another body, but this one is just outside Abbunex. They already have an identification. Julian Stover, some bigwig at Abbunex. Have you met with Doc G's husband yet?"

I nearly dropped the phone upon hearing the name of the victim literally minutes after hearing it the first time from Dr. Grove. "I'm at their place now," I replied, loud enough for Patti as well as Elise to hear. Both women looked up to me and were instantly tied to my every word.

"Then question him hard about it," stated Carter. "There are too many coincidences and too much bullshit to not be related. Once you're done there, get your ass up to the accident site. I'll have the address texted to you. I have instructed those on site to sit tight until you arrive."

As I hung up the phone, Alan reentered the room and appeared agitated. "I have to apologize, but something has come up and I'm going to have to ask you to leave. I'll be glad to speak more later, but I do have a work issue that I need to address."

"Does your work issue have anything to do with Julian Stover?" I asked.

He froze in his tracks. "How the hell do you know that?"

I was growing angry with his vague responses, and it was clear in my tone. "My question is, how the hell do *you* know about it, and why were you not going to say anything to me?"

He opened his arm to guide me toward the door. "At this time, I have nothing to say. Obviously you know more than I do as I just received the call. Besides that, I have much bigger things to worry about than whether you're getting what you need to solve a murder. Now we have a car accident on top of it, and a second member, this one on the senior leadership team, is dead."

"Julian is dead?" asked Elise. Her voice was soft and caring mixed with shock and concern. "How?"

"Darryn said it was a car accident. That's all I know." Alan was still motioning Patti and me out the door but neither of us had moved. "Now, Detectives, I'm trying not to lose my patience, but I need to get to work immediately."

"So," I began, "I want to give this whole thing one formal run-through, if you'll humor me. It won't even take a minute and it may give everyone a real taste of what we're looking at." I paused and when it appeared Dr. Grove was not going to leave immediately, I continued. "So last night I show up at a party I had no business being at because your wife invited me. During that party, I come to find out that your wife has some concerns with things going on at your place of work, and she wanted my opinion. Within twenty-four hours, two of the people at that party, both fairly high up in rank at Abbunex, are dead." I paused and locked my stare on Dr. Alan Grove's eyes. "I would say your wife's concerns were justified, wouldn't you, Doctor?"

He did not break his stare with me. "I can't speak for my wife, but my concern is for the company. Whatever Randy was involved with, I cannot say. Julian having a car accident was just bad timing. However, when word gets out that two members this high up in Abbunex are dead, it will drive the stock down, and that, my friends, is something the world watches."

"I suppose so," I replied, now moving to step past him. "We can show ourselves out."

"Nonsense, Tommy, I will walk you out," added Elise.

Alan grabbed her arm as she passed him and whispered at a level neither Patti nor I could hear. "No more talking to your colleagues about Abbunex." He then released her arm and she continued behind us.

I could see the white finger marks left on her arm clearly depicting a very tight grip. Maybe this guy was not the awesome husband I had always believed him to be. He did nothing to help his case today, that much was certain.

6 When we arrived at the scene of the accident outside Abbunex, we were immediately struck with the severity of what had taken place. There were multiple police cars and an ambulance. The medical examiner from North Chicago was already present. He was very competent. I knew him fairly well as he had been in his role for as long as Doc G, but because I was in downtown Chicago and he was up north, our paths did not cross very often. Unfortunately for us, several killers moved throughout Chicagoland so our murders did overlap more times than either of us would like to admit. I had been told on the phone that it was as Alan said—a car accident. However, based on the number of emergency vehicles around here, it was very clear upon first look that it was pretty bad.

This was not my official jurisdiction, but all the detectives from the different areas worked together on related cases. Although these were not connected by the type of death, when two people linked this closely die within eighteen hours of each other, they instantly become paired. Sergeant Carter had spoken to Sergeant Jeff Dalponte of North Chicago, who I knew from the Polino-Moretti Case and worked with before he took the promotion up north. Jeff paved the way for me and Patti to take part in this case, at least until we confirmed it was an accident.

"O'Malley, long time no see," stated Sergeant Dalponte.

I shook the large man's hand. By large, I do not mean overweight, fat, or anything derogatory. I mean he was 6'8" tall, a former army rat, and basically a brick shithouse. His grip was like someone squeezing a bottle of ketchup to get the last drip out of the bottom, and I was sure he had no idea those he shook hands with often left with nearly broken fingers. I warned Patti but not in time. She cringed as their hands released.

"Hello, Jeff, good to see you. This is my new partner, Patti Halterman." I motioned to Patti who was still looking at her hand and stretching her fingers.

"Partner? Something happen to Franky? Did he not come back after the shooting?"

It had been a while since I had crossed paths with Sergeant Dalponte. Jeff was handler for the undercover vice lieutenant who got in over her head with Moretti and Polino. He was also with us during the raid on the closed batting cage warehouse where that undercover lieutenant and several others, including my girlfriend, Tammi Hutchins, were found murdered or close to it.

I shook my head and pressed my lips together before replying. "No, Franky is still hanging in there. Carter just thought it would be good for us to disperse all of our great wisdom to some younger detectives and split us up."

Patti rolled her eyes. "Yeah, wisdom dispersement—that was the reason."

Dalponte smiled. "Don't worry, Patti. I've known O'Malley a long time, and I can smell his bullshit from a mile away."

We all started to grin, but we also knew the small talk needed to end. "What do we have here?" I asked.

He turned and we walked toward the cars. "Well," started Dalponte, "It seems the blue car T-boned the Vette at a high rate of speed. Being a '70 Corvette, the body is fiberglass and buckled at impact. The driver was thrown from the car about twenty-five feet on the embankment. We don't believe he was wearing his seat belt which was only a lap belt at best anyway. For some reason, even in the cold, he had his T-tops off."

"Jesus," Halterman said as she looked across the scene.

"You said it, Halterman," Dalponte replied. "Though I don't think Jesus had anything to do with this one."

We arrived at the cars. The Corvette was nearly split in half. The driver's side door was pushed more than halfway across the middle of the passenger compartment and almost the entire frame was splintered and broken. The fiberglass body was a total loss. I'm fairly good at estimating speed in accidents by only looking at the scene—one of my inherent traits that not only made me what everyone called the best detective in Chicago, but also fun at parties, like guessing someone's weight. Without any other facts, I would guess the speed of the car doing the T-boning was at least 50, possibly 60 mph.

"This doesn't make sense. Where was this car going? There's no road in the direction of its impact."

The second car, the one that did the T-boning, was perpendicular in the road. It had pushed the Vette off onto the shoulder and grass by at least twelve feet. Dalponte pointed. "Good eye, Detective. However, that is not the most interesting fact."

The comment was open-ended and I could tell he wanted one of us to fish for more. It was like he was increasing the drama or something. "I'll bite," I said. "What is the most interesting thing?"

"Would it change your thoughts to know that the car causing the impact, the Bonneville, was stolen?"

Patti rolled her eyes. "Then it was not an accident."

Dalponte nodded. "We are not ruling out the possibility of a drunk driver, but all signs in my opinion seem to point to this being a targeted situation. The Bonneville was used as the weapon to commit a murder."

"Just the same as pulling the trigger on a gun," added Patti.

"Yep," Dalponte replied. "I have the forensics team checking out the car, but it was amazingly clean. We are also reaching out to the owner of the car, although it was reported stolen about five hours ago."

"I assume no sign of the driver?" I asked.

"Nope, but there was some sort of red paint on the airbag."

I raised an eyebrow, almost turning the comment into a question. "Red paint?" I asked. "That's definitely different. What would have caused paint to transfer to the airbag?"

Dalponte nodded. "That was our question too. My forensics team will find the source. Other than that, we don't have anything yet. We're reaching out to the family of the victim. I think I heard on the radio they arrived a few minutes before you."

"How do you want to work this, Sergeant? Do you want us alongside your team? Do you want us not involved and you share what you discover?"

He smiled. "This is not some jurisdictional bullshit, O'Malley. Carter walked me through what you have been working on the last twenty-four hours. This is your case. Unless you determine it's just an accident, a drunk driver hit-and-run, or something similar, you and Halterman will be running point. I will introduce you to the forensics team and get you access to our department information. I would request you run your activity through me, meaning if you are serving a warrant or meeting with witnesses, let me know what is happening and when. Other than that, go find this killer."

I don't think I hid my smile well, but regardless, I was pleased. "Thank you, Sergeant, we'll find out what happened here."

He reached out to shake my partner's hand again and she reluctantly complied. I held up my fist and exchanged a very manly fist bump. Halterman glared at the action and I knew I would hear about it later. We parted and Dalponte exited in the direction of the forensics team. I would meet with them later. My first stop would be the family of the victim. I wanted to get to them before they had time to think this through. I was pretty sure I knew who they were. I saw a woman crying and what looked to be a teenage boy staring at the Vette.

We approached slowly, as they were talking to a uniformed police officer who I think was simply trying to find out where to send them. I had not seen the condition of the body, but it most likely was not good so I hoped she didn't send them there. We arrived just as they were being asked to wait while the officer went to find the right person. "I can take over if you like, Officer?"

"Peterson," she replied. "Kristin Peterson." She paused, looked closely at me, and realized she had no idea who I was nor my partner for that matter. "I need to speak with Sergeant Dalponte," she added reluctantly.

"Why don't you do that, Officer Peterson?" I reached out my hand to her. "I'm Detective O'Malley and this is Detective Halterman. We're from Chicago. Sergeant Dalponte has asked us to be point on this case as it ties back to our case in the city."

She seemed to instantly relax upon hearing this, and although I did believe she was going to verify our story with Dalponte, I think she was happier to simply release these individuals to us. Younger officers never like giving notices to families. Hell, nobody liked giving notices. However, when someone had not previously done it often or at all, it could be overwhelming. We would take that burden for her today.

I turned to who I presumed was Julian Stover's wife. "As you may have heard, I'm Detective Tomas O'Malley and this is Detective Patti Halterman. Can I ask who you are?" I was certain this was Julian Stover's wife and son, but I needed them to confirm this before we could speak about what happened.

The woman's voice was frail. She was clearly distraught and worried, but it did appear she was still holding onto some hope that although her husband's car was nearly split in half, her husband was still alive. "I'm Wilma Stover...Julian Stover's wife. This is our son, Russell." Her voice cracked and she took a break from speaking. I used the time to control my instant thought—Russell Stover. Who the hell would name their kid Russell Stover? "We got a call that there was an accident," she finally continued.

"Yes, ma'am, there was an accident, and it involved your husband. They have cordoned off an area over here. Will you please join me? They have some chairs and

I think it will be easier to talk." I was trying to be empathetic, but I kept thinking about Russell Stover. I wondered if there was any chance he could meet and marry Cindy Hershey or Reese S. Piece.

Wilma's voice got stronger. "I don't want to go anywhere until I see my husband."

I glanced to Patti and she nodded. My candy thoughts quickly left my mind and instantly I was back on task. "Well, Mrs. Stover..."—I turned empathetically to her son—"Russell." Oops, the minute I said his name the thoughts came back. "I regret to inform you that your husband, and father, was killed in a two-vehicle accident as he left the facility."

Russell looked down immediately. I don't think it had occurred to him that his dad had been killed. He was clearly fighting away tears that he didn't want to show. I wished there was a way to tell teenagers not to worry about what other people do or say. If you need to cry, then cry. But teenagers, especially boys, will do everything they can to not let that show. Wilma was not so reluctant. Her tears came immediately and came hard. She dropped her head into her hands and tried to talk and ask questions but the words were not recognizable.

I assumed what I thought she was going to say and answered as appropriate. "We don't have any facts at this time. All we know is a car broadsided your husband's car at a high rate of speed. The driver of that car did not remain on the scene. Your husband was thrown from his car and is believed to have died upon impact." The truth is, I didn't know if that last statement was true, but people should always believe their loved ones did not suffer.

She continued to cry. It was the type of crying that was hard to listen to because it sounded like it hurt. Patti and I sat in silence and let it happen. Russell moved next to his mom and put his arm around her. He whispered something we couldn't hear but it did seem to give her some strength. She lifted her head to us. "I want to see him."

Patti looked immediately to me and I thought she was going to protest, but she held her tongue and allowed me to reply. "I'm not sure the medical examiner is done on the scene. To be honest, we have not even seen him yet. We also have several questions we need to ask. However, at some point we will need to perform a positive identification. If you're sure you're ready, we can walk over there now."

She did not answer other than a nod. I glanced toward Patti who seemed content with the direction. I then looked to Russell who appeared to be reluctantly following. We approached the accident scene. The local police had affixed some temporary lights which ran on a generator. Besides the obvious ability to see, it also created an ability to not hear. The gas motors churned loudly and the smell that would be expected was strong, but I don't think either Wilma or Russell heard or smelled anything. Their attention was focused on one area. A pair of medical professionals were working over a body. When our approach was noticed, one of the individuals tapped the other on the shoulder and pointed. When our eyes met, he instantly softened his annoyed stare and stood to walk our direction.

"Detective O'Malley, what has it been, two years?" asked the chief medical examiner.

"Unfortunately, I think it has been less than half of that, but who's counting?" I turned to Patti. Red Ayres, this is my partner, Patricia Halterman." Turning to my partner, I said, "Patti, this is Dr. Red Ayres."

She reached out her hand. "Red, it's a pleasure to meet you, and please call me Patti."

Red removed his glove and they shook hands while both Wilma and Russell stood almost hiding behind us. I moved apart from Patti so they could also be introduced. "Red, this is Wilma and Russell. Wilma is the spouse of the deceased and Russell is the son. They wanted to perform a positive identification before they go any further."

The medical examiner frowned. "I really would not recommend that. We should wait until I get him back to my lab and can better prepare..."

Wilma raised her hand. "With all due respect, Dr. Ayres, I need to see...I need to see my husband."

Red pressed his lips together and clearly did not want this to move forward. He looked to me and I nodded slightly. "Okay," he replied, his tone still depicting this was not a good idea. "You are going to see him as an accident victim. We have not been able to clean him up at all as we're still trying to determine the specifics."

She did not respond and slowly began walking past us toward where they had been working. Red motioned to his assistant to back away, and he complied without comment. When Wilma and Russell got close enough to see, Wilma fell into her son's arms. I walked up behind the two. "Is this your husband?" As I said it, I looked to the body and had to turn away. For someone who had seen as many crime scenes as I had, even I was taken by this one. Julian Stover's body was twisted like a pretzel. One of his arms was bent back behind his torso and one of his legs was no longer attached at the knee. His face was blood-soaked and you could barely make out his hair color.

Through muffled tears, Wilma replied, "Yes."

We spent the next ninety minutes interviewing Wilma, her son Russell, and any other witness or person of interest we could find. In the end, I felt like we had less evidence than when we started. Wilma and Russell thought the world of Julian, and everyone else we talked to had nothing but positive things to say about him. Although Dr. Alan Grove was supposed to be coming to Abbunex at the same time we were, we never saw him. We did meet with several other Abbunex employees initially, and all had wonderful things to say about Julian Stover. However, none were very high up in the ranks so I don't know if they really knew him or not, and none were witnesses of the accident. At some point, I believe word was spread that no employees were to speak with the police and our options got less and less. It was late and we still had a long drive back to Chicago.

"So, what do we know?" asked Patti.

I glanced over at her and then back to the Interstate. "We know that two individuals, one very high up in rank and one on his way there, were killed within eighteen hours of each other, and both within twenty-four hours of concerns being brought up about the company."

Patti nodded. "What else do we know?"

I shook my head. "Not much. What do you think?"

Her body response seemed to match my tone telling me she did not have much to add. "Well, Doc G's husband was lying or at a minimum hiding something."

"I would agree with that, though we have no proof."

"Agreed," she replied. "Also, where was he? If this was one of his close colleagues, why the hell was he not on the scene? The press were there. The police were there. But there were no representatives from the company."

"I was thinking the same thing, but is it because right now it's still just an accident? Two cars collide. If the same people were in an accident in Naperville, we would not expect a company representative. Is it only because it was outside their entrance that this brings the question to mind?"

She thought a minute. "I guess so, but this is two executives in the same day. One essentially in their parking lot. Someone should have been there and we know Grove was on site because he left before us."

"I'm not disagreeing with you, I'm just playing devil's advocate."

"And perhaps most importantly," she began, "who names their kid after a candy company?"

"Thank you," I stated flatly. "I couldn't get it out of my mind every time his name was said."

She smiled. "I know you couldn't." Her tone changed. "Do you want to get a drink?"

Her question completely blindsided me. Patti and I had had a strange relationship. She had become my partner on essentially the same day my girlfriend, who I thought I might marry, told me she took a job in California and had a flight to catch. When Tammi left, Patti entered. We had not crossed any lines, but there were several occasions where I thought we might, and I was sure she thought so also. I did find myself thinking about her, just like now when I'm driving thinking about a case and she asks me for a drink.

She appeared concerned when I didn't answer. "I wasn't trying to scare you or anything. I just think I could use something with some kick."

"Sorry," I replied with my voice showing my slight embarrassment. "I was just thinking about the case. I would love a drink. Do you want to stop somewhere around here or wait until we get downtown?"

"Let's wait. I want to get back to my comfort zone."

"Sounds good to me," I answered. "Do you want to call Franky? I'm sure he's available." I smiled a little when I said it thinking about him sitting in his recliner with Darth Vader on his lap.

"Nah," she replied. "Franky is not needed tonight."

I wanted to say, "Bingo," but in truth, I was suddenly scared shitless. In a voice that sounded more like a romance novel audible reader, I replied, "Sounds good to me."

She smiled at my tone, but did not comment further.

7 We had just pulled into the Loop when Patti fired this zinger across the bow. "Sure, Flap Jaws sounds good, but I'm sure you have a stocked bar at your place. Why don't we just go there? Cheaper, and prevents you from driving or having to leave your car at the bar."

"Ah, sure, we can do that," I replied. I wanted to say, *Yeah baby, I'm down with that. Let's go back to my crib and let things happen. Ya know what I'm sayin'?* But I simply did not have the guts.

We arrived at my apartment, and it was already 10:45 PM. "You sure you don't want me to just take you home? It is late."

"Shut up, O'Malley. We need to talk so shag your ass inside and let's talk."

We got out of the car and began walking toward my building when I saw her. Patti had not seen her yet but I was sure the connection was coming.

"Tommy?" she said in a voice loud enough to be heard by us but muffled enough to not bother anyone else.

"Doctor Gerstenberger? What are you doing here?" I asked. When we got close enough to see expressions, it was clear she had been crying. "Are you okay?" I added.

"What are you doing here, is probably the better question?" my partner interjected.

I shot her a quick glance, but I also knew she was right.

Elise looked to me and then to Patti. "I'm very sorry to interrupt. I assumed you would be alone."

"Are you talking to me or Tommy?" Patti replied.

Elise glared at her. "What do you think, Patti?"

I was not going to let whatever this was to continue. "What do you need, Elise?" I asked.

She seemed hesitant. "I shouldn't have come. I just wanted to talk to you about..." She paused in mid-sentence then added, "I should go."

"You might as well stay," Patti added. "I was simply going to Uber home."

I swung my head over to her and she gave me the, *it's about solving the case*, stare, and I didn't respond. However, I still wanted to have that drink. "Before you leave, Patti, let's hear what Elise has to say."

"No, I need to get going. It's late." With that, Patti turned and walked toward the corner pulling out her phone in the process. I watched her walk away and whether Elise's presence caused it or not, my attitude was now salty.

"What do you want, Doc?" I said with more than just a touch of tone.

She cowered and her response was very timid. "I'm sorry. I didn't know you guys were—"

"We're not," I interrupted abruptly. "I spent the day, my birthday mind you, at two murder scenes, one of which led to a shooting, on a weekend I did not intend to work. She drove back from a short trip only to be forced back into work. Then, to top it off, we interviewed a couple I thought were friends only to be given the runaround. We thought it would be nice to grab a drink and talk through things but didn't want to deal with driving, so we stopped here since Patti didn't have her car anyway and she would take a taxi home from wherever we went." I paused and narrowed my stare. "Now, one last time, why are you here?"

She still was timid when she answered. "Can we go inside? I just..."

She didn't complete her sentence and it was not because I interrupted her. I didn't know what this meant, but I needed some answers. I motioned her toward my door and after unlocking it, I pushed it open and guided her inside. "Elise, this is obviously not quite the same as your house so please don't patronize me with comments about how much you like my place. I'm not in the mood for bullshit tonight. Frankly, I'm not happy you're here and it has nothing to do with missing a drink with Halterman. I'm going to have that drink whether she's here or not. I don't like it because I think you're going to ask me about the case and I thought I made it clear in the beginning that we would not have those discussions."

Elise walked into the living room while I was talking and turned back hard at my last statement. "Damn it, Tommy, I'm not here to ask you about the case. Get over yourself. I am not here to save my marriage or protect my husband. I'm here to help you *solve* this case."

I'm sure I gave her an, *I'll believe it when I see it*, look. "Okay then, Elise, help me solve this case."

"Where do I begin?" she started, causing me to roll my eyes again. She saw the reaction and did not ask again. "So, after you left, I pulled Alan aside before I let him leave and asked him point blank what was going on. I truly don't believe he knows anything. I asked every question I could, drilling him about the company performance, specifics about each of the victims, and everything else I could come up with. He didn't know anything."

Wow, I thought. *This is really helpful with the case and you definitely are not trying to protect your husband.*

Elise continued. "But the way he answered, or maybe it's better to say the way he did *not* answer, your questions, it just didn't sit with me. So I asked him what everyone had in common. What was the link between Randy Thompson and Julian Stover? And you know what he said?"

She stopped talking so I wasn't sure if this question was rhetorical or not. Because there was a pause, I thought I would give a very in-depth and well-thought-out answer. "No."

"My husband, the president of manufacturing for one of the largest pharmaceutical companies in the world, replied by saying, *I don't know*. Can you believe that? I don't know, my ass. I was so mad I wanted to tear him apart."

She was almost yelling now so she was either putting on one of the best performances I had ever seen or she was really trying to find the truth about her husband and these murders. Surprising as it was to me, I believed this was just a performance. "So what did you do?" I asked.

"Before or after I slapped him?"

"Either, if it helps me on this case."

She smiled. "I told him that you didn't believe him, and I told him *I* didn't believe him."

"What did he say to that?" I asked.

"He told me to fuck off. He said I should have never brought you into the case."

"Interesting," I replied. To be honest, I was now intrigued. "Why don't you come into my study and grab a seat? And by study, I mean *kitchen*."

Through everything, I still made her smile at the study reference before she walked into the kitchen and took a seat at the table. "Look, it is a study, you have a book."

I had left a book on the kitchen table which she proceeded to pick up. "I didn't know you read books, especially dragon fantasy. *The Return of the Dragons, Hidden Magic Volume 1*. Is it good?"

For some reason I was embarrassed, but at this point, I didn't care. "Yes, it is very good. The writer is very talented and I can barely put it down. It's the first book of a trilogy."

"Nice, I will have to keep it in mind for my reading group."

Okay, this was going down a path it should not. I needed to redirect it. "So what did you say after he told you to fuck off?"

She smiled at the abrupt conversation change away from award-winning dragon fantasy books. "I asked him why. I asked if he was scared about what you might find?" She paused and let that sink in but did not give me a chance to respond. "He then looked right at me and said, absolutely he was scared. He said no matter what the cause of these tragedies, we stand to lose millions if the stock price goes down, especially right before the results of the Phase 3 trials for Emplex."

"He said that?" I asked. "He used the word *millions*?"

"Yes," she replied. "That caught me also. How the hell could we have millions of dollars' worth of exposure on one company? Even with the company he works for, we agreed from the start to diversify everything. So I asked him that question straight-up, and you want to know what he said?"

"Yes, I do," I replied, whether that was rhetorical or not.

"He told me it was below my understanding."

I could tell that did not sit well with her. "Below your understanding?"

"Oh, don't get me started, Tommy. I just about flew out of my skin."

I smiled at her response but I needed to know where this was going. Right now, we really did not have anything new. "So what happened next? What did you say to that?"

"He didn't give me a chance. He told me to stop talking to you and to not worry about anything. The company had done nothing wrong and neither had he nor anyone on his senior leadership team. Then he left, without any other comment."

"And you came here?" I asked.

"Yes, I knew you would be at the accident scene for a while but I had to get out so I came here."

I looked at her. "Elise, you know you really gave me nothing new. I already thought your husband was lying, or at minimum withholding information. I still believe that."

She shook her head. "Tommy, it's about money. I still don't think Alan is involved, but we would never have millions riding on anything. If he was serious about the money, and I believe he was, then you need to figure out who has exposure other than us and where that exposure is."

"I hear you, Elise, but those you're talking about all must have millions in stock. If the price goes up or down a few dollars, they lose or gain more than I will make in my lifetime. He could simply be talking about bad press from two high-ranking company representatives being murdered."

"Two murders?" she asked immediately. "I thought Julian was a car accident."

I smiled but didn't respond on the subject. "Are you okay to drive home?" I asked.

"Of course I am," she replied.

"Then I think it's time for you to head that way." I stood, causing Elise to do the same. "Elise," I began.

"Yes," she replied as she took a step toward the door.

"Thank you for coming to me with this. I know it was probably not an easy decision, and although you didn't give me a smoking gun, you did give me a direction."

"Tommy, I meant what I said. I am not here to protect Alan. I don't want him to be involved in this, but I will not protect him against anything that involves murder. That is very black-and-white to me."

I understood but did not want to talk about it any further. Her tone was passionate and her words clear, but something still told me she was playing both sides. I wanted to believe her at her word, but it was millions of dollars and it was her husband and the father of her children. She wanted info. She was a brilliant woman. She was going to give me a little, not much, but a little to build trust. Then she would continue to be present in the investigation and ensure she gathered the information needed to keep her family intact. That was my theory. I didn't resent her for it and I had no reason to believe it was the case, but I simply felt it. Dr. Elise Gerstenberger had a great life. I truly did not think she would jeopardize it. She wanted me on the case and she got me on the case. Now she was going to manage me on the case. The same way I thought she was using me, I would see if Patti and I could use *her*.

When we reached the door she gave me a deep and long hug. "Thank you," she whispered then turned and walked out.

I shut the door without even watching to make sure she had a car or cab ready for her. To be honest, I was a little pissed. It had nothing to do with Patti, and everything to do with Doctor Elise Gerstenberger. Who am I kidding? It had a little to do with Patti and the fact she was not in my apartment right now telling me whatever it was she needed to tell me.

•　　•　　•　　•　　•

"What do we have, O'Malley?" asked Carter.

"We have a high profile pharmaceutical company with two fairly high-ranking officials killed in the last twenty-four hours," I replied before taking a sip of coffee during the morning briefing. Like normal, Halterman did not sit next to me. She arrived as the doors closed and instead of coming up to the front as I would have liked (but would have drawn further attention to her slightly disheveled appearance), she simply stood in the back.

"Who are your suspects?" Carter replied, trying to draw more out.

I had not expected the question. The case was less than a day old and it was a weekend day. "To be honest, Boss, I don't even have a theory on a motive yet. I mean, everyone involved are millionaires. It's tough to see one of them killing two people over money."

Carter was not pleased with this response but it was all he was going to get. Franky smiled to the side. He seemed to enjoy seeing me put on the spot.

"Halterman, do you have anything to add?" Carter asked, turning his attention to my partner in the back.

"No, Sergeant," she replied, with a hint of tone that possibly only I heard. "I think Tommy really said it all."

Carter found no humor in her response, though some was intended, but it seemed to end the discussion. "Very well," he said. "Let's have both of you and Sullivan and Huston join me in the Bulls Room after this."

The rest of the briefing was straightforward. I think the use of the Bulls Room was directed toward me. Carter, like everyone else, knew I preferred to work in the Royals Room, but I felt I had asked for enough favors. We would set up in Michael's domain today.

Sitting around the conference table was Carter, Franky, Halterman, and me. Huston was at the whiteboard adding the photos we had pulled from our investigation.

Carter took a big drink of his Paul Bunyan sized Diet Dr. Pepper. "So, what do we know for sure?" he broke in after his first swig from the 7-11 plastic cup.

Halterman stood and took the lead, pointing to pictures of the individuals she referenced as she mentioned them. "We have a major pharmaceutical company in North Chicago with two individuals high in rank murdered over the weekend. We have a chief medical examiner married to another high-ranking individual who came forward prior to the murders with concerns about the company. We have a modern-day pimp who may have witnessed the first murder, who in turn was killed in a shootout with police. The only other possible witness is a prostitute who arrived after the murder and allegedly saw nothing. The car used on the second murder was stolen hours before to run down the CFO. There was a strange red substance on the airbag but other than that, the car was wiped clean, according to the report I glanced at during the briefing."

That caught my attention. How the hell did she get that report? She finished abruptly and the room fell silent. It was an odd silence. It felt like an interrogation. I wasn't sure what Carter's angle was on this. It was like he wanted us to have a list of suspects already lined up.

I let the silence linger there for a while before responding. "Let's talk about our direction today."

Halterman looked toward me. "Tommy, did you learn anything new from Doctor Gerstenberger last night?"

I know why she said it. I know the whole situation was bothering her. I wasn't sure why, but I knew it did. Why she said it right now, in this setting, was my question. All eyes fell on me. I coughed slightly, buying time, then answered. "Uh, well, uh...yes, Doc G came by my place last night. I thought it was to simply pry into the investigation, and I do think that was one of the motives. However, she seemed more interested in claiming to provide me key information but not actually providing anything."

Before I could continue, Carter interrupted, clearly pissed at my comment. "O'Malley, goddamn it. I broke every rule putting you on this case because you said you could be objective. I don't want to hear..."

Now I cut Carter off. "Just a minute, Boss." I am not sure why I called him Boss at this time as that is not a term I had used in the past, but I did. "Doc G may have come over, but she was not invited and I asked her to leave right after getting there. She tried to share info about her husband, which was bullshit, and pried impertinently for me to share in return. When I refused, she left in a huff and I didn't hear from her again."

"Impertinently?" Halterman whispered to herself but I heard.

"Yes, Halterman," I shot back, still pissed we were even having this discussion. "I took a shit today and learned a new word."

Franky actually spit slightly in his attempt to hold back his laugh. Carter was not amused and Patti simply stared at me. Her eyes burned like daggers. To her credit, Huston wrote the word on the whiteboard. Even Carter had to turn his scowl into a bit of a grin.

"We should all use this word today," stated Huston. "It's not just about solving crimes, it's about bettering ourselves intellectually."

"Jesus Christ," stated Carter. "What the hell has happened to you four? Has O'Malley turned you all into minions of him?"

"Minions?" questioned Franky. "I may be a lot of things, but a minion of Tommy, whatever the hell that is, is not one of them."

Carter stood and was clearly not amused, regardless of the small smile that had started when Huston wrote the word of the day on the board. That brief brush of humor had immediately passed. I was not sure what the story was, but Carter was not acting like his typical self. He knew we had only been on the case for twenty-four hours and most of that time was a weekend day. He paced the room and all eyes were on him, like watching the slowest-moving tennis match in history. Back and forth he walked without saying a word until he stopped, turned, and faced the group. "Fuck all this shit. What are you doing today?"

An odd intro to his question, but when all eyes fell to me, it was clear I was being nominated to respond. "Sullivan and Huston should chase down the hooker. We need to know if Teague said anything to her and drill a little further into what she may have seen. Halterman and I will make a run at Abbunex. It may be tough to get in front of the CEO, but I think we need to give it a shot. Someone on his staff was run down just outside their parking lot last night and regardless of where Thompson falls in the org chart, his death has to be related."

Carter seemed to accept this but was confused by the second part of that statement. "What do we know about Dr. Thompson's death?"

I answered without looking to any of the others to respond first. "I have not seen the M.E.'s report, but at the scene, it appeared to be death by multiple gunshot wounds."

"Wait a minute," broke in Franky. "Multiple wounds?"

"You got something, Franky?" asked Carter.

"Well, you know as well as I do, multiple gunshot wounds is personal. I was assuming if this was related to big pharma business, all of these crimes would be professional, not personal. The death by the Bonneville up north definitely was. Stolen car, timed to a tee, according to Patti there was not a latent print anywhere— all about that scene was professional. Killing a guy under a bridge by shooting him multiple times, not so much. What do we know about Thompson? Could he have just been down there scoring drugs or something and the deal went bad?"

"Or maybe he was the man meeting the hooker. What was her name? Mandy?" added Huston.

"Both good points," I replied. "We need to do a full run-up on Thompson. I want to know his history, financial and personal. I want to know about his kids, wife, ex-wife, boyfriend, whatever he has now or has had in the past." Turning more to Franky and Huston, "And find out what Mandy's real name is and get the same history on her. Verify that she didn't have any large cash deposits recently. Maybe she knows more than we thought. And it might be worth a quick call to Officer Duncan. She drove Mandy home. The woman was wigged out on some kind of drugs. Maybe she got a little loose with her speech in Duncan's car."

Carter seemed to accept these actions and nodded appropriately. "Okay, let's touch base again this afternoon. I'll place a call back to Dalponte in North Chicago. He might have a better path in to speak with the CEO."

"Or you could reach out to Doc G's husband, Dr. Grove," added Halterman. "If he truly wants to make himself not look so guilty, he should be open to facilitating a meeting."

Carter agreed. "Yes, let's do both. CEO's by definition are pompous and impertinent." He struggled slightly on the word but kept going nonetheless. "Any roadblocks we can break down on the front end will help. And if you get in there, I assume Thompson lives up north. Why don't you run by and talk to his wife? I'm sure the local police already talked to her, but we need to collect our own information and background."

"Sounds good," I replied. Turning directly to Carter, "And that is not the proper use of the word so it doesn't count."

●　　●　　●　　●　　●

The man again stuck his hand across his mahogany desk. "I don't know how you did it so quickly, but having your guy get rid of Thompson in less than twenty-four hours is amazing. It was a little dangerous with all the activity around it and unlucky with the accident the next morning, but what's done is done and in the end the problem was solved. How do we get him his money?"

One of the two men in front of him paced the floor before turning back to face him. "Well, in that statement, there's a fairly big problem, sir."

Instantly his eyes turned up and he stood in front of his desk. "With what we are talking about, don't tell me there's a problem."

His voice cracked and he took a few steps closer, the other man beside him doing the same, though it was clear he did not need to hear what was about to be said because he already knew. In a soft voice, the man answered. "You see, I wasn't able to get ahold of our guy. I put a feeler out for him the way we had done before, but I didn't get a response. I never provided Thompson's name."

"You mean we're not responsible for his death?" the man behind the desk questioned.

"That's exactly what I mean," he responded softly.

He stood tall and smiled. "Yes!" he exclaimed.

The other two men stood back in surprise. "Not what I expected to see," the other one stated.

"Don't you get it?" the man replied. "Whatever Thompson was into did it for us. His death can't be tied back to us. Tie that in with the accident involving Julian and we're in the clear, and even more rich than before. His options will roll back to the company and we can in turn roll them to us, and the issues with the samples are back to being our little secret."

The two men seemed skeptical and the first one who had responded continued to drive the conversation. "That may very well be the case, but the police are involved and the two deaths so close to each other are bringing the investigation to us. I already received a call from a North Chicago sergeant to set up a meeting. Further, there's something else which has cast more suspicion on us."

"Dr. Elise Gerstenberger," the man said.

"Yes," he replied.

"I will handle that situation myself," the man behind the desk stated.

"What do you want me to do about the meeting that was requested?"

"Set it up for this afternoon. I want to speak to some people first."

8 Franky pounded on the door again. He was standing to the left of the doorway and Huston was on the right. They had spoken to Officer Duncan. She basically said the woman known as Mandy had told her nothing during their short ride to her place and when they arrived, she learned it was a real pit. That being said, her son was very glad to see her, and he seemed healthy and happy. There was no sitter there, but to bring her in on negligence would serve no purpose at this stage, in her opinion. Franky was not sure he agreed, but he would use this visit to draw his own conclusions. Now it was just past 9:00 AM, and he and his partner stood outside the door knocking, not knowing if anyone was home.

A small rustling was heard inside and then the sounds of someone walking toward the door. A dead bolt clicked open and the handle turned slowly. "Who is it so goddamn early in the morning?" The stale smell of old cigarettes blew out immediately as the door opened. A face with deep-set and wrinkled eyes with skin like worn leather greeted both detectives. She coughed and Franky actually stepped back, fearful he might get struck by something expelled from her mouth. "What the hell do you want, pigs?"

Pigs? Franky thought. *What was this, the '70s*? "We just want to have a brief word with you, Mandy."

"Mandy? Who the fuck is Man..." She paused as the synapses in her brain connected. "Oh yes, I'm Mandy. What can I do for you?"

Huston stepped forward peering in the door as she spoke. "May we come in? We have a few more questions for you regarding the murder the other morning, and the death of Jimmy Teague."

She took a step back and appeared as if she may collapse. "Jimmy is dead?" she asked.

"May we come in?" Huston repeated again.

Mandy was mumbling as she stepped aside and began walking in. "Shit, shit, shit, shit. He's dead. He's dead. Goddamn it, he's dead." She began frantically grabbing some clothes and stuffing them in a pillowcase. "I got to get outta here. I got to go."

Franky looked around the small studio apartment. It was a shithole. The smell was atrocious and the crap all over the floor and counters made the place almost impossible to traverse. It appeared Mandy, or whatever her name was, slept on a double bed on the far end of the single room. Her son, or someone who was not there, slept on a futon that was folded up into couch form because there was no room to lay it flat. The bedding was still in place. The kitchen ran along the side, as a single counter with a sink which was overflowing with dirty dishes, a single door fridge which must have a freezer compartment inside, and a stove top. There was no oven that he could see. There was one door that must be to the bathroom and whether it had a shower or bath was not able to be determined, but by the smell of old food, cigarettes, and body odor, the chance that it was ever used was low.

Franky watched as the woman pushed by him and continued to grab clothes. "Ma'am, can I ask you to sit down so we can speak?"

She swung her eyes to him. "If they killed Jimmy, then they have to be coming for me. I need to get my son and get the hell out of here."

Huston looked to Franky and both seemed to question how best to play this one. Franky being more senior took the lead. "Jimmy was not killed by someone who was after him. He pulled a gun on the police and in the exchange was fatally wounded."

She stopped what she was doing and turned to face the two detectives. "You guys killed him. You fucking assholes." She flung her bag of clothes at Franky from which he ducked. Huston moved quickly and had the woman on the ground. "Get off me, you bitch. Get your fucking hands off me!"

Huston had her hands behind her in cuffs before Franky could even get down to assist, but it was Franky who spoke. "Now, ma'am, a move like that could be considered assaulting a police officer. By making that choice, you could end up in jail, and if that happens, the chance you will see your son at night becomes less and less. Are you sure you want to go that direction?"

His voice was calm and unemotional. Huston was still on the woman's back holding her down with her head turned to the side. When Franky positioned himself to see her face, he saw tears streaming down her cheeks. Immediately he understood. Jimmy was not just her pimp. She cared for him, and by all appearances, cared for him deeply.

Through her tears, she replied, "Don't take my son. He's all I have left."

Franky motioned to Karen to stand up and help Mandy up to the futon. In a soft voice, he replied, "If you want us to forget about the assault, then you have to help us."

She shook her head. "I ain't no snitch."

"We are not asking you to snitch. We simply want to understand a few things. Nothing you say will get anyone in trouble and it will keep you and your son together. Don't you think that's worth it?"

Huston pulled out a pen and notepad as the woman replied, "That's what you said when I told that other cop where Jimmy was going. Now he's dead. Why should I believe you?"

"Because it's the only way you will keep your son," Franky replied.

There was an extremely long pause. The woman was crying, but Franky didn't know from what. Was it her loss of Jimmy Teague, or the potential loss of her son and going to jail? It could be anything. Then, she looked up and stared right at them. "Anything to keep my son."

"Good, good," Franky said softly. "Now, let's start with your real name. We know your name is not Mandy."

She paused as if contemplating if she should say so or not. "Julie. Julie is my name, but most everyone calls me Jules."

"Well, hello, Jules, it's nice to meet you. Can you tell me your last name?"

"Hanrahan," she finally stated after another pause.

"Well, Jules, why don't you tell us what you know about everything that happened Sunday morning?" Again, Franky's voice was calm almost drawing her in. He was one of the best at getting information from individuals in the field.

She looked up to him. He believed she didn't even know what she was going to do. "I can't lose my son."

"Then you need to help us," Franky stressed, taking a more firm tone.

"I didn't see nothin'. I was late. My first appointment was long, you see. The guy wanted more and was willing to pay. Then, it was a bitch to get an Uber that would bring me there. By the time I got there, I was thirty minutes late."

She stopped and gave Franky the impression she was done. From his perspective, she had given him nothing he cared about yet. "So that's really the key, Jules. What happened after you arrived?"

She was still a little jumpy but had calmed down significantly since she first heard Jimmy was dead. She had stopped crying and seemed to actually be focusing. However, it did appear to both Franky and Karen that she did not want to say anymore. Her voice cracked followed by a fit of guttural coughing common with years of smoking. She cleared her throat and continued. "That was really all it was, Officer. I arrived, Jimmy left, and I saw the body. Then I called 911."

"But you had to have spoken to Jimmy. The other detectives said you told them on the scene that you spoke to Jimmy." Franky was not sure that was the case, but he was sure Jules would have no memory of it one way or the other.

She immediately cowered back into the futon. "Uh, well, uh…"

"What, Jules?" Franky interjected. "Just tell us what you saw. Jimmy is dead. He can't hurt you."

"Jimmy would never hurt me. We was going to get married. We was going to give Trevor a good family life." She started to cry again as she thought about Jimmy.

Franky may have underestimated how strongly she believed in Jimmy Teague. Whether he really intended to or not was immaterial. The fact was, Jules believed he was going to do exactly what she said. "I understand, Jules, and I'm very sorry for your loss. But we need to find out who killed that man and to do that, I need to know what you and Jimmy saw. Unfortunately, I can't ask Jimmy so I have to hope he told you something. It may be the one way he can still help you. By telling me what he said, it may allow you to keep Trevor with you."

That caught her. Her eyes swung up and locked on Franky's. "He said he saw a car."

Now they were getting somewhere. "What kind of car, Jules?"

"He said it was way out of place here. You know, one of those fancy cars with the initials."

"BMW?" Karen asked.

She looked back toward Huston who she had really not acknowledged since Franky had started talking. "Yeah, something like that. BMW."

"Did he say what color?"

"Black. He said it because it had a big scratch down the side from somebody keying it, and he could see it against the black side."

"So he saw a black BMW. Did he see a driver? Did he see something happen with it?"

She wore a look of confusion on her face, but Franky thought she was telling the truth. Something about her tone and her need to protect her son.

"He just seen it drive away. He said the truck was open and bouncin' up and down, like it didn't latch or somethin'."

Franky looked directly into Jules' eyes. "I want to be certain I'm clear. Jimmy showed up at the regular time. He learns from you that you're going to be late. At some point while in the area, he sees a black BMW drive away with the trunk open. Is that about it?"

She shook her head. "Yep, that's what he told me."

Franky now shook his head negatively. "That is not going to do it for us, Jules."

She reacted immediately. "What the fuck, Detective."

Franky subconsciously was pleased as it was the first time she had called him Detective. "Where was the guy you were supposed to meet? What about him? If Jimmy was there, where was he? Also, what about the gunshots. I believe the individual was shot seven times. How did he not tell you about that? There's no way he hears a car leaving but not gunshots."

"I don't fucking know, and I guess you can't ask him since you already killed him."

She was getting jumpy again but Franky thought that might make her talk even more, so he thought he would fire one right off the bow. "Did Jimmy kill that man, Jules? Is that who you're protecting? There was no goddamn BMW, was there? Just Jimmy and his gun."

"Bullshit! Jimmy never killed nobody."

"He took shots at other detectives in a crowded restaurant. Don't tell me he never killed anybody. He's a killer. We have his gun and I'm going to match up ballistics on his gun with the bullets in that man you found. They are going to match, aren't they, Jules? Tell me why he killed that man."

"He didn't kill him. I know he didn't." Her voice was high-pitched and full of emotion.

"How do you know he didn't kill him? Did he tell you that?" Franky shrugged and his voice faded as he spoke. "You can't believe anything a murderer says."

"I was there," she shouted out, cutting Franky off with her words and tears. "He told me not to tell anyone. If anyone asked, I was to say I got there late." She put her head in her hands. It was an odd pose for a woman who appeared so rough and hard.

Franky smiled and placed his hand on her hunched-over shoulder. "So, Jules, now you just need to tell me what you saw."

She was still crying. She lifted her head when Franky's hand touched her shoulder. Through tears, she continued. "I did get there late, but only about ten minutes. Jimmy had met my date,"—both Franky and Karen smiled at the use of "date" for what really was her John—"and sent him to get a room at No Where." She was referring to the No Where Inn that everyone in the area knew for selling all the way down to fifteen-minute room rates. "When I got there, the black car was right there, like it followed me. The guy drivin' didn't see me. I think Jimmy knew somethin' was up and called me over. We ducked behind a pile of shit and watched. He gets out of his car, does a quick look around then goes to the back. He hits a button on his keys and the fuckin' trunk just opens. Jimmy said he heard somethin' but I didn't. The next thing I see is that fucking driver pulling out a gun and swinging it down like a hatchet ten or fifteen times on somethin' in his trunk. Then he bends down and grabs it. I knows it's heavy cuz he has to set his gun down to move it. Right then we seen it was a body. He dumped the body down on the ground, looks around again, and then gets his gun. Then *bam, bam, bam, bam*—he just shoots the guy on the ground. Then he runs back to his car and peels out, not even shuttin' his trunk."

That was not what Franky expected to get from this visit. "Jules, is there anything else, even if you think it's not important?"

She shook her head, then stopped, and her eyes showed something. He wasn't sure what, but something.

"Did you just remember something, Jules?"

She smiled a little. "Just that Jimmy said the guy probably had not fired that gun very much."

"Why did he say that?" Franky asked.

She smiled again. "Well, just that the first shot kicked back near his head. He said it just looked like he didn't know what to do."

Franky nodded understanding. "Again, Jules, I'm sorry for your loss. Enjoy your night with your son."

She looked up to him and this time her lips clearly turned upward. "Thank you, Detectives," she said.

Franky and Karen made their way back to the door until Franky turned to her. "And Jules, why don't you stay out of trouble, stop getting paid for dates, stop smoking in your house, and clean the place up? If you truly want to keep your son, you will need to do better than what I see here."

She didn't reply but Huston did see her nod slightly.

•　　•　　•　　•　　•

"Nice job in there, Franky. I never thought she knew all that." Huston was finishing some final notes as they entered Franky's car.

"Yeah," he replied. "I had no idea we would end up where we did either. I guess that's why you go to each place and ask all the questions."

"I hope Tommy and Patti have the same luck," Huston added.

"I hope so too," he replied. "But my gut tells me talking to a CEO won't be nearly as revealing."

9 I had made several calls to Dr. Grove to set up a time to meet with his counterparts at Abbunex. Additionally, Carter had greased the wheels with Dalponte, who in turn dialed right into the senior executive team's office at Abbunex. Even with all that prying, we ended up only getting a 3:00 PM appointment and that would be with the CEO, Darryn Hermann, Dr. Alan Grove, as well as a man named Joseph Reingold, who evidently was Randy Thompson's boss. I requested meeting with Julian Stover's boss as well only to learn that I already was meeting him. Julian Stover was the Chief Financial Officer and he reported directly to Mr. Hermann.

We took my car. We did this because, well, it was cool. Both our phones dinged with messages. Halterman checked hers as I was driving, but using your phone while driving was against the law, and I would never break the law. By the way, I was using my flashers and driving well above the posted speed limit.

Halterman pulled her phone and said, "Looks like the final report from the lab is back on the car that hit Stover."

"I thought you had the final report?" I asked. I was annoyed that she got a report and didn't tell me about it, and actually brought it up with Carter at the same time as me.

"Yeah, I was doing police work while you were entertaining one of our suspects."

I was about to protest but she didn't give me the time.

"This doesn't make any sense," she added, her voice showing some confusion.

"What?" I asked, my interest piqued.

"It says there was no DNA anywhere in the car."

I arched my head back. "No DNA? The car was stolen. Nothing from even the previous owner?"

"It says it was completely wiped clean. There was residue from bleach and possibly another disinfectant they haven't identified. They identified the red paint on the airbag as being from a motorcycle helmet—Harley Davidson to be exact." She paused. "Wait," she added still reading through her phone which took longer due to the size of the screen and the ability to scroll.

"Something else?"

"Sand. The only material they found was sand on the seat."

"What the hell does sand mean?" I asked. "The killer had been at the beach prior to stealing a car, wiping it down, and then using it to kill a pharma exec while wearing a helmet?"

"The helmet makes sense," Patti replied.

"Why?"

"It was a professional hit. The perpetrator steals the car, completely wipes it down, and then uses it to murder the CFO. However, because of the type of murder, he doesn't want to get injured so he wears a helmet. He would not have time to clean the airbag. He T-boned the car and then got the hell out of there."

"That, partner, makes perfect sense. It was all preplanned down to accident protection." I paused and continued to think then asked, "But what about the sand?"

"The sand has to be a plant, don't you think?" Halterman asked. "Nobody would be so meticulous to completely wipe down a car and then so careless to leave trace amounts of sand behind. Would they?"

I nodded taking in everything she said. "So, we have someone with the means and ability to steal a car and wipe it clean. Then the fortitude to use that car to kill someone in a violent way that, in all honesty, has no guarantee of death. Very often people survive car crashes."

"Not to mention, there was no guarantee the driver of the stolen car wouldn't be hurt, even with a helmet."

"Right, it's a very dangerous way to murder someone," I agreed. "Then, to top it off, the killer leaves some calling card behind. What the hell would sand mean?"

"Wait," Patti broke in, her inflection clearly showing a question was coming. "Wasn't there a calling card at the downtown murder also?"

Instantly my mind connected the dots. "There was—a rabbit's foot."

Neither of us said another word for several moments then Patti asked, "What the hell does a rabbit's foot and sand have to do with each other?"

We ended the discussion there and just finished the last ten minutes in silence. We made it up to the North Chicago campus, which was really a small city, and had gone through two security booths with, you guessed it, men and women working them who dreamed of being police officers. But in most cases, they just didn't have what it takes. The campus had a *no firearms* policy but they waved us through with no questions asked. With everything going on, I was surprised. However, they were equal to mall security so what did I really expect. Then we had to get by the ever-threatening 18-year-old receptionist who took our identification, called someone, and then directed us, unescorted, to a bank of elevators and told us to go to the top floor.

When we arrived on the top floor, the elevator opened into what I can only describe by saying I was uncomfortable walking on the carpet for fear of tainting it. I felt like I was walking into Willy Wonka's candy room, not the remake with Johnny Depp, but the original Gene Wilder version. The place was amazing. It had oak and mahogany everything. The oak was stained darker than what I would say was standard, making it accent the deep mahogany furniture with an unbelievable touch of class. It had a waterfall—not one of those six foot high decorative things you buy at Sharper Image, but one that must be twenty feet high and dropping water three to four feet across its face. It appeared to be built into a rock wall making up the center of the office area, and water fell across both sides. There was a separate reception desk directly in front of the elevator and it did not have an eighteen year old wearing whatever she just picked up at Old Navy the night before. Behind the immaculate mahogany desk was a mature woman, I'm guessing about 62 years old, in a business suit that cost more than my entire wardrobe, including my special sports coat I had worn twice in the last five years. Circling around the waterfall was a bank of glassed-in offices and conference rooms. The woman could tell we were starstruck because the elevator doors began to close and we were still partially inside.

"Come on in, Detective O'Malley and Detective Halterman. We're very glad to have you visit. May I take your jackets?"

I was wearing a suit and tie today but my jacket did cover my firearm so I opted to keep mine. "No, thank you, ma'am, I'll hold onto it."

She swung her eyes to my partner who was wearing a department-issued jacket over her pantsuit. She removed the jacket and handed it to her. "Thank you very much," she answered. "It's still needed outside but it will be nice to be without it for a while."

She smiled. "I'm June Meyers, but please call me June. May I get you anything to drink? Water or perhaps a coffee or tea?"

"Why, thank you, June," I replied. "I would think water would be very nice."

"Why don't I just make that two waters?" she answered, looking toward Patti as she spoke. She spoke softer and with a slight smile when she added, "Even if you don't want it, those men in there will talk your ears off and you may be screaming for it later."

Patti nodded. "That would be very nice, thank you."

She hustled off to a small room behind the elevators away from all the windows. Refreshment area, I thought. The least desirable room on the floor. No windows and right behind the elevator mechanical room. I'm still not sure why I always think these things, but I do.

As I was turned away from the front desk watching where June had disappeared to, I felt a hand on my shoulder. The touch was a surprise but I hid it well. "Tommy, glad you could make it. Any trouble finding the offices?"

I turned, smiling as I did so, and reached my hand out to greet his. "No, Dr. Grove, no trouble at all." I paused, released my hand, and motioned to Patti. "You remember Detective Halterman, I assume."

"Of course I do," he said slightly louder than I think was natural. It was almost as if he was trying to show everyone that this was not a big deal, and he was friends with both of us. "Patti, how are you doing?" He gripped her hand and then wrapped his other hand around the top in a double grip which clearly meant...I have no idea what the hell it meant.

"Very nice to see you again, Dr. Grove, and I am doing well. Thank you for asking."

He broke hands and I believe I saw Patti pull hers back closer to her side as if protecting it from a future grab. "Please, stop with the Dr. Grove. Call me Alan."

I smiled but did not respond. He began walking around the front desk which in turn took us to the other side of the waterfall. It was more spectacular on the back side and when we got around and could see the office area, it was like walking into an Amish furniture store. I had never seen more dark hardwood in one area. The place was top-notch. I glanced toward Halterman, and I knew she thought the same. Alan led us through a few sitting areas, and then by a large conference room that I could barely see inside but what I saw was just plain amazing. The wood sign with black etched letters on the side of the entry read, *Boardroom*. I wanted to go in there but we continued by. It appeared we were headed to a corner office.

Alan peeked his head around the corner office door and then continued in after making what I assume was some sort of eye contact with whoever was inside. We followed. "Darryn Hermann, may I present to you Detective Tomas O'Malley and Detective Patricia Halterman." He motioned with his arm then continued.

"Detectives, this is Darryn Hermann, the Chief Executive Officer for Abbunex Labs."

Darryn stood and it took him close to five seconds to navigate around his desk, but he made it safely. When he reached us, I was amazed that I was at least twelve inches taller than him. He extended his hand. "I know what you're thinking, you thought I would be taller."

I was instantly embarrassed. I stuttered slightly. "Ugh, well, I—"

He cut me off. "Stop it. I do that to everyone. You can't be in my position at a whopping five foot four inches and not have a sense of humor about it."

"Five foot four inches?" I questioned.

He stopped in his tracks and Patti actually coughed to cover her smile. "Nice one, Detective O'Malley. Let's call it five foot three and a half." He shook both our hands and motioned for us to join him at the conference table. "It's good to see you again Detective O'Malley. We barely met at the party, but I am very surprised to see you again so soon. I can't believe what has happened in so short a time."

I was surprised I didn't notice his height when we met briefly on Saturday evening. However, I quickly forgot my thought as I took my seat. When I sat down, I realized the chair was more comfortable than what I watch television in at my apartment.

"Nice, aren't they?" Darryn stated, seeing my face. "I love watching people sit down the first time."

I nodded. "Yes, it's like sitting on a marshmallow, but still holds you high enough at the table."

He acknowledged my response as he and Grove took seats across from us. His face turned instantly serious. "Now, Alan tells me you would like to discuss the recent tragedies we've faced and if they may in some way be tied to Abbunex."

Cuts right to the chase. Guilty guys do that to give the impression they are willing to share everything, when in reality they're not. "Yes, that is part of it. We also want to discuss the individuals in general. We want to learn as much as we can about them and who might want them dead."

He appeared to understand but seemed caught by something. "Julian was in a car accident? Nobody wanted him dead, did they? It was just a freak drunk driver or something, correct?"

"I can't go into details, Dr. Hermann, but we have reason to believe it was not an accident and Dr. Stover was targeted." I paused and let that sink in. "Now, since you brought it up, why don't we start with Dr. Stover? Do you know anyone who would want to hurt him?"

Hermann and Grove looked at each other. Grove lifted an eyebrow during their stare as if in deep thought or intrigue, and then they turned back to face me directly. Hermann started. "Nobody. Absolutely nobody. His home life was good. His work life was good. I don't think I ever heard anyone say a negative word about him." He turned to his counterpart. "Alan?"

"I concur," he said flatly. "I mean, you never know what goes on behind closed doors, but everything I saw with Julian, his wife Wilma, and son Russell was very positive."

There it was again—Russell Stover. I just couldn't get by it. "Positive?" I asked. That seemed like a strange choice of words. "What do you mean?"

He fumbled a second or two then found the words. "Ugh, you know, positive. They had a healthy, strong marriage and family makeup. I never heard a bad thing about the kid either, for that matter."

"So, Russell Stover was good?" I said smiling, but nobody returned the smile. It was like they had something against chocolate.

"He was a great kid. Julian always talked about his sports and grades and all that." Alan was doing most of the talking now.

This was the second time sports had come up. I flipped through my previous interviews in my mind and remembered a conversation with Alan and Doc G previously. Dr. Randy Thompson was a coach and had a parent that complained about playing time. I didn't think this was the reason he or Julian was killed, but it was worth keeping the conversation going. "So, Alan, you mentioned the other day that Randy Thompson was a coach. Hockey, I believe. Did Russell play hockey?"

"Not that I'm aware of," he answered immediately. "Baseball and basketball were his sports, if memory serves."

So much for expanding the conversation. He simply shut it down. "So Thompson did not coach Julian Stover's son?"

"Not that I'm aware of?" Alan replied. "Does this really have anything to do with their murders, if in fact they were murdered?"

"Well, Dr. Grove, since I don't know who murdered them or why, I can't tell you if it does or it doesn't have anything to do with the murders." I let that stand for a moment. "So, leaving the subject of sports, how was Dr. Stover's performance at work?"

"Maybe a better first question is, what did he do here?" added Halterman.

Alan looked to Dr. Hermann to take that question. "He was my chief financial officer, probably the best CFO I have ever worked with. He protected the company from any and all financial issues, he was sensitive to stock movements, and handled the majority of our quarterly financial announcements."

"Was he honest?" I asked, firing it across the bow.

"To a fault," he answered without hesitation, leaning in slightly as he answered.

"How do you know? If we looked into his finances, which we are, what are we going to find?"

"Listen, Detectives, I don't know about the personal lives of my direct reports, but we are all at professional levels in our lives where we don't need to break the rules. We all have incomes that surpass ninety-nine percent of the US population. I'm not bragging, I'm simply telling you that Julian Stover was not only the most honest man I've ever worked with, he was a Boy Scout. He kept us all in line."

"The most honest man you ever worked with?" I repeated, using inflection as if it was a question. "What does that mean? Have you worked with dishonest men? Did you guys try to do something illegal, and he prevented it?" I wasn't being serious, but I was interested in his answer nonetheless.

"Of course not, Detective," he replied smiling. He was trying to determine if I was serious or not. "Unfortunately, in our world, everything we do is scrutinized by the media, Wall Street, our board, and especially our investors. We would not risk it."

"Do you agree, Dr. Grove?" I asked.

Alan shifted in his chair. "Do I agree that we would not risk doing anything illegal, or do I agree that Julian was above reproach in all his activities?"

"Both, I suppose," I said.

"Both answers are unequivocally *yes*," he answered firmly.

"So," I began, "we have a CFO who's great at his job, high profile, honest, and great at home. I can see why he would be a target for murder."

Hermann rolled his eyes. "Why can't it just be a drunk driver hit-and-run? I saw the accident scene. The guy who hit him was nowhere near the right lane. Don't you think Chicago's finest are barking up the wrong tree because of what happened to Thompson?"

"Well, Dr. Hermann, the car that hit him was stolen. It was also wiped clean, and I mean bleach-wiped clean. No DNA at all, even from the original owner who reported it stolen. The car was also seen in a parked area before it left for its target."

I paused, then said completely from left field, "So, Dr. Hermann, what goes into making a new drug?"

He was surprised by the question. "Why do you need to know that?"

I shrugged. "Since you were asking me multiple questions about doing my job, I thought I would ask you how to do yours."

He got the message. "Okay, Detective O'Malley, I get it. I just don't know of anything either Julian or Randy could have done to put them in harm's way."

"But they did, didn't they?" I stated and asked respectively.

"Did what?" Hermann asked.

"Did something that put them in harm's way," I repeated.

"Not because of their jobs," he stated flatly.

I didn't pursue it further. "Listen, gentlemen, I don't know what's going on here. I've sensed since I first began speaking to you, Dr. Grove, about Dr. Thompson's death, that you've been hiding something. Is there anything you can say that will change my mind?"

Dr. Grove did not flinch. His tone was raised slightly usually depicting someone on the defensive. "Tommy," he said, causing me to smile that we again were on a first-name basis. "I can't do anything to change your mind. I told you before, I have one concern, other than for the families of my peers, and that is the welfare of this company. The stock was down two percent following news of the two deaths. If Julian's death is also publicly called a murder, it will drive it down another three to five percent before the open tomorrow. It is—"

I cut him off. "Do you think I care if your stock is up or down? I have two dead bodies and a company putting up some sort of strange shield around them. Just tell us what the hell is going on."

"Nothing is going on, Detective," replied Hermann, "and I think our conversation is done here. We have made ourselves available to you. We have provided you with background and information, and you continue to badger us with accusations. The problem I have with these accusations is they are not based on facts. Then, someone spreads one of those accusations into the media and it could cost this company millions in market cap. So, with that, I think we will conclude our discussion, and going forward, let's arrange any conversations through our attorney." He reached out and handed me a card.

"You're kidding me. Staci Lambda?" I asked.

"Yes, do you know her?" Hermann replied.

I smiled. "Yes, I have worked with her in the past. She worked for Ross Moretti."

"Yes. When I heard he was released and cleared of all charges, I just had to have her on my staff." He paused then added a touch of sarcasm to his tone. "That was your case, wasn't it, Detective O'Malley?"

I nodded. "Yes, it was," I replied proudly. "Brought down one of the largest crime bosses in Chicago and saved the lives of a huge number of individuals held against their will."

"Yes, but one did get away," he added. "I suppose, anyway."

"I suppose he did, Dr. Hermann. I'll have to make sure that doesn't happen again."

Hermann stood from across the table causing Alan to also stand. "If there's nothing else…"

Halterman and I both followed suit and rose, taking a few steps toward the door. I outstretched my hand and both men shook it. As we headed toward the office door with Alan in tow showing us out, I stopped and turned back to Dr. Hermann. "You know, let Mrs. Lambda know that we'll be issuing a subpoena for some of the company's financial records tied to Dr. Thompson and Mr. Stover's finances related to Abbunex."

"I will let her know," he replied. "And for your own well-being, you should know that she prefers to be called Ms. Lambda."

"I know," I replied.

•   •   •   •   •

We got off the elevator and exited the executive building. Immediately, Halterman laid into me. "So, who the hell is Ms. Lambda, as she prefers to be called?"

I shrugged, knowing I had to give credit where credit was due. "She's a fireball attorney that works for whoever has the biggest bankroll. I met her on the Moretti-Polino case. She represented both of them. The case gained her some notoriety when Moretti got off and most likely paved her way to the corporate big boys."

"It doesn't get much bigger than Abbunex in Chicago," stated Patti in return.

"Yeah," I said. "But my question is, what has Abbunex done that they want the hottest attorney in Chicago on their team?"

"Or more accurately, what has the executive team done?" added Halterman.

"You think they're hiding something?" I asked.

"You think?" she replied sarcastically.

"I think so too, but I don't know if they both are." I paused and stopped walking for a moment causing Patti to stop next to me. "What if one of them is guilty of something? They bring the other in the room with them to add legitimate tone and argument to their discussion."

"So you think one of them is lying and the other doesn't know it so they support it unconditionally?" She seemed puzzled by my suggestion.

Breaking the short silence, I said, "I don't know. I just thought it was odd how each would lead the other."

"Whether one led the other or not, it definitely would be a method to hide deception." She paused and then asked, "Who do you think was lying?"

"I don't know, but with these guys, if we can see their finances, I think some things will come to light."

"Do you think you can get a subpoena?" she asked.

"We definitely can for Thompson and Stover. Any additional will be a stretch unless we can find something to tie them to some sort of fraud that they were all involved in."

We started walking to our car again and as we reached the doors, Halterman asked, "Where to now?"

"Let's go talk to Thompson's family. I want to know what she thinks about her husband's death. I want to probe a bit further into this sports thing and make sure we can rule that out. I need to make sure there's not a link outside of Abbunex between the two men."

Halterman began typing on her phone as she climbed into the car. "I have the address and phone number. Do you want me to call ahead?"

"Do it," I stated, as the engine fired up.

10

We arrived at the Thompson house fifteen minutes later. It was several levels down in financial standing from Doc G's mansion, but still well above the norm. It was a very traditional house with a large— probably an acre-plus—yard, which was huge in any suburb of Chicago, and some beautiful landscaping. I remember my first impression of Dr. Randy Thompson. I believe I said he was a rich, smug, and a born-again asshole. Based on this house, I may not have been as accurate as I always claim to be.

We walked up to the double front door and I moved to the side motioning Halterman to do the same. Then we rang the bell. There was some noise inside, typical of someone getting up and walking to the door. When the door opened, a movie star was behind it. Long blonde hair with a body that looked like she just filmed a Pilates video. She smiled but it appeared she was covering for something, maybe the fact her husband was killed less than forty-eight hours ago.

"Hello, Detectives. I assume you're the ones who called a short while ago?"

"Yes, ma'am," I replied removing my ID. "I'm Detective Tomas O'Malley and this is my partner, Detective Patti Halterman. Would we be able to speak to you for a few minutes?"

There was pain in her demeanor. It was hidden, but still present. "I'm Abigale Thompson," she stated, pressing her lips together but still opening the door further for us to enter. As we passed, she added, "I'm not sure what information I can provide. I've told the police everything already. Both me and Myron did."

"Myron?" I asked.

"Our son. Myron Green Thompson. He was named after Randy's grandfather." She paused and appeared to be fighting off tears. "I'm sorry, this is just so hard."

Myron Green Thompson, I thought. What the hell was it with these families and names? *Russell Stover*...and now using all three names at once? Who identifies their child with all three names? I could tell my momentary delay made everyone uncomfortable so I instantly changed my direction.

"I can never fully understand, Mrs. Thompson," I replied, carrying as much empathy in my voice as possible. "And I know you've told others so many things, but Detective Halterman and I are taking over the case and we would be very interested in hearing directly from you. So many times one comment someone thinks isn't important clicks and solves a case. Can we have a few minutes with you and Myron, if he's home?"

She led us to a beautiful but not extravagant entry and then down a step to arrive at an open living room. There was a stone fireplace along the center and a large-screen television hung on the wall. Bose speakers were affixed around the room which I'm sure provided a very nice surround sound for any movie or sporting event. The mantle was full of family pictures and on the opposite wall were several long frames with what had to be pictures of each year of Myron's life. It was actually very nice and would make a lonely divorced man like me a bit jealous.

"Please, have a seat," she broke in. "I did let Myron know you would be coming by based on your call. He was going to play some video games. It's all he's been doing for the last two days since..." She paused and both Halterman and I knew no further comment was necessary.

Patti said, "The last thing we want to do is bring difficult feelings back to the surface, but when it comes to a situation like this, very often, time is critical."

"I understand," she replied. "And there is nothing you can say that will bring any new negative feelings forward. We can't get by them right now." We both nodded understanding, before she continued, "Do you want us here together?"

I was about to answer before my partner cut me off. "You know, maybe it would be easier on Myron if I simply went up and talked to him while he played. It may help him keep his mind on something else but still be able to share anything he might know."

I was surprised at the idea, not because it was a bad one, but because she had thought of it. Everyone considered me the best detective in Chicago, and now twice in two days I had found myself a little off. Was I losing it? I believe I was actually looking in the air pondering this when Halterman poked my side. "You good with that, partner?"

Shaking out of my stupor, I replied quickly, "If Mrs. Thompson is comfortable with it?"

"She already said she was," Patti replied.

"Of course she did," I answered proudly to the hard stare of Halterman which clearly said, *what the hell is wrong with you?*

Patti kept her stare on me for her first few steps out of the room. Evidently during my lapse of consciousness, Abigale Thompson had not only agreed to the separate interviews but already told Patti how to find her son. I turned back to Mrs. Thompson who also stared at me with a bit of wonder or concern, I couldn't tell which. "So, can you tell me about your husband?"

"What do you want to know?" she replied, but continued before I could answer. "He was a good man. He was smart and had a very good job. He was a great husband. You know, he knew how much I loved black shoes. Every time he traveled anywhere, he would always bring me back a pair of black shoes. I bet I have fifty pair upstairs." She started to cry a bit and stopped.

"I'm sorry I have to ask, especially after what you just said, but it is important to hear the answer. Were there any marital problems?"

She smiled. "No. Randy and I barely fought. Occasionally about things involving Myron or stress he felt at work, but not the things most couples fought about. We are fine with money. We could have a much larger house than we do, but we put over twenty percent into savings each month. It was really a good marriage, compared to most, I guess."

"Did Randy have anyone he did not get along with? At work or personal?"

She shook her head. "No, not that he ever talked about. He always talked positively about the people at work as well those we knew personally. He was a coach and with that, some parents were less appreciative of him and his efforts, but to be honest, we really don't know most of them that well. I mean, you're together through a season and then everything resets. Randy did say he would not coach again. I know there was one parent that was especially upset at him at least one time in the past."

"Do you think it bothered him—that parent being upset at him?" I asked.

"I think it did at the time," she replied. "But the season is over. When the season ended, so did the issue."

"Would it surprise you to know that as recently as Saturday night, your husband was complaining about that same parent at the dinner party he was at?"

She reacted immediately, "Yes, that would really surprise me. He had not mentioned it in weeks to me."

Interesting, I thought. "You said he was often stressed at work. When was the last time you saw that?"

She thought a minute. "Well, on and off as things would happen. He was in charge of R&D on new projects. So, when new trials were coming out, his group would handle much of the testing. Testing for new drugs could go on for years and when one bad series of results came in, it could nullify years' worth of work. If the drug got cancelled, it could cost the company millions."

"Interesting," I replied. "But I'm not sure you answered my question. When would you say is the last time he was stressed?"

Her eyebrow lifted and clearly she remembered something.

"What is it?" I pushed slightly harder.

"Well, actually, his last day of work. He came home concerned about something he had discovered. He said he was fearful he would have to work all weekend but when he talked to his boss, he was told to sit on it till Monday. I don't think he wanted to but he also didn't want to work all weekend so he accepted the direction."

"Interesting, do you know what the problem was?" I asked.

She shook her head. "No, I just know the results he got were not what he expected, but that was all he would say." She paused, then added, "And I don't even know if he actually said that, or if I just inferred that from his comments."

I understood. "So he talked to his boss about it, though. What is his boss's name?"

She replied without any tone one way or the other, "Dr. Joseph Reingold."

"Did they get along?" I asked.

She smiled and nodded. "He's a huge supporter of my husband. Gave him the position in the department and has mentored him for the last five years. He's a good man."

"So they got along well then?"

"Absolutely," she replied smiling.

I nodded understanding and let that sit for a second or two as I thought about my next question. "Why didn't you go to the party Saturday night with your husband?"

I think the question caught her off guard at first, but her answer still came easily. This is a key step in questioning witnesses. Keep them slightly off guard with questions and watch how they respond. Do they have to think about how to answer, or do they just answer? Mrs. Abigale Thompson had nothing to hide. She just answered, "To be honest, I don't like those big company parties. They're always at one of the bigwigs' houses, and don't get me wrong, I'm thrilled that he's included at his level, but he is the lowest on the totem pole. He tries to fit in as best he can, but even he says he comes across sounding more pompous than he truly is. He feels obligated to go."

"So what did you do instead?"

"Myron and I had movie night. He likes those dragon movies so much. We watched the third one."

"*How to Train your Dragon?*"

She smiled. "Yes, that's the series."

"They're very good," I replied smiling. "Right up my alley also."

We talked for another five minutes or so before my partner and a young teenage boy came into the room. Patti spoke during one of our short breaks in conversation. "You have a wonderful son, Mrs. Thompson. You should be very proud."

She smiled and Myron walked over and sat down next to her on the couch. "Thank you. I am."

"Are you both finished?" Patti asked, speaking mostly to me.

"We are," I replied. "Unless you have anything else you wanted to say," I added, turning back to Abigale.

She had placed her arm around her son. "Just catch the person who did this. Please catch the person who did this," she repeated a second time softer.

As we walked to the door, I turned and asked one more question. "You know, one piece of information I didn't get was the name of the parent who was not pleased with your husband's coaching. It may be worth a quick follow-up with him also to help with the background."

"That's easy," replied Myron immediately, speaking before his mother could answer. "Colin Larson's dad. I think his name is Ryan."

"Ryan Larson," I repeated back to him. "Thank you both for your time, and we'll do everything we can to catch the person who did this. I can promise you that."

With that, we left the house shutting the door behind us.

11 As we drove back down south toward Chicago, Patti immediately broke in with conversation, "I meant what I said. Myron Thompson was an extremely well-spoken and mature kid. However, other than speaking very highly of his father, he really provided nothing." She paused and looked toward me as I drove. "How about the mother? Any useful info there?"

I kept driving without turning to her. "A couple interesting items. She too was very positive about her husband. In fact, I have to believe that whatever caused his murder, it had nothing to do with his home life. The marriage was strong and she wasn't lying or sugarcoating it. I could tell by the way she spoke. However, something happened at work his last day, that Friday. His boss told him not to worry about it until Monday but Abigale also shared that when his team found issues, sometimes it cost the company millions, even could cancel years' worth of research on a new drug."

"Millions," Patti restated softly. "That would cause some eyes to raise."

"My thoughts exactly."

"So, he told his boss. Did he tell anyone else?"

"The impression I got was he went to his boss and it all stopped right there because his boss wanted to sit on it till Monday."

"Who is his boss?" Patti asked.

"A Dr. Joseph Reingold."

"We should talk to Joseph Reingold," she said.

"Yes, we should," I replied. "I want to know what was so unimportant it could wait until Monday but lo and behold, Dr. Randy Thompson didn't make it until Monday."

"Do you think Dr. Reingold is involved?" she asked.

"I don't know enough right now, but it's definitely worth asking the question."

"Where to now?" Patti asked.

"Well, we have burned through most of the day. I know Carter wanted us back to download at the department. I say we skip that and go for a drink. I could use one. We could maybe even swing by my place and pick up where we were going the other night, when Doc G stopped by."

Patti pressed her lips together. "I need to head back. I have plans tonight."

My eyebrows raised. "Plans?"

"Yeah," she replied hesitantly. "I was asked out to dinner by a mutual friend. I wanted to talk to you about it the other night but things just got in the way."

"Are these romantic plans?" I asked inquisitively.

She shrugged. "I don't know." She paused. "Maybe. I just..."

I was actually getting angry and I didn't know why. "Who is it?" I sounded abrupt and jealous. Why the hell did I sound so jealous?

"Swanny," she replied softly.

"Swanny? From the lab? Give-him-a-Clark Bar-and-get-anything-you-want-Swanny?"

She smiled. "I guess I will have to bring a Clark Bar."

I realized how stupid I sounded. I didn't know why I sounded that way so I needed to recover quickly. "Good for you two," I replied, staring directly forward through my window, entranced by the road. Maybe she wouldn't drill into me about my response if I could sound pleased.

"What is with the reaction anyway? Is there some reason you don't want me going out with Craig?" She paused then added in a tone which got quieter as she spoke, "He asked like a little kid in school."

"No reaction. I just thought..." I stopped. "Hell, I don't know what I thought."

Nothing more was said on the subject. I headed straight to the department and I couldn't get there fast enough. I called ahead to Carter and he let me know Franky and Huston were already back. He wanted to debrief with everyone when we got in. I let him know Halterman may not stay and that was not an issue as long as I could relay all the information in full. Patti heard the conversation but didn't speak.

We arrived at the department and I parked in the lot. As we both got out, I opted to break the monotonous silence. "So, where you guys going tonight?" I tried to remain light and act like a friend or partner normally would act, not the jacked-up a-hole I had been thirty minutes earlier.

"Nothing is decided. He just asked about grabbing dinner."

"Well, I hope you have a good time. Swanny is a good guy."

"Thanks, O'Malley, I appreciate that. And thanks for covering for me with Carter."

"No big deal," I replied. "I'll be more accurate relaying the info than you anyway." I smiled as I said it and she knew I was kidding. Or was I?

* * * * *

I walked into the Bulls Room, grabbed all the files, and proceeded to the conference room next door. "Damn it, O'Malley, we are not moving. Everything is up on the whiteboard in here and this is where we are going to have our meeting." I did not reply so Carter continued. "And that is a goddamn order!"

I slowly walked back and poked my head in. "You're lucky my partner isn't with me or there's no way we'd be having this meeting in this room. I will say it this one time and one time only: If the Royals Room is available and I am to present any information, then that is the room I will use."

Carter got up from his chair and walked over to me. "I will say this one time and one time only: If I hear one more peep from you about that goddamn Royals Room, not only will the name be permanently changed back to the White Sox, you will be working two weeks on desk duty and I'll set up your desk right inside the goddamn White Sox Room. Do you get what I'm saying?"

Franky stood and walked over. "I'm sure what Tommy meant was that he would prefer the Royals Room remain as such and today he's fine meeting in here. Isn't that right, Tommy?"

I don't know why I was so pissed. I think because of Halterman, but why? I didn't answer but pushed by Carter and took a seat at the table. "What did you guys find out with Mandy?"

"Shouldn't we wait for Halterman?" asked Huston.

"She won't be coming. I have all the information anyway."

"But we prefer hearing..." She stopped in mid-sentence to the piercing stare from Franky.

"What was that?" I asked.

"Nothing," she replied more quietly. "Now, what do we know?"

Both groups downloaded all their information. It was interesting to hear what Franky learned from Jules, formerly Mandy, combined with what we learned from the executives at Abbunex as well as the Thompson family. We opted to call it a night and regroup in the morning, all agreeing to toss around options for the plan of attack tomorrow. I knew Franky was headed for a beer so I nodded I would join him, just as my phone rang. I looked at the number. It was blocked.

"O'Malley."

"Hello, Tommy." I instantly recognized the voice but couldn't believe it.

"Marco Filini. I can't say I expected to hear from you."

His voice was deep and cold. "I think we need to speak. In person."

"And why is that, Marco?" I asked, with everyone still in the area now taking notice of my conversation, Franky and Carter at the forefront.

"Because there's something going on that doesn't involve me but you may think it does, and I don't wish to be tied to it."

"Where do you want to meet?" I asked.

"I already have a table at the Chop House. I figure it'll be like old times."

I took a deep breath as I remembered everything to do with Marco Filini, the Chicago Chop house, and my old girlfriend. I cleared my throat. "Sounds good. I'll be there in fifteen minutes."

"Fifteen minutes," he replied. "See you then."

I hung up and lifted my head to see Carter and Franky only feet from me. "There's no way in hell you're going to meet Marco Filini alone," Franky stated.

I started to protest to Carter's raised hand. Carter's voice was hard and unforgiving. "We all go or nobody goes, and that, like previously, is an order."

I stammered a bit and then answered, "Fine, but we do this my way. Marco called me for a reason. He only would do this if he wanted something from me. I speak to him alone. You can be in the restaurant, but Filini and I meet alone."

"You will wear a wire or you won't go," Carter added.

"Then, unless you can get a wire on me in less than five minutes, I won't be going and we will lose a chance at gaining information on something. I'm not sure what, but something."

"There's no way I can get a wire that fast," said Carter. "You know that."

"Then meet me at the restaurant."

"What restaurant?" Franky asked.

I turned to face him. "The Chicago Chop House."

"That asshole," he replied.

"Yep."

I prepared to walk into the Chicago Chop House about twenty minutes later. I was not wired nor escorted, but I already knew Carter and Franky were inside. They both knew what Filini looked like—hell, he was impossible to miss. At well into six foot and African American, he was a daunting figure. He also spared no expense with his clothes. He looked the part, that was the easiest way to say it. For a murderer, even I had to say he had class.

The engine of the 1974 shit-brown Camaro roared to life as the valet drove it away. I pulled open the door and was immediately greeted by a face I knew well. "Tommy? It's been a while. How are you?"

I smiled and outstretched my hand to the Chicago Chop House general manager and former boss to my long-time girlfriend, Tammi Hutchins. "I am well, Keith, and good to see you."

"Good to see you as well." He released my hand. "Hey, I heard from Tammi the other day. Sounds like she's doing well. Have you two remained in touch?"

"Not so much really," I replied, my tone clearly showing we should not go there. I don't know why I didn't want to go there. It really was no big deal. Couples break up every day. It's a normal progression. Just because I didn't want to break up, and that wonderful woman who lived with me who I was considering asking to marry me found a new job in San Francisco told me about it the day of her flight—what the hell, that was normal, right? We should have been able to do the long-distance thing—yeah, whatever. The word that comes to mind is not on the *Word of the Day* toilet paper—*bitch*.

Kaplan sensed my hidden message and didn't pursue it further. "I didn't see you on the reservation list. I can find you a table in the bar?"

"No, I'm actually meeting someone here," I replied. "A large man, African American."

"Oh yes," Kaplan stated. "He has a table in the corner upstairs. I can take you there."

Kaplan led me up the stairs, although I could have easily found it on my own. This is what he did. He shook hands, spoke to everyone, and wanted to make sure everyone saw him doing this. It sent a message to all patrons that you wanted to get to know this man, because he knew everyone. And his message worked very well as this was one of the most popular restaurants in Chicago. As we rounded the corner, I saw Marco, his back to the wall, facing the room.

"There you are, Detective," Kaplan said, extending his arm as he pulled out the chair with his other hand. Enjoy your dinner, gentlemen. He walked away actually giving us a small bow.

Filini stood up and reached out his hand. "O'Malley. I would say it was good to see you but part of me never wanted our paths to cross again, other than what you owe me, that is." He smiled as he said this last part, and as always, I had never seen such white teeth on anyone. Marco Filini was a black belt, as was I. In fact, I was the highest-ranked US-born black belt in the Midwest, even at my age. Marco Filini had trained as long as I had. In fact, we evidently were slated to fight in the US Nationals in Las Vegas until the tournament reorganized and we ended up in different brackets. Marco was disqualified by some unrelated issues and we never faced off. It's worth noting that I won those Nationals and that was the last time we would have met. It's also worth noting that I have no knowledge of Marco Filini being there or the reorganization of the brackets. Marco believes Master Yi, my coach and mentor, purposely arranged those changes to avoid us meeting. Marco is full of himself.

"Marco Filini, I can't say that I had no intention of ever seeing you again, because if I did, it would be to put you behind bars."

He actually laughed out loud just for a second. "O'Malley, you never change. Still too afraid to meet? I'll be glad to come by your dojo. I've gotten to know Master Yi quite well."

That actually caught me just a bit. "I will have to talk to Master Yi about the company he keeps."

Again, Filini only answered it with a smile. "Take a seat, O'Malley. My soup is getting cold."

We sat down and I slid my chair to the side slightly so I wasn't looking directly into the wall. "Why did you call me here, Marco?"

He lifted his spoon and took a sip of his soup. "I thought you would come alone. I didn't realize you would bring Carter and Sullivan, and who the hell is that monster with your partner?" He pointed to a table across the room.

My eyes followed his direction. "Shit," I said to myself as our eyes met. "I'll be right back."

I got up and walked over to the two at the table.

"O'Malley, what the hell are you doing here?" Swanny asked, almost smiling proudly that he was being seen out with Patricia Halterman.

"I just want to say hello, folks," I replied. "I got called to a meeting with someone and didn't know you'd be here also."

Patti still hadn't spoken and was staring toward the table I had left. Swanny continued, "Yeah, we just decided after we got in the car." He paused. "This is Patti, my date." He started laughing at his implied comment that I wouldn't know Patti.

"Really, great to meet you, Patti. You having a nice dinner?" I was trying to continue the joke, though I was not laughing at all.

"Who the hell is that?" Patti asked. "Does it have to do with our case?"

My smile quickly faded. "Don't worry about it. Enjoy your dinner. Carter and Franky have my back tonight."

"Shit!" Swanny interrupted. "That's Marco Filini. I remember his picture from the Polino case. What the hell are you—"

"Take it easy, Craig. Stay at your table. Enjoy your dinner. We got this." I put my hand on his shoulder and turned my eyes to Patti. "Seriously, partner. I'll talk to you about this in the morning." My stare told her clearly to not get involved and not be overly observant. Any hinky feeling he gets could end this meeting before it gets started. She got the message.

"We're almost done anyway so we'll be leaving," she stated. "Call me tonight, why don't you?"

"Will do, partner."

I returned to the table and took my seat. "Believe it or not, she's on a first date."

Filini nodded. "I actually believe that because she was here before I even set it up with you. I found it ironic." His voice was very deep but he spoke softly. I'm sure it was habit. Marco Filini most likely never had a conversation that he did not want kept quiet so he simply learned to always speak that way.

"Why am I here, Marco?" I asked.

"Straight to the heart of it," he replied. "Let's wait for our food. I took the liberty of ordering for you."

"Now who is on a date?" I asked.

He smiled that white-toothed smile. "Yeah, but your date is better looking than Mr. 5X over there."

"You commenting on someone's size...that's something I never thought I'd hear."

He held his smile. "You know, O'Malley, nobody but you could ever say something like that to me. I appreciate that." He paused. "From anyone else, it would disrespectful, but I sense that is how you show respect. I have had to learn that about you."

"If you say so," I stated in rebuttal.

He ignored my return and continued with his thought. "You know, I think I learned it with Ricardo. Do you remember Ricardo?"

"That numb-nuts you had as a doorman at one of those clubs. The guy that continually got in my face no matter how many times he ended on his back. That guy?"

"Yeah, that guy," he replied, now smiling even larger as he thought about those exchanges outside the strip clubs his boss owned.

"No, I don't remember," I said, now smiling myself.

"I don't either," he replied.

Just then, a waiter who was tall, thin, and appeared to be homosexual (but that really wasn't a factor), walked up carrying two large Caesar salads and two tall drinks that looked like whiskey.

"Here are your salads, gentlemen, and two double McNaughton's on the rocks. Can I get you anything else?"

We both looked toward him and nodded we were good. "McNaughton's, huh?" I said to Marco. "How did you know?"

He knew the question was rhetorical. Marco did his research. There was nothing Marco Filini didn't know if he wanted to know it. "Someone is killing pharmaceutical executives," he stated.

"I know," I replied nonchalantly, grabbing my fork and stabbing a large bite of salad.

"They might be trying to frame me," he added, now taking a bite himself.

That actually caught me a little by surprise. "Why do you say that?"

He continued eating, not seeming to notice that I had stopped on his last statement. "I can't say, but I also have no reason to lie about it."

"Then why are you here, Marco?" I asked.

"To tell you that it wasn't me who was doing this." He took another bite. He wasn't even looking at me, as if he didn't care if I believed him or not. He just wanted me to know.

"Okay," I replied. "Thanks for letting me know." My intended nonchalant return did get his attention.

He smiled again. "Nice, O'Malley. Very nice."

I smiled in return. "You wouldn't have told me this unless you had a reason. What's your reason, Marco?"

"The reason is, if it's not me, ask yourself, who is doing it?" He had stopped eating.

"The murders are not professional. In fact, they are amateur," I replied. I stopped eating as well to focus on him and this conversation.

"Listen, I can't tell you everything, but just know two things: First, I am not behind these murders. Regardless of what it looks like, I am not involved."

"Fair enough," I interjected. "What is the second thing?"

"After this is all done, and assuming you are still alive, then you will owe me what I have been asking for."

I shook my head and went back to eating my salad. "Are you serious? All this bullshit is still just about you sparring with me." I paused as I shoved a forkful into my mouth. "You need to get a life, Filini. We're old shitheads now. We're too old to worry about the Nationals like when we were kids."

"When it's over, Tommy."

We finished the multicourse meal and even knocked down a crème brulee. Marco paid our bill without question, stood, shook my hand, and winked. It was not a, *you're lookin' good,* wink. It was a, *you know I'm not fucking with you,* wink. He then walked over to Carter and Sullivan and bid them well, and then he left. Just like that. No further comment. Have dinner, tell me he is currently not killing anybody but someone is, and then leave. The guy is eccentric—that much is certain.

I joined Carter and Franky, and their first question was exactly what was expected due to the serious nature of the situation. Franky led and went directly to the point. "What the hell, Tommy. Patti and Swanny? Why didn't you say something?"

"I know, brother. I just found out today," I replied.

"How long has that been going on?" Carter asked.

"From what I hear, he just asked her out today. This was their first date." My lips were pressed together and I was nodding as much as speaking.

Franky added, "I always thought you and her might make an item, but Swanny? She must like 'em big, huh?"

I didn't answer as much because I too was starting to think Patti and I would possibly make an item, or at least give it a run. My gut instinct was to simply deny it, but both Franky and Carter were long-time interrogators. They would have seen through me. It didn't matter anymore anyway. Carter pushed his stool over at the bar to make room for me to drag another stool between them.

Carter grabbed his club soda, took a drink, and flagged the bartender over. "Two McNaughton's and a Boulevard Pale Ale, please." Turning to me, he said, "Okay, what did murder-for-hire have to say?"

I probably raised my eyebrow at the title as I thought about the proper response. "Well, it seems he was concerned that we might have thought he was behind the murders of the pharmaceutical executives."

"Why the hell would he think that?" asked Franky. "Are they even professional hits?"

"I sure as hell didn't think so," I replied, "but it might be worth taking another look at them."

"There's no way the Thompson murder is professional. The description from that hooker said he barely knew how to use a gun," stated Carter.

I paused then said, "But what if the individual knew he had a witness? Maybe he was, I don't know, putting on a show for the crowd. Couldn't use the gun. Shot way more than necessary. In short, he made it look amateur and personal, rather than clean and professional. There was no trace, according to the evidence. Only a handful of fibers they haven't been able to positively match yet from a trunk that are common to about a thousand of the cars currently on the road in downtown alone."

Carter nodded. "I suppose that is possible, but I still say it's a stretch. No professional would have killed Thompson right out in the open. My gut still tells me it was personal."

Part of me had to agree, but I just didn't understand what Filini's purpose was in calling me. "I have no reason to trust Filini, but for some reason in certain instances I do. So, why the hell would he set up this meeting, be so cloak-and-dagger with the discussion, but in essence tell me these are professional murders and it's not him doing them?"

We sat in silence and drank letting that one float out there for a while. Out of the blue, Franky said, "Maybe he has a competitor."

"What?" I asked.

"Think about it," he returned. "Remember the Polino and Moretti case. Moretti and Polino were partners, but in the end they were competitors. Moretti's whole plan was to take over the Chicago underground and in turn put his competitor, and partner, out of business. He set up the evidence such that we did his dirty work for him." He paused letting his thoughts catch up with his mouth. "Maybe Filini has someone else who's trying to get into the business and he simply wants us to get rid of that someone for him."

I thought a minute but then shook my head. "Nope, Filini would simply kill some amateur that was making him look bad. He wouldn't need us. He would kill him and the body would never be found." Right when I said it my mind flashed back to something Moretti had said to me when I went to meet him the day he had been released. He said, "*I could do it, you know. Kill you right here in my office, and your body would never be found. I guarantee you there would be no evidence and no witnesses. Your disappearance would simply go through as an unsolved cold case. Detective Thomas O'Malley, Never Been Found.*" I didn't like the phrase, because I knew it was true.

Carter nodded agreement. "You're probably right, but this case just doesn't add up. We don't even have a motive."

"There is so much money involved with these people," I replied. "It has to be tied to money somehow, because there seems to be one rule that always rings true. No matter how much money you have, you always want more."

"That was a quick dinner, gentlemen," stated Kaplan from behind, causing all three of us to jump a bit as we turned to face him. "Oh, sorry, I didn't mean to startle you."

"No problem, Keith," I replied. "My food was excellent as always."

"Great, great to hear. Let me know if you need anything." He motioned to the bartender. "Paul, these are all on me." He shook our hands and as quickly departed, immediately being grabbed for a discussion at an adjacent table away from the bar.

"Damn," stated Carter. "He's like an eagle. He swoops in, does his thing, and gets the hell out."

"He is an entertainer," I replied. "And everyone here wants to show they know him."

Franky smiled. "But he paid for our drinks, and in my book, that makes him okay."

"Let's finish these drinks and run by Flap Jaws. I think Roy needs a visitor." I smiled slightly as I was sure that Roy Pura, the Flap Jaws bartender and owner, was perfectly fine whether we came by or not.

"Sounds like a plan," replied Franky. "Maybe when we're there you can tell me why it bothered you so much that your partner was out with Swanny." He laughed and even Carter turned a small smile.

I said nothing and left.

12

"So what is our next plan?" asked Franky.

"We need to determine a motive." I replied.

Carter said, "Maybe tomorrow we all sit together and run through every scenario we can imagine. We play out every option."

I nodded. "I know Doc G, whether she wants us to believe it or not, thinks her husband is involved. If we assume he is, what could be his motive?"

"Money?" asked Franky.

"Maybe, but they have so much of it. What other motive could they have?" I thought a minute and then stated, "Maybe we're thinking about the wrong letter."

"What the hell does that mean?" Franky asked. "What letter?"

I turned to stare directly at Franky just as Roy Pura walked up. "Another round?"

"Do you have to ask?" Carter said.

"Since I brought another round with me, I guess not." Roy set down three more drinks.

"Very good," Carter replied. "You are detective material."

"Nah, too easy," replied Roy sarcastically as he walked away.

I continued to answer Franky's question, "What do you think is a lot of money?"

Franky answered after just a little thought, "Ten million dollars."

"How about you, Carter?" I asked.

"Sounds good to me," he replied. "Ten million."

"What if this deal is about a B?"

"What do you mean, B?" asked Franky.

"Do you mean billions of dollars?" asked Carter.

"Yes," I stated. "To most every criminal in the world, millions is enough to get them to do certain crimes. Maybe to these guys, it takes exponentially more. What could they be tied to that could involve billions of dollars?"

"Well," said Franky, "Google says Abbunex has a 154 billion dollar market cap. I guess that would be billions."

Carter shook his head. "No, I don't think that's right. What is the one thing rich people fear?"

I looked at him. "Not being rich anymore."

"Right," he replied. "I think there's a better chance they did something that could make them poor than something that could hurt the company. The company pockets are just too deep. It can weather any storm."

I nodded my head in agreement. "We're just guessing anyway. We need some evidence. We need to figure out what the hell is going on. What besides the pharmaceutical company links these guys?"

"And we need to find that out before any more Abbunex people die," Franky said.

"Why the hell is my glass empty?" I asked, motioning to Roy in the process.

He smiled and brought over the bottle rather than another glass. "Here, gentlemen. Finish this bottle and then call it good." He turned to Franky. "Another IPA?"

He nodded. "And hey, Roy, do you think O'Malley is shitty at finding women?" Franky asked.

Roy looked to me but did not reply. I nodded. "The answer is yes, Roy. Yes, O'Malley is shitty at finding women." Roy smiled but had no idea what conversation he had walked into and quickly turned back to the bar.

"You going to still bring Swanny Clark Bars?" Franky asked.

"Jesus, guys. Patti and I don't have any relationship. Why the hell are you acting like we do?"

They just smiled, but took it no further. Thirty minutes later we were headed out. Roy got us all cabs and we headed out with plans to regroup in the morning. As I was walking into my place, I texted Patti to let her know to be in early. To my surprise, she replied.

Sounds good, she wrote.

You still on your date? I wrote back. Shit! Why did I write that? Why did I care?

No, she sent back, with a smiley emoji.

Smiley emoji? "Bingo," I said out loud, and I fumbled with my keys for the front door.

Did everything go all right? I expected either a yes or a no, but she one-upped me.

Why do you want to know?

Damn woman. She should not be smarter than me with her questions. *Just wanted to make sure you were okay?* I typed.

Without hesitation, she typed back, *Why wouldn't I be okay?*

I thought about not replying and letting it drop, but as always, I ignored the right thing to do and pulled an O'Malley. *I guess you caught me off guard by having this date.*

"Do you want to talk about it?" she said from behind me, causing me to jump out of my skin and drop my keys. She laughed. "Some detective. What if I had been a mugger?"

I bent down to pick up my keys and smiled. "Then you could have had the four dollars in my wallet and my maxed-out credit card without a fight."

She walked right up to me, put her hands on my hips, and whispered, "That was not the answer to my first question. My first question was, do you want to talk about it?"

"No," I replied, my voice actually trembling just a bit.

"Then what do you want to do?" she asked.

"I'm not sure I can say…" I paused then added, "and keep my job."

She gripped her hands tighter on my hips and pulled me slightly closer. I put my hands on her hips and then it happened. This is where I talk about how I nearly broke down my door and we fell over furniture in each other's arms fighting through each other's clothes. My stereo was somehow already playing soft jazz and the lights were automatically dimmed. A fire crackled in the fireplace but that was not what was creating the most heat. The most heat was in my bedroom, I can tell you that for sure. We were like two wild animals in the jungle roaring at the passion nature had brought between us. However, since I did not have a fireplace or a working stereo, that version did not happen.

So, back to my doorstep. I leaned in closer as she squeezed my hips and just before our lips touched, our noses hit so hard I thought mine might bleed. "Jesus," she exclaimed, pulling back and grabbing her nose.

"Shit," I replied, pulling away as well. "That moment was perfect."

"Nice job, you killer ladies' man," she added. "Let's go inside where nobody can see us."

"I am absolutely a loser."

"Yes," she replied. "But soon, you will be *my* loser."

"Bingo!"

•   •   •   •   •

The night was simply incredible. The first three minutes were magical for me, and then about an hour later, Patti was absolutely taken away with my abilities, or so she said, multiple times. High five. We didn't go to sleep till well past 3:00 AM. We also knew we had an early morning, but this was one of those times that I could have stayed up all night. I had asked her once about her date. She told me Swanny was incredibly nice, but when she saw me at the restaurant, she knew where she wanted to be. What can I say, when you got it, you got it.

Now it was 6:30 AM and the choices made last night did not seem as intelligent as originally thought. To her credit, Patti had brought an overnight bag. To my credit, my bathroom was clean.

"Almost ready?" I asked.

"Aren't you even going to shower?" she asked. "We"—she paused thinking of the right word— "got dirty last night."

"There's no time. Carter will have my ass if I'm late again."

She walked out wearing her slacks and no shirt. "That's your problem. If you weren't late sixty to seventy percent of the time, being a little late today would not be a problem." She got right up next to me pushing her body against mine and then rapidly pulled away. "But there's no way you're going to work smelling like that. You smell like a strip club."

I let out a long sigh that clearly demonstrated I did not like her statement. "Perhaps that is my cologne."

"What are you wearing, Polo, or Pole? Because you smell like a stripper has been using you to dance around all night."

I smiled broadly because she did not make the connection. "Actually, someone has been riding up and down my..."

She raised her hand. "Get in the f'ing shower. Now!"

The tone changed enough that I wasted no time. I checked my phone and saw it was conceivable I could take a shower and still make it to the morning briefing on time, though the odds were against me. To my credit, we walked in two minutes early and without even talking about it, Patti went straight to the back to stand next to Franky and I moved to the front by the whiteboard next to Carter.

"What the hell is the occasion, O'Malley? You're two minutes early." Carter shook his head, dug out his wallet, and walked over and handed Franky a twenty. "You guys set me up somehow. I know you did."

I had no idea what they were talking about but quickly understood that my beloved sergeant had no faith that I would be on time, much less early. "I'm just dedicated, sir. Been turning over a new leaf for some time now. I'm surprised you would bet against me."

"I will bet against you tomorrow as well. Now, let's cut the bullshit and get down to it."

The morning briefing was uneventful and then the five of them regrouped in the interrogation room.

Carter again led the way. "We talked last night." He briefly glanced at Huston and Halterman and adjusted his comment. "Sullivan and O'Malley met me briefly last night and we ran through some things. I wanted everyone together this morning to organize our actions. In short, we don't have shit to solve this case right now and need to come up with all our options."

Halterman replied, "Can you run through everything we know at this point for our benefit?"

The "our" was clearly meant for the two women which included my partner who was not pleased to have been kept out of the meeting last night. "You were busy last night, partner, or I would have called you to join us."

Huston looked toward Franky. "And what's your excuse, Franky?"

"I just didn't call," he replied. "Never even thought about it actually."

She clearly did not like that response but both Carter and I had a slight smile neither of us could hide. Carter responded, "I wanted to run through everything again anyway so there's no harm."

He then proceeded to review everything we knew on the case. He used the evidence board and added to it where he could. He was very thorough and I was impressed with how he hit every point, and in the end, we all looked at each other and without saying another word, all agreed we had nothing. We really did not have a viable suspect because we still had no motive. Money was clearly an easy factor to include in the discussion, but everyone had so much of it we didn't know for sure it was an issue.

"What is our next move?" Carter asked.

"There's one name that's been brought up in our interviews and is not on the board," I stated.

"Who is that?" Carter asked.

"Well, I don't think he's a factor because it's too long of a reach, and he's not linked at all to Abbunex that we know of, but Ryan Larson is tied to Randy Thompson."

"Who the hell is Ryan Larson?" asked Franky.

"Really?" questioned Halterman. "The parent who didn't like the way Dr. Thompson coached? You think he could be a suspect?"

"Hey," I replied, "at this point, I'm reaching for any name that has come up." I paused. "What if Larson is somehow linked to Stover and we just don't know it yet? Then what would your reaction be?"

"Very well," Carter replied, writing his name on the whiteboard and drawing a line from Randy Thompson to him. "Let's find out what we can about Larson."

As I looked across the suspect board, I saw Russell Stover's name below his mother's. Suddenly I thought about his name and smiled again.

"What the hell is so funny, O'Malley?" Carter asked.

"Nothing, sir," I replied quickly, removing the smirk from my face. "Just thinking about chocolate actually."

He didn't know what to do with that so he let it drop. "O'Malley and Halterman, look into Ryan Larson and why don't you two"—he motioned to Franky and Karen—"do a full financial review of Abbunex, Thompson, Stover, and everyone else on this board? Tommy said he didn't really trust Hermann so dig deep into him as well."

"Now that you've had the night to think about it, what are your thoughts on what Filini said?" I asked my question toward Carter, but it was meant for everyone.

"Marco Filini is nobody I would give the time of day to," Carter began. "He's a killer who somehow avoids ever being tied to a murder. His motives are for him and him alone. Therefore, all I think about Filini is we need to arrest him sooner rather than later."

I did not mean to, but my shoulders dropped and I clearly showed disappointment in the response. In fact, I thought the response was bullshit, but I should have kept those feelings to myself.

Carter saw the reaction immediately and pounced like a cat on a wounded mouse. "What the hell, O'Malley. You think differently?" He paused and lifted his eyebrow almost as if an idea was pouring into his mind out of nowhere. "Oh, wait," he said, the sarcasm growing with each syllable. "You and Filini are Kung Fu buddies. He wants to meet up with you in some sort of rematch from your high school days."

He let out a breath and although the word was not stated, it clearly came across as, *whatever*. "O'Malley, we don't have time for any bullshit from that murdering asshole. He is fucking with you. More than likely, he did kill one or both of our victims and is trying to see where the investigation is at."

I did not react to Carter's tone or sarcasm. I simply stared back at him taking his words at face value. "First, if that were the case, he would have slyly asked about the case in some way. Instead, all he said was that he didn't do it. Secondly, we are not Kung Fu buddies, nor have we ever been. He's under some disillusion that I ducked facing him in a championship when I was a teenager, but that is not a factor in any of our discussions. Yes, he wants a rematch and to be completely honest, I don't."

You could feel the tension in the air carried in my cold tone in the wake of Carter's sarcastic rampage. Sensing this, Franky broke in, "Is it actually a rematch if you two never met the first time?"

I did not expect this response, and I liked it. I smiled. "I stand corrected, Franky. He would like a chance to make up for the alleged missed opportunity from our childhood."

Carter was having nothing of it. "I don't give a shit if it's a rematch, a reunion, or a goddamn bar mitzvah..."

"Bar mitzvah?" Franky whispered almost to himself, but not completely. The *not completely* drew a stiff glare from the sergeant.

"I also don't give a shit where you stand, O'Malley. Filini is not a part of this investigation."

"Well, sir," I answered. "With all due respect, he made himself part of it when he called me for a meeting. Regardless of his motive, he's a person of interest, and I will continue to keep that in mind as I evaluate the evidence."

Carter let out a sigh but I think my last comment made enough sense that he had to let it go. Filini was personal for Carter. Not that Marco had done anything personal against my boss, but because he was a criminal that flaunted his criminal activities in front of the police force and nobody seemed able to touch him, he held a different spot in Carter's world. He was the one that always got away clean, no matter how dirty he was.

13 We arrived at Ryan Larson's house two hours later. Patti had done a workup on him and found that he was pretty normal. He was on his second marriage; his first marriage produced one child who was in the armed forces and currently overseas. He and his second wife had two children, a boy, Colin, who was the same age as Randy Thompson's son, Myron Green Thompson (I had to say it again for sheer three-name opportunity usage), and a girl, Chelsea, who was two years younger. Their house was upper middle class with a decent-sized yard and a three-car garage, both of which were rare in the Chicagoland area and added value to the home. The neighborhood was nice and friendly. As we pulled up, there was a car running in the driveway and a woman sitting in the driver's seat. We pulled along the road, parked, and just looked around.

"That is not one of the Larson's registered cars. Do you want me to run the plate?" Patti was already taking down the plate number.

"We will run it, but let's just get out and introduce ourselves. That should tell us who this is much faster. They have no reason not to say."

"I suppose," Halterman replied. "Unless they do have a reason, I suppose."

I smiled. "You're starting to sound like me now."

She returned the smile. "I should. After last night you left enough of you in me to make us twins."

Immediately I was caught between smiling broadly and amazement that she had just said that. "Nice," I replied, opening my door. "Maybe I need to leave a bit more tonight?"

"Maybe," she replied, pleased with the exchange as she too exited the vehicle.

I walked up to the window of the car and lightly tapped on the window causing the woman in the driver's seat to jump. She had been focusing on her phone and nearly dropped it at the sound. When she looked up, she had an extremely annoyed appearance but quickly softened when she saw us holding our badges and recognized this wasn't some random kid banging on the window.

"May I help you?" she asked after she had lowered her window about halfway so we could speak.

"Can I ask what you're doing here?" I said, still holding up my badge. I looked at the woman. She was exactly what I would expect. Probably in her early forties, either a stay-at-home mom or she had a mid-level career. Most likely 2.5 kids in the family, a dog, and their other car was a gas-guzzling SUV that her husband drove to his job. They more than likely lived in the same neighborhood or at least school district. In short, she was another mom.

She stuttered a bit not knowing what was going on. "I just dropped off my son to hang out with his friend. Is there a problem?"

"No problem," I replied. "We just don't often see cars idling in a driveway for that length of time. We just wanted to make sure everything was okay."

Her entire body dropped and relaxed as if a weight had been lifted off her. "Oh, that's all." She smiled almost embarrassed. "I was actually..."—she paused and then her tone depicted her being reluctant to finish—"I actually was just playing on my phone."

I returned her smile. "Well, at least you were doing it in a driveway and not while driving. For that, I would have given you a ticket." I liked pretending I could write a traffic ticket. I couldn't remember the last time I had written one; even when I was a policeman, I didn't write many. Truth is, I did not like writing citations.

"I would never text or play or use my phone in any situation when I drive, Officer," she replied, her voice confident as if speaking in a court case.

"Good," I replied. "It's illegal in Illinois and my partner and I take it very seriously. I once had a third-time offender spend several days in jail."

"Oh my," she replied, now almost uncomfortable with the discussion. "I absolutely will not, sir."

We bid her farewell and she reached down and motioned to me to watch her put her phone in a holder attached to the air vent. She slowly backed out of the driveway. "You are such an asshole, O'Malley," my partner said smiling.

"Yep."

"How long do you think it will be before she pops that phone out of the holder?" Patti asked.

"She probably has already. Texting her friends about her run-in with the law."

Patti smiled. "You might be on Facebook already."

We continued up the front walk to the double doors. Patti was standing in front of the door when I reached out to ring the bell and then stopped. I grabbed her arm lightly and pulled her behind me. Then I rang the bell.

"What, Tommy? You think they're going to come out shooting?" She was trying to sound lighthearted and funny but she quickly saw that was something beyond my ability to joke about, even this many years later.

"I supposed you can say that about every house, until the first time they actually do," I replied, my tone clearly showing my feelings. My comment came across harder than I intended, but it was something I just could not hide. My last official partner, not Franky but the one partner I was assigned, got shot and killed through a door just like this one when we innocently walked up to a house to follow up on a lead. His cousin was in the FBI. At the funeral, that FBI agent told me directly a statement that I will never forget and I live with every day: *You failed your partner, Detective O'Malley. You failed my cousin. You were the experienced detective and you let him walk into a bullet. You should never hold a gun again and if I have anything to say about it, you won't.*

Patti knew the story so I didn't have to repeat it now. She saw in my face that was where my mind was. "Hey, Tommy, I didn't mean to…"

"Nonsense, Patti," I interrupted. "Just don't step in front of doors."

She nodded and let it drop, just as the door opened. "Mrs. Larson?" I asked.

"Yes, I am Sharon Larson," she replied. "May I help you?"

Sharon was attractive in her own way. She had long blonde hair with tight curls that I imagined were natural. She was short, around 5' 2" and probably 110 pounds. She was not a model or anything, but fit the house, the neighborhood, the life. "I'm Detective O'Malley and this is Detective Halterman. We would very much like to speak to Ryan Larson if he's home."

Her face clearly showed concern. That is natural when detectives come to your door, but usually it appears more as wonder about the visit. Her facial expression said, *Oh shit, what did Ryan do now?* But it quickly faded as she fell to an easy answer. "Ryan is at work right now. He won't be home for several hours."

Patti answered in a much softer voice. "No problem, would you have a few minutes to talk? It might give us all the answers we need."

She was caught for a minute and appeared to be struggling to come up with a reason why this wouldn't work. After a few seconds that more than likely seemed like minutes to her, she slowly opened the door further and agreed to let us in. "I suppose that would be fine," she stated, then paused and actually stepped in front of us preventing us from entering. "Can I ask what this is about?"

Again with her soft tone, Patti answered not missing a beat. "We really would be more comfortable speaking inside, if that's all right. We think it would be better for everyone involved."

She still seemed uncomfortable but was also unable to deny us entry. Maybe it was curiosity as much as concern. She again moved to the side and motioned us in. The house was nice. It opened directly into a family room with stairs going up to a second level loft directly adjacent to the door. It was all hardwood flooring that looked to be bamboo. It echoed when we stepped but had a very rich look. The furniture was black leather and family pictures were on shelving all around a brick fireplace which had an opening into what I assumed was the kitchen. The house felt warm. I thought about my apartment. It did not feel warm. It was not a bachelor pad by the stereotypical definition of the word, but it was not warm either. I made a note to change that. I might now have someone in my life worth making something better than it currently was. I would love to do it for my kids, but they were at an age where they didn't care how my place looked as long as it had good Wi-Fi. Maybe I should make my apartment a home. *Oh my God*, I thought. *I'm becoming a woman.*

Sharon's voice broke my momentary thoughts. "Why don't we go to the dining room? The table is larger and we can sit. I can try to answer your questions there."

We took our seats and I looked around the room. It was a continuation of the entry and living room. Very nice, upper middle class, and well kept. I turned my eyes to face the woman who stared back with a questioning gaze. "So, Sharon...may I call you Sharon?"

"Of course, Detective," she replied.

"So, Sharon, can you tell me if your husband owns a gun?" *Bam*! Sometimes I just like to throw it out there and see if it sticks. When questioning someone, you have to evaluate the best direction to go. Sharon Larson was uncomfortable. Sharon Larson was already wondering what her husband was involved in. Sharon Larson needed the in-your-face question that kept her uncomfortable and also caused Patti's jaw to drop.

Sharon let out a gasp. "What? A gun. Just what the holy heck is this about?"

Well, golly, Jethro, I just don't know what all this craziness is all about, I thought. Who the hell were we interviewing, Mary Poppins?

"Well, Sharon, a man was murdered and we need to rule out anyone that had any beef with that man. We have confirmed witnesses that say your husband was one of those people." I paused and leaned back. I know I had just slapped her across the face, so now it was time to reel her back in and let her see I was the nice guy. "Do we believe your husband had anything to do with this? No way."

When I said this, I turned to Patti to get her acknowledgement as well. Without missing a beat, she added in that same soft caring tone. "Of course not, Sharon. This is all just procedure. Our boss makes us check out each name we're given. Your husband just doesn't fit the bill."

I nodded to her comment. "You see? My sergeant hears a name and until we do the background work to clear it, it stays on the board."

Sharon sucked this story down like she was drinking bottled water for the first time after two days in the desert. Her shoulders dropped, eyes softened, and I think she even smiled. "Oh, that makes so much sense. I thought for a minute I might need a lawyer or something like you see on TV." We all smiled but I did not acknowledge the lawyer comment. That was territory I did not want to go down. She continued, "What do you need to know?"

I was about to ask about the gun again because we were never given an answer but Patti cut me off. "Well," Patti started, "the easiest thing to start with is if you knew where your husband was on Sunday, particularly in the morning?"

Sharon seemed to be in a short moment of thought. "Well, that's easy. We went to church at seven-thirty, stopped to get donuts, and then came back home. Church was about an hour and our stop was short so I would assume we were home by nine o'clock. We were here the rest of the day."

"So everyone was together the entire day?" I asked. "Nobody left?"

"Well, Ryan did run out to get milk and some beer," she added.

"About what time was that?" Patti asked.

She thought again. "I don't know, maybe ten or so."

I glanced at Patti but she didn't show any signs of giving away that 10:30 was about the time the murder took place. She jotted down the time quickly on her notepad and continued. "And about how long do you think he was gone?"

Then her eyes twitched, just a bit. She was suddenly uncomfortable. I was not sure why she would be uncomfortable. She had no idea what the timing was for the murder nor did she even know who was murdered.

Patti interjected again during this pause. "Mrs. Larson? Is something wrong?"

"No," she quickly replied sternly, too sternly for my liking. "He was just gone a bit long. Maybe forty-five minutes."

"What store did he go to?" I asked.

Again, she paused longer than I thought she should. "Um, I'm not sure. Probably Dominick's."

"Probably Dominick's?" I asked again.

"Well, it's not like I was with him," she stated defensively. "He could have gone all the way to Walgreens for all I know."

Patti took over again. "Let's assume he went to Dominick's, but please note that we will pull his credit card receipts. About how far is Dominick's?"

She answered smoothly again, back to someone not hiding anything on the distance of a grocery store to their house. "Maybe ten to fifteen minutes." She ended it there and Patti was about to speak when she added, "What do you mean that you will check his credit card receipts?"

Patti again didn't miss a beat. "Well, Sharon, although we would love to take spouses' words for everything, the truth is often spouses are not honest with us. That is why we like more physical proof—credit card receipts are good, but both Dominick's and Walgreens will have video surveillance. That will truly prove his whereabouts." She let that sit for a bit while she began striking some keys on her phone. I had no idea what she was doing but it did provide a nice period of silence to let Sharon Larson simmer over that last comment. It did seem to be bothering her as she shifted slightly in her chair. Then, without any warning, Patti set her phone down in front of Sharon so she could see the screen.

"Would it surprise you that Dominick's is six minutes from your house and Walgreens is five?" She pointed to the Google Maps app opened on her phone. "You see, I mapped them both."

Damn, I thought. I am truly becoming an old-timer. I would have left and driven both of them to verify the time. To be honest, I still may.

"Well, uh..." Sharon was clearly caught off guard as she stuttered toward her next comment. "Like I said, I don't know where he went. He may have gone to get gas as well."

"Fair enough," Patti said, "but his credit cards will tell us that, won't they?"

Now it was my turn. "Mrs. Larson, I sense you're hiding something. Do you want to tell me what that is? We are going to find out. Your husband obviously did something out of the ordinary. I know if I left on a Sunday morning after church and didn't tell my wife where I was going, she would stop me in my tracks and find out what the heck I was doing. Why don't you just tell us? Your husband did not go to Dominick's or Walgreens, did he, Sharon?"

She looked away and a tear may have even formed in her eye. I had no idea where this was going. I was bluffing all the way around. For starters, I wasn't married. Secondly, the timing was not that far off. I know sometimes when I was married, I would leave to go to the store and take much longer than I should simply to get the hell away from my family on a Sunday morning.

She turned back to us and said three words. "White Hen Pantry."

Patti reached her hand out and placed it on Sharon's as it laid across the table. "What about White Hen Pantry, Sharon?"

"He went to the White Hen Pantry," she answered.

"You mean the one that's at the corner before we entered your subdivision?" I asked.

"Yes," she replied, a sadness carried in her voice that was not there before. "My husband is having an affair," she blurted out, now with tears flowing. "Are you happy? My marriage will be over, and all because you have to verify how long it took him to go buy the darn milk."

What can I say? The woman just won't swear.

Patti held her arm. "Now, Sharon, don't jump to any conclusions. We don't know anything."

"Jiminy Cricket, he was gone for more than an hour and the store was two minutes away. He came back with White Hen bags. He's sinning with another woman, I know he is."

I actually choked slightly when I heard "Jiminy Cricket." I didn't know who the hell Jiminy Cricket was, but this was the first time in my twenty-plus years of doing interviews that a witness used that exclamation. Patti noticed my, let's call it a cough, and glared my direction. "Sharon, there are hundreds of other options for the time he took other than he's having an affair."

Yeah, I thought. Like going to our victim's house, clubbing him over the head, driving his unconscious body to a remote area of downtown Chicago, and plugging him full of a shitload of bullets.

"He is having an affair. Our sex life is horrible. He is filling his devil desires with some trollop."

What in the hell is a trollop? I thought. I was going to turn through an entire roll of *Word of the Day* toilet paper to see if that one came up.

Again, Patti was calm and soothing in her response. "So, if I'm hearing you correctly, your husband did go to the store on Sunday and he did bring back the items you needed, but he went to a store very near here and was gone much longer than he should have been. Because of that, you believe he's having an affair?"

"I know he is," she said now speaking through tears. "He has needs and he told me I was not filling those needs. We argued on Saturday night and he didn't even speak to me at church."

"So," I broke in, "would you say your husband has a temper?"

That question caused her tears to stop immediately and she turned to me. Her entire demeanor changed and she seemed to go back into protective mode. "No." She tilted her head and shrugged her shoulders. "No more than anyone else, I guess."

"So he does get mad sometimes?" I asked.

"Doesn't everyone?" she replied coldly. "I just told you we argued on Saturday."

"Right," I replied. "Has he ever been violent?"

"What do you mean?" she asked, but appeared more to be buying time to formulate her answer than really seeking to understand my question.

"Has he ever hit you? Have you ever seen him get in a fight with another man? How about your family?"

"No. Never." Her answer was immediate and without room for interpretation.

"How about just arguing with other people *not* part of your family? Other adults or teachers, or even coaches?"

Boom, there it was. The *tell*. She was looking toward the table through my entire question until I said the word "coaches." She instantly looked up at me. Her eyes narrowed and her shoulders slumped. "Is this about a coach? Is this about Colin's hockey coach, Coach Thompson?"

"What about Coach Thompson?" I asked.

She seemed to realize her change and reverted back to her former self quickly, but she couldn't take back the immediate reaction. But when she spoke, it was clear she didn't want to. "Listen, there's one thing I have not told you about my husband."

Now we were getting somewhere. "And that is?" I asked inquisitively.

"He speaks with a lisp and a stutter."

Okay, not what I expected. "And what does that have to do with anything?"

"That coach was terrible. The league says equal play, and our son never got the same playing time. When Ryan talked to him about it, he told him to go..." She paused and it was clear she didn't want to say it but continued anyway. "You know, he told my husband to go F himself." She shivered when she said it.

Not the kind-hearted Dr. Thompson that had been described to me previously. "What did your husband do when he said that?" I asked.

She remained timid when she spoke, as if she was embarrassed to have to say what took place. "Well, I told Ryan it would come back to bite him, but he swore right back at him. My husband was picked on his whole life for his speech. He has been to countless doctors and speech therapists, but it only seems to improve when he gets mad. I had never heard that side of him. He called him names I didn't know the meanings of and he did it with the fluency of a salesman. He told him he was a horrible coach and the league was going to hear about it. He told him that when he was through with him, he would never coach again." She leaned back and actually smiled. "You know, I never told Ryan, but I was so proud of him standing up to that..."—she took a deep breath and finished with—"man."

"So there was nothing physical, just words?"

"Yes, just words." She smiled a little. "My husband may have been upset and ready to blow, but he would never get into a fight. He is...how can I say this without sounding rude...not the biggest man."

"What did Coach Thompson do when your husband said all this?" Patti interjected.

"He raised his middle finger right to my husband's face—you know what that means, don't you?"

I smiled ever so slightly. "Yes, we are police officers so it's our job to know such things," I replied.

"Oh, I suppose it is," she responded. "Well, he raised his middle finger right to my husband's face and said, 'Go for it, La-La-La-Larson. Your kid can't play so we might as well make a court case out of it for the world to see and you can ar-ar-ar-ague your way through the whole'..."—she paused again—"that F word again, 'thing'." Her voice got softer. "He threw in some more expletives toward my husband at the end of that statement also."

"Then what did your husband do?" Patti asked.

"He turned and walked away," she said. "I was so proud of him for that as well. Everybody on the team was watching and nothing good was going to come from it at that point."

"He probably made the right call," Patti agreed, making Sharon Larson very pleased.

"Is there anyone else your husband ever argued with or complained to you about?" I asked.

"Not really," she replied. "I mean, he would get upset when someone was in the right lane at a traffic light but wasn't turning right and he would have to wait for the light to change to green and that car to go straight for him to make his turn, but nobody he ever talked to."

Oh my God, I thought to myself. This guy is not a killer. He *is* actually married to Mary Poppins. I turned to my partner. "Any other questions for Mrs. Larson, Detective Halterman?"

Patti smiled. "I never did hear if he owned a gun." *Nice job*, I thought.

"Absolutely not," she now replied, this time without any delay. "We know the statistics. You are ninety percent more likely to be killed or injured with a gun if you own one than if you don't."

"I don't know if that is the case, but I respect your position, Sharon. Thank you for your time." I turned again to Patti. "Anything else?"

"No, sir, Detective," she replied very formally. "But we do still need to speak with her husband."

"Yes," I agreed, turning to Mrs. Larson again and pulling out one of my cards. "Why don't you have your husband give me a call when he's available? We can swing by again or he can come by the department, whichever is easier."

"Is my husband in trouble, Detective?" she asked in return.

"My gut tells me no, ma'am, but we still need to talk to him."

She seemed to understand and stood as both Patti and I got up from our seats. Sharon Larson, who was married to a stuttering, disgruntled father, led us over to the door. She wore a small smile, but it appeared to be forced. "I will have Ryan call as soon as he gets home." She bid us farewell and shut the door behind us.

"What do you think?" Patti asked as we walked to the car.

Without missing a beat, I replied, "We just interviewed a nun."

"That's helpful, Tommy," she replied sharply. "What do you think about Ryan Larson being good for Thompson's murder?"

I shook my head. "There's something off there, but his history and the situation doesn't strike me as someone bent on murder. I struggle over why she's married to a stuttering, not-well-built man who can only speak clearly when he's angered or stressed."

"Love works in mysterious ways," she replied, smiling a bit as she said it.

There was no chance I was asking another question after that.

We got in the car and headed back to the department.

14 "So, what the hell was this text about?" the man asked, placing his hands across the mahogany desk.

"What do you mean?" the other man answered. "You texted me, and why so early? What couldn't wait that we had to meet at five a.m.?"

The two men looked at each other perplexed. The first man whose office they were in pulled out his phone. "Are you saying you did not send this text?" He held his phone up with the face out showing his text message.

The second man read it out loud. "Meet me at the office at five a.m. Don't call tonight or tomorrow morning. Just come. No questions." He turned his face back to the man holding the phone. "No, and I have the exact same message sent from your phone." He paused and then in a concerned voice, he said, "What the fu—" The desk phone rang and interrupted his comment.

The first man reached down to see the display stating the call was coming from the other man's office. He pointed so both men saw. The second man shrugged as the first reached down to push the speaker button to answer. "Yes?"

A deep and even raspy voice replied, "I suggest you don't come out of your office or things will get messy."

"Who is this and why have—"

"Shut up," he interrupted immediately. "Right now it's your job to listen. Do you understand?"

"Yes, but I want..."

"It doesn't sound like you understand. Your answers should be as follows: 'Yes,' 'No,' or 'I will make that happen.' Unless I tell you to answer differently, don't respond differently. Do you understand?"

The two men looked at each other. The second nodded to the first. In a weak voice very alien to his normal self, the first man replied, "Yes."

"Good," the voice on the phone said. "Now, you imbeciles are probably wondering why I brought you here." He paused and seemed to wait for an acknowledgement but when none came, he continued. "I'm the man you hired to take care of your problem, and we have two *new* problems." Again he paused but because this statement didn't permit one of the predetermined replies, the two men on the other end remained quiet. "The first problem is my funding has not been secured. You were provided directions to transfer the funding. It is my expectation the funding will be transferred as directed by noon today. Will that occur?"

The first man looked toward the second man. The second man did not wait for a response. "I can make that happen."

"You can or you will?" the voice repeated back.

"I *will* make that happen," he returned.

"Good," the voice said. "So you are aware, if you don't, it would be very bad for you and your families. Do you understand?"

"Yes," the second man said.

"Good," the voice repeated.

"The second issue is a question you may answer using whatever you need to say. Why is there someone looking to determine who I am?"

The two men looked at each other and the first pressed the mute button. "What the hell is he talking about?" the first man said. "Who the hell is this?"

The second man paced back and forth. "We had to find someone to handle the issue with Julian. He was going to the authorities."

"Jesus Christ. Now he's in our building. You fucking idiot. What the—"

"Gentlemen," the voice on the phone broke in. "I should let you know I disabled your mute button. You will want to get that fixed after I leave." He paused as both men considered shitting their pants. "Now, if you will quit the pointless bickering and tough-guy talk, I need the question answered. Why is there a murder-for-hire killer asking questions about me?"

The second man stopped pacing and placed his hands on the desk on both sides of the phone. "I don't know. I reached out to one man whose name I had from a previous situation. When he didn't reply, I did some work and came up with a second name. I never spoke to anyone directly. I just left messages as instructed. That's the only thing I can think of."

There was silence on the phone. Then, the other man added, "And the police were here asking questions. Maybe it was them."

"I know about Detectives O'Malley and Halterman. They are of no concern. Should they become a concern, they will be dealt with. Make sure the payment gets to me by noon. The other issue you asked about will be handled shortly."

"Wait," stated the second man. "What other issue?"

"You provided me two names. I have only handled one."

The second man's voice was louder. "But both men are dead already."

Now there was a long silence. "You mean Thompson is already dead?"

"Yes, he was murdered Sunday morning. He—"

"Shut up," the caller interrupted. "Now it all makes sense. It seems you have two individuals solving your problems for you. I don't like competition, and I really don't like the competition looking for me."

"I understand," the second man replied. "I can make this second man discontinue his actions. Just give me today."

"Not your concern. I'll handle what is overdue. Pay me for both issues by noon. It's because of me that he killed Thompson. He's sending me a message."

"Is that all you need from us?" the first man asked.

"Stay in your office. You don't want to try to see me. It would not end well for you."

The second man responded in a stronger voice. "The last thing I want is to see you, but I have a third name for you." There was silence again. A long silence. "Are you still there?"

"What is the name?" the voice returned.

"Doctor Elise Gerstenberger, and it needs to look like an accident, just like Julian, only better," the second man stated. Just as the words came out of his mouth, the first man stared at him in horror.

"What the hell, Reed?"

"Shut up!" the second man, Dr. Reed Anderson, stated in return. "She's too close and you know it."

"No!" the first man said.

The voice on the phone was calm and deliberate. "I don't care who, as I'm only interested in payment. For that one, I want more than my fifty percent up front. I want to be paid in full, by noon today."

"I will make that happen," Dr. Anderson replied. "But I have one more question."

"I am not here to answer your questions," the voice replied.

"If you want to be paid, you will need to listen to my question," Reed said.

There was more silence then finally he replied, "I'm listening."

"I reached out to two individuals. At this point, I don't know for sure who to pay. Who am I talking to?"

"Just call me Sandman, and if you don't pay me in full by noon, Trinity won't make it to her one p.m. accounting class at Northwestern today."

The phone went dead. The two men heard a door open and close in the adjacent office and then their office was engulfed in silence. The first man grabbed Dr. Reed Anderson's shirt and pulled him close. "You put a stop to this, *now*."

"I can't. If I do, we're all dead or in jail for life. You knew the risks when we got into this. It's too late to turn back now. We have some loose ends. Elise is asking too many questions and she's too close to the police. I'm sorry, but it's her or us."

The second man released his shirt pushing him backward. Reed straightened his shirt and looked toward him. "Now, we have an immediate concern. How do I transfer a quarter of a million dollars before noon to keep my daughter alive? Once we take care of that, we can figure out what else we need to do."

The other man did not reply.

●　　　●　　　●　　　●　　　●

Patti and I walked into the department together. It was easy to walk in together because we had slept together, and when I say "slept together," there was not much sleeping going on, if you know what I'm sayin'. We were early. In fact, we were very early mainly because she had woken me up at four a.m. with her mouth, again, if you know what I'm sayin'. There was a jump in my step. One that only Franky would notice.

"Jesus, you had a good birthday week," Franky said.

"Franky," I replied with Patti still standing next to me. "I have come out of my fifty-fifth birthday with a new fortitude toward life in general."

"Really," Franky replied. "You're going to dump the *Word of the Day* toilet paper on me at six-thirty in the morning?"

"I believe he just did," answered Patti, "and he did it with fortitude."

He smiled and shook his head. "Carter is in also and wants to regroup at eight a.m. on the Abbunex case. You have anything new?"

"Not much," I replied. "Let me get my shit together and we can talk before the briefing."

"Sounds good, Tommy." He noticed Patti walking toward the break area. "Are you getting coffee?"

She turned. "I am, and yes, I have a hot chocolate coming for you."

He smiled in return but said nothing. I headed to my desk which was currently right next to Franky's, though they often got moved around as needed. "Where's Huston?" I asked.

"She'll be in for the morning brief. Not before. She texted me she was on her way." He paused for a second and added, "I guess she met someone."

"Really," I replied. "Good for her. I was starting to wonder about both of them, if they were spending too much of their lives on the job and not actually living. You and I are old. I'm fine alone and you have your new wife, Vader..." I paused before adding, "You did finally tie the knot, didn't you?"

"Fuck you, O'Malley. You're just jealous."

"Franky, I may be jealous of you for a lot of things, though I can't think of any right now, but the fact you sleep with a two-hundred-pound dog and base your evening decisions on taking care of him is not one of them."

"Whatever, O'Malley. Vader and I understand each other."

I could have pushed it further, but to be honest, I was glad for Franky. He had not dated anyone since his wife died of breast cancer and without his dog, I don't know if he would have made it. More power to him for his loyalty to his late wife and his dog.

The briefing came and went. We shared the short version of what we had on our case, which was basically nothing, but we also knew we would dive into it further after the meeting. The detectives disbanded and we all headed to the Royals Room, where I had moved all the evidence for our case.

"So," Carter began, "you two said you had some information on the financials of our suspects."

"Suspects?" I questioned.

"Anyone we have not formerly cleared of involvement in these murders is a suspect," Carter replied.

I stood up, walked to the whiteboard, and wrote down Craig Carter's name.

"What the fuck, Tommy?" Carter asked.

"Where were you the morning Randy Thompson was killed? I haven't formerly cleared you yet."

"Do you just like wasting everyone's time, O'Malley?" Carter asked.

"Is that a rhetorical question?" I asked.

Carter walked up and erased his name. He did not want the brass from upstairs coming in and seeing it and opening up the questions. "Sullivan, what do you have on the financials?"

"Well, Sergeant, it's actually Huston who seems to understand this more. If you don't mind, I'll defer to her."

Without responding further, all eyes turned to Franky's partner. She pulled out a file and flipped through several pages until she found what she was looking for.

"Well, I spent the better part of five hours with a financial investigator. She educated me on a world I never knew existed—the world of multimillionaires." She walked up to the whiteboard and slid the front board to the side revealing an entirely new blank board behind it. "We all know about retirement plans, bonuses, and other forms of income and benefits. Well, when this investigator began digging into the financials of the top individuals at Abbunex Labs, several things became very clear."

"What types of things?" I asked.

"Well, for starters, they all have multimillion-dollar base salaries. The CEO, Dr. Darryn Hermann, has a base salary"—she stopped, wrote his name on the board, and then glanced at her notes before continuing—"thirty-two million dollars."

"Wow," I replied. "Who needs that much money?"

Huston continued, "And the husband of our medical examiner, Dr. Alan Grove, has a base salary of fifteen million dollars."

"Jesus," stated Carter. "Why the hell does Doc G even work?"

"Interesting enough," continued Huston, "Doctor Elise Gerstenberger, if you include her income as Chicago's Chief Medical Examiner as well as her medical practice in North Chicago where she also owns the land and collects lease income on the building, clears north of nine million on her own."

"Are you fucking kidding me?" I replied, not meaning to react so strongly but in disbelief that the woman I had shared an Old Style with several times at a Cubs game, which I had insisted on paying for, made more in one year than my entire family would make in a lifetime.

"And the list continues," Huston said. "Every name on that list makes significantly more money in a year than all of us put together."

"Yeah, but being rich doesn't make someone a murderer. In fact, it doesn't sound like any of them would be influenced by money as they all have so much of it," Franky said with conviction. I tended to agree, but I also had seen in my career people with plenty of money still making decisions based on getting more.

Karen nodded. "Well, there is one thing that links a small group of them."

Now all our eyes turned back to her. Carter was the only one who spoke. "What, you found something?"

"I don't know if we found anything important," she replied, "but we did find something that puts about five of the senior leadership of Abbunex in a different pool than the rest."

"What is that?" I asked.

"The financial investigator called it a deferred option bonus."

"Sounds like the word of the day," Franky said. "What the hell is a deferred option bonus?"

"Well," she replied, "it's hard to believe, but these guys all receive a minimum bonus of about twenty-five percent. For Dr. Hermann, that by itself would be a one-time check of more than eight million dollars."

"Eight million in a bonus?" Carter said in disbelief. "I'm definitely in the wrong profession."

"And that's not even all of the bonus. It could be more if the company does well."

We all just shook our heads, and if the others were like me, I was thinking about what I would do with that much money—1969 Camaro came immediately to mind.

"So that doesn't answer what a deferred option bonus is?" Franky stated, breaking me away from my Camaro I had already named Daphne after the foxy Scooby Doo detective.

"So, what these five individuals did was defer one hundred percent of their last year's bonus to stock options. Using Dr. Hermann again, that equals more than 11.5 million dollars of options. If our information was correct, the option price at the time of transfer was $132.75 per share, or roughly 86,629 individual stock options."

"Is that unique?" I asked, not really knowing what this meant or why someone would do it.

"Well, out of the 50,000 plus Abbunex employees across the world, we have only found five that did it," she replied. "However, we haven't been able to verify everyone at this time."

Carter smiled. "That seems to be more than just a coincidence to me, but why would they do it?"

She lowered her voice to prevent some elation that this was a smoking gun. "Hold on, everyone. Although this is not common across Abbunex, it is common in these circles. What I learned is that very often senior executives will continue to put money back into stock. It demonstrates to the shareholders that they believe in the company. If the leaders of the company are buying stock, it's a message to the public that they believe the stock price will go up."

Now I was starting to understand better. "So, these five individuals were banking on the stock price increasing so their bonuses would increase with it?"

"That is the theory, and like I said, it is a common practice. This really is no evidence of any wrongdoing and it's definitely not illegal. In fact, it's all public information which is how we found out so easily."

I was still intrigued. "So, if it is so common, why do you bring it up?"

"Because in this case, in the next quarterly report following this deferral that the company provided, or should I say Dr. Darryn Hermann provided, they announced the initial results and success of the IGB100 Emplex Phase III Trials. The stock went immediately from the low $130's to over $200 per share. Since that time, with the continued solid reports on the trials, the stock is tipping all-time highs at greater than $345. My quick math has Dr. Hermann's stock options valued at close to thirty million dollars today."

Carter whistled in such a way as to send the message without speaking, *Shit, that's a lot of money.*

Huston added, "And each of the other four, though to a slightly lesser extent because they were dealing with a smaller bonus, have the same percentage gains."

"Wow," I replied. "Is there anything else?"

She smiled which told me immediately there was. "Well, Doc G's husband did something the others didn't. He liquidated a great deal of free cash he carried in his portfolio and in addition to the options, purchased another 40,000 shares in the open market. Purchases like that from insiders also have to be reported as required by the Securities and Exchange Commission. The total purchase was over five million total."

I walked up to the whiteboard and slid the board back over blocking where Huston had been writing her numbers. "So, five senior leaders of Abbunex Labs each made multimillion dollars on reports of successful drug trials, and one of them dipped into the pie a little extra." I circled Dr. Alan Grove's picture on the whiteboard. I turned back to Franky's partner. "Obviously, the CEO, Darryn Hermann, made the same deferred option purchase. Who were the others?"

Dr. Reed Anderson, President of Research and Development, Joseph Reingold, Vice President of Lab Testing and Quality, and Dr. Dennis Child, Head Pharmacist for the site."

I circled each name as she said it. "Interesting," I stated, looking at the board.

"What do you see, Tommy?" Franky asked.

"It's not so much what I see versus what I *don't* see. How come our two dead Abbunex employees aren't on the deferred option list?"

Franky pointed. "And why is the chief financial officer one of those missing?"

Carter rose from his seat and stepped up to the board. "I don't care if this is common practice or not for big multimillion dollar companies. This smells bad. There's more to this deferred option thing." He turned back to Huston. "Karen, great work. Who have you been working with to get this info?"

"Her name was Emma Nelson. She's on the second..."

"Yes, I know Nelson. Brilliant, to say the least, when it comes to numbers. Go get with her some more. Dig up everything you can. Look into the history. I'd be willing to bet there's more here than what you already have. Great work."

"Should we get the SEC on the case?" I asked. "They have access to more detailed information."

"Not yet," Carter replied. "Let's see what we can find first. If we bring in the SEC they're going to identify some money transfers, most likely out of the country. When that happens, it becomes a federal case and our murders take a back seat if they're ever prosecuted. These guys are guilty. That first murder was done by someone who didn't know what the hell they were doing. Then they brought in someone from the outside."

"Bingo," I stated. "I get where you're going, Sergeant."

"What?" asked Patti.

"Two murderers," I replied.

Patti tilted her head not understanding. "I thought you said you thought they were related?"

"I did," I answered, "but I was hung up on that belief because they had to be performed by the same person. There was no way two individuals from the same company would be killed the same day, after I received a warning that there was something going on from the spouse of another individual from the same company. I don't believe in coincidence, but that had to be more than a million to one odds." I paused and took a breath. "But what I wasn't taking into account was two killers being directed by the same source. Let's say these five guys discovered they needed to remove Thompson. They drew straws, or someone volunteered to do it or something, who knows. They're not killers. They don't know what they're doing. They kill him in the open, with witnesses, and leave some goofy rabbit's foot. The guy is probably having nightmares now and going crazy. Then they find out whatever

Thompson discovered he told Stover. So they then need to remove the CFO as well. They realize they're out of their element trying to do it themselves."

"So they hire it out," stated Franky. "One inexperienced, reckless murder, and one professional—looks like an accident with no evidence left behind."

"Right," I replied. "Then add to that the strange insertion of Marco Filini claiming innocence and you definitely have some new factor involved. I say you look into money transfers from all of them when you do your financial analysis. If they set up a professional hit, they would have had to pay for it."

"You still trying to clear Filini, O'Malley?" asked Carter, not so much a question as a statement.

"No, Sergeant, but I am taking him at his word for now," I replied. "I agree, had he not come to me and told me he wasn't involved, and we had come to this conclusion today, my first instinct would be to bring up his name as a possible professional behind this. So, like you said, by coming forward, is he trying to throw us off the chase?" Carter seemed pleased with the direction I was going. "I still don't think so because it's not his style, but it definitely does not rule him out."

"Fair enough," Carter replied, accepting that I was open to all options.

The discussion was interrupted when Huston's phone rang. "This is Huston."

There was a pause while the person on the other end spoke. Then Karen continued, "You don't say?" She paused. "Thanks for the information. Hey, I'm glad you called. I was just speaking with my team and we want to dig deeper. Any chance you're available today?" Again a pause. "Great, I'll be down within the hour." She hung up.

Karen turned back to the group. "I assume you gathered that was Nelson in Finance again. I'll get with her shortly but she found something else that may throw a question into the mix."

"What did she find?" Carter asked.

"There was a sixth person at Abbunex who did the deferred option plan. She didn't catch it originally because she was looking through the public records required by the SEC. Those records are only required to a certain dollar amount and this individual was below the threshold."

"Who was that?" I asked.

"The first deceased—Randy Thompson."

"Thompson was part of this thing?" Franky asked. "Then why was he killed?"

"To answer your first question, the dollars he's talking about are less than one hundred thousand. He could be part of it, but if he is, he's at a much lower level."

I added, "There could be a ton of reasons. If there is something illegal going on, maybe he was getting cold feet. Maybe he wanted more of a cut, who knows? By making him part of the deferred plan, it actually would give more reason why he would have been removed."

We all seemed to agree on that one.

"What are you three going to do while Huston is busy solving the case?" asked Carter, getting his soft jab in to us while also complementing Karen, a trait he excelled at.

"I want a run at Dr. Grove," I replied. "I want to see his face when I ask him about the deferred options and the additional purchases."

"We also need to check all of these guys' alibis for Thompson's murder," added Franky. "If our theory is correct, one of these guys had to commit the first murder, and that means one of their alibis is bogus."

"Good call, Franky," said Carter. "You go back through the file and find solid verification for all of them. No family member corroboration. I want a street camera or security camera or something. Hell, get a picture of them pumping gas for all I care. Verify the M.E.'s report on the time of death and corroborate it for all of them." He stopped in mid-sentence and then continued in a noticeably softer tone, "And why don't you verify it for Doc G as well?"

"You don't think Doc G is involved, do you, Carter?" I asked.

"No, but I want to follow up on every angle. Our witness says it was a man, but Doc G would know how to make things look one way when they were another. Maybe that whole murder scene is a setup." Carter went back to the whiteboard where I had written his name as a suspect at the start of our meeting. "Remember what you said. Everyone is a suspect until they're cleared." He wrote Doctor Elise Gerstenberger on the board.

"Point taken," I replied.

15 Patti and I left the department and headed back to North Chicago. We were not going to announce our intended visit. I wanted to show up and corner Dr. Alan Grove. I wanted him off guard and not in a position to have a lawyer present. When we arrived at Abbunex Labs, however, we were not allowed to pass without being escorted, and that meant we needed to let him know we were there. To my surprise, he sent someone down to get us right away.

"I assume they're scrambling to decide which direction they will take," said Patti after hearing someone was on their way to get us.

"We'll see when we get there," I replied. "We have already been told to speak to their lawyers, but not by Alan. We need to limit our discussions with him today."

"Agreed," she replied flatly. "How do you want to play this?"

"I've been thinking about this for a while. I think I will start with a shot right across…"

Just then, a thin and attractive woman walked in. "Are you Tomas O'Malley?"

"Yes," I replied. "Are you our escort to meet Dr. Grove?"

She nodded. "I just need to give this authorization to the security office." She gave authorization and in the process was given two temporary badges to be used while on the grounds. She motioned to us to follow. "You know, it will go much faster and smoother if you call ahead for an appointment."

"Thanks," I replied. "We'll keep that in mind for next time." She was smiling as they walked and really appeared to not have a care in the world. "What do you do here?" I asked, breaking the silence.

"I'm in sales. I just happened to be in the corporate office area when security called. I volunteered to come and get you. Dr. Grove says you guys are old friends."

I smiled but didn't respond to the friend comment.

They won't be after this meeting, Patti thought to herself.

"Have you worked at Abbunex long?" I asked, trying to keep some sort of conversation going. I had not lowered myself to talk about the weather, but if I got desperate, it was coming.

She continued to smile as she walked. "Not as long as most of the people I work with, if that's what you're asking. I'm only twenty-nine. I started here when I was just out of college at twenty-two. I haven't worked anywhere else."

"Nice," I replied. Again there was silence. She wasn't offering anything. "So, you know if this weather is going to hold?"

"I haven't heard, but I hope it does."

And that was it. Not another word was said during the walk.

● ● ● ● ●

"Hello, Dr. Grove," I said as I was escorted directly to his office behind the magnificent waterfall that still amazed me. We took seats opposite Alan who was behind his huge mahogany desk, identical to all the desks up here.

He smiled broadly. "What is with this Dr. Grove crap all the time, Tommy? Please call me Alan. Only newbies at the company call me Dr. Grove."

"Okay, Alan, but I do want to stress that Detective Halterman and I are here on official police business." I used the term Randy Thompson had used the first time I met him at Alan and Elise's party. Thompson was concerned I was there on official police business. In hindsight, maybe I should have been.

Alan seemed instantly annoyed. "Jesus, Tommy, what now? We're still in recovery mode with the recent tragedies. The stock has already fallen five percent and Darryn is going to have to make a formal announcement today on the incidents and our plan to move forward."

I nodded that I understood. "That's really what I'm here about—the stock, that is—not the announcement."

He lifted his hand. "Whoa, Tommy, I can't comment on our stock prices and possible direction."

I smiled. The thought that I could afford a $300 stock was very humorous to me. With the exception of the surprise birthday check my family gave me, I would not have been able to purchase one share. "No, Alan, I am more interested in what you're going to do with the millions you made in recent stock purchases and deferred option plans?" I paused as I watched his face go from a smile to an immediate level stare. "Secondly, I want to know why you and your fellow cronies on this floor murdered

Randy Thompson and then arranged to have Dr. Julian Stover run down." I know what Patti was thinking—*Boom! There he goes again.*

That level stare went immediately to a frown and he stood up from his desk. "Get the hell out, Detective. Now."

He did not tell me to speak to his lawyer, so I thought I would fire another shot broadside. "Can you at least tell me how you paid the murder-for-hire man? You know, following the money will be easy. I found out about your stock plan without even trying too hard."

He walked around his desk to face me. Alan was not a large man, but he was in shape. Like his wife, he exercised every day. Between running and riding his bike, the guy was toned. That being said, I was a black belt and I would tear his ass apart if he even tried to throw one punch. Plus, I would throw his ass in jail and see what turned up from that. He stood inches from my face when he spoke in a slow, deep voice somewhat uncharacteristic of his own. "Detective O'Malley, less than a week ago I thought of us as friends. I didn't know you well, but I know my wife respects you tremendously. What you just said throws any chance of future friendship out the window. I have two words for you and I want you to hear them very clearly. *Get out.*" When I waited without moving or responding, he added, "And don't come back without a warrant."

I smiled and turned. I motioned to Patti to join me and as we got to his door, I turned back to see the anger growing within him turning his face a deep red. "I'm the best chance you have to finish the rest of your life with your family, Dr. Grove. You may want to remember that while you're talking to your lawyer."

"Hey, Tommy," he replied. "That instruction goes for Elise as well. No talking to her without our lawyer present. When she hears what you just said to me, she will never speak to you again."

I pressed my lips together, nodded, and walked out.

It took ten minutes to walk back to the guard shack and then reach our car. We did not make any additional stops or speak to anyone else on the way out. Because Alan had specified speaking with an attorney, before we started doing any additional investigation around the site, I wanted to make sure we had our legal requirements lined up. The last thing I wanted to do was find a new witness or a bit of evidence and have it not stick because of a formality. I didn't believe there would be much solid evidence left behind. Therefore, having anything thrown out was not acceptable.

When I got to the car, Patti finally asked, "Are you going to call Doc G?"

I nodded. "Yep, after I get in the car. I hope I reach her before Alan. His story will be one-sided and will most likely shut her down. His description of how she'll react is probably accurate."

"Wouldn't he have called her already?" Patti asked.

"It depends," I replied as I climbed into my car.

She sat down in the passenger seat. "Depends on what?"

"On if he is guilty or not," I replied.

"What would his guilt have to do with it?" she asked, questionably.

"If he's guilty, he would go immediately to those who are in on it with him. He would know that he could always call Elise, but he would need to let the others know first thing." I started the car but before pulling out, dialed Elise. The phone rang four times then went into voice mail. I did not leave a message.

When Patti saw me hang up the phone, she asked, "What does no answer mean?"

"Could go either way." I pulled out without further comment.

• • • • •

"How are you doing, sir?" Andre stated as Marco Filini walked into the top floor high-rise office. Marco lived in one-half of the top floor building overlooking Lake Michigan, and the other half he used as his main office. Filini did his special type of work all over the country, but ever since his lucrative time spent in Chicago with Ross Moretti and Joey Polino, he found he liked the downtown city. He had homes in five other countries and financial stability in accounts all over the world.

As Andre saw the scowl on his face, he already knew exactly how his boss was doing. "Not good, Andre. Not good at all." He paused and removed a vitamin drink from his refrigerator and took a long swig. "I need you to do some work for me." Marco's voice was cold and direct leaving nothing to be discussed.

"Name it, Boss," Andre replied, now standing to meet him. Marco moved to sit on one of his lounge chairs in what would normally be a living room, but he used the area to discuss business with clients.

"There is someone active in Chicago. I need to find out who."

Andre shook his head not sure if he understood. "Active, sir?"

He turned toward the toned, African American man dressed in a $3,500 tailored Armani suit and pressed shirt. His tie was a sharp red and gave the presence of absolute power. The shoes he wore were black and shined to a level such that he could see his reflection. Andre had been with Marco for more than ten years and they were more than a team—they were one and the same, except in build. Marco was a large man, refined, and in excellent shape. He claimed to be a fourth degree black belt but he had never been officially tested. He was talented with his hands and deadly in a variety of ways. He had served in the armed forces and was an excellent marksman. He had killed more than a hundred people and had never once been brought up on charges. Andre was taller, skinnier, but toned like a professional basketball player. He had no desire to train in the martial arts. He killed with a gun, but most of all, he made sure Marco Filini didn't get killed. When anyone looked at them, all they saw was raw power.

"Andre, someone is doing what we do in Chicago. I want this to be my city. I need to find out who it is."

Andre understood. He also knew no other individual who got involved in Marco's line of work would ever really affect his livelihood. However, it would affect his pride. He just couldn't let things go. It was the same reason Marco had a bug up his ass to face Tommy in a martial arts showdown. He felt he was cheated back when they were kids, and he never forgot.

"Have you checked your contacts with the police?" Andre asked.

Marco choked on his vitamin drink. "They don't even know he exists. They didn't even recognize the Abbunex murder as a professional hit until I planted the seed." He paused and took another drink finishing the plastic bottle. "No, I need you to do some research. Reach out to your connections. I want to know who the hell is out there. I've already made some calls and come up empty, but I did not like the feeling I got from one of our investigators."

"What do you mean, Boss?"

"I mean, one of our guys was lying to me. I'm sure of it."

Andre smiled. "Which one was it? I think I should start there."

"Donly. Steve Donly." Marco nodded agreement as he said it.

Andre stood and walked over to a desk. He opened a drawer and pulled out a small cylinder. He reached inside his suit, removed his gun, and twisted the silencer onto the end. He returned the gun to his inside holster. "Donly is still on the West side, correct?"

"Yes, sir," Filini replied. "Downers."

"I'll be back in four hours," Andre said and walked out.

Patti and I returned to the precinct with no further discussion. A few questions and comments surfaced, but for the most part we just thought about how things were lining out. I believed Alan was guilty of the deferred bonus action. I didn't think that by itself was illegal, but when people involved in it started to die, that begged the question as to why. If someone involved committed murder around it, then all parties were guilty.

We walked into our lavish fourth floor department digs and Patti immediately grabbed my arm. "You have company."

I turned my eyes toward my desk and greeted the burning eyes of Doctor Elise Gerstenberger. "I guess that means Alan was able to speak to her before me."

Doc G did not give Patti time to respond before she walked at a pace that could only be called *aggressive* toward me. "Who in the hell do you think you are?" Elise exclaimed. She reached up her hand to slap me and Patti grabbed it.

"Just hold on, Doc," Patti said. "Don't do something that will get you in trouble and that you and your husband will regret later."

I stared at my friend and saw the pain in her eyes. I wanted to reach out to her but I couldn't. I had to stay separated from this. I had to stay unbiased, and right now, I believed her husband was guilty. My voice was soft, but not in any way submissive. "Elise, let's go talk in private. You know I would not say or do anything without evidence. I can't share what we know with you, as I told you several days ago when you asked me to take this case." I wanted to add that statement to remind her that only a few days ago she begged me to take this case because I would seek the truth, not railroad her husband or anyone else through the process. "But I can share with you a few things which will help you understand."

I think Patti was slightly uncomfortable with this statement, but I also knew she trusted me. Patti still had hold of Elise's arm and as the doctor slowly lowered it and relieved the tension holding it against hers, Patti released it. I motioned to the other side of the room where several interrogation rooms were empty. She issued a slight huff as she turned and followed me. We went into the Bulls Room. I was not about to move her to my more comfortable spot especially since it included a board with her name on it. Elise took a seat on the far side making it easy for me to sit down directly across from her.

Patti followed us in and Elise immediately turned to her. "I want her gone, Tommy. What I have to say I will say to you." Her eyes were still like daggers pointed toward me. "And I want the cameras and recording devices off."

I held my soft but unrelenting tone. "You know I can't do that, Elise. I will have Patti step out"—I motioned to her and then continued—"but this is an active investigation of a multiple murder case, a case which you are intimately involved with. You also just attempted assault on a police officer. Had my partner not stopped you, we both know you would have gone forward with it. Right now, I am your best friend, but if you continue down this path, there will be nothing I can do to help."

"Help? Help!" she exclaimed again. "Tommy, you are not helping me or my family. You are doing exactly what I asked you not to do. You are taking the easy answer and railroading my husband to jail."

"Doc, I don't know what you're talking about," I answered. "I don't have any evidence that would send your husband, or anyone else for that matter, to jail. Further, you told me directly a few days ago that if he was guilty, you would not stand in the way. You came to me with suspicions. You're the one who, and I will use your words, 'knew something was wrong'. I told your husband the exact same thing—that I am his best chance to finish the rest of his life with his family. He is definitely hiding something. You know it and I know it. Until he comes clean, there's nothing I can do for him." I paused and then in a softer tone, added, "And your husband stated we were not to speak to you without a lawyer. Are you waiving that right?"

"I don't need a lawyer, Tommy, but I am done speaking to you." She stormed out of the room and pulled the glass door closed hard in her wake. She continued through the office and repeated the glass door slam leaving the department. I watched her pacing in front of the elevators. She was pacing with a purpose. She was pissed. I wasn't sure I had seen her this mad before. She felt I was letting her down. At this point, I hadn't done anything serious. I mean, I had accused her husband of murder, but that was just a fishing expedition. She knew that. She was mad about something else. What really was driving her emotion? I hoped I would find out before anyone else ended up getting hurt.

Then, out of nowhere, she stopped pacing. She looked back at me and our eyes met. She was fighting with herself about something. She paced another step or two and the elevator door opened. Then it closed and she was not in it. She turned, reentered the office, and walked right by me back to the Bulls Room.

Her entire body seemed to deflate. Her shoulders fell limp and I believed for a moment she was going to collapse. It was such a huge migration away from the strong woman I thought I knew so well. I didn't think she was going to cry. She looked more like a deer right before a wolf takes it down for the last time, that moment of truth when you simply give up. Then, without warning, she looked up and her voice was back to being strong and decisive.

"Tell me what you have," she stated. Not a question, a direction.

"You know I can't do that, Doc, and you told me at the start you would not ask."

"Fine," she replied. "Tell me what you can tell me, or tell me what I can do?"

"What you can do is easy," I answered. "Go home to your family. Talk to you husband and find out what he's hiding. Both of you need to come clean. It's the only way."

"Come clean about what?" she asked. "I don't even know what's going on."

There was a long silence. It probably wasn't that long, thirty or forty seconds is all, but when you're in an interrogation room, one-on-one, it feels like an eternity of silence. I thought a moment or two longer and I knew she was going to wait me out. The questions were in my lap. Interrogation was not supposed to go this way. Doc G was good. I would need to remember that. She played the angry, out-of-control victim and then switched to interrogator like nothing happened. Damn, I was being played. I saw it in her eyes. "Are you playing me, Doc?"

Instantly back to victim. Her eyes shot down and her hair tossed slightly to the side with the movement. She was a beautiful woman, but I had never thought of her that way. She was a professional, by far the best M.E. I had ever known. She was not a beautiful woman, she was a friend. There was no attraction there, but when she played this victim, she gave the appearance of a puppy in the rain—someone you just wanted to help.

"Tommy," she said softly, "I am not playing you. I just don't know what to do. I'll find out what's going on. I just need a direction to look."

That was brilliant. She was asking for a direction. By asking for a direction, she was fishing for what evidence we had. "I can't help you, Elise," I replied. "I would like to, but I can't. At this point, I can't even tell for sure if you, not just your husband, are involved or not."

That caught her just a bit. She pressed her lips together and then smiled slightly. "I'm sorry I came, Tommy, and I'm sorry for what happened out there." Her eyes went to where she had approached me in the office area.

"No problem, Elise," I replied, again in a gentle tone. "Just go home to your family. You need to talk to your husband."

She nodded. "What do you want me to ask him?"

Damn, she was still pushing. I thought I would give her one thing that I had already asked Alan about directly so there would be no surprise. Maybe, however, if she wasn't involved, it would bring her into the mix. "Why don't you ask him about his last bonus?"

Doc G was a professional, but she was not a professional actress. Her immediate response was one which clearly told me that was not what she expected to hear. Every muscle in her face demonstrated surprise. "Bonus? What about his bonus?"

"Just talk to your husband, Elise, and if you hear something that connects some dots, why don't both of you come in?"

16

"What the hell do you want?"

Andre's voice was hard and cold. "Well, I don't know, Steve. Maybe I just want to know why you're lying to my boss?"

His shoulders dropped and instantly he was more attentive. They were in an auto repair shop—Don's Body Shop, named for the owner, Steve Donly. He specialized in foreign cars but he would work on anything. The store was actually profitable, but it was also a shop that handled stolen cars as well as large sums of money that needed to be cleaned. Steve recognized the situation. This was serious. Andre's boss was not someone you crossed. "What do you mean? I would never lie to anyone?"

"I checked you out before I got here. You know what I can do with a computer. I found the money transfer, Steve. I just want to know who it was from?"

Steve tried to fake relief, but Andre didn't buy it. "Wait, is that what this is about? I handle money all the time. That's no big deal."

Andre was not smiling nor did he show any reduction in tone. "Now you're lying to me, Steve. You are not making things better."

"Wait," Donly pleaded, now taking a step back to match Andre's step toward him. "You have it wrong. I wouldn't cross Filini for anyone, and I wouldn't lie to you."

Andre stopped and inspected the entire shop. He had waited until a few minutes before closing to enter. He now walked over to the door and turned the lock. There was a neon *Open* sign hanging in the window which he turned off with a pull string. Then he lowered the shades. When he turned around, Steve Donly was holding a gun pointed directly at him.

Donly's voice trembled a bit as he started, "Go ahead and pull your gun, Andre. I have to make this look like a break-in anyway. You can do it now or I can do it for you when you're dead."

Andre's voice was smooth and without fear. "You ever kill anyone, Steve? You ever pull the trigger that takes a life?"

Donly's voice was still shaky. "Well, I never fucked a chicken either but there's a first time for everything." He paused and took a step out from behind the workbench where he had grabbed his gun when Andre had turned around. He was about to speak when Andre cut him off.

"You haven't thought this through, Steve. If you kill me, what do you think my boss will do to you? Now put down your gun and let's talk. If you give me the answers I want, we can both go about our business and continue to make incredible money in this great world we live in."

Donly thought about what Andre had just said. He was right. Filini would kill him immediately if he killed Andre. Again, Andre spoke, "Steve, I can see in your face you know I'm right. Just lower the gun before it accidently goes off, and let's talk about what was done and why."

Steve slowly lowered his gun to his side but he did not set it down. Andre very slowly and without even making it noticeable, moved his right hand to his side and then to his back where he had moved his gun, silencer in place. Steve looked down to the ground and softly stated, "Okay, we can talk, but I didn't do..."

The first bullet struck his wrist with precision marksmanship. The gun fell to the ground and Steve let out a cry of pain. The second shot struck his opposite shoulder knocking him back against the workbench. Andre moved quickly forward and recovered the gun on the ground and with the butt of the handle, struck Steve across the face sending him to the garage floor.

Andre leaned over Donly's body as he twisted to lie on his back and face the man leaning over him. "Steve, you are a stupid man." He struck him again with the gun across his face. "Now we're going to talk. I am going to ask the questions, and you are going to answer them. If you answer correctly, I won't shoot you again. If you answer incorrectly..." He stopped and noticed a large pair of what appeared to be bolt cutters in the toolbox on the bench. He set down the gun he had taken from where Donly had dropped it and grabbed the cutters. He lifted the tool in front of Steve Donly's wide open eyes. "I will cut off a finger until you give me the correct answer."

Steve was trying to push himself up but the hand below where the wrist was shot was useless. The other arm where the shoulder was hit was also useless. All he could do was lay on his back and stare up at the man who held a gun in one hand and a set of bolt cutters in the other. "Goddamn it, Andre, I didn't do anything!"

He took his foot and stepped on the wrist that had been shot pinching it between the garage floor and the full weight of his body. Donly screamed in pain as Andre set his gun next to the other on the bench, took the bolt cutters, and in one quick motion removed Donly's little finger. The digit laid loose and bloody on the ground next to him. Donly screamed until Andre struck him again across the face, this time with the end of the bolt cutters.

"Shut the fuck up, Steve. You lost that first finger for speaking without being spoken to. If you scream again, I'll cut off the whole hand." Andre pressed down firmly against Donly's wrist. "Now, let's talk about why you pulled a gun on me if you've done nothing wrong, or can we just skip the bullshit and go right to who the fuck paid you the money and made you lie to my boss?"

"Nobody paid me any money." Blood dripped between his lips but was lost in his broken speech. "All I did…"

Andre cut off a second finger without saying a word. Donly started to scream again but bit his lips to try to muffle the sound. "Good," Andre said. "Now, how attached are you to your remaining fingers? Who the fuck paid you the 50K that was transferred into your account?"

He looked up at him. His eyes were bloodshot and the floor was filling with a large puddle from his severed hand. "I can't tell you anything. I don't know anything." He screamed this time, not able to muffle it, "What he fuck?"

"Oh, sorry," Andre said sarcastically. "I guess I cut off three at one time. Go figure."

Donly's body curled on the floor in an almost fetal position. "I don't know anything," he cried.

"Okay, Donly," Andre said softly. "If fingers don't do it, then maybe I should start with another appendage." He lifted his foot off Donly's wrist and rolled the man to his back. There was no resistance. The man lay limp on the ground, his fingerless hand curled into his belly trying to restrict the pain and slow the bleeding. Andre bent down and undid Donly's pants.

"No," stated Donly softly. "Don't."

Andre moved the blood-covered bolt cutters in front of Steve Donly's face and then began to lower it down his body to his now completely naked lower half. Last chance, old friend."

"Sandman," he replied, spitting through blood as he talked. "That's all I know."

Andre jabbed the bolt cutters through his chest with unbelievable force and Donly's body surged upward and then lay motionless.

"Who the fuck is Sandman?" he said to himself. Twenty minutes later he left the auto shop, the dead body still spilling blood in his wake.

•   •   •   •   •

"Sandman?" Filini said. "That's all you could get out of him?"

Andre nodded. "Yeah, boss, sorry I couldn't get more, but surprisingly enough, the guy wouldn't talk. I got through a whole hand and had to move to his dick to even get that. He was going to bleed out so I had to end it. I was lucky he offered anything."

"Five fucking fingers? Are you kidding me?" asked Marco. "Damn. You haven't gotten to five fingers in a long time. Remember the Texas rancher down in Mexico?"

Andre laughed. "Fuck. That guy was nuts. All ten fingers and four toes and he didn't even die."

"This Sandman must have something over on him."

Andre again nodded. "Or he just scared the fuck out of him, more scared than from us. I'm telling you, boss, this guy was not going to fucking talk."

Marco pressed his lips together and picked up his phone but didn't dial anything, and instead, stared back to his associate. "So, we have someone who was able to turn one of my informants to a level they would not even give him up without the use of extreme force. Further, this Sandman is doing business in my backyard without a care about me."

There was silence in the room. Andre nodded, but he didn't know for sure if Marco was asking him a question for feedback or not, so he opted to not comment on the statement. Instead, he asked, "Do you know Sandman?"

Without answering, Marco pressed a button on his phone. Although it wasn't on speaker, Andre could hear it ringing.

"Well," a voice said through the phone, "you must be desperate to be calling me."

Filini's voice was as cool and low, but calm as always. "Let's put the past to the side right now. I've stumbled on something that might be a problem for both of us."

There was silence through the phone, then Marco heard the sound of a door shutting. Footsteps coming back to the phone told him the call was still connected, until the voice finally responded. "You have piqued my interest. If I've learned anything from you over the years, it's to trust your instinct."

"I need to know what you know about someone who goes by the name of Sandman?"

Again there was silence, a much longer silence than before. The voice on the phone was quieter than it had been and more reserved, as if he no longer wanted anything to do with pleasantries. "Listen, Marco, I respect you. Hell, I trust you, and there are probably very few people out there that can say that." He stopped talking for a minute which gave Filini a chance to respond but he said nothing. "Whatever you're involved in that involves Mike Sandman, get out. You're clean, refined, and you do our delicate business with a code. Sandman is not the same. I won't work with him, and that has cost me in the past." He paused again. "Marco, I am telling you this as a friend. Not that we are friends, but if we were, I would say, stay away."

"Where can I find him?" Marco asked.

"That is what I am telling you, Marco. You don't want to find him. Whatever it is, let it go."

Marco repeated his question, his voice deeper and slower than previously. "Where can I find him?"

The voice on the phone let out a long sigh. "I don't know, but do you remember Amos?"

"The property guy up in Northbrook?" Filini asked. "Yeah, I remember him. What about it?"

"He told me once that he had done some work for him in the past. He provides him vacant buildings for his work. If anyone would know where he is, Amos would."

•   •   •   •   •

It was only thirty minutes later when Marco and Andre walked into the offices of Amos Simms Real Estate. Amos was African American, had played football in college for Purdue, dressed nice, and shaved his head. He was what even current pro football players would call a big man, and how he carried himself spoke it with every move. His voice fit his body and he never showed fear, not even to Marco Filini. Marco always respected him for that, not that their paths crossed often. Amos stood when Andre and Marco entered.

"Well, I guess something pretty fucking shitty must be happening for you to come in here," stated Amos.

Marco did not outstretch his hand or even acknowledge the large man's greeting. "Amos, I need your help and I will make it worth your while."

Amos smiled. His teeth were white against his extremely dark skin. "I don't help people, Filini, and who is the hired muscle? Is he supposed to scare me?"

Filini smiled. "No, he's just my wedding planner."

"Wedding planner, huh," replied Simms. "That's a new one."

Andre smiled. "Yes, I'm looking for some empty warehouse space to hold a wedding. My associate, Mike Sandman, might be using it now. I wanted to meet him there."

The minute Andre said his name, all pleasantries ended. "Gentlemen, you need to leave. I can't help you."

Andre smiled and drew his weapon at the exact same time Amos drew his. Marco remained with both hands free but did take a step closer to the large black man. "Listen, Amos, this does not need to get messy. I need an address. You have an address. It's as simple as that."

"Not going to happen, Marco," he replied, his voice showing no sign of stress or fear. "Tell your boy to lower his weapon."

Filini paced sideways, making it appear that he wasn't getting any closer to Amos, but in actuality, he was slowly moving within range. "Amos, Amos, Amos—there are two things I'm sure of. First, there's no chance my counterpart is going to lower his weapon. Secondly, I will leave here with the information I need one way or the other." He stopped right there and did not leave room for interpretation.

"Well now," he began as he turned his gun off of Andre and directly at Marco's head. "Your partner may leave with the info, but you and I will both be dead unless he drops his fucking gun right now."

Before another word was said, Filini moved. He dislodged the gun from Amos' hand and with one quick and short jab to the throat, the big man was on all fours choking. Filini grabbed the gun and put it to the big man's head while Andre moved over and locked the door and drew the shades. "Jesus, Marco, you're not going to live past this one. Get the fuck out now. Sandman does not fuck around."

"That's what I keep hearing," answered Filini, "but when was it assumed I *did*?"

"Ah, shit, man," stated Simms. "You think you're a fucking badass. Fuck that, man. You're a fucking killer, we all know that, but that fucking Sandman is goddamn crazy. The last thing I wanted to do is work with his fucking ass, but he didn't give me a fucking choice." He paused and spit on the floor as he gagged for breath. "Now that I am helping him, I will sooner die than give him up."

"You will die if I you don't," stated Marco in a deep slow voice.

"There are many ways to die, Filini, and I choose you every fucking time."

This statement caused Marco to turn his head directly up toward Andre. Marco had, albeit remotely, just been part of a murder where the victim's fingers were removed one at a time to obtain information. Now he was hearing someone would choose that over answering to this Sandman. "I guess I need to work on my reputation," answered Marco. "Now, let's start from the beginning."

Marco nodded to Andre who walked over, removed a small rope he carried in his pocket, and pulled the large man up by putting the rope around his throat tethering it tight. Amos choked again but Andre tightened the rope preventing even a choke from being allowed. Filini stepped closer to the man whose face had almost immediately began changing colors. "Amos, my beef is not with you. If you answer my questions, you have a chance to live. If you don't, you will die. Regardless of whether you feel there are different ways to die, it's the one sure thing in life. I suggest you help me now, and live, but that's just my opinion."

Andre was cool and calm, but still had feeling when he spoke. Marco was just cold. There was nothing there. Amos recognized that, as his life began to fade. He motioned with his eyes toward a file cabinet. Andre saw the response and slightly loosened the rope, only enough to allow a swallow and a brief sound. His voice cracked and lacked the previous strength, but in all honesty, it was stronger than either Andre or Marco expected. "Over there. Bottom drawer. Under the file, Beach Property."

"Beach Property," Marco replied, then smiled as he recognized it. "For Sand?" He walked over to the file cabinet and pulled the drawer. It was filled with files that appeared to be labeled for different addresses, areas, and properties. Near the front was the file Simms referenced. "Beach Properties it is," Marco stated as he removed it. He quickly flipped through a half dozen buildings that all had dates on them. The one dated yesterday was on top. Marco held it up to Amos who nodded affirmatively. "Thank you, Amos. We will leave you now."

Amos smiled just for a brief second before the rope again tightened around his throat, this time not being released until his body fell limp.

17

"Ya-ya, your ska-ska-ska-skin is so soft," the man's voice stuttered as he looked over the woman bound and tied to the table.

Her face was beaten. She was naked. "Stop," she pleaded. "Please stop."

"Nuh-nuh-nuh-no. Pre-pretty lady. Yuh-yuh-yuh-yuh..." There was a pause and he really fought to find the words and it seemed to be making him angry. "You need to juh-juh-juh-just tell me again how great I am." He was touching himself between his legs. He was sore. He had already raped her numerous times and he was going to again.

She was crying and almost unconscious. "You are not great. You were horrible. You sucked in bed just like you suck at talking, you fucking freak."

"Nuh-nuh-nuh-now you juh-juh..."

"Shut the fuck up, you fucking freak."

He turned to the adjacent table and grabbed a large knife, the same knife he had used to abduct her hours ago. The same knife he had used to penetrate her, but only enough to cause bleeding, not enough to seriously harm. The same knife he had used to draw on her chest. "You are the one who nuh-nuh-needs to shu-shu-shut your mouth."

She spit on him a mixture of blood and saliva. It landed in a spray across his face.

He wiped his eyes with his sleeve. "Nuh-nuh-nuh-now, now, bunnies can't spit." It was as if that event changed what he was looking at. His eyes lost focus and seemed to squint at the beaten and bloody woman before him. He raised the knife and without another word plunged it ten times into her chest. She was dead after the first strike. He then carefully decorated her and left.

. . . . .

Andre picked the simple lock in a matter of seconds opening the side door to the Northbrook warehouse. There was power to the building as the outside lights were on and they could hear noise from inside. There was a woman's voice, though muffled and not forming words, and what appeared to be the deep, steady hum you hear by a large electrical panel. However, the building itself appeared to be vacant. Andre walked up to a nearby overhead door and released it allowing it to come up several inches, just far enough for a body to slide through.

"What are you doing?" whispered Filini.

"I have found it's faster to run full speed and slide under a garage door if you need a fast escape than dealing with a door that may lock when it shuts."

Although Marco thought it was overkill, he was not about to argue. They walked quietly toward the noise. The building was dark, but there was some natural light from the moon through skylights and what appeared to be emergency solar lighting that charged during the day and then stayed on through the night. Regardless of the source, it was enough.

They made their way through the receiving area and came to two large swinging doors. They were lightweight and had no way to lock. They had large black curved bumpers on them that Marco assumed were to enable fork trucks to drive into them and push them open, but they would swing closed behind, most likely to keep the cold of the warehouse confined to that area. They tried to look through the windows on the doors but they were covered with duct tape on the other side. Andre and Marco looked at each other and it was Marco who nodded to move forward. Both had their guns drawn and Andre even used his to push the swinging door forward.

Just as the door opened about three inches, a loud beeping sounded. Marco looked down to see a thin red laser beam whose path was broken on the inside of the door. "Shit."

. . . . .

"Tell me, Dr. Gerstenberger, and this is the last time I'm going to ask you, why am I being hired to eliminate the senior leaders of Abbunex Labs?"

Elise was tied to a chair in the middle of a large empty building. There was a man speaking to her that she didn't know. There was another man standing next to what appeared to be a portable battery used to jump-start stalled cars. The jumper cables coming off the battery were each attached to one of Elise's fingers. She was mostly naked and wet. Her skin was also bruised. It appeared she had been beaten, tortured with some sort of submersion or blasted with water, and now electrocution. Her head hung straight down with her chin almost resting on her chest. The man who had spoken grabbed a wad of her hair and pulled her head back up to look at him.

"Goddamn it. Wake her up. I need her to talk to me."

The man next to the jumper box grabbed what appeared to be a small vial and stepped up in front of her. He broke the vial under her nose and the pungent smell caused her head to jump. He patted her lightly on the cheek as he did it. "Elise. Elise. Wake up, Elise."

She lifted her head but could not seem to focus. She uttered some noises but nothing coherent. The man with the smelling salts held her head upward by grabbing her under her chin. "I don't know, boss. That last time I hit her, I may have charged it too much."

The other man did not respond but looked over at the machine then back to her. "Fuck it. We need to get out of here. Let's throw her back in the car and dispose of her body. It should never be found."

"I thought the instructions were to make it look like an accident?" the second man said as he dropped her chin to let her head fall back against her chest. He walked over and began closing down his electrical system.

"Well, I changed the..."

His comment was stopped when one of their motion detectors sounded.

"Fuck! Get your shit together. Let's get out of here."

"What about the girl?" he asked as he grabbed his battery and headed toward the door.

The first man removed his gun and shot her in the head. "Leave her."

• • • • •

"Gunshot," stated Andre.

Marco was already breaking through the door. "It wasn't shot toward us. We just interrupted something. They're clearing out."

Andre followed suit and both men ran through the room toward the far side where they saw another double door. These doors had a larger gap and there was light inside. Filini peered through the gap in the door and saw a body sitting limp in a chair. The door on the far side was open and appeared to be the front entrance. They heard an engine start, rev higher, and then silence.

Marco looked up to Andre. "Follow me through. Clear the sides in case any stayed behind. My gut tells me they're gone."

"Will do, Boss."

Marco burst through the door with his gun raised. He scanned the main area knowing Andre had the rest. The room was silent. After a few moments making sure the room was clear, he ran up to the woman on the chair. Marco was sure she was dead but checked for a pulse nonetheless. "Holy shit," he stated. "She has a pulse."

"How?" Andre asked. "She was shot in the head."

"Look at the back of the chair. Because her head dropped and the idiot who shot her was in a hurry, he just scraped her." He paused. "She still won't live, though."

"Who is she?" Andre asked.

"Dr. Elise Gerstenberger, the Chief Medical Examiner," Marco answered. "I've seen her interviewed at crime scenes—some of *my* crime scenes," he added.

"What are we going to do with her?" Andre asked.

Marco appeared perplexed. "Here," he stated. "Help me tie this off so it will apply pressure to the head. Pull her body down and use her own weight to help hold it in place and control the bleeding. Then we're going to leave her like that and get the fuck out of here. Then I'm going to call O'Malley."

"Let's go," replied Andre. "This has big pile of shit written all over it." They started to walk toward the door and felt something under their feet causing them to slide just a bit. "What the hell is that?"

Marco did not look down. "It's sand."

•　　•　　•　　•　　•

I sat with Patti, Franky, and Huston at Flap Jaws. They served pizza there and I would often partake in a pepperoni or sausage, or on those really crazy nights, a combo. Tonight, however, Roy gave me the okay to bring in four Dagwoods from Mr. J's. All the other patrons were clearly jealous, and by all, I mean both of them. We dove into the food keeping the talk going as we did. Franky and Patti were good with the Dagwoods, though I think Karen would have preferred less grease and more greens. As I thought about how she felt, I realized I really didn't care.

"What do you want the plan to be tomorrow?" Patti asked.

"I'm not sure," I replied. "I'm concerned because our leads have started to dry up." I turned to Karen. "Anything new with the financials?"

She had just taken a bite and had to wait to fight through the chewing before she could respond. "Only that the list of names of those that deferred their bonuses last year didn't get any longer. Everyone else in the entire company took their bonuses as normal. However, there was something extremely odd with Dr. Grove's finances."

"Odd? What do you mean?" My eyebrows lifted as I spoke, an involuntary response that made me appear like Mr. Spock on *Star Trek*. Instantly, I wanted to be able to do it again, but I could not recreate it.

"What the hell is the matter with your eye and forehead?" asked Franky. "You having a spasm or something?"

"It's nothing," I replied. "Go on, Karen."

She too was looking at me like I was an idiot but did not comment. "Well, just recently, a great deal of money has been moved around in accounts in his name."

"Okay," I said. "What makes it odd and how great was the money?"

"The odd part is one of the accounts was just opened, only in his name and not his wife's, and the volume going in and out of it is in $9,999.99 increments."

"Under ten thousand," I said. "So it won't be flagged by the government."

"Yeah," Karen replied, "that's what we thought also. However, it's odd because the money is coming from other accounts that we traced either to his name, or we were unable to find the original source."

"Unable to find the source?" asked Franky. "How can that be?"

"Nelson hasn't given up, mind you, but to use her words, these guys are 'incredibly talented at keeping money hidden.' Certain countries don't allow the United States government to have full access to their systems. Criminals know what countries to use and when they use multiple ones with the same poor relationship with the US, it becomes almost untraceable."

"Did she find any of the original sources?" I asked.

Karen continued. "Yes, several were, like I said, tied back to new accounts in Dr. Alan Grove's name. Other accounts went to a large corporate account in the Caymans, but we've been unable to identify the true owner at this time. Then, several other unknown owners were from Swiss and German banks. The first name we can find on any of the accounts falls back to the new Alan Grove accounts. However, as quickly as they were filled, the money was moved."

"What do you mean, moved?" I asked.

"I mean, at eleven fifty-five this morning, a quarter of a million dollars was moved in twenty-five transactions. All out of Alan Grove's accounts, all to one account that goes by the name of 'Sand Enterprises.' It's an exploration company in Saudi Arabia. Everything about it appears legit. In short, before anyone starts drilling for oil in the desert, they call this company to determine the best location. The company is private and near as we can tell makes millions."

Just then my phone rang. I looked at the screen and could not believe what I saw. I showed my phone to the others who immediately drew the same surprised expression. I answered, "Hello, this is Detective O'Malley."

"Tommy, this is Alan Grove." His voice was nervous and cracked when he spoke. I could tell he didn't want to be calling me, but something was forcing him to make the call. "Is Elise with you?"

Instantly my expression changed. "No, what is it?"

"She said she needed some time earlier today. Then she told me she had just met with you at the department and the exchange went poorly. We talked through everything you had said to me and the conversation she and you had, then we spoke candidly with each other. It was a good conversation. She told me she was headed home but she hasn't made it. Her phone is turned off or dead. Tommy, I'm worried." There was a pause then he added, "And I wouldn't have called you if I didn't think it was serious."

"When was the last time you spoke to her?" I asked.

"Let me check my call log." There was a brief silence when he pulled the phone from his ear to scroll through his call history. "Three forty-five. We talked for fifteen minutes."

"That was right when she left the precinct." I checked the time on my phone. 8:45. "She should have been home by five with the worst traffic."

"I know, Tommy," he replied. "What can we do?"

"We have all her car information on file as she is a government employee. Let me put a trace on her car and then let's see what we can do to turn on her phone."

"You can do that?" he asked.

I ignored the question. "Alan, is there anyone who would want to hurt Elise?"

"Damn it, Tommy. Enough with the bullshit interrogation. All I want is my wife back."

Again, I ignored the comment. "Alan, let me rephrase. Is there anyone who would want to hurt Elise to get to you?"

There was a long period of dead silence. Then finally, his much weaker voice broke in, "I don't know. Just find her."

"Stay near your phone, Dr. Grove, and I'll do the same. I'll call if we find anything." I hung up without further comment.

I turned to the others who stared blankly toward me. "If you didn't guess, that was Doc G's husband. She never made it home after her visit earlier. Dr. Grove is worried to say the least, but he offered nothing to me as far as cause."

"I already called it in when I heard your call," answered Halterman. "Swanny was still at the lab. He said he could handle the phone trace. He said it might take about ten minutes. He also said he could turn on her phone remotely unless the battery was removed or it was dead."

"What do you want to do, Tommy," broke in Franky. "We've all been drinking. Do you want to Uber up to North Chicago?"

"Nope," I replied. "But it is Doc G. Let's head back to the station and see what Swanny digs up and make sure the APB on her car gets released to all villages."

They all agreed without actually speaking. The immediate grabbing of jackets and waving Roy Pura over to settle their tab was a full discussion on its own. When it came to protecting their own, the police department rivaled no group other than the military, and since a huge percentage of the police department was former military, it simply was the way it was.

It was less than fifteen minutes later when the group arrived back at the department, and not to anyone's surprise, Sergeant Carter was there waiting. Carter greeted them at the door. "I heard the call. I already spoke to Swanny. He has the phone on and is tracking its history. Says he will have it in minutes."

"Let's hope she just stopped by a restaurant or bar to clear her head," Huston replied.

"Let's hope," I repeated, though I did not have a good feeling. People have patterns, ways of doing things. This was not Doc G's way. She was refined, precise, and did not let emotions govern her actions. However, the situation was definitely like none she had been in before. Her normal actions may have been thrown out the window. Let's hope, I thought again to myself.

My desk phone interrupted my thoughts. I looked at the screen. "It's Swanny," I said to those around. "What do you have, Swanny?"

"I got her phone, Tommy. A warehouse north of downtown. By what I can find, it's vacant."

"Oh shit," I replied.

"Oh shit is right, Tommy. She would have no reason to be there. The place hasn't been occupied for more than ten years."

"Text me the address," I stated firmly.

"It's already on its way, Tommy," added Swanny. "I'll stay here. If I can help, just call."

"Thanks, Swanny. Find out everything you can about that building."

"Do you want me to call the phone?" Swanny asked.

I thought a minute. "Will anyone know you've turned it on?"

"Only if they look at the screen, Tommy." He paused. "Or if it rings, I suppose."

"Then no," I stated flatly. "Don't alert anyone we have activated the phone."

"Ten-four, but I can't stop anyone else from calling."

"I understand," I replied.

I hung up with Swanny and then turned to the others. "I have an address coming my way for Elise's phone. Swanny got it turned back on and located it. It's in an abandoned warehouse up north."

Franky grabbed his keys from his desk. "That doesn't sound good. I can drive. I only had one drink."

Carter now moved closer. "You four all ride with Sullivan, but I don't want you going in unless we have no other choices. You've all been drinking and nothing good can come from that."

"Jesus, Sergeant, it's Doc G."

"Damn it, O'Malley, that's an order." Carter's voice was raised and firm. "Just be glad I'm letting you go at all."

"He's right, partner," added Franky. "Just ride with me. We'll see what the scene is before we commit to anything."

My phone beeped meaning I had a text. I looked at the phone. "I have the address. 610 Waukeegan Road in Northbrook."

"I'll meet you there," stated Carter. "Huston, Halterman, I changed my mind, you both ride with me."

I swung my eyes to Carter and knew instantly what he was doing. He wanted to hear exactly how much we all had to drink and he believed his two first-year detectives would shoot straight. I said nothing on the subject. We all headed to the door when Parker and Hannifin broke through.

"What are you guys doing here?" asked Carter.

"We got a call for a dead body," Parker replied.

Instantly we all stopped and stared at the two.

Parker saw the response and recognized it as odd. "What? Something we need to know?"

"Where is your body?" I asked, almost fearing the answer.

"Downers Grove. Don's Auto Shop, I believe was the name," Hannifin replied, after pulling his phone up to read off the name. "Downers PD says it's like nothing they have seen and wanted us to come in. Why?"

We all collectively let out a breath. Carter moved between them as they held open the glass door. "Read the APB. Stay in touch with O'Malley. If we need support, then finish your scene and head up to Northbrook."

This cloak-and-dagger short response I am sure sparked their interest, but Carter was going to waste no additional time. Northbrook was at least fifteen minutes away and he wanted to get there as soon as possible. Parker and Hannifin did not seem to mind and let the door shut behind only watching the four of us get in the same elevator they had just exited. Within two minutes, we were on the road heading north.

I scanned through my recent calls and hit the call button when I found the right number. The phone was picked up on the first ring. "Tommy?"

"Hey, Alan," I replied. "I need you to listen to me and listen to me good. Don't call your wife's phone without calling me first. We turned the phone on and if it rings, it could bring attention to whoever turned it off."

"What are you saying, Tommy? Somebody turned her phone off?" Alan's voice was strong, not typically what I would have expected.

"No, I'm saying it was off and now it's on, and it's not worth the risk to call."

His voice now actually seemed even stronger. "So you have found her?"

I should have anticipated this response. Shame on me. "Listen, Alan, I'm going to cut to the chase. We located the phone. It's in a location she would not typically be. We will know more in the next ten minutes. Stay by your phone but under no circumstances should you call her. Do you understand?"

My question was returned with only silence until finally Alan answered more softly now. "Yes, I understand."

"Good," I answered. "I'll call you back when I know something." I hung up, not giving him another chance to reply.

Franky turned to me. "Do you think you should have called? What if he calls to warn whoever that we have located her?"

I nodded as I understood where he was going. If Alan was involved, then I just gave him the opportunity to protect whoever was behind it. However, for me it was worth the risk. I did not think Alan would hurt his wife, so I was banking on the thought that if he was involved, he would not be to that level. If he did, we would know immediately with his phone records. "Yeah, partner, it is a risk, but I think the positives by making the call outweigh the potential negatives." Nothing more was said as we soared up Lakeshore Drive with Franky's flasher blazing and Carter's car breaking our path as we went. Neither car had sirens going, which was often my preferred choice. Why give criminals a heads-up that we were coming?

We pulled up to the building and saw exactly what we expected—a building that looked to be completely abandoned, with three exceptions. First, there was an outside light above the front door that was on. Some buildings left electricity on when they were trying to sell. Based on the info Swanny had sent me on the drive, this building did not fit that mix. It was not for sale or lease and was simply sitting vacant. Further, there was a fence around it that was closed. However, the second thing which caught our attention was that the chain around the fence was cut and the gate was unlocked. Finally, there were several cars outside the fence. There was street parking so they could have a reason to be there, but still it begged the question—were they there for this building or something else nearby? That would need to be checked out.

Carter did not even get out of his car to push the gate open. He drove straight through causing it to lurch and swing violently around 180 degrees to bang against the inside of the fence. We both drove inside taking opposite positions with Carter going to the far side of the building and Franky and I heading straight toward the front door. My phone rang.

"How do you want to play this, Sergeant?" I said immediately upon answering.

"Huston and Halterman confirmed nobody had more than two drinks and it was more than two hours ago. I say you guys are good to go. Do you agree?"

I smiled as that was the answer I wanted to hear. "We do, sir."

"Then you two take the front and we'll take the back. The loading dock overhead door is open about ten inches. Think we can get in there? What does the front look like?"

"Well," I replied, "it's a glass door so worst case, we can break through without issue."

"Okay, then, when you're in position, let me know," stated Carter. "We'll go on my word and my word only."

"Ten-four, Sergeant."

I hung up and as quickly my phone rang again. I looked at the caller. It was Marco Filini. "O'Malley."

"Hey, Tommy, Marco."

I could tell he was in his car. I heard the car noise and the sound as his phone was blue-toothed tied to his radio which made the clarity slightly different. "I know who it is. What do you want? This really is not a good time."

Marco's voice remained flat and without emotion. "Hey, listen, I need to let you know I stumbled on something, something I didn't do, but it involves a friend of yours."

My heart stopped. "What are you talking about, Marco?"

"I have my own problem brewing here in the city. It involves what we talked about before. However, upon following up on that issue, I found the chief medical examiner in a bad situation in a warehouse up north. I'll text you the address but you need to get an ambulance there right away."

"Is it 610 Waukeegan?"

There was silence on the phone. His normal flat tone was slightly higher. "You surprise me, but I'm glad you're on your way. I would hurry."

"If anything happens to her, I will kill you."

"Be careful, Tommy. If I was behind this, I would not have called you. Just hurry. The building is empty. I surprised whoever was there." He paused then added, "Hey, I didn't need to call you—remember that." He hung up.

I grabbed my radio instead of my phone and direct connected to Carter. "Don't ask questions. I just received a call. The building is clear and Elise is inside and seriously injured. Go in now." I turned to my partner. "Call for an ambulance. Officer down."

We all burst through the doors with me blasting through the front glass door with multiple shots. Both groups reached the large open warehouse space at about the same time from opposite sides. The women had to look away, as I ran to Elise's motionless body on the ground. "*Elise*," I hollered. "Elise. Can you hear me?"

There was no response. I examined what I could. She had been moved to rest where she was now. Tape had been affixed to her head to prevent it from turning. Some clothes, the ones she had been wearing previously, were pinned under and around her head injury. Combined with the tape, they were preventing her wound from losing too much blood. She was mostly naked and clearly beaten to near death, but she did have a pulse. "Goddamn it, where is that ambulance?"

"Does she have a pulse, Tommy?" asked Carter.

I nodded. "I think so. It's hard to tell." I looked back down at her and used my thumb to hold open one of her eyes. It was like holding open the eye of a dead person. Blood still appeared to be seeping from her head, but the injury seemed to be more on the surface of the scalp. "Elise," I called again with no response.

The sound of sirens filled the area. I don't remember much after that. I remember the medics coming in and pushing me aside. I remember seeing her wheeled away back toward the front door. I don't really remember anything else.

At some point later, I found myself sitting in a chair in the same room where Elise was found. Several folding chairs had been brought in from a nearby storage area and the forensics team was doing their thing.

"Tommy? You with me?" asked Carter, his voice soft and foreign for his normal speech.

I looked up at my boss. "I don't know, Craig."

Franky and Carter looked at each other, probably as much from me calling him Craig as my tone. Carter put his hand on my shoulder. "We need you to be part of this, Tommy. Franky said Filini called you with the address. Said she was here. How did he know? How is he involved?"

I didn't answer right away. I stared straight by both of them, my eyes locking on the forensics team taking samples and pictures in and around the chair that my longtime friend had most likely been tortured in—my friend who may already be dead. "I don't know, Sergeant. All I know is he called. He had already been here, but he said he didn't do it. He's chasing the same person we are."

"Do you believe him?" asked Franky.

Carter turned to Franky and his tone turned much harder and less reserved. "I don't give a crap if Tommy thinks he did it or not. He's clearly involved and I want to bring him in."

I didn't respond. I agreed with Carter. I wanted to talk to Marco too, but not at the precinct. I had his number. We would talk. I pushed myself up. "Whoa, Tommy," stated Franky putting his hand on my shoulder. "Just sit back down. You went a little south on us. No hurry to get back in gear."

"Jesus, Franky, I'm fine. I just needed to get my breath. You get that heart going, that adrenaline, and sometimes it just catches up to you. I've got someone to meet."

"Not without me, partner," stated Halterman as she walked up from the side.

I turned to her and instantly felt a calm come over me. Shit, what she was starting to do to me. "Not this time, Patti. This is something I have to do alone, but I'll follow up with you the minute I'm done."

"No fucking way," responded Carter. "You will have a partner with you and if it's not Halterman, it's going to be me or Franky. You make the call."

"Can't do it, Sergeant. You know who I have to see and it won't work if anyone else is with me. Just not his style."

"I don't give a fuck about the style of Marco Filini. We'll do this one by the book or we won't do it. You take a partner or you don't go."

Before Carter could add anything, one of the individuals from the forensics team came over to him. "We found motion detectors at every door to this building and at internal doorways closer to the area. Someone was in here doing their work on the victim—"

I interrupted this investigator because I did not know who he was and I did not like him referring to Doc G as just another victim. "She has a name, asshole. It's Doctor Elise Gerstenberger, and she's one of us."

"Hey, Tommy," said Franky. "Let the kid talk. He's just doing his job."

I waved my hand down at him. "Ah, fuck it." I started to walk away but stopped because I really did want to hear what he had to say.

The young investigator continued, though his tone was much lower. "As I was saying, whoever was in here harming Doctor Gerstenberger had the place staged to prevent any surprise visitors. The one on the other side of the adjacent room was tripped. It was the only interior one tripped. Several of the exterior ones were tripped but it's impossible to know if they were tripped during the evacuation or when our guys were coming in. The interior one was not tripped by our team as I confirmed none of our guys came through these doors."

I turned back to Carter. "Let's assume Filini is the one who tripped the interior sensor. That would have caused whoever was in here to end their plans early. Filini realizes what he's done, possibly heads directly to this area and finds Doc G. He helps control her injuries, gets the hell out of here, and then calls me. He has no issue with Doc G and would always look for an opportunity to gain some good points with the police. I don't think Filini is involved, but I would bet my salary he knows who is."

The investigator was listening intently to me, although I was speaking to my team and he just happened to be present. He turned from me to Carter. "I don't know this Filini, but whoever was fulfilling their plans, as you say, on Doc G, it was full-out torture. She was beaten with some blunt object, burned, and electrocuted. It even appears she was blasted with a high-powered water gun or dunked. I don't know what information they needed from her, but I can't believe she didn't share it, if only to bring about her death sooner. The other thing we have not figured out is the reason for the sand. It doesn't appear to be part of the torture."

I nodded agreement about the sand, but my mind was on something else. "What was her head wound?" I asked.

He seemed surprised by my question. "I believe it was a gunshot wound, but you will need to verify that at the hospital. There was a gunshot casing and bullet hole in the back of the chair."

"I don't understand," I replied. "Why the hell would he shoot her in the head but not kill her? I can't believe this guy would leave a witness." The investigator shrugged but offered nothing more. He shook Carter's hand and used the opportunity to walk back toward the crime scene without further comment.

There was a brief silence as he left, then Franky stated, "He wouldn't. I'm sure whoever did this meant to kill her." He paused, then turned to face only Carter and me. "Hey, what if he got rushed? Take your theory a bit further and tie it to what Huber said."

"Huber?" I asked.

"The investigator you just broke down for not respecting Doc G."

"Oh, got it," I said with a touch of an apologetic tone even though Huber had already left.

Franky continued, "What if the perpetrator is doing what he's doing to Doc G and then Filini, who somehow found out about this location, tripped that wire before he was done. The perp panics, fires a shot at Doc G who has the wherewithal to drop her head. He packs up in a rush and exits not realizing his shot wasn't fatal. This whole setup was done by a pro. Pros use one shot, to the head. He would have had no reason to believe she wasn't dead. She wouldn't have been moving regardless."

My interest increased with each word. "Yes, and does that mean Filini may have seen the perpetrator?"

"Maybe," Franky added. "We won't know until we talk to him."

I looked over to Halterman and she already knew what I was asking without saying a word. "Fine, O'Malley. Take Sullivan. I'll stay here and see what they find out and what they'll share with us."

I smiled at her. "Thank you, partner. It's just that if I have to take someone, Franky has the same history with Filini that I do." I suddenly stopped and turned to Carter. "You okay with that, Boss?"

"Only if you agree to never call me Craig again," he stated with a smile. His voice went instantly back to serious. "Be careful—both of you. Marco Filini is not someone we work with or trust. He's a killer and has dodged the law for more than twenty years. If we can bring him down, we will, and I want you to bring him in."

"But if he can help bring us Doc G's perpetrator, I'll use him all day long," I replied.

"Fair enough, Tommy, but keep your guard up," Carter repeated.

"Yes, partner," stated Patti. "Keep your guard up, and call me when you know anything."

"Will do," I replied to both of them. "Did anyone call Dr. Grove?"

"We did," replied Carter. "He's on the way to the hospital."

"Someone should get over to interview him as well. He's involved, I know it."

Carter stared back at me. "We got it covered, Tommy. Now go find Filini."

I turned to Franky. "You ready to go?"

"Let's go." He then stopped before taking a step. "Do you know where we're going?"

"Yep. I think it's time for a workout."

I turned away as Franky looked to Carter, shrugging his shoulders. "Yeah, a workout. Makes perfect sense, Tommy."

I did not respond. I heard Carter's phone ring as we walked away.

18

"Jesus, Hannifin, you ever seen anything like this?" Detective Parker whispered.

"Yeah, partner," Detective Hannifin replied as he looked across the auto shop. "This guy was murdered for information. I wonder what he knew."

A woman sat off to the side with her head in her hands. Occasionally her cries were loud enough to break the monotonous silence that engulfed the auto shop after hours. The two detectives had already called in the forensics team. Unfortunately, they were busy at the warehouse where Doc G had been found. The second team originally dispatched to assist at the warehouse was redeployed to Downers Grove and should be arriving any minute. A young Downers police officer sat next to the woman. Parker tilted his head to the officer. "The DG cop looks a little green."

Hannifin glanced over. "Do you mean he looks like a rookie, or he looks like he's going to be sick?"

"Both," Parker replied.

"This is a tough scene, partner. It wasn't that long ago you would have been uncomfortable with torture and dismemberment."

Parker accepted the description of his relatively short status as a detective. "What do you want our next step to be?"

Hannifin pressed his lips together. "Well, based on the fact that the scene up north with O'Malley is similar, and we haven't had anything like this in a long time, I believe they have to be related. Therefore, we're going to interview the woman who made the call and learn everything we can about this victim. Once we do that, we'll get O'Malley's team over here."

"Should we call Carter?" Parker asked.

"You bet your ass we should call Carter." He pressed his earpiece to activate his phone. After a few simple voice prompts, Carter's phone was ringing. Less than a minute later and after hearing the word "fuck" seven times through the conversation, the connection was dropped.

"What did Carter say?" asked Parker.

"For starters, we are to work this case completely and brief everyone as soon as we wrap it up."

"And secondly?" Parker asked.

Hannifin smiled slightly. "Well, if you couldn't tell from my end of the conversation, he was glad we told him and he felt mildly disappointed that this is what we found."

"Really?" replied Parker.

"No, partner, not really."

•   •   •   •   •

"Okay, Tommy," said Franky as I fired up the engine of my 1974 shit-brown Camaro. Franky had driven us back to the station which was very near where I said we were going. I wanted my car because Marco knew my car. "Why the hell are we going to work out?"

"We are not going to work out, but I think that's one of the only places Marco will meet me."

"How do you know he will meet you there?" Franky asked.

"Because he has wanted something from me for a long time, and for the first time since I met the man, I need something from him that I'm willing to trade."

"Ah, shit, Tommy, you're going to fight the guy? What the hell for?"

"Doc G," I replied. "I will do whatever it takes to find out who's behind Doc G's attempted murder, and he knows who it is, I'm sure of it."

"Why do you think that? Just because he called you?"

I turned to my partner as we waited at a downtown traffic light. "Because he went there to find the guy. I believe finding him with Doc G was a coincidence. I think he got some sort of lead to put the man we're looking for at that warehouse and Filini was going to meet him. To his surprise, he got more than he expected."

"I don't know, Tommy. There's no reason we should trust this guy. He's dirty all the way through. How do you know he wasn't the one who did that to Elise?"

"Is that what you think?" I asked.

"I don't know what the hell to think, Tommy, but I know I'm not going to blindly believe Marco Filini is here to help."

"Fair enough," I replied, my tone starting to show a hint of my annoyance with his continued arguments. "Carter didn't want me going in alone. If you don't want to join me, I can drop you off anywhere. I need to know that you're not going to put Filini in cuffs and haul him in." I pulled the car to the side of the street and turned to face him. "I mean it, Franky. What are your intentions? Did Carter give you separate orders?"

Franky looked down and did not immediately reply.

"Shit!" I stated. "Get out of the car, Franky."

"No can do, partner. I may have been given other orders, but my partner comes first. If I hear Filini say anything about a crime he has committed, he's coming downtown. If he only provides us information on Doc G's situation or anything else for that matter, not admitting any fault himself, then I will let my orders from Carter fall to the back."

"I can't put you in that situation, partner. We are not going to bring Filini in today, but we are going to meet him. If you're supposed to bring him in, then you will be openly defying a direct order. You can't do that."

"Shit, Tommy, I'll be in another room. I won't actually meet him. Whatever bullshit we want to say, we will say it." He pointed for me to start driving again. "I am not getting out of this car and there is no way you are going to meet him alone, so just put your pretty little foot on the gas and let's get the fuck to the dojo."

I pulled out but actually started to smile, even laughed under my breath.

"What is so fucking funny, Tommy?" Franky asked.

"Put my pretty little foot on the gas?" I repeated, the humor in my voice clear.

"Yeah, it didn't sound too cool, did it?" He joined the smile. "But I followed it up with two fucks—those sounded manly, didn't they?"

I nodded. "They did, until you had to ask if they did."

Like clockwork, my phone rang. I looked at the number. Blocked. "Right on time," I stated. "This is O'Malley," I answered into the phone.

"Hey, Tommy, how are you?" the deep slow voice said.

"Just fine, Marco. I was expecting your call."

"We need to talk," Filini said, holding that same deep slow speech. "Alone," he added before I could reply.

"I agree, but my partner is with me."

"You mean Sullivan, or the one you're banging?" Filini replied.

That caught me. Is there anything this guy doesn't know? "Sullivan is with me."

"Fine," Marco replied. "Bring him along. I like Franky."

"We're almost to my dojo. Do you want to meet us there?"

"I'm already here with Master Yi," he replied. "Come to the back room. We might be able to fit in a little workout after we're done."

"My partner wants to bring you in. I don't think we'll be able to fit in any workout, Marco."

There was a brief pause and then Filini continued in a very slow, clear, and even threatening tone. "I wouldn't recommend bringing me in, O'Malley. I am the only thing keeping you alive."

Now I paused, just long enough to realize the phone was dead. "Shit," I said softly to myself.

"What is it, partner?" Franky asked.

I briefly turned my head to him as I drove. "I don't know, but that asshole thinks he has something on us or for us. He's not worried at all about us taking him in. When we hear what he has to say, it seems he's confident it'll be more than enough to let him walk."

"He's probably right," Franky replied, to my surprise.

"Why do you say that?"

Franky smiled. "Because right now, we don't have shit. We got three dead bodies, one of our own beaten and near death, and our only lead involves some legally transferred stock options."

"Since you put it that way..." I said sarcastically. Then I paused and added, "Wait, what three bodies?" Instantly my mind went to Elise. Was she one of them? Did Franky know something?

"Thompson downtown, Stover up north, and the body Parker and Hannifin found in Downers. And I'm not even including the pimp you chased down on Sunday."

"Parker and Hannifin found a body?"

"Yep," Franky stated. "Carter called when we were switching cars at the station. I assumed he called you too. Some guy was tortured and killed in an auto shop—cut half his fingers off while he was alive and kicking. He's not kicking now though. A cold one through the head."

"Just like they tried to do to Elise."

"Right," Franky replied. "But the problem is, the initial word I heard from Carter was they took place at approximately the same time."

"The same time?" I questioned. "You mean there are two sets of murderers?"

"That's the only answer possible," Franky replied, turning his head back to face the road. "Carter says up north is too drawn out to have captured Doc, performed the Downers hit, then finished with Doc."

"What does that mean?" I asked.

"Maybe that's what Filini wants to talk to you about."

I shook my head not understanding the new information. "Maybe? But it begs the questions, who and why?"

Franky did not answer.

•   •   •   •   •

We arrived at Master Yi's Academy five minutes later. I parked in my reserved spot. I was the highest-ranking black belt in the academy and had been for nearly twenty years, other than Master Yi, that is. He parked in the first spot, his wife parked in the second spot, and I parked in number three. I saw a brand new Mercedes parked one spot over. I knew whose car that was, but I think we all agreed, mine was nicer.

We walked in and Mrs. Yi greeted us both with hugs. As always, she tried to give us some sort of health snack, the likes of which I had never seen and would never put in my mouth, after which she bowed her head as we exited toward the workout areas. We passed through the first area that had an adult class finishing up. I knew the trainer. She was good, and young—and hot—and married. As we passed by, she bowed to me, which I returned. A few others in the class who knew who I was also bowed respectfully. I would teach classes on occasion. I was not a good teacher, but over the years when Master Yi asked, I would go. We came to the back training room and the door was closed. I reached out to the handle and just as I began to turn it, the door ripped open and a hand grabbed my wrist and pulled me in.

Instantly I was on the mat with a fist coming toward my face. I kicked my legs up, arched my back, and landed on my feet. I had not done that in years and my back muscles instantly told me as much. I looked up to the smiling white teeth with one gold crown up front, of Marco Filini.

"Impressive," he stated.

Damn, his teeth were white against his black skin. "Jesus, Marco, I'm too old for that shit."

"Obviously not," he answered. "But being able to pop up from your back does not make you able to defeat me."

"I am not going to fight you, Marco," I answered. "Not today anyway."

Instantly he smiled even larger, if you can believe that. "That is the best news I've heard in over thirty years—ever since you ducked me in Vegas."

Now it was my turn to smile. "Still won't let it go. You need a new set of disappointments."

"Oh, I assure you, O'Malley, I have been disappointed every day since."

"Very well," I replied. "Believe what you want, but right now I need to know what the hell you were doing at that warehouse?"

"How's the doctor?" he asked flatly, his voice carrying concern.

My shoulders relaxed. "I don't know anything. She didn't look good, but you may have saved her life."

He began walking toward the far wall where there was a bank of mirrors and a small table and chairs. He turned to Franky, who stood with his gun drawn in the doorway. "Sullivan, good to see you. Let's all sit."

Franky nodded but didn't return the greeting. He must have drawn the gun when I was pulled inside so abruptly. I motioned for him to holster his weapon by putting my fingers in the shape of a gun and pointing them to my pocket. He reluctantly did as instructed. We walked over to the table and Marco motioned for us to sit.

We all three looked at each other until Filini finally spoke. "Okay, gentlemen, there's no need for me to beat around the bush. There's someone working in the Chicagoland area and I need to explain to him that he should not be working here. I followed a lead to that warehouse. When I arrived with my partner, we inadvertently tripped a wire allowing this individual to escape. Moments after tripping the wire, we heard the gunshot. When we arrived, the good doctor was slumped over in the chair and the room empty. We heard a car leave so I assume we were close. So close as his amateur ass didn't even finish the job. His rushed attempt to kill your doctor friend missed. We did a short-term patch to try to limit her blood loss and support her body to keep it in place. Then we headed after our target and called you." He paused and leaned closer to me. "I need to talk to your doctor when she wakes up."

"Are you kidding me, Filini?" Franky interrupted to a glare from Marco. "There's no way you're going to..."

I raised my hand to him. "Let's say I set up a meeting, what can you offer me in return?"

Marco leaned back now. "I can't give you the person behind it. He is for me to deal with."

"So you know who he is," I stated, not as a question.

"I know a name, or a nickname, I'm not sure."

"What is the name?" I asked in a stern voice.

Filini just smiled. "Yeah, right. You're going to break me down using your big detective guy tone." His voice was deep and slow and sounded more like Darth Vader than a human. He won the tough voice contest.

Even Franky recognized the distinction but did not speak, leaving it open for me. "Listen, Marco, you wanted to meet. You came here ahead of us. I need to know what the hell is going on."

"You don't have anything, do you, O'Malley?" he replied.

"We have a whole bunch of events that don't go together, ending with the murdered auto shop dealer in Downers Grove." I said that for one reason and one reason only. I wanted to see his reaction. In short, I wanted to know if he knew about it.

"Everything is related, O'Malley," Marco replied without hesitation.

He was completely unfazed. Yep, he knew about it, I thought.

"I have led you right to what you need to be looking for. How can you have nothing?" He paused and looked down, then turned back to stare directly at me. "Tell me about the murders."

I glanced to Franky who gave me a very slight side-to-side headshake. "What do you want to know?" I asked.

"Was there sand at all the scenes?" Filini went right to the punch.

"No, just the hit-and-run and Doc G."

He started to ask another question, but I raised my hand to him this time. "No, now it's my turn," I interrupted. "What lead brought you to the warehouse?"

He pressed his lips together almost in a smirk. "What, now we're doing a quid pro quo game. Are you Clarisse and I'm Hannibal Lector?"

"If the shoe fits," I replied.

He took a deep breath, then answered slowly, "You already know the answer. I have contacts all over the city loyal to me. Nothing happens in Chicago that I don't know about. The minute the man was killed down south, I was informed." He paused and let that sit in, but then something connected in his mind. I could see it in his reaction.

"What?" I asked.

"Are you saying the murder in South Chicago did not have sand left behind?" he asked.

Again I glanced to Franky who, as before, shook his head no, this time more pronounced. "No, there was no sand in South Chicago."

"Are you sure?" he asked. "It was the first one. Is there a chance it was missed? Is there a chance forensics thought it was just sand on the street?"

I thought a minute, not sure where he was going. "I don't think so. The sand at the other scene was different than sand used on the streets. It was white, like Normandy Beach." I had never been to Normandy Beach, but I was familiar with it. My father had fought there in WWII. He was not one of the first marines that stormed the shores, but came in after to help hold it. His stories were amazing and horrible at the same time.

Marco actually stood and paced around making both Franky and me just a bit uncomfortable. One thing about Marco Filini, he was a daunting figure. He was a very large man, at least 6'4". He spared no money on his dress, always wearing the nicest suits. He was by no means fat, but he was extremely large, easily over three hundred pounds. Marco never has scared me because of his size, but there's no way I did not recognize him as a threat. Not a threat should we ever meet in the way he wanted to meet, but a threat because he was an extremely dangerous man. I knew he had murdered more people than I would care to imagine. However, there was never a chance for any evidence. He was that good.

Marco turned back toward us. "We have multiple killers. Whoever killed the man in South Chicago did not kill the victim in the hit-and-run or kidnap and torture your doctor. This man is too precise to not leave his card. It's his way of saying he's above you."

"Do you have a card?" I asked Marco.

He smiled. "I'm not sure what you're asking. Other than occasionally speeding in my brand new Mercedes, I don't break any laws, but if I did, I guarantee you I would not leave evidence of any kind. The last thing I would want is anything tying events together."

"So what is this guy's card? The sand?" I asked.

"Here's what I will give you right now," Filini replied. "There's something going on at the senior executive level at Abbunex Labs. Someone put out a request to make some issues go away. I don't know who that person is. I learned about the request after the order was already filled. That order was your South Chicago murder. Tell me about that murder."

"We can't do that, Marco," I replied. "You know that."

He sat back down in the chair in front of us and slammed his hand on the table. "Goddamn it. Do you want to find this guy or not?"

"We will find him with or without your help, Marco, but I won't provide you information on an unsolved murder."

"Jesus, O'Malley. I can have the full file sent to me within the hour. We don't have time to fuck around."

I knew he was telling the truth. I knew he had contacts in the department that would get him information in exchange for large sums of money. He had previously assumed the same guy did all the murders. Now, because of this sand thing, he did not. I wondered if I should tell him about the rabbit's foot. "Fine, I can tell you this much. The murder in South Chicago was reckless. It appeared to be unprofessional."

"How so?" Filini asked.

"Multiple shots. The killer left a witness." I paused. "It just seemed impulsive."

Filini did not respond so I used the opportunity to continue. "We believe the killer is someone who hired a professional but took matters into their own hands on this victim."

"Are you sure it was unprofessional?" Filini asked. "Could it be a true professional who made it look unprofessional on purpose?"

"I thought about that," I answered, now standing and pacing a few steps. "However, the issue I have is the witness. No matter how they wanted it to look, the actual murder took place directly in front of one and maybe two people. We know that for sure."

Filini shook his head showing understanding. "Okay, so the witness then got a good look at the killer?"

"The witness is unreliable at best, but it's not a dead end. We're still working it."

"Then the question you need to ask yourself is, who killed your guy in South Chicago?" Filini responded.

I was not sure I was tracking his comment. "What do you mean? I have more murders than South Chicago to solve."

"No, you don't," Marco replied firmly. "I'll be taking care of the others."

Franky moved and stood beside me. I knew he was coming out of his skin. I knew this was not going to work for him any more than it was working for me. "Forget it, Marco. I have half the department looking to bring you in. My partner is most likely not going to let you leave this building. There's no way either one of us is going to accept you taking the law into your own hands."

Marco actually laughed out loud, and I couldn't blame him. What the hell were we going to do about it?

"What the hell are you going to do to stop me?" he asked.

"For starters," began Franky, "you're going to tell us what the sand means, and then you're going to tell us who is calling the shots at the big pharma company."

"No, Franky, I'm not." Filini's tone changed and he stood, squarely staring down at Franky, and then turned his scowl on me. The tone change was not drastic, but I heard it, and I was sure Franky did as well. He was not bluffing. He truly meant the message to be, *there's no way I'm telling you any more, and I dare you to say another word about it.*

Silence engulfed the room. It was as if a major war was taking place and one general just played a card and everyone was waiting to see if the opposing general would call it a bluff.

"Where are we going with this, Marco?" I asked, breaking the silence.

He did not respond but nodded strangely, almost through us. I reached for my gun but Marco raised his hand. "Easy there, O'Malley. Let's call this one a draw. Believe it or not, I'm here to help you, but there's no way I'm going to be taken in. Too much in action right now. I will come to the station when my work is done."

I did not pull my weapon but I also held my hand in the same position, inches from it. I heard the gun cock behind me. I began to turn but again Filini spoke.

"Keep your eyes on me, both of you. When I start to leave, you keep your eyes forward." He turned his eyes in the direction of where I had just heard the noise. "Andre, keep your gun pointed down. I don't want anyone hurt and I don't want anyone falsely arrested for some trumped-up charge of assault or something. My partner here is simply ensuring I'm able to leave safely from this meeting."

I let my hand fall down my side. "Marco, I need to know who we're looking for up north. You have to tell me what you know."

He began to walk away leaving me and Franky remaining locked staring forward. "There is much at work here, Tommy. The killer up north is too big for the police. Let me do what I do and all will be well."

"You know we can't do that, Marco." I heard the door open and then I hollered, "How about a trade?"

The door did not shut. I could tell because I knew the sound that particular door made when it was released to freely close. "What kind of trade, Tommy."

"You include me in North Chicago, and I'll give you what you've wanted since we were teenagers."

"I'll be in touch," was returned just before the door shut.

"What the fuck, Tommy!" exclaimed Franky. "Guys can pull guns on us and walk now? Not only that, you give up a deal after they do it?"

"Nobody pulled a gun, Franky. He cocked a gun—for effect."

"Effect, my ass. I thought I was going to have to change my pants."

"I get it, Franky, but we need to find out what the fuck is up with that sand. Filini didn't say it, but the sand is the key up north. Further, we need to pin the auto shop murder on Filini."

"Why the hell do you think he did the auto shop murder?" Franky asked.

"Because he made a mistake. He said we have multiple killers. He said that whoever killed the man in South Chicago did not kill the victim in the hit-and-run, or kidnap and torture your doctor. Then he ended it."

"Holy shit, Tommy," Franky replied. "He didn't say anything about the auto shop because that was his informant."

"Right, that's where he found out about the warehouse."

• • • • •

I knew we needed to go back and check in with Carter and the team, but to be honest, I didn't feel like it. Filini may be a lot of things I didn't like, but for whatever reason, I trusted him. Maybe a better way to think about it was respect. Criminals don't play by the rules. That, usually by itself, makes them criminals. However, Marco Filini may not follow the rules of law, but he did follow a code of criminality—yep, *Word of the Day* toilet paper, but only because I used more than twenty squares and got two words today. An El Famous Burrito yesterday created the extra need today. He would break the law in the most serious ways, but he only did it if it was justified. His justification may be tied to someone not liking someone else for whatever reason, but as long as he was paid and the other person was in some ways bad, then he would handle it. That's why the first time our paths crossed and he could have killed Franky and me, he didn't. He put a body in my trunk and made it look like I was guilty of murder, but he did not put a gun to my head and pull the trigger—code of criminality.

I called Patti on our drive back to the station. I let her know I was not coming up and would simply head home. She informed me she was already at my house and wasn't sure if she'd be in the shower or in the bed. "Bingo."

"What the hell is bingo, partner?" asked Franky as we drove. "Some bar calling numbers tonight? I'll go. I love bingo."

I stuttered a bit. "Ugh, no. She just agreed we shouldn't go back to the department. Carter was on a rampage and she and Huston got the hell out of there also."

"Great, Flap Jaws then?" Franky replied. "You want to head straight there in one car so we don't both leave one downtown?"

Again my stuttering continued. "Ugh, I don't think so tonight. I think I'll just head home. It's been a long day and we're going to have to hit it early in the morning. Don't you have to get home to Vader anyway?"

He pressed his lips together tightly and tilted his head. In an inquisitive voice, he replied, "I think Vader will be fine, but what's your strange tone for?" There was a long pause and then he added with a large smile, "Oh shit, you may be going home, but you're not going home to an empty house, are you, Tommy?"

I actually think I blushed. Why the hell was I blushing? We were two grown adults and there's nothing wrong with us spending the evening together. As I was about to answer, my phone rang. I saw the caller and rolled my eyes. "Fuck," I said as I hit answer. "What do you need, Sergeant?"

"She's waking up. I'm headed to the hospital now."

"Franky's with me. We're on our way."

19 "I'm Doctor Kessel," the older male doctor said introducing himself. "I've spoken to the husband and he's with her now. What do you need to know about Doctor Gerstenberger?"

I took the lead in responding. "First, are you a good doctor?"

"Jesus, O'Malley, what the hell kind of question is that?" stated Carter.

Doctor Kessel stared right at me. "Well, I was called to repair Paul George's leg when he broke it during practice before the Olympics, so somebody must think I'm okay," he answered without hesitation.

I nodded. "Then fine, is Elise going to be all right?"

His tone did not change. It did not get softer or more reassuring. He was all business and like many doctors, had a shitty bedside manner. I hated doctors like this, so f'ing full of themselves.

"We have no way of knowing at this time. She had extensive internal injuries— several broken bones, bleeding, a ruptured spleen, and a rib that punctured her left lung, among other issues. My biggest concern was the gunshot wound to the head. Fortunately, my speculation is that her head dropped at the time of the shot because the damage was clearly from close range but only skimmed the scalp. We were able to repair the injury but she doesn't seem to be responding. She's been in and out of consciousness and when she is awake, she's not able to speak, much less determine where she is or even *who* she is. She has been through extensive trauma. You'll have to give her time. Only time will tell how long her recovery will be."

Now it was my turn for my head to drop. Halterman walked up behind me right as the doctor finished his statement. "How is she?" Patti asked.

"We're just hearing now," I replied to her then turned back to the doctor. "May we see her?"

He thought a minute before answering. "Normally I would say no to police at this point, but I can tell this is not about an investigation, she is one of your own."

He turned to the room and then back to us and added in a softer voice, "Okay, one at a time, if it's okay with the husband, and no more than five minutes each."

"I don't need to go in," stated Patti. "You all know her much better than I. You three go." She motioned to me, Franky, and Carter.

"I'll stay out. Let her know I'm here, O'Malley," said Carter. "And let her know we're going to find the bastard who did this."

I nodded understanding and began walking to the room behind Doctor Kessel. In my wake, I heard Carter continue, "Now Franky, what the hell did you learn from Filini?"

"Shit," I said to myself.

"What was that?" asked Kessel.

"Nothing, Doctor," I replied. "Just worried about my friend."

He stopped and turned causing me to stop and face him. "She's very lucky, Detective. Are you the one who dressed her wounds at the scene so quickly, or did the paramedics get there that fast?"

"It wasn't me, but I was first on the scene. The paramedics didn't arrive for ten minutes or so."

"Whoever did that was brilliant—using her clothes in that fashion. They completely controlled the blood loss. She owes them her life." With that, he turned and continued to the room.

I looked in through the window of Intensive Care and saw Dr. Alan Grove sitting next to the bed. With tubes and wires going every direction in and across her body, I saw my longtime friend. Alan must have heard us approach as his eyes turned and made contact with me. His head dropped and he waived us in. Doctor Kessel continued, "Looks like it's okay with him."

Before he could leave, I handed the doctor my card. "My cell phone is written on it. Call me if there are any changes."

He smiled. "I got the same message from your sergeant." He turned then added before walking away, "Remember, no more than five minutes, and no questions. We want her to wake up on her own time. It's better for her recovery."

I walked in and shook Alan's hand, though after our last meeting, I was concerned if he would even let me in the room, much less shake my hand. "How is she?" I asked. The question sounded stupid, but what else do you really ask when you walk into that situation?

It was clear Alan had been crying. "I don't know, Tommy. She has woken up a couple of times, which the doctors say is good, but she doesn't speak or appear to hear anything, and the noises she does make are just gibberish."

"She's been through a ton, Alan. Extreme trauma. Her body will recover when it's ready."

He stared back toward his wife. "You sound like you know what you're talking about. You must see this all the time."

I thought about the time I had been caught and tortured during a case more than ten years ago. To this day I would say I was not fully recovered. I also remembered my time in Afghanistan when I was sure I would be killed. Both fresh in my mind like they happened yesterday. "No, not like this."

He did not answer, but only continued to stare at his wife.

After an acceptable length of time, I fired one off the bow. "You ready to tell me what the hell is going on at Abbunex?"

He immediately stood from his chair and paced around behind me. "I don't have any idea, Tommy. All I know—"

"Stop with the bullshit, Alan," I interrupted. "They almost killed your wife over it. If a friend of mine hadn't intervened, she would be dead. I'm not even considering that you're not involved anymore. I don't see any scenario where you're not. Therefore, before you and your family are destroyed, tell me what the fuck is going on."

He grabbed my shoulder and turned me to face him. We were eye to eye. He was skinnier than me but in excellent shape, like his wife. They trained, ran marathons and the like. He was toned. This was not a move to create tension or initiate a fight. This was a move to get my attention. What he was going to say next was supposed to be given the utmost importance because he had initiated contact to turn me to him.

"Damn it, Tommy, I don't fucking know." He fell into my arms in a hug.

Okay, not what I expected. I reluctantly put my arms around him. I could not have been more uncomfortable. I rarely hug my kids, and unless we are about to have sex, Patti and I don't touch. Hugging another man, especially the husband of a coworker, not in my wheelhouse. I moved my hands to his shoulders and pushed him away. "Alan…"

"I'm sorry, Tommy. I just don't know what to do."

"To do about what?" I asked, trying to draw anything out of him I could.

"Abbunex stock is plummeting. My wife is in the hospital near death, several of my friends are dead." He paused, looked toward his wife, then back to me. "How can these all not be related, but how can I have no idea what's going on?"

For the first time since I started suspecting him, I heard something in his tone that made me question his involvement. However, I also knew he was a seasoned executive whose job it was to make others believe what he wanted them to believe, so one emotional comment wasn't going to be his get-out-of-jail-free card.

"Alan, we have money in your accounts moving in and out in huge sums. We have multiple members of your executive team already dead. We have the bonus deferment in which you stand to make millions when the stock price goes up. And I'm not even mentioning the fact that your wife, who is now fighting for her life, came to me before everything happened to say something was wrong in your company."

His demeanor changed immediately. "What do you mean she came to you beforehand?"

There was no reason to hide it. Elise was near dead now and protecting her actions seemed far from high on the importance ladder. "Why the hell do you think I was invited to your party? You think I fit in there?"

"Are you saying she invited you to spy on me?"

He actually appeared as if he was going to be angry with her. His wife, her life hanging by a thread due most likely to something he did. "No, jackass. She called me there to talk about concerns she had with how you had been acting." I paused and let that sink in. "Fears she had that you were getting involved in something with Abbunex that was a concern for her, and you."

"Well, I guess that answers it for me."

"Answers what?" I asked.

"I thought we were friends. I thought you were someone who could help. Now I see that not only are you against me, but my wife is as well."

"Did you make the call to have the hit put out on her?"

Now he stepped forward and got right in my face. "Watch your mouth, you asshole."

"Watch my mouth?" I replied. "Why, you going to put a hit out on me as well?"

I did not move back and I could feel his breath and he could feel mine. I could barely see the whites of his eyes because we were so close. I could smell his dinner—Mexican, I think.

"Alan?" a voice said softly.

"Elise!" He turned immediately and leaned down by the bed. "Elise, can you hear me?"

"Alan?" she whispered this time, the sound fading then she fell back unconscious.

He looked up to me. "Get the fuck out of here, Tommy. And don't come back."

I could have said a lot of things, but now wasn't the time. I placed my hand on her sock-covered foot. "We're here for you, Doc. Everyone is praying for you." I turned to Alan. "You need to figure out your priorities, Dr. Grove. They got her right after leaving the precinct. You don't think they can get her here too? Ask yourself, what does she know that someone wants information from her or simply wants her dead? Ask yourself, who? From my perspective, that finger points right to you."

"Don't come back until you have who did this to my wife, Tommy, and that goes for the whole fucking department."

"That is the first thing you said that I agree with. I'll be back for you when I know who's behind this."

●   ●   ●   ●   ●

I relayed the exchange between Dr. Grove and me to my team. I could tell Carter wanted to bring him in right now. I talked him out of it. I wanted him there should Elise wake up. She was asking for him. She loved him, and nothing was going to happen with him by her bed. Even with that, Carter authorized security outside her door. It was probably not called for, but I liked it as it sent a message to Alan that I thought was good.

We departed the hospital and agreed to meet at 7:00 AM to run through the case. I already knew Franky had filled in the others on our discussion with Marco and the little info he provided. I also knew that Alan was not going anywhere. Whether he was guilty or not, he was not going to leave her side. I didn't believe Alan put a hit out on his wife, but someone had. It was my best clue. If I could find why she was targeted, it would be very easy to determine who targeted her. If I was right and Alan was not responsible, then he knew who was. My gut tells me he works with the person. The catch for me was, if I did believe Alan was involved in the other murder-for-hires, which I did, why then did someone go rogue against him and his family?

I entered my apartment five to ten minutes after Patti. I took off my jacket and set my badge on the entry table and then looked up. In front of me stood my partner, 100% naked, with a slice of pizza in her hand. "Ready for bed?"

"You are my dream girl."

She smiled. "Why, because I'm naked or because I'm naked holding pizza?"

"Yes."

• • • • •

We walked in at 7:00 AM and I would be lying if there was not a spring in my step, which was not typical of only getting three hours of sleep. We had actually arrived early and it helped us blend. I think Franky knew. His comment along the lines of, "Well, both of you look like you didn't get any sleep," simply was out of place. We looked fine and he was just fishing. My response, "We look better than you and Vader. What the hell did you both do last night?" That shut him up flat.

The morning briefing was completed and then we all proceeded to the Royals Room to discuss the case. We asked Parker and Hannifin to join us. We didn't know how the Downers Grove auto mechanic murder fit in, but because of the nature of the death, we all felt it was at least worth pursuing. We sat around the conference table and in all honesty, the silence was deafening as we simply stared at the three boards.

Finally Carter broke in. "Anything new on Doc G, O'Malley?"

"I called the hospital on my way in. Still not conscious, and although there are moments she is awake, they're not increasing in frequency or length. It's basically one word or sound and then nothing. I spoke with the security guard as well and he said her husband was there all night."

Nobody reacted too strongly to this, but all seemed pleased to know the status. Carter then continued. "So, O'Malley, why don't you run through what we do know?"

I started to run through everything, start to finish. We had done this several times but it was always good to repeat it. Things you forget come up; items you did not know were related, suddenly become related. Today, however, nothing I said connected any dots. We all felt Alan Grove was involved, but none of us understood how. There were still some pieces missing.

"What about the guy at the auto shop?" I asked. "Donly?"

Parker stood up and taped some pictures to the newest board. "It was pretty nasty. The blood spatter was all over the shop. His fingers were cut off while he was alive. The guy was being made to talk. What about, we have no idea."

"Criminal history?" asked Franky.

"Yeah, some small-time stuff. Tax evasion is the only thing he even got probation for. He cut some deal to avoid jail time. Other than that, mostly moving violations and one charge that was dropped for buying stolen car parts." All seemed satisfied with the summary. In short, a normal small-time criminal that doesn't do anything to end up in prison, but repeatedly cuts every corner he can.

Franky stood up. "That doesn't make sense."

I was surprised by the comment, but wanted more. "What do you mean, Franky?"

"There's no way a guy who's doing those things gets tortured and killed."

I stepped toward him. "What are you saying? He was in deeper than those crimes imply?"

Franky walked to the board. "I am saying, we all agree these are related. Downers Grove never has this type of murder. Then it happens the same time as Doc G. No way that's a coincidence. What I'm saying is, what don't we know about Steve Donly?"

"No shit!" stated Halterman, somewhat out of character.

"I think she speaks for all of us," broke in Carter. "What Franky says makes sense. We need to find out what Donly was into that put him in the know about something. He had information somebody wanted, and wanted badly."

"Tommy thinks Filini did Donly," Franky stated.

I immediately glared at him as I did not want to bring this theory out. I wanted the heat kept off of Filini right now.

All eyes turned to me but it was Carter who spoke. "You want to share, O'Malley?"

"No, sir, not at this time," I replied.

"Let me rephrase," answered Carter. "Tell me how Marco Filini is involved with Donly or you will be very disappointed with your new assignment."

I knew he was bluffing, but I also knew I needed to say something. "Just a gut feeling, Sergeant. He knew about the murder but didn't include it when he ran through everything. It was how he said it, but nothing we can use. Just a theory."

That seemed to pacify him, at least for now, but I knew he still wasn't happy.

Parker broke the tension and pointed but did not speak.

"What is it, Ollie?" I asked.

He remained silent for a moment. He was working things out in his mind. I recognized it. I did it all the time. I start to speak before I'm ready. I used to do that with Tammi and she would get so pissed. I can hear her now—*What? You can't start something and then stop. That is so rude.* Fuck you, Tammi. I wasn't sure if I had said that out loud.

Ollie interrupted my self-conversation. "If you put it all together, I think I know who killed Donly."

All eyes turned to him in surprise. "Jesus, Parker, how the hell would you know that?" asked Carter.

His voice softened. "Well, I don't obviously know, but I have a theory that I think is making sense."

"Shoot, man," I stated.

"Well, like I said, it's just a theory, and you guys know these players better than I do."

"Yeah, yeah, we get it, Ollie," I said. "But if you have something, let's hear it."

"Two brutal tortures took place at the same time. Have you guys considered that we have two suspects that would partake in such events?"

I thought I was starting to see his train of thought. "What are you suggesting?"

"You have the sand killer who was the perpetrator to Dr. Gerstenberger. I believe we are all in agreement that that individual was not Marco Filini. Although he was clearly there, if he was behind it he would not have made the call to O'Malley, nor would he have clearly worked to save her after he inflicted the torture. The crime scene investigators said an alarm was tripped which we're assuming was done by Filini as he entered."

"Yeah, I'm following you. Where are you going with this?" I asked.

"How the hell did Marco Filini know to go to the warehouse where Doc G was being held?"

"Shit!" I replied, although we all got it at the same time. "Filini got the information from Donly."

"Right," Ollie replied. "You need to find the connection between either Donly and Filini, or Donly and the sand killer."

I knew right away where Carter would go.

Carter stood. "Bring Filini in. I want to pin this fucking thing on him and get him off the streets once and for all."

"We can't do that, Sergeant," I replied.

I could see Carter's face turning red. He was going to let me have it.

I continued before he could say a word. "Wouldn't it make more sense to tail him, that is, if we could find him?" I went up to the board. "There's a name involved that's not on the board."

Carter was about to protest to my first comment but my second shut him down. "Who?" he asked.

"Andre," Franky answered.

Carter threw some papers down on the table. "Damn it, I know what you're saying. Filini will have an ironclad alibi because he didn't kill Donly for information."

"Andre did," Halterman answered for him.

"Find Andre?" Carter replied. "And bring Filini in anyway. He called for the order, whether I can prove it or not."

"No," I stated flatly.

Carter's head swung hard to stare directly at me. "What did you say, O'Malley?"

"I said I am not bringing Filini in." Surprisingly enough, my voice was a little shaky. Carter hated Filini, I knew that. But the truth was, I needed him to figure out who the sand killer was.

Just then there was a knock on the door and another detective peeked in.

"There are two detectives from GiST here for you, Sergeant. They said to have O'Malley join as well."

"Fuck," I said.

"Ass One and Ass Two," Carter replied.

It was the first time I had heard him use my names for them. I liked it. He should use it, I thought, since they tried to have him removed on the high school bullying case we cleared several months ago. I hated these guys, and so did Carter.

Carter waved to the young detective. "Very well, we'll be right out." He turned to the group but spoke mostly to Franky. "I don't give a shit what O'Malley says. You find Marco Filini and bring him in. If Andre is with him, bring them both in. You got me?"

Franky did not reply and glanced over to me.

"Don't look at him. The last time I checked, I was the fucking sergeant and he was a twenty-five-year detective." The length of time I had been stuck as detective was supposed to be a shot at me not promoting—by the way, it was.

"No problem, Sergeant," Franky replied, giving me a quick wink as he did.

Carter and I proceeded out of the room and toward his office. I could see the two already in there. I assumed one would be sitting behind Carter's desk, just to fuck with him, but they weren't. They were both simply standing, staring out the windows in our direction.

We entered the office and Carter immediately headed to his desk, almost like a dog claiming territory by pissing on the floor. "To what do we owe the pleasure?" he asked.

Detective Adam Only stepped toward the desk and reached out his hand. "Good to see you, Sergeant Carter. How have you been?"

Carter reached out his hand. In a gruff voice not really like his own, he stated, "Now that we have the bullshit handshake out of the way, you want to tell us why you're here?"

I liked Alan Toose, at least I liked him a little. I hated and did not trust Adam Only. There was a reason I called them Ass One and Ass Two. They had both been detectives in the department for three years. They did not solve many cases but they kept their noses clean. When the opportunity arose, they joined GiST—the Governor's Special Task Force. Any crimes in Illinois that needed this "elite squad," the governor called in GiST. Only was not just a horrible detective, he was an asshole. I think everyone agreed on that.

Only paced a few steps back, slightly caught off guard by Carter's curt reply. Toose stepped toward me. "Hey, Tommy, good to see you. Things been going well?"

It was a tension breaker. Carter had smacked them in the face, and Toose, playing his role perfectly, was trying to lessen the blow. "I would say it's nice to see both of you," I started, "but usually it doesn't work out in our favor. You guys trying to get both of us fired again, Only?"

Carter actually coughed just a bit on that one. Toose lessens the blow, and I throw in a new haymaker from the outside. Only smiled. "Well, I can see it's going to be the same old bullshit in downtown Chicago, so why don't we forget trying to pretend we like each other and simply cut to the chase?"

"Sounds good to me," stated Carter. "I didn't realize we were pretending to like each other though."

Only let out a sigh and I could tell he was losing his patience.

In short, Governor Little requires us to work together when asked, but we don't have to like each other. However, neither party had the authority to get the other fired, so when Only played that card with the FBI several months ago, all hope for a positive working relationship was lost. Carter had weathered the storm, but still at a cost to his career nonetheless.

"Listen, Craig—" Only began.

"I am listening, Adam," Carter interrupted, also using his first name.

Only caught the reply but ignored it. "What does your team know about the Elmer Fudd Killer?"

Bam, that one came out of left field. "The who?" I asked.

"The Elmer Fudd Killer," Only repeated.

I looked at Carter and Carter back to me. It was clear we both had no idea what he was talking about. Carter replied, "I don't think we've heard about any Elmer Fudd Killer."

"That doesn't surprise me as we've done everything we can to keep it under wraps. It will most likely hit the media soon. Usually, however, you and your team dig things up before our team thinks you should." There was a short pause as both Carter and I realized that was as close to a compliment as we would ever receive from this guy. He continued, "I asked you"—he nodded to me—"to join us because you were assigned the case of one of his victims, we believe his first. We didn't realize it until this morning when we reviewed all the open cases in Chicago."

I was surprised by the comment. "What case? The only case I'm working is the Abbunex murder case."

"Your dead body by White Sox Stadium—Thompson was the name."

"That is part of my Abbunex pharmaceutical case," I replied.

"Are you sure? When we read the report, it was noted that there was a rabbit's foot left on the body. Is that correct?"

I glanced at Carter and he gave a slight nod. "Yes, that is correct."

"Does that fit your pharmaceutical case?" Only asked.

I shook my head. "Not that we know of at this time, but the victim sure does." I paused and stared at Only not sure where this was going. "Who is the Elmer Fudd Killer?"

"We don't know," Only replied. "But there have been two victims killed in a suspicious fashion. Your dead guy in South Chicago and another body in a downtown Joliet apartment. Your guy had a rabbit's foot and the other had a fuzzy tail added to her back."

I saw where they were making the connection, though in my opinion it was a bit of a leap. "Are you sure they're connected? Seems like a stretch to try to link them over a rabbit comparison. And you already named it the Elmer Fudd Killer?"

"We didn't name it," replied Toose. "The media made the connection and we've simply worked to bury it. Little still has some pull around here with the media. He didn't want a panic about some bunny serial killer on the loose."

"A killer wabbit, huh?" I stated, though nobody thought it was as funny as I did.

"What do you need from us?" Carter asked.

Only replied, "Just an overview of your South Chicago case. We want to confirm if they're related or not. We need to put this thing to bed before it starts, if we can."

"It's O'Malley's case and it's up on the board in the Royals Room. He can run through it with you right now."

"Sounds good," Only replied, but he looked like he had more to say.

Recognizing the look, Carter asked, "Anything else, Only?"

"No, just let your detectives know to keep their eyes out for anything related to rabbits should more murders occur. We really don't know what we may be dealing with."

"Will do," he replied.

I turned and led them out of the office and back toward the Royals Room. Franky and Huston watched me lead them in. I was sure they thought they were taking over the Abbunex case. Little did they know they were simply chasing a wabbit. I was running through the case when my partner peeked her head in the door.

"Hey, Tommy, you got a minute?"

"Hello, Detective Halterman, how have you been?" Only said before I could reply.

"Just fine, A-one," she said, causing his face to instantly lose its smile. "Tommy?"

I nodded to both detectives and then moved over to meet her at the door. She motioned me outside and let the door shut behind us. A few minutes later, I was back in the room. "You guys up for a ride?" I asked.

They looked surprised. "Why?"

"Because we have a woman's body in a warehouse downtown. From my understanding, she was beaten before being killed."

"Why do you want us to join?" Toose asked.

"Because according to the report from the scene, she's wearing bunny ears."

20 The warehouse was older and much more run-down than the one where we found Doc G. That warehouse was in a condition to be sold and started back into a business. This place should be condemned. It was dirty, smelled of feces and urine, and had clear signs of homeless squatting. In fact, it was a homeless person who found the body, according to the report.

The body, however, was like nothing I had seen before. If this was the same killer involved in the Randy Thompson murder, then in a very short time, they had refined their craft. Only and Toose were with Franky, Halterman, and me. This was way too many detectives on one scene, but it was Only and I who took the lead. The others were there simply to see what the hell was going on. The body was on a table. It had been beaten to a point where I would call it mutilated. From the bruising, even I could tell much of it had been while the victim was alive, but it was also clear some work had been done postmortem. But the most distinguishing characteristic on this body were the ears. Large bunny ears, like on a jackrabbit from the southern United States, the kind that taxidermists with a sense of humor put antlers on and call jackalopes, had been sewn onto the ears of the woman. When the first report had come to me and I heard the body had bunny ears, I assumed it was simply some costume ears held on by a C-clip that fits over the head. Nope, these were actual ears taken from a jackrabbit and then sewn onto the head of a woman. It was a combination of disgusting and weird.

The room was dimly lit. It had a natural light coming from a window high up on the wall. I would have said this was a shipping and receiving office if the building was still in operation. Most of the squatters appeared to have found homes in various areas of the warehouse, so this room was segregated from the rest. Even if we had a witness, they most likely would not be willing to speak or be at all credible. Our best work would be to investigate the scene, learn what we could about the woman, and figure out the link between Randy Thompson, the other victim Toose and Only spoke about, and this new victim.

Franky came up beside me as we looked at the body. "What do you think, Tommy?"

"I think if this killer is also responsible for Randy Thompson, it pulls that murder from our Abbunex investigation. I also think if that is the case, then this killer is advancing at an alarming pace. He would have gone from an uncontrolled shooting on a public street to a sick and well-planned murder of a woman in a controlled fashion. I mean, look, for this much bodily damage there's no blood spatter. It's like the room was wrapped in plastic and when he was done, he just cleaned up and left."

"Could he have brought her here after he killed her?" Franky asked.

"I doubt it. There's still significant blood loss on the table, and why tie down a dead woman?"

"If it is the same killer, he got a taste of it in South Chicago and is perfecting his craft now." He shook his head. "What about those fucking ears?"

"Where do you get rabbit ears?" I asked. "And those look like a jackrabbit. Like what you would find down south in Texas or Mexico."

"I'm not sure, but my gut tells me he got them from a rabbit," Franky said. Although he tried to say it as if he was serious, the ever-so-slight smile crept up on his face.

"Good call, Sullivan. Make sure you put it in the report."

Just then, Toose and Only walked up and Only had heard me praise Franky as he approached but had not heard why. "What was the good call? You guys got something?"

We both were caught slightly off guard. "No, just wondering where someone gets jackrabbit ears in Chicago," I replied, breaking the stare between me and Franky.

"We thought the same thing. I have my team working on it now," he replied. "What do you think about this as a whole?"

I pointed. "Well, you said your second victim in Joliet had a bunny tail and this victim has ears. I would say it holds that our first victim with the rabbit's foot is related. I want to know more about your second murder. Was it as planned out as this one? Were forensic countermeasures taken? Our murder down South was not. It was a random shooting on a public street with witnesses. Our murder victim was a male, whereas this and your previous were females. What can you tell us?"

"We only just made the connection this morning, so I've only been briefed on the first murder. I haven't been to the crime scene or read the report. The governor has, and he feels strongly that they are connected." Only lit a cigarette during this short pause. He coughed a few times upon his first breath and then continued, "From my understanding, the Joliet victim was a hooker and was found in a motel. The motel was run-down and had hourly rates. With that, it also didn't have any security cameras. The couple checked in at four o'clock for one hour. The man then came back out when the desk clerk was in the bathroom and left a note saying they would stay the whole night and left cash for the room. The clerk pocketed the cash and by the next day it was used, so no chance of fingerprints. Also, the note was tossed."

"Then I'm guessing when the time expired, they went to clean the room and found the girl dead?" I asked.

"Pretty much. They don't actually clean the room until they get down to so few rooms they will need it. The manager felt it could have been two days or maybe three. The clerk said the same. The M.E. confirmed the time of death so we determined it had been two days, which puts it right after your White Sox murder." Toose blew some smoke directly in the air and my guttural cough at being disgusted by smoking finally got through. "Oh, sorry—I thought all detectives smoked."

I ignored the comment. "What kind of description do you have for the perpetrator?"

"Well, to be honest, nothing. I'm pretty sure the clerk was high on something while at work. All he could tell us was the girl set up the room and did all the talking. The guy with her was male and white,"—he paused then added—"or Hispanic or black."

Franky and I both smiled. We were not criticizing anything. We had experienced numerous times when witnesses were far from useful. "So, we have a male, any age, possibly white, Hispanic, or African American in Chicago?"

Toose and Only also smiled. "Yep," started Toose. "You're welcome. We just cut about fifty percent of the possible suspects off your list by ruling out women and Asian American men."

Sullivan continued to smile. "Well, the individual didn't speak to hide their voice. Perhaps it was a woman dressed like a man, meaning you can't rule out women completely."

We all realized we had shit. I saw Dr. Denise Bitty, Doc G's counterpart and replacement, enter the crime scene and immediately my thoughts went to Elise. I made a note to swing by the hospital on my way back to the station. "Let us know what you find, Dr. Bitty."

She glared at the four of us. "Listen, Tommy, I know how Doc G handled her crime scenes and there's no way you're going to tell me she shared any information with you until everything was confirmed at the lab. You tried to pull this down South and it's not going to work here either. Move along and I will get you our information when—"

"Your investigation is complete?" I interrupted and completed for her. Changing my tone, "Have you heard anything new on Elise's condition?"

Her shoulders dropped and I could tell this was hitting her hard. They had worked together for a long time. "Last I heard was no change, but that was three to four hours ago."

I nodded but did not speak further.

Only shook his head since the original exchange had taken place. "You still have a way with people, O'Malley. You do realize you will catch more flies with honey rather than shit."

"Why the fuck would I want to catch flies, Only?" I replied, as I saw Huston and Halterman emerge from a door on the far side of the warehouse. "Franky, let's go talk to our partners." I turned back to Ass One and Ass Two. "We'll keep you in the loop about these cases, if you do the same." Out of nowhere, Carter slapped his hand on my shoulder causing me to jump. "Where the hell did you come from?" I asked.

"I'm like a goddamn ghost, O'Malley. You never know where I might show up." I rolled my eyes but did not speak. "And I just got off the phone with the governor. He wants his guys on the rabbit case, and you two to focus only on the pharma case. He wants all information to be shared and"—he paused and cleared his throat emphasizing what was coming next—"none of the bullshit from the past getting in the way." He smiled and stared right at Only. "You got that, Only? No bullshit."

I put my hand on Carter's shoulder now in a comforting fashion. "No bullshit from me, Boss, but that's not really my style."

With that, Franky and I walked off. I did not look back but I was sure that Only used the opportunity to reassure Sergeant Carter he was committed to the process and the team. That is what Adam Only did—ass-kiss. Maybe I should start calling him Ass-Kiss One.

Sensing my thoughts, Franky said, "You really need to learn how to get along better. You are a one man career-limiting machine."

I had to admit, I liked the title.

Dr. Reed Anderson sat in his office waiting for two others to join him. He was alone at his desk, but he was sweating. Not the under-the-arm workout sweat, but the drip-down-the-forehead cold sweat. He could feel his heartbeat. It was not beating obnoxiously fast, but he could feel and hear it. The sound only added to his anxiety. Just then his door opened and the two others walked in.

"It's about time you made it. The shit is falling apart here," stated Reed, the tenseness in his tone clear to both of them. "What are we going to do, Joe? This all started with your guy figuring out the goddamn samples."

Joseph Reingold moved and sat down in front of him. "Relax, Reed. You have to keep it together. Everything is fine. I'm working on the paperwork for the test samples. Thompson has been handled. We all have to keep it together."

The other man also took a seat across from Reed. "The police don't know anything yet. They're tracing the money, but money is not traceable, I've been assured of that. Further, I've also been assured it's not enough to pin anything on us. Our stock transactions are legal. We notified the SEC when we made the option exchange and it's all on record. That's the best part about this, it's legal."

"Legal to falsify trials. Legal to have people killed?" Anderson said. "You of all people should care about that."

The other man continued to speak. "I checked on Elise's status. She is not dead. In fact, this is probably the best of all outcomes. Even if she comes to, she'll be out of commission for weeks at best. Next week we announce the phase three results and the stock will skyrocket. We all exercise our options and this is all done. No more killing and no more false trials."

"Are you sure the FDA won't be able to find the discrepancies?" asked Reed, the question more directed to Reingold than the other man.

There was tension in Dr. Reingold's voice. His nerves showed clearly in his speech and demeanor. "I have doctored the paperwork to tie it all to Thompson, like you asked. If the FDA finds anything, we can make him the fall guy." He stuttered a bit and wiped a bead of sweat off his face as well. "Worst case, we will redo the phase three trials to confirm the results. The stock will take a short term hit but we would have already sold our options. The drug doesn't work. We all know that. How we got past phase two is beyond me. Eventually it'll catch up to the stock price. Like you said in the beginning, we need to capitalize when we can."

Reed sat back. He was nervous. He could feel it inside, but Reingold was coming apart. "I can't believe it might work. Do we have any more loose ends?" He looked toward the other man when he said it, wondering if he saw the same thing in Reingold.

"Just the guy doing the killing," the other man replied. "Sandman."

"And how about the other killer, the one who killed Thompson?"

"Sandman says he will take care of him."

Reed smiled. "Then we just stay status quo?"

"Yes," the other man replied. "Other than to get your financial guy ready to move some stock options for you. Next week is the quarterly announcements. I predict favorable phase three Emplex trials."

They all smiled, but it was Reingold who replied, "I just want this whole thing to be over."

"Don't come apart on us, Joe," the other man replied, signaling Reed that he saw the same thing. "We need everyone together on this one. Are you okay?"

Joseph Reingold stood and paced the room. "Jesus, we're having our friends killed. Hell, Thompson worked directly for me. Not only that, we're having innocent people killed. What the hell did Elise do to anyone? We are paying for a murderer. Do you really think I'm okay with this?"

The other man stood and walked up beside him. "Hey, Joe, take the day off. Go home. In fact, take the week off. Things will be fine around here. Clear your head and wait this thing out. All will be fine if you just be patient."

He nodded. "Okay, that might be best. I'm really worked up right now."

"Head out now, Joe," Reed said. "I'll let your team know."

He nodded again and walked out without another word. The man walked over and shut the door and turned back to Reed. "You want to make the call or me?"

"Jesus," Reed stated. "Really? Are we sure he won't stand strong?"

"You heard him. If the police bring him in, we're all going down. We need to take care of him. His stock will fall to his wife and we will advise that she sell. She'll be fine, she'll have millions."

Reed picked up his phone and dialed the number he had been given. A voice mail picked up. "This is Dr. Smith's office, please leave a message."

"Hello, Dr. Smith, I have another name for you. Dr. Joseph Reingold. He should be at home for the next week or so." And he hung up.

"Amazing," the other man replied. "Just like that."

"Just like that," Reed Anderson said, more softly than previously.

Back at the station, we regrouped in the Royals Room. Huston and Halterman had remained at the scene of the bunny ear murder until Dr. Bitty was done to try to gain any information they could from her. Upon discussion, we all agreed they would have the best chance of a successful exchange. Franky and I went by the hospital. To our surprise, Alan was not there. He had told the nurse on duty that he had to run to work to finalize some things in his absence. Made sense to us and it was actually good. We got some time alone with Elise and the doctors. We learned there had been no change. The brief periods of consciousness continued, but nothing coherent other than a name. To my surprise, she had said "Tommy" during the night in front of the nurse.

I started the discussion in front of the group. "Okay, are we saying it was simply a coincidence that Thompson was murdered?"

"Well," Huston replied, "he doesn't fit with the others. He was lower on the executive team, and he didn't have the stock option deferral. He took his bonus last year as normal."

"Wait," I replied, "remember, the financial investigator found his name late because his total was less and he didn't have to report it to the SEC. He also took the deferred bonus. He was part of it..." I paused then added, "Let's pretend that although he's involved with the stock plan, his murder is not related and was just random. He left Dr. G's party late at night after drinking. Let's say he stopped somewhere, even the side of the road. He becomes an easy target for a first-time killer. He is grabbed, thrown in a trunk, and then driven around. Eventually, the killer gets his courage up, drives to a somewhat remote place, opens his trunk, and kills him right there."

"It's possible," Franky said. "But what are the odds someone who works for this company is killed at the same time as these other killings?"

"Wait," I replied. "What if it's *because* of his murder that the other killings happened?"

"What do you mean?" asked Patti.

"What if Julian Stover, the chief financial officer, learned something and was planning to go to the police? What if they used the random murder of their other employee to camouflage Stover's murder? We immediately went to them being related. We're fighting the theory now trying to talk ourselves out of it. What if, because of the first one, they moved on to the second one?"

"So we need to determine what Julian Stover discovered before he was murdered?" Huston said. "I should go spend some more time with Officer Nelson in Finance."

Carter nodded to Huston. "Go." He turned to me. "Let's bring them all in. No more meeting with lawyers at their office. Bring them down here, separate them, let them all see each other, and let's talk through this bonus." Before Karen had grabbed all her stuff and headed down to the second floor, Carter added, "And, Huston, ask Nelson what we should be probing for from these guys when we get them in here. We need questions that will trip them up."

"Do you want to bring in Dr. Grove as well?" Halterman asked.

"He is first on my list, and I don't give a shit if he wants to stay with his wife. My gut tells me he's the reason she's in the hospital in the first place."

My gut was telling me the same thing, but I did not vocalize it. "Let's make some calls, Franky. Let's start with the lawyers and go from there."

●   ●   ●   ●   ●

"Now hold on, Detective," stated Alan Grove's personal lawyer, who was not Staci Lambda which in turn pleased me. "The fact that he legally deferred his bonus and legally purchased additional stock is no reason to be throwing out accusations. My client's wife is in the hospital fighting for her life and you want to accuse him of putting her there."

"I don't want to accuse him. I *am* accusing him," I replied. "And all I need your client to do is explain why he chose the deferred bonus of which he stands to make more than twenty million dollars even at the reduced stock price today. And while he's at it, why not explain why he added another six million on top of that?" I was on a roll. "Finally, why the hell did he just transfer two-hundred fifty thousand dollars to offshore accounts that are untraceable? If he would just answer those questions, maybe I wouldn't be so quick to accuse him of trying to kill his wife, who was trying to bring evidence against him."

The lawyer leaned over and whispered in Alan's ear after which Alan whispered back. The attorney turned back to me and Franky. "Are you bringing charges against my client, Detectives?"

I glanced to Franky and then to the one-way mirror where Carter and the team sat watching. The phone on the table rang and I picked it up. "Yeah. Yeah. Okay." I hung up the phone. "To answer your question, if you refuse to answer our questions now, we'll bring you up on charges of conspiracy to commit murder. If you answer our questions now, and no additional evidence is obtained linking you to any of the crimes in question, then we will release you at that time, but ask you to submit your passport."

Again the attorney leaned over and whispered to Dr. Grove. Alan returned the whisper. His lawyer stared back toward Alan and pressed his lips together. Alan stared back at him and replied for all to hear. "Say it, David."

The lawyer turned back to me. "My client wishes to say, and I quote, 'Fuck You, Tommy. Arrest me then.'"

He called my bluff, but it meant I had to call his. "Gladly, Dr. Grove. I guess you won't be spending much more time at the hospital."

Alan put both his hands on the desk and I saw a look in his eyes I had never seen before. It was the look of defiance. It was the look of a killer. "I'll be out before the afternoon is over, Tommy, and when my wife wakes up, we are going to ensure you never work in Chicago again, if it takes every goddamn penny I have."

"Well, after all this shit you've pulled, you have a lot of pennies to spend. We'll see if you get to spend them or not." I paused and my tone softened. "I just don't get it," I said, changing my direction. "Stover didn't take the deferral. Why the hell did you guys have him killed?"

"Don't answer that," spouted David, the name I heard for his attorney.

"I'll be glad to answer it. Julian was our CFO and was killed in an auto accident. Although certain things were allowed legally, he wanted to keep his position clean. He didn't participate in any stock plans or trading activity around Abbunex. That's because we are above reproach." He stopped talking and sat back, proud of what he had said.

I was just glad I had him talking. I wasn't going to let this stop now. "Above reproach, huh. Then why are you wanting to be arrested rather than help us find whoever tried to murder your wife and did murder your CFO?"

"Julian is the one who taught us about the deferred option program. He just couldn't do it but he wouldn't prevent us from doing it."

"What?" I asked. "He knew about it?"

"It was public information, Tommy. Everyone knew about it who wanted to."

"Then why kill him?"

"Jesus!" exclaimed Alan.

"We're done, Detective. Do you intend to arrest my client or not?" Attorney David now stood.

"Goddamn it, Alan. Don't you want to find the person who hurt your wife? What if it's someone you work with? Someone at Abbunex called these shots. Stover, Thompson, your wife." I did not want to tell him that we already knew Thompson may not be connected. "How many more have to die? Or, if you're not involved, are you then next on the list?"

Somewhere in that statement I got him. I don't know if it was when I said it could be someone he worked with or he might be next on the list, but he changed. I saw it in his look. "What do you mean, someone I work with?"

"I said that's it," David replied. "You can process him now. We'll submit his passport and post bail immediately. Let's move quickly as my client would like to return to the hospital to be with his wife. Your evidence is all circumstantial and no judge is going to keep my client here."

I knew the attorney was correct. We had enough to build a weak case. The $250 thousand was key. If he could not define where that money went, we could probably convict him. The team had already talked about options. This questioning had gone almost exactly as scripted. We had two other executives already at the station, but I was not ready to let Alan go. He was starting to appear connected to our conversation. "Alan, let's say I believe you and your wife aren't involved. Then someone at your work tried to have Elise killed. You have to see that."

He was standing in the doorway and I had my cuffs out but I had not placed them on him. He glanced toward his lawyer and his lawyer did not stop him from speaking.

"I don't believe you, Tommy. Nobody at Abbunex would have done that."

"Alan," I replied, "this is not a hypothesis or theory. There's no way your wife's abduction, torture, and attempted murder did not originate from your work. I think they're sending a message to you to keep your mouth shut." I did not necessarily believe that, but as I said it, I did accept it could be true.

"Not possible, Tommy." He ended it there, turned from me, placed his hands behind his back, and did not speak again.

As we escorted Dr. Grove out in handcuffs, we would take him in front of the two rooms the others were waiting in. We had Joseph Reingold and Reed Anderson at the station now. Supposedly Darryn Hermann, the CEO, was on his way.

As Grove went by the window in handcuffs in front of Joseph Reingold, I saw a look of pure terror across my next suspect's face. I knew immediately, Reingold had something to hide.

"Hey, wait," Alan said. "What is Joe doing here?"

"We are questioning most of the executive team. You have a problem with that, Alan?"

"No, but I want to talk to him," he said flatly.

"No can do, *compadre*." I'm not sure why I went Spanish, but it did sound cool.

"Seriously, it's about work." Alan tried to turn and go to the conference room but with his hands in cuffs, he was easily stopped, though he put up a noticeable fight. It was clearly noticeable to Joseph Reingold. "Damn it, Tommy, five minutes. That's all I need."

"You want to tell him, or do you want me to?" I said to Attorney David.

"You can't talk to him, Alan, but I can. What do you need me to say?"

After a brief exchange of whispered remarks, I continued with Dr. Grove, and Attorney David went into the Bulls Room with Joe Reingold. Carter saw the exchange. Speaking to Franky, "I think we just lost Reingold."

Joseph Reingold had his own lawyer. Lawyer David spoke to him briefly and then to Reingold directly. The conversation was short and to the point. The men shook hands and Lawyer David left.

As Dr. Grove was printed and photographed, I headed back to the interrogation rooms. He was going through the full booking, which would take about an hour. After that, I suspected he would be walking out of the station in no more than two. I poked my head into the Bulls Room. "Dr. Reingold, will you come with me please?"

His attorney stood and held up his hand. "I have instructed my client to not answer any questions. If you wish to Mirandize and arrest him, please inform me of the charges. At this point, we feel there's nothing he can provide that will help in your case because he doesn't know anything."

"Pardon me for saying so, Mr..." I started, holding onto the last word hoping to get a name this time.

"King. Nathan King. I'll be representing Dr. Reingold."

I stepped into the room and shook his hand. "Well, Mr. King, I would like to be the judge as to what is or is not valuable to this case. Your client is not a suspect. We're trying to understand why two individuals at Abbunex, one of whom reported to your client professionally, and the wife of another executive, have been targeted for murder. Two are dead and one hangs on by a thread. Doesn't your client wish to help?"

"As I stated," King replied, "my client cannot help you. He does not have any information about these murders. He simply wishes to be left alone."

I turned to Reingold. "You realize that by refusing to answer any questions, plus the bonus deferral you participated in, you're looking very guilty for the murders of Julian Stover and Randy Thompson. Not to mention the attempted murder of Dr. Elise Gerstenberger."

It was as if I had turned on a hose. Beads of sweat began to roll down Reingold's face. I saw it, my team standing outside the door saw it, and his lawyer, Mr. Nathan King, saw it.

"I said no questions, Detective O'Malley."

"That was not a question," I replied.

King thought about what I said, and then smiled. "If you're not going to detain my client, then we'll be going."

I opened my arms to them to bid passage by me and out the door. "One request, don't leave town without calling us first."

"It's okay, I'm not—" started Reingold before he was cut off by Mr. King.

The lawyer took over the response. "There's no reason we can't leave town, as my client has done nothing wrong."

"Again, gentlemen, just a professional request," I replied smiling.

King returned my smile. "At this time my client has no planned travel. However, I want to stress, we are under no obligation to inform you should that change."

This guy reminded me of Staci Lambda. She also had been hired by Abbunex Labs. I was sure when Darryn Hermann arrived, Ms. Lambda would be by his side. She almost got Jamal Jackson killed last spring. Now I would be dealing with her again. As fate would have it, however, Ms. Lambda never showed nor did her client. She did have the courtesy to message ahead and inform us she would not be showing. There was nothing her client could provide, and we should focus on finding the killer instead of harassing the victims' coworkers.

"We didn't accomplish much in there, did we?" asked Halterman.

"I disagree," I replied. "We stirred the soup. We arrested Grove. Although he didn't seem to care, I believe he really did. Everyone saw Reingold start to melt. He's our window into whatever is going on. Let's let him get home and then pay him a visit tonight to see if he will talk then. If we can get him to waive his rights, he might bring down this whole thing."

Franky added, "What about Hermann, Anderson, and Child? They all ducked the questioning. How do you want to handle it?"

"I think we have to go to each of their houses and if they won't talk to us there, we have to obtain a subpoena to compel them to come in."

"Wait a minute," stated Carter. "These guys are all lawyered up. We've been told they're refusing to help."

"None of them want to go to jail. We have more than enough with the deferred bonuses to bring them in for questioning. We have to keep stirring the pot."

Just then a loud bang was heard outside the windows from the street. "What the hell was that?" asked Halterman.

"Gunshot," I replied. We ran to the outside window overlooking the street below from the fourth floor. "There," I said pointing. "That car crashed into the parking meter—where the people are gathering."

"Get down there, O'Malley," stated Carter. "See what the hell is going on."

Patti and I got to the accident in fewer than five minutes. Because it was in front of the police station, there were numerous police already on the scene. I saw someone I recognized immediately. "Pete, is that you?"

"Hey, Tommy. You hear the shot?"

Officer Pete Schram was a good cop. We ran into each other on several cases. He had always been in downtown Chicago, and it didn't appear he would ever leave. He was kind of like the police officer version of me. I liked the guy, but I didn't really know him. "Yeah, Pete," I stated. "We heard the shot. What happened?"

"Looks like a sniper. The guy was dead on impact. Right between the eyes."

"Who is he?" I asked.

"His wallet says the last name is Reingold. Joseph, I believe."

21 I hated cases that could not be solved. There were not many of them, but every once in a while one crossed our desks. Franky and I had cleared more cases than any other team in Chicago. We had opened and closed more cold cases as well. Actually, the department did not keep those stats, but if they did, everyone would know what we had accomplished. I wasn't stupid. I could see the writing on the wall. These guys had more money than they could ever spend, and I was sure they were breaking the law to get more. What the hell would motivate someone who had everything to get even more, I thought to myself. How the hell did they know Reingold was going to cave so quickly? The only one who really saw him was Dr. Alan Grove.

•   •   •   •   •

"What the hell would motivate these guys to murder?" I asked Patti as we sipped our wine. Yes, wine. I know what you're thinking. I was only drinking wine with the hopes of pleasing Patricia Halterman such that she would allow me to repeat some of our recent encounters. And guess what, you're right. I don't like wine but I drink it when needed, and right now, it was needed.

"They already had more money than they could ever spend," she answered and then paused. "I don't know," she added. "Before, I would always say money, but it seems like they would have cancelled whatever was going on before murdering someone if it was just about money."

I looked at her. "Let's keep going with that…"

She appeared surprised at my interested response. "Come on, Tommy, let's just have a nice dinner. We can talk about this tomorrow."

"No, seriously, I like what you said. All this time we've been acting like the motive was money. Maybe that was the motive originally, but what could have changed to take that motive off the table and up the stakes so much?"

"They've already shown they don't care about family. Thompson was a family man, a coach to other boys for that matter. Stover had a family, and you know what happened to Elise." She stopped. "Have you ever considered that Elise was involved?"

I glanced at her then looked down. "Yes, and I still believe it."

"So you think she was playing you?"

"From the start," I replied.

"Why?" Patti asked.

"Why was she playing me or why is she involved?"

"Both, but mostly why would she play you? Why invite you to the party in the first place? Why share the concerns about her husband? Why any of it?"

"I don't know," I answered. "To throw suspicion off her maybe."

"That makes sense, but by doing so, she directly threw suspicion on her husband."

We looked at each other. "What is the oldest reason in the book?"

She looked right at him and her eyes lit up. "He was having an..."

"Affair," we both said at the same time.

"So," I continued, "let's walk through this. Doc G finds out her beloved husband is having an affair. The money is not important to her because she's already a millionaire on her own."

"Right," Patti said. "All along we thought money was the driving force. What if it's just about a cheating husband?"

"Then why all the killing?" Half the executive team is dead. Doc G may be a lot of things, but she's a doctor first. She's not going to kill anyone."

"Exactly," Patti replied. "Things started to go south. She wanted to set up her husband, but there was something illegal at Abbunex. Because of her, this whole thing was going to blow up so they got rid of her, not because of her reason for being involved, but theirs."

"Jesus," I stated. "Every time we plug one hole with an idea, another opens up. We need the one that ties it all together. Did she devise this plan to get back at a cheating husband or was it about money? Why did Stover have to be killed and what the hell was Reingold hiding? Too many questions without answers."

"Let's talk to Stover's wife again," stated Patti.

"Why?" I asked.

"Because nobody knows why he was killed. He didn't have the deferred bonus; in fact, he suggested it to the others. I would be hard-pressed to believe he would have found some evidence against the deferred plan if he was the one who suggested it."

"Fair enough. Do you want to finish dinner first?" I asked.

"Absolutely. Then I want to go to bed and continue where we left off last night. Then tomorrow morning, I want to talk to Wilma Stover."

"Oh," I replied, "that sounds like a good plan."

"Just a *good* plan?" she questioned.

I smiled. "I'm open to a reevaluation later, pending your effort."

"That sounds like a dare, but since I know you're only drinking wine for me, I accept the challenge."

I don't remember much that scares me, but suddenly, I was freaking terrified.

✦   ✦   ✦   ✦   ✦

The next morning I called Franky and told him where Patti and I were headed. I asked him to relay our theories to Carter and pass on our morning schedule. He seemed intrigued by our discussion but not overly confident. On a hunch, I asked Franky to pull all the cell phone records for everyone involved as well as get a court order for the records from each of their office phones. Some companies pooled their phones into a single number, but with Abbunex being so large and these being the executives, I was certain when they dialed out, they wanted the caller ID to identify their individual office. I also wanted records that included spouses and kids. I wanted to know who was talking to who. These guys were rich, but they were not crime smart. They would have used their own cell phones or office phones for setting up these calls, or affairs, or anything else they were doing. They would not see things as a threat. One thing I always liked about *The Sopranos*—even though they had cell phones and burner phones, Tony Soprano always used a pay phone for critical calls. What a great show.

Patti had pulled the address and set up directions. I realized when she plugged in the address, we had never been to their house before. We had interviewed Wilma and her son, Russell Stover (I just had to say it again) at the scene of the accident. They made a positive ID at the scene and that was it. This interview was long overdue. We had a dead body that we had thrown into the mix with others and never performed our due diligence. I was absolutely losing my touch.

We arrived at their Barrington, Illinois, residence outside Chicago, and like the others, it was beautiful. Not quite as extensive as the Grove's, but well out of my price range. We had called on the way to make sure Wilma was home. She was.

She greeted us in sweats and a T-shirt. Very down-to-earth for what I would have expected.

"Please come in, Detectives. Excuse my house. I just haven't had the energy to do anything."

Her voice was soft and gentle. There was still pain there, but it was greatly reduced or filtered from when we had first met at the scene of her husband's death. "Mrs. Stover..."

She raised her hand. "Please, call me Wilma. Everyone does. And let's go sit at the table. I just heated up a pot of tea."

"Wilma," I continued, "if it's all right, we're trying to do some additional background on your husband, trying to determine who might have wanted to kill him. Would you be able to answer some questions?"

"I can try," she said softly. She poured some hot water into her cup and added an Earl Grey tea bag. "What would you like to know?"

"Please understand," I started. "Some of my questions may seem personal, but we need to cover every angle." She nodded but did not speak so I continued. "Did your husband ever have any concerns about his job or the company?"

She thought a minute. "Not that he ever said to me. I mean, sometimes he would come home clearly stressed from his day, but no more than any other job. He was the chief financial officer, so in some ways he said he was the policeman of the company finances. I can tell you, he would never bend the rules when it came to financials. He always said it would eventually come out. Everyone always followed the money."

I smiled. "We use that motto as well." I was trying to show support for her comments and in truth, the picture I had of Julian Stover was exactly as she had described him. "So, if there were no issues at work, can I ask if there were any issues at home?"

Instantly her facial expression changed. Usually the spouse of the deceased does not want to damage their spouse's memory by sharing negative comments. I instantly thought something was there and was extremely interested in what she would say.

"No, no problems at home. We were extremely happy. He was the model husband."

Model husband, I thought. Who the hell says that? And what about the instant look of concern on her face? That was bullshit. "Wilma, I sense in your expression you're not telling me everything. Are you sure there's nothing you can say? It may help us find…"

Her voice was stronger and more agitated. "No, Detective. There's nothing more to say."

Patti rested her hand on Wilma's as it laid across the table. She turned to me. "Tommy, will you run out to the car and get my pad and paper?"

I swung my eyes from Wilma to my partner. "What the…" I paused, understanding her direction. "Yes, I'll run out to the car for you."

"Thank you, Tommy," she said softly. Turning back to Wilma, I heard them talking as I exited but I could not tell what was said. The walk to the door and then the car was probably thirty yards in total. It took me twenty minutes.

When I arrived back, without any pad and paper, mind you, the two women were laughing and drinking tea. I walked in and they both turned and immediately laughed at me. I turned around and looked behind me because there must have been something funny going on that I hadn't seen. I wanted to check my fly but it was too obvious to do so then. What the hell was going on? Wilma's eyes were red. She had been crying. I wasn't sure what just took place, but I was sure of one thing—my partner was one hell of an interviewer.

"Come on over here, Tommy," stated Patti, motioning her hand at the same time. "Wilma and I had a nice talk. Would you like some tea?"

I was still not sure what the hell was going on because both women were still smiling, almost laughing. "Can I ask what you two talked about?"

"Most of it was about you, boo-boo," Patti said.

Oh shit, I thought. What the hell did she say? Wilma poured me some tea even though I never actually asked for any and giggled softly as she did it. "Will you sing me the 'Do You Want to Kiss My Nose' song?"

My eyes shot like daggers toward my partner as both women broke into laughter again. The "Do You Want to Kiss My Nose" song is nothing that will ever be discussed in this book. It happened alone in a bedroom between two people and was to remain private. End of discussion. "No," I replied, still glaring at Patti. "That would not be appropriate for this discussion." I paused and turned back to Wilma. "Now, if it's all right, I do have a few more questions…"—I paused then added—"about the case."

"Oh, Tommy," Patti said smiling and moving her hand to rest on my arm. "The interview is over. I may be coming back for a girl's movie night with Wilma, but we can be leaving now."

I glanced to my phone. "It's been twenty minutes. Now you two are going to have a movie night?"

Patti looked back to Wilma and they both smiled. "Girl's movie night. Not just a movie night."

They both stood and walked together still whispering comments back and forth. I had no idea what had just transpired, but I was sure it was not good for me. It might be good for the case, but somehow I was the fall guy.

When we got to the front door, the two women hugged tightly. Patti handed Wilma her card and pointed to the cell phone number she had written on it. "Use that one. I'll always answer if I can."

"Thank you, Patti. I really enjoyed our talk." She turned to me. "And, Tommy, I do *not* want to kiss your nose."

Oh, the two of them just laughed and laughed. My new rule, which I obviously have to spell out to my partner, is, "what happens in the bedroom, stays in the bedroom."

We got in the car and my tightly pressed lips told the story. Patti smiled. "Oh, don't get your panties in a ruffle. I had to build some rapport. I talked about our relationship, and then she opened up about hers. Contrary to her initial response to your question, their marriage was not perfect."

Instantly my previous annoyance was lessened, but I was going to revisit the breach of privacy she exhibited in her rapport-building exercise. "What was not perfect?"

"He had stopped showing interest in her in the bedroom. She didn't think he was having an affair, but she was lonely."

I knew where this was going. "Are you saying *Wilma* was having an affair?"

"She wouldn't tell me with who, but she was. They had been seeing each other for over a year."

"Did she tell you anything about the man?"

Patti nodded. "Nothing specific. She did say he wasn't happy at home either. He was married as well and his wife was never home."

"Did she say if this man thought his wife was having an affair too?"

"She didn't say, but I'm not sure she would have known." Patti paused a minute. "I think she was willing to leave her husband for this man."

"The questions are, who was he and was he willing to leave his wife?"

"She talked about the things they did—the romantic walks, the calls throughout the day, the stuff newlyweds do. That's how she described it."

"Who do you think it was?" I asked.

Patti didn't answer at first, but asked another question that told me where her mind was. "Do you know how Doc G's marriage was with Alan?"

I shook my head as I entered the tollway. "I always assumed it was good, but what goes on behind closed doors, nobody knows." I swung my head to her briefly. "Do you think it was Alan?"

"I asked her directly. Although her immediate reaction was questionable, all I can confirm is that it was inconclusive. She wouldn't admit it."

"But did she deny it?" I asked.

"Only by saying she wouldn't say as he's still married. She said, and I believe her, that she would not be a home-wrecker. She feels very guilty about the affair, but until he's divorced, their relationship is on hold."

"Interesting."

"What is interesting?" Patti asked.

"Well, you know I have Franky pulling all the phone records. Assuming this man would prefer the relationship to continue, he would have called her recently. Further, they should have a pretty clean paper trail of calls. She told you they called each other throughout the day, so he should be easy to identify."

"That was my thought exactly," Patti said. "How long do you think it'll take to get the records?"

"That all depends on your old boyfriend, Craig Swanson," I answered, smiling. I brought up their one date whenever I could.

"First off, please don't call him Craig. The name just doesn't fit."

"Agreed," I stated. "That all depends on your old boyfriend, Swanny."

She actually flipped me off. "Sometimes I wonder what might be different if I pursued that relationship further," she said flippantly.

"And miss out on all of this?" I motioned my hand across the front of my body as if displaying it as a model.

She smiled. "Yeah, that would be a loss that would tear me apart." There was a brief pause and we both smiled. Then she continued, "Back to my question. How long will Swanny take to pull them?"

"He probably has some of them done already. There were a lot of names but it's a simple process. Getting the authorization will take longer. If I was there, we could cut through some of that red tape with two dollars at the vending machine."

Patti turned toward me. "You know you're a loser, right?"

"Not the word I would have chosen, but yes, I know."

We arrived at the station about thirty minutes later. Franky had requested all the phone and text logs. Carter had approved the order but due to the nature of the suspects, it required court approval. That could take days. However, with the proper influence, we could run them now, review them, but not use them until the order was approved. I was going all out on this one. There was a White Hen Pantry across the street. They had king-sized Clark Bars on their shelf. I had only used this method once in the past, and it paid off. I walked into the downstairs lab alone, the way I wanted it to be.

"Jesus, O'Malley, you got a lot of nerve coming in here," Swanny stated, the anger in his voice clear.

I was caught completely off guard so my planned entrance discussion was thrown out the window. "What?" *Yeah, that was smooth.*

"First you steal my girlfriend, and now I hear you reported to Internal Affairs that I take bribes to gain information before it's approved."

"What? I didn't..." Then I saw his face.

"Got ya, you asshole. How are you doing with my sloppy seconds?"

"I'll tell her you said that," I replied.

"Oh, I wouldn't do that. You still need me, and to be honest, I don't need you."

I reached in my pocket and pulled out the king-sized Clark Bar. "Are you sure you don't need me, Swanny?"

"Where did you get that?" Swanny asked. "I thought they stopped making them in that size."

"You are that important to me, Swanny."

Craig Swanson was easily three hundred pounds. He had gone on several diets over the last two years, but in the end, he just was what he was. He loved life, he loved food, but most of all, he loved the thirty-third most popular candy bar in the United States, the Clark Bar. And I made sure I always had some available. I even had them stocked in the vending machines on our floor. I pushed White Hen to keep them on their shelves, and at times, I even ordered directly from Boyer, the candy company nobody has heard of that bought the patent to the bar in 2018.

"Yeah, I can see that," he replied. "What do you need, Tommy?" he asked while holding out his hand for the candy bar.

"I need those phone records Franky asked for."

"You mean the ones we're waiting for court approval to get? You mean the ones I was specifically told by the lieutenant not to run until we had said approval? You mean the ones the captain actually called to verify I wasn't running them without approval?"

"Yes, I suspect those are the same ones," I replied.

"Good, because I would hate to give you the wrong ones."

I smiled broadly. "You mean you have them? I only want to review them. We won't use them for anything..."

Swanny raised his hand. "You know, it just dawned on me that information like this, so highly valuable and restricted by so many upper-level individuals, probably has a higher cost than one measly Clark Bar."

"King-sized Clark Bar," I added.

"Yes, than one measly king-sized Clark Bar."

I reached in my packet and pulled out a second king-sized bar. He took it without comment. "Now are we good?" I asked.

He smiled. "I appreciate the gesture, but I need something more that doesn't involve candy bars, unless you have another one in your pocket, that is."

"Quit circling the airport, Swanny. Land the plane. What do you want?"

"I need your girlfriend to go to my family reunion with me as my date."

If I had listed out a hundred things I thought he would say, that would not have been one of them. "You what?"

"I need Patti to go to my family reunion. They all think I'm desperate for a girl. I need to bring someone home. Strictly platonic, of course."

"Uh huh," I interjected.

"Will you talk to her about it?"

"Do you have the phone records?" I asked.

"I have some of them," he replied. "The rest will have to wait until the court order comes through. I'm serious, the brass are all over this one."

"Okay," I replied. "I'll ask her."

"Yes!" he replied like a kid, pumping his fist in the process. "You don't know how big this will be in my family. You don't care if we hug and maybe kiss a little, do you?"

"Excuse me?"

"Never mind. We'll just wait and see what happens naturally—if you know what I'm sayin'?"

Jesus, he used one of my lines. That fucker. "What phone records do you have?"

He walked over to his desk and pulled a file. "As you know, I keep copies of everything. These were requested months ago. I recognized one of the names."

"What do you mean, requested months ago?" I asked.

"The case at the start of last month. Doc G requested them as part of her investigation. You know. Your name was on the request as well. I was disappointed you didn't come down here and try a Clark Bar trick to speed up the process. I held the file an extra two or three days waiting. Finally, I just gave it to her when she stopped by."

"Oh, that's right," I said. "I forgot. What name did you recognize?"

"Wilma Stover. Other than the Flintstones, you just don't see the name *Wilma* anywhere anymore." He paused and handed me the file. "Since this is from the other case, there's no issue with me handing it over to you."

"Right," I replied. "And also no reason I need to bargain with my girlfriend for your family reunion."

He smiled. "That could be correct, from a certain point of view."

"A certain point of view," I replied questionably. "Remind me, what names did you run from before?"

"For starters, with all the hoopla around these numbers, I went ahead and ran them to current—that could get me in a little trouble, but I thought it would save some time. I'm sure this will all be approved eventually. She wanted Wilma and Julian Stover, her husband Alan Grove, which I thought was weird, and this office number at Abbunex Labs." He pointed to a number on the page with a prefix from North Chicago. "There they all are, as of yesterday."

"Thanks, Swanny, I appreciate it."

"No, Tommy, thank *you*, if you know what I'm sayin'?"

"Stop using my line, Swanny."

22

I wanted to tell everyone the news, but my anxiety on what the hell Elise was doing exceeded a potential break in the case. My gut was telling me one thing and one thing only—Alan Grove was having an affair and his wife, Dr. Elise Gerstenberger, found out about it. I went straight to my desk and began tearing through the reports. I started with the text messages Elise would have seen from approximately two months ago. It didn't take long to confirm my fears.

Alan: *I want to see you tonight. Elise is downtown on a call.*

Wilma: *I want to see you too. Julian said he was going out after work.*

Alan: *I know. I set it up with a group from the executive team. I will leave early.*

Wilma: *Same place?*

Alan: *Yes, 6:30. Heart emoji.*

I leaned back in my chair. So Dr. Alan Grove and Wilma Stover were having an affair. What does that mean? What would Elise have done when she found out? Why did Elise devise the elaborate scheme with me at her party? Why was she targeted for murder?

"What's up, partner? Did you get the call logs?"

I nearly jumped from my seat when Patti came up behind me. "Ah, yes, I got some of them."

"Great, do they show anything?" she asked.

I motioned for her to whisper. "Two things. Yes, they confirm something very pertinent to our case. Wilma Stover and Dr. Alan Grove were definitely having an affair."

"Interesting," she replied. "And second?"

"You need to go on a date to a family reunion with Swanny." I said it quickly like ripping off a Band-Aid.

"Okay," she replied smiling. "I would like that."

"What?"

"I'll give Swanny a call on his personal cell so we can set it up."

I did not like how she could always say things to get under my skin. She should have reacted like a normal person. She should have been pissed that I bargained with her personal life to get information. Instead, it was just fucking fine. Well, it was just fucking fine with me too then. The hell it was.

"What's our next move?" she asked, completely changing the subject.

"Well, I don't want to bring everyone in the loop yet. I want to find out what the hell Doc G is involved with. I want to talk to her husband about the affair and I really need her to wake up."

"I called the hospital. She has taken a turn for the worse. She has had no periods of consciousness for almost twelve hours and her vitals are falling."

"Maybe we need another run at Filini as well."

She nodded. "Let's go to the hospital, check with the doctor and see if Dr. Grove is there. Then, see if you can connect with Marco again."

"Sounds good to me. Let me tell Franky where we're going. He doesn't need to know about the phone records yet. Let's let the delay with the court approval delay that conversation."

• • • • •

At the hospital, we ran into the doctor before making it to the room. I still did not like the pompous ass. However, it gave us the opportunity to probe deeper than Patti had previously, and to our displeasure, the news was worse, not better. Elise's body was shutting down. They had put her in an induced coma to combat the degradation and give her body time to heal, but the outlook was clearly worse today than yesterday. The doctor did say Alan had been there all morning. It was now bordering on lunchtime, so Patti had the idea to talk to Alan over lunch. I liked it for two reasons. First, it would be harder for him to simply leave if we had food present; and two, I was hungry.

We entered the room and his eyes met mine. We had not spoken since we had arrested him. The new information did not change any of my feelings on his guilt, but I did need him to answer some questions. I needed him to be willing to talk to me. I was not sure if lunch would be that reason, but it was worth a shot.

"I'm sure you're here to check on Elise. Well, she's worse. Much worse. She's not waking up at all and they've put her in a chemically-induced coma." I could hear the tone of his voice change slightly showing he was getting choked up.

"We know, Alan," I said softly. "We ran into the doctor before we got to the room. He gave us an update."

"Then you know there's nothing you can do, and I'm not about to..."

"Hang on, Alan, we are not here to interrogate you. We do have some information that we think you'll want to hear, but if you don't, then we can go."

"Information on what?" he asked.

"Your wife," I replied. That caught his attention. "Have you eaten?"

He shrugged negatively.

"Then let me buy you some lunch and we can talk." It seemed funny, me offering to buy him lunch when he and his wife made millions.

"I'm sure I should call my lawyer, but right now, I don't even care." His voice had no enthusiasm, no hope.

We headed out and as we passed the nurses' station, he had a brief word with the nurse which I assume was him telling her where he would be. We then proceeded to the elevator and back down to the main floor cafeteria. The three of us went through the line, which was more like a deli than a traditional cafeteria. I was actually impressed with the layout. It had been a few months since I had come to this place to eat, and the improvements were considerable.

We filled our plates and found a table off to the side. After a few bites and Patti leaving and returning with some salad dressing, I dove in. "What can you tell me about Wilma Stover?"

His eyes turned directly to me. I could see he was thinking about his answer. I didn't care. I let him think in silence. "She's Julian's wife."

"Do you know her well?" I asked.

He leaned back from his food and stared directly at me. "Why do I think you already know the answer to that question?"

"Would it surprise you to know that I found out today that Elise also knows the answer to that question, and has known that answer for several months?"

His eyes dropped. He lowered his head into his hands and rested on the table. He was not crying. He was simply giving up. He slowly lifted his head. "I'm so stupid. I should have just told her. I should have had enough guts to face her."

"Now for the tough question, Alan." I leaned slightly closer. "What do you think she would have done with that information? Obviously she never told you."

"No, she never told me," he said softly. "She probably hired a private investigator to follow me to compile evidence to ensure a positive outcome for her in the divorce."

Interesting he went straight to the "what's in it for her" position. "I could see that," I replied. "But would any of this mess that Abbunex is in now be her doing as a way to get back at you?"

"What mess?" he asked. "The murders? I can tell you for sure, she is not capable of murder."

"What about the financial mess?" Patti asked.

"There isn't one without the other. These murders have thrown the senior leadership in question. That will drive the stock down. When the new leaders are assigned, it'll recover quickly. It's actually a good time to buy the stock, but you did not hear that from me."

"We are not interested in any stock tips, Alan," I stated. "We only want to know what's going on at Abbunex. There's something with the stock deferral. There's something with your additional purchases of stock. I just need to..." His eyes came up right when I said that, but he didn't speak. "What did you just remember?"

He shrugged his shoulders. "It's probably nothing, but if she found out months ago about my affair, that's right at the same time she convinced me to buy another six million or so in stock."

"Is that out of character for her?" Patti asked.

"Out of character?" Alan repeated. "She never had any comments on our retirement or stock portfolio. In our entire marriage, it's the only time she ever said anything, much less pushed for a large purchase." He smiled and his voice trailed off slightly. "So yes, I would say it was out of character."

"Why do you think she did it?" I asked.

"I don't know," he replied. "We had had the executive team over for a party and I suppose she heard us talking about the projected stock activity following the upcoming results. I know she had talked to Darryn about it at some level as well, or at least she mentioned how he thought it was a good idea."

"Do you mean Darryn Hermann, your CEO?"

"Yes, I asked him about it, and he said she had asked him in passing when we were having hors d'oeuvres that night. He gave his blessing and said just to make sure it was reported. I let Julian know and we did the purchase."

"Was it a good purchase?" I asked. "Are you going to make money?"

He nodded. "My best ever. Even with the drop in the stock price, it's up over one hundred percent. We will more than double our investment."

"You do realize that fact alone makes you our prime suspect. You were having an affair with a woman whose husband is now dead. You have significant wealth so a divorce could be messy. You get rid of your mistress's husband and your wife, and now both issues are cleaned up. Tell me how you are *not* guilty."

"I can only tell you that I loved my wife and would never hurt her. The main reason I couldn't tell her about my affair was I didn't want to hurt her. I could never have had a hand in what happened to her. Never."

"So, who do you think did?" I asked flatly.

"Some strange serial killer. That's all that makes sense."

"Serial killers don't target points of employment, Alan, but I like your imagination." I motioned to his food. "Take your plate back up to your wife and be with her. She needs you now."

He stood and acted like he was about to shake my hand and then recanted. As he walked away, I asked one more question. "Hey, Alan, are you still seeing Wilma?"

He stopped and turned back. "No, she cut it off two days ago." He turned and walked out of the cafeteria.

●　　●　　●　　●　　●

"What are you doing to me?" the woman screamed.

"I-I-I just want tuh-tuh-tuh-talk to you," the man said.

"Stay away from me!" she screamed. "*Help*!"

"Nuh-nuh-nuh-nuhbody ca-ca-can hear you, Mindy," the man replied. He walked up to the table where she was tied down and ran his finger across her naked body. "So-so-so-soft. Like a buh-buh-buh-bunny."

"Don't touch me," she replied, her voice softer now as it was coming through tears. "Please..."

He walked over to the counter next to him and picked up a box of cereal, Trix. The rabbit logo displayed large on the front. He took the box of Trix and poured them over her naked body and began to giggle uncontrollably. The woman glanced down and saw he was aroused through his shorts. "What are you doing, you freak? Don't touch me."

His speech suddenly got better. "I am not a freak!" he exclaimed. His tone softened. "I-I-I like you. I thuh-thuh-thuh-think you a-a-are pretty and so-so-soft, like a bunny."

"I am not a bunny," she screamed. "Please, I just want to go home!"

He bent down and ate some of the cereal off her belly. He pressed his shorts against her leg and began to giggle again. He walked over to the counter where the cereal was and pulled his shorts down. "Tuh-tuh-tuh-time to multiply."

"*No!*" she screamed. "*Help!*"

He reached under the cabinet and pulled out a bag. It was dripping with something thick and red, like ketchup.

"What is that?" she exclaimed, her head turned straight to the side watching his every move.

He reached in the bag and pulled out a large dead rabbit. It appeared that its neck had been broken and blood drained slowly from its nose. "Muh-muh-must clean first."

He walked up to the terrified woman holding the rabbit out closer with each step. He started at the feet, and like a sponge cleaning dishes, he wiped every square inch of the woman's body with the rabbit, its blood streaking up and down her body as it passed. She fought and twisted as best she could but the bindings were too tight. He had used cable ties around every limb and throat. Each time she moved, they cut into her skin. She screamed several times and then simply went to a quiet place. She laid still and motionless and the dead rabbit slowly moved into and out of every crevice of her body.

The man walked back over to the counter carrying the dead rabbit sponge with him. Its fur was matted with blood and nearly unrecognizable. He carefully put the rabbit back in the bag and turned back to the woman who had slowly turned her head to the side to watch him. The man was still naked and erect. "The bunny is ready to multiply now," he said in a soft and sinister tone. "Thu-thuh-thuh-thank you."

He walked over to the woman on the table with one hand behind his back. He pulled his hand forward revealing a large butcher's knife. The first stab went right through the heart. The next eighteen went wherever he decided to hit.

23 "What do we have?" asked Patti as we sipped our drinks at Flap Jaws. Carter shrugged. "We have a bunch of shit that doesn't fit together."

"We're starting to find those ties," I added.

"What do you mean?" asked Carter.

"Well, let's take the fact that we know some of the suspects involved. If Doc G and her husband are just random people and not our friends, what would we be considering?"

Patti lifted her red wine and took a drink. "I would want to look closer at Elise."

"Why?" I asked.

"Because when we talked to Dr. Grove in the cafeteria, he didn't even know what the mess at Abbunex was. He acted like there's nothing out of the ordinary there. He went straight to the deaths of two of their senior leaders causing the stock to fall. In fact, he didn't change his tone at all when he talked about his stock deals. Further, without realizing he was implicating her, he brought up that Elise drove the stock purchase."

"My thoughts exactly," I replied. "If we pull the murders off the table—because I do agree with Dr. Grove that Elise could never orchestrate a murder—could she have tried to set him up for some SEC violation somehow?"

"It makes sense, but we still can't find anything illegal," Carter stated.

Franky had been silent since we arrived and now placed his hand on the table. "What if the stock deferral is illegal? Something about what they're doing is going to artificially drive the price up, and what if Elise found out about it? By convincing her husband to buy more stock, she would highlight his involvement."

"Who would she have gotten this information from?" I asked. "Shit! Let me see those phone records we finally got from Swanny after everything was approved." I turned to Carter. "Thanks for making it happen so quickly, Boss."

"No problem," he replied. "What are you thinking?"

I grabbed the file he had brought with him when he left the station to meet us. I flipped through several pages and came to what I was looking for. "Look here. Look at all these calls from this number at Abbunex to Doc G's personal cell phone. They started about three months ago."

"What's the big deal? So her husband started calling her a lot from work. He doesn't have to always use his cell phone," Franky said.

I nodded. "Correct, if these calls were from Dr. Alan Grove's work extension."

Patti nodded. "CEO Darryn Hermann."

"Bingo!" I said.

"Alan even said it was Hermann that Elise talked to about the stock purchase in the first place and recommended it," Patti added.

"Are you saying Doc G and Darryn Hermann are also having an affair?" asked Carter.

"I don't know about a full-blown affair," I replied, "but there's more going on than just acquaintances through her husband's work."

"Tonight, go through those phone records with a fine-tooth comb. Then tomorrow morning, go see Darryn Hermann. If his lawyer says he doesn't need to come in, then arrest him." Carter was not mixing words.

"On what charge?" I asked.

"Conspiracy to piss me off, O'Malley," stated Carter. "You figure it out, but I want him in."

I glanced toward Patti. "I guess I'll be working tonight."

"I can help run through these phone and text logs. There has to be a hundred pages there," she replied.

"I can help too, Tommy," stated Franky. "Do you mind if I bring Vader over?"

I smiled. "What, you miss him already?"

"Maybe I do, asshole. Plus, he's been alone almost every night."

"Oh, your dog has been alone in the evenings. Sounds almost unbearable for him." I finished my McNaughton's and placed the empty glass on the table. "I'll bet he's still sleeping fine cuddled up next to you."

"You got that right, partner," Franky replied proudly.

I turned to Carter. "Thanks for ruining my night, Boss. You can get the tab."

"No problem," he replied proudly, "on both accounts."

• • • • •

We split up the file. I was actually not happy about Franky coming over to help. However, after he arrived, I quickly realized we needed all the help we could get. Karen Huston also came by but only for about an hour as she had another date. She had found herself a fireman who seemed to be heating up her free time just fine. Vader was here as well. He was not helpful. My apartment allowed dogs up to thirty pounds. He exceeded it by about 150. The good news was I believe he lost at least five pounds while here in drool alone.

"Well," I said, looking at the text file for Dr. Darryn Hermann. "It's not one hundred percent clear to me if they were having an affair, but it is clear to me that he was open to one. He continues to reach out to her time and time again. He keeps talking about stock and financial stuff from the party, but it seems fishy, and what party is he talking about?"

"Here you go," Patti said. "It looks like she's replying to another message because the one before this doesn't make sense with the answer."

"What's it say?" I asked.

"Well, the text before it says, *I think it would be a good decision.* The she replies, *Last night was very nice. Thank you.*"

"What was the date and time of that text?" I asked, flipping through my pages.

"Saturday, March 30th, ten a.m."

"So, about two months ago, a handful of weeks after she found out about her husband's affair."

"And look at this," Patti added. "Look at these texts from all these numbers asking about the party. It looks like they had another one of their parties at the house, like the one you attended."

"That's where she did it," interrupted Franky. "That's where she made first contact with Dr. Hermann."

"What do you mean?" I asked.

Franky stood and paced a bit, a trait he always did when he was trying to work through something in his head. "You told me when you described the party that there were hundreds of people. You said they had some jazz band from Kansas City. Let's assume Elise found out about her husband's extramarital affair and used that party to connect to one Darryn Hermann. You've met the guy. You said he was pompous, condescending, and an outright ass."

"I don't think I used those words exactly, but I'm with you. Go on."

"I think we all agree, Elise is beautiful, in great shape, and in short, a real catch. Any guy would be thrilled to have a woman like that express an interest in him."

I looked embarrassingly toward Patti wanting to immediately deny it until she interrupted. "Forget the guys, any woman would feel the same way."

Damn, she was the perfect woman.

Franky nodded and continued to pace. "Let's say Elise approached Dr. Hermann and asks him to join her in some side room. They talk, she flirts, and she talks down about her marriage, which immediately opens up Hermann's eyes to the possibility of her not being happy." He turned to me. "You know how guys' minds work."

"Everyone knows how guys' minds work," Patti added.

Franky smiled and continued, "One thing leads to another, and before you know it, he's giving her vital information about something. Who the hell knows what, but maybe it's something illegal that she can exploit with her husband?"

I interrupted, "You just lost me a little, but keep going, and maybe it will come back together."

Patti raised her hand. "Forget it, Franky."

We both turned to her. "What?" Franky asked.

"I think you're going down the wrong path," she answered. "You're implying she got information from Darryn Hermann. He had no motive. He may not even be that smart. We know Dr. G. She's brilliant. She's a doctor but also owns her own business, the medical clinic up north. She owns the land, pays a lease to herself, and never sets foot in it and brings in millions. If she pulled Darryn Hermann into a meeting, it wasn't because he was going to give her some financial tips. She was telling him what they were going to do."

"Patti," I said, "it's Elise we're talking about."

"And you said before to take our relationship with everyone off the table," she replied. "What is the cliché, 'a woman scorned' or some bullshit?"

"Hell hath no fury like a woman scorned," I stated.

"And you said you were always a good husband or boyfriend. You sure knew that one right off the top of your head."

"I might have stated that a bit too quickly," I replied to Patti's glaring eyes. "Go on though, I like where you taking this."

"If we can all agree that Doc G is a financially-savvy individual, then why can't we assume she came to Dr. Hermann with her plan? She was going to create some evidence against her husband, something that would put him in legal trouble and create a situation where a divorce would be required and most likely be in her favor."

I now stood. "I like it with one exception. Why the hell would Darryn Hermann go along with it? He was friends with Alan. They worked together. There would have to be some loyalty there."

"Wait," stated Franky. "There's something in his texts and phone calls."

We both stared at him as he ruffled through some papers. "What, Franky?"

"I got it," he finally said, although he just threw the papers down instead of reading off something he had just seen. "Nothing."

"What do you mean, nothing?" I asked.

"I mean, nothing. He has no texts to a spouse or friend or anything. He has nothing."

"Our paperwork showed him as married," Patti said.

I nodded and replied, "Yeah, but at the party I went to the other night, he came alone and if I remember right, I read somewhere that he owns a condo downtown also."

"Separated," Patti said.

"Most likely," I replied. "Elise would have known that. She could have flirted her way into making that pompous asshole do anything for her in the hopes of removing Alan from the picture."

"It still doesn't explain the murders," Patti added.

"No, but it gives us a shitload of questions to ask Darryn Hermann tomorrow."

◆   ◆   ◆   ◆   ◆

The next morning came quickly. I texted Carter that we were going to head straight up north and try to catch Dr. Hermann at his home. We were on the tollway by 6:30 AM and entering Barrington before 7:00. Patti, as always, had his address mapped and the only question we would have was whether we would be able to approach the house or would it be gated. To my surprise, we drove right up the driveway.

The house was very nice, but also surprising to me, it was nowhere near the mansion of Dr. Grove and Dr. Gerstenberger. It did have a circle driveway in which I parked my Camaro dead center in front of the door. When I turned the key off, I noticed Patti just staring at me. "What?"

"For whatever reason, you really love this car, don't you?" She paused. "You sat there for an extra five seconds just listening to the engine."

"I continue to impress you, don't I?" It was my turn to pause as she slightly rolled her eyes. "Play your cards right, and you might get to start it in a few years."

"Don't you mean drive it?" she stated, trying to correct me.

"Oh, hell no. You can start it and sit in it, but no woman has ever or will ever drive this car." I rubbed the dash. "It's against muscle car etiquette."

She coughed. "Did you say *muscle* car?"

I turned with daggers on the woman. "Be real careful, Patti. You may be going down a path you don't want to go."

"Get out, tough guy. You and your muscle car can have all the time you want tonight. I have a date with Swanny."

Jesus, she knew how to get under my skin.

We walked up to the door and without even knocking, the door swung open. "Detectives?"

"Expecting us?" I asked.

He frowned. "No, the noise from your car as it came up my driveway is not typical in this neighborhood. I thought I was being robbed."

Patti tried to prevent the instant laugh but could not completely.

I was going to speak but Dr. Hermann cut me off. "Listen, I believe I made it clear last time that I wouldn't be speaking to you without my lawyer. I provided you her number which I believe you already knew. Staci Lambda."

I ignored the comment. "Tell me about your relationship with Elise Gerstenberger." I paused then added, "You know, the wife of your coworker and one you've been texting constantly for the last three plus months. We were going to go straight to Alan and ask him about the texts, but I thought we would give you the courtesy to explain first."

Instantly his face changed. He looked around as if someone might be watching him. What the hell was that for, I thought. "Okay," he said reluctantly. "Come on in. I can talk about that, but only that."

We walked into a very spacious entryway. It was larger than my entire apartment. Elise's house was better, or at least larger, but this house was equally finished. There was marble and granite and plants, and a fountain, and...well, let's just say it was really nice.

"Is your wife home?" Patti asked, causing me to smile now. "We would like to speak to her as well."

He looked back to us as he led us to what I wanted to call a study, because I liked every house that had a study. But he called it an office. "My wife and I are separated, but why do I think you already knew that?"

We all took seats in the study. Yep, did it on my own. "Dr. Hermann, we have reason to believe you were in some sort of extramarital relationship with Dr. Elise Gerstenberger, and now since Elise has been severely injured in an attempted murder, you have vaulted up to the top of our suspect list. We are not here to arrest you at this time. We're simply gathering information to determine if you *should* be arrested. Do you understand?"

"I do understand, but I had nothing to do with her attack. Alan is a friend of mine. I couldn't do anything to harm his wife."

Patti leaned forward. "You don't think sleeping with her would harm your *friend*?"

"Goddamn it," he replied. "She came on to me. He was cheating on her and Elise found out about it. I thought she just wanted to get back at him, and who was I to argue? My wife had moved out, Elise was gorgeous, and by the way, I did not sleep with her."

"Why not?" I asked. It didn't have any bearing on the case but I felt like going there.

"Well, she kept having to leave right when we got close." He seemed slightly embarrassed.

"So she was using you," Patti said.

"What do you mean, using me?"

"She kept promising you the final prize, but pulled it each time. She didn't want to completely cheat, just get what she needed from you and go."

I smiled because I was sure of two things: I was right about Elise using this asshole, and two, I had just driven a stake through his ego because he never realized that was the case.

"That bitch," he said under his breath.

"Hey now," I replied. "That bitch is one of my best friends and she's hanging onto life by a thread, so keep your opinions to yourself. You're the one who tried to play Dr. Playboy." I have to admit, just thought of that title as I spoke, and I liked it. "So the question I need answered is, why *you*?"

"What do you mean, why me?" he asked.

"Let me rephrase it so it'll be easier for you to understand. Why you?"

"Fuck you, Detective," he replied. "I'm the CEO of a company. Alan had everything. He had a huge salary, a great job, and a successful wife. Her clinic was hugely successful and she held onto that medical examiner job as well to fill her time. She was doing what she liked and she was good at it. And she was a wizard at stocks. When she came up with the stock deferral plan for us, it was huge. I just can't believe Alan was against it."

My eyebrows raised, but I needed to play it like I already knew that. "Yeah, why was Alan against it? It seems like a no-brainer now."

I try not to ever show my surprise at a response, but that one tested me. Elise came up with the stock idea? I wondered what it had to do with everything?

"Yeah," he said slowly. "I'm sure Alan told you. At the swimming party at their house—we were all having drinks and we started talking about what the stock was going to do if the trials went well. It was right around bonus time and she knew what type of bonus we were all getting. She suggested the deferral. We just needed good results from the trials. If that happened, we all knew the stock would take off. And it did." He paused. "But we didn't just take her word for it. I checked with Julian and he said she was completely right. As long as we properly notified the SEC of our trades, it was completely legal."

"Why wasn't Alan on board?" I asked.

Hermann shook his head. "He said there might be some issues with the trials. If it failed, the stock would fall the same as it would increase with success in the other direction."

"Why did he think it was going to fail?" I asked.

Hermann suddenly appeared a little skittish. He stuttered briefly and then pushed through with his comment. "I don't think he did. I think he was just being cautious."

I was sure Patti saw the same thing I did. It made sense. The five leaders of the company doubled down on the results of the Emplex trials. Alan was against it because he's in manufacturing and knew things were not as perfect as they were being led to believe. The guy in charge of performing the trials was the late Randy Thompson and his boss was Joseph Reingold. But Thompson was part of the rabbit murders. Or was he?

I looked right at Hermann. "Tell me about Reingold and Thompson."

"I don't know what to say," Hermann began. "Both long-term employees at Abbunex. Both solid. Joe was on the executive team and Thompson oversaw the trials."

"So," I said, "if something was going south on the trials, they would know about it?"

"I suppose so," he replied. "But I am the CEO, I would know immediately as well."

Bingo, I thought. You did know. "And now they're both dead."

"They are," he replied.

"You just said the only thing that would make this deferral thing not work is if the trials went south, and the two people in charge of the trials are now dead. Don't you think that seems suspicious?"

"I don't know what to tell you, Detective. However, I do know that this conversation has gone much further than my possible indiscretions with Elise Gerstenberger. Therefore, I think we will end it and as I said before, let's take all future conversations through my attorney."

"No," I replied. "I think we will continue this downtown. "Darryn Hermann, we are placing you under arrest for conspiracy to commit murder. Please place your hands behind your back."

"Shit, Detective, you don't have anything on me. This is bull and you know it."

"When the shareholders find out you've been arrested, what do you think will happen to the stock price?" I asked.

"Exactly, Detective. Think of all the 401Ks. Think of all the people living paycheck to paycheck that have put money into this company. None of this will stick, and you can cause them to lose their savings. Take a step back and think about the impact of what you're doing. There's no evidence here that will find me guilty."

"You know, Dr. Hermann, when you say that, you make me feel like the evidence *is* there and you *are* guilty, I just haven't found it yet."

Patti was the putting her handcuffs on him as this conversation took place. She added, "You know, you could resign and name Julian Stover as your replacement. Oh, wait, he's dead too."

I did not expect it, but it was a nice shot. I looked right at him and said, "Perhaps you're the one who needs to step back and consider all that's going on. How many people have to die before you own up to all you've done?"

"Don't do this, O'Malley. There's nobody I can't get to."

"What did you say?" I asked, moving to stand right in front of him.

"You heard me," Hermann replied, staring directly at me. "I'll be out on bail in two hours. Then we'll see who made the right choice."

It was a different Darryn Hermann than I had seen previously. He was confident and cold. He was standing like he was untouchable. I was not sure where he got his confidence, but he definitely had it. Patti recognized it too. It was also clear that neither of us liked it. I know I didn't like it at all. A man with unlimited funds was absolutely dangerous.

We walked him to my car. "You're kidding me. You're taking me back to Chicago in that?"

"Make yourself comfortable, Dr. Hermann. The back seat is roomy." I smiled as I held his head down to avoid the top of the car.

"Call my lawyer, O'Malley."

•   •   •   •   •

On the drive back things started to fall in place for me. I usually call it "the jazz." Stolen from Hannibal on *The A-Team*, an 80's TV show starring of all people, Mr. T. "The jazz" is the thing only those solving crimes or lawyers can feel when the critical piece falls into place and they're about to solve—or for a lawyer, *win*—a case. I was on the jazz and this case was coming together. I still did not know who was guilty, but I did understand the crime. My only thought was to ask for help from a source nobody on my team would agree with. It was a risk, but I believed two things: this individual was innocent, and this individual was the only one who could prove my theory.

It took us close to an hour with traffic to reach the station. I had called ahead to Franky and he met us in front to take Hermann in. His lawyer was already there as well. I was not sure how she already knew, but she did. I had Patti join Franky and Dr. Hermann upstairs and told them I had a lead to follow up on. She could see in my eyes that I was jazzing, but with Hermann in the car, we were not free to talk.

As he walked away, Dr. Hermann looked back to me and said, "Watch your back, O'Malley. I can touch you where you never thought possible."

This guy went from a suspect having a mild affair with a coworker's wife to a South Chicago thud in twenty minutes. It was crazy. He was so rich and so entitled, he thought money could buy his way out of everything. I was going to make that belief false. I pulled up my phone and dialed a number. After a brief conversation, the plan was in motion. It would take most of the day. I needed Hermann to remain in our custody. I called Carter and filled him in. He said he would work his magic, and I believed him.

24 Hermann sat in the Royals Room. It was late in the day and he had been there for nearly ten hours. We could tell he was agitated. Actually, we could tell he was pissed.

Carter motioned to me to join him in his office. "What do you have, Tommy? Esson is telling me we can't hold him much longer. We have pulled every string."

Just then the district attorney himself burst through the doors. "Hey, O'Malley, good to see you. Esson, James Esson. How are you?"

Why does he always do that? He is not James Bond. He's not even a great district attorney. "I'm good, Jim, we were just talking about you."

"I bet you were," he replied. "Listen, I've done everything I can. That Lambda is one hundred percent in the right. We've delayed this longer than I ever thought possible. Do you have your evidence?"

"I just need a little more..." My comment stopped when I saw him exit the elevator and come through the glass door into our department. "Wait right here, gentlemen."

I left Carter's office and walked up to meet the man coming my direction. He looked tired. He looked completely beat, but he appeared beneath that demeanor to be pleased.

"Did you find it?" I asked.

"I found it," he replied.

"We don't have any time. Can you do what we talked about? If not, it's okay. I just think this is our best—"

"I can do it. Just put me in there."

I nodded. "Let's go into my boss's office and get everything set up."

We walked into Carter's office. I did brief introductions and so forth, and then headed to the Royals Room. As we approached the room, I saw Dr. Darryn Hermann sitting at the table with my old friend Staci Lambda right next to him.

"Somehow I knew when my client was stuck here against his will for so long, you would eventually show up."

"Hello, Staci," I said. "Mixed up any good potions or brew lately?"

"If I had, do you really think you'd still be walking upright?"

I smiled, but did not take it any further. Staci Lambda was an absolute pit bull. She had gotten some of the worst and most guilty criminals off in the past, with several of them being my cases. She and I were not, and would never be, friends. She was about everything I was not. I agreed everyone needed a lawyer, but she did not play by the rules. Her middle name should be loophole. It worked well for criminals, but not so much for those who put their life on the line every day to stop crime.

"This man showed up and wants to talk to your client. They work together. After they're done, we should have the paperwork and he can leave."

"Under no circumstance is my client talking to anyone you bring in," she stated flatly.

"Hey," I replied, "this is not part of the case. This guy came in pissed and wants to tear your client apart. I think it's better they speak here than on the street, but to be honest, I don't care where he kicks the shit out of him."

Hermann leaned over and whispered something to Ms. Lambda. I suppose it was something like, *I slept with his wife and then tried to have her killed.* Ms. Lambda then whispered back something like, *Are you sure you want to talk to him? I can keep the room clean if this is a better location for it.*

Hermann turned back to us. "I will talk to him, alone."

"No problem," I replied.

Staci smiled. "You agreed a little too quickly, Detective. I want the cameras off and the speaker turned down. I also want to be in the adjacent room while they're talking. I want to be sure nobody hears their conversation except these two. Are we clear?"

I smiled in return. "Mrs. Lambda, this meeting would not fall under attorney-client privilege, but to be honest, all I want to do is watch. I don't need to hear anything."

"Good, Officer O'Mallet, then we understand each other."

She always has to one-up me. I came up with the *Mrs.*, and she fires back with the *officer* and *mallet*. Well played, Senorita Lambda.

Not only did I turn off the camera, I walked over to the wall and unplugged it. The speaker box on the table that connected to the recording devices in the room was disconnected. Ms. Lambda seemed satisfied with the action. She grabbed my shoulder and turned me to face her. "No funny business, Detective."

"I don't have a sense of humor, Staci."

"Alan is not going to become some state's witness because he's looking to blame someone. My client has agreed to talk to him here only because he feels the environment is safer based on accusations Dr. Grove may have heard about my client's relationship with his wife."

"Understood, Ms. Lambda. Like I said, this is not part of the investigation. I just don't want to be called to a Barrington home tonight to solve another murder. Let's have these guys talk it out here first."

She seemed to accept that answer. As we walked out, I added, "By the way, Dr. Elise Gerstenberger died today. Your client is going down for conspiracy to commit murder. If we can tie him to the killer, he will be an accessory. Second degree murder at best."

To my surprise, she ignored the threat of additional charges and as we left the room, she placed her hand on my shoulder. "I'm sorry, Tommy. I know you were close to Dr. Gerstenberger. My condolences."

There was no hint of joking or insincerity. Maybe this pit viper had a heart after all. I almost felt bad about what was to take place—almost. Without another word, we walked into the adjoining room and although there was no sound as requested by Ms. Lambda, we could see the whole thing. Franky began making up words to go with the lip movements like a poorly dubbed Chinese kung fu movie.

"Oh yeah, well, I did steal the gold and put it in the wagon, but then it all vanished."

In a different fake Chinese voice, he continued, "Vanished, huh, well, I don't believe you. I think you ate it."

"Ate it. I could not eat all that gold. It was laced with hot pepper sauce."

"Pepper sauce, huh."

"Enough, Franky," I interrupted. "Funny, but enough."

It was clear we all agreed because everyone was smiling, even Ms. Lambda, but also nodded that he had taken it far enough.

In the room, Hermann and Grove were both leaning across the table.

"Did you sleep with my wife?" Alan Grove asked Hermann, his voice deep and carrying anger.

"Listen, Alan, it wasn't like that. I did not sleep with your wife. We talked. We met a few times outside of work. She was a great lady and she knew you were having an affair. She was looking for someone to talk to."

"What did she want to talk to you about, Darryn? Money? The bonus? The trials?"

"Listen, Alan, I'm not going to talk to you about those discussions. They don't matter anymore. We announce our results next week. Hell, we announce them in four days. We will all make more money than we know what to do with. Just sit tight. Let the announcement happen. Sell the stocks and let's put all this behind us."

"She's dead, Darryn. My wife is dead."

"Damn it, Alan. I am so sorry. This is so..."

"Shut the hell up, you asshole. Did you make the call to have her taken out? Did you kill my wife?"

"Wait a minute, Alan. What the hell are you saying? I loved your wife. I would never have..."

"You what? You loved my wife. She was my fucking wife, you asshole."

"No, no, no. Not in that way. I loved her the same way I love all my friends. Your wife was a brilliant lady. She's the one who pushed us into this deal. You didn't even want to do it, if you remember."

"Do you remember *why* I didn't want to do it?" Alan asked.

Hermann nodded. "Just like always, you were fearful that something would go wrong with the trials, but as predicted, the trials have gone through flawlessly."

"I checked the results, Darryn. I've been at the plant the whole day, going through every ounce of paperwork. The tissue samples we used for the phase three trials did not meet the requirements. Not only were they not random, they were all from the same person. The reason the results showed such a high success rate is the one sample that turned positive was used on all samples, hundreds of times. Joe thought he had cleaned the paperwork but my team backs up everything. He didn't know. How many people did you kill to have this info stay buried?"

He leaned in close to me. "You listen to me, you fucking Boy Scout. You're the only one with shit to lose here. Do you think we're fools? All six of us had the deferrals, and I have a ton of evidence that ties the orchestration of this to your wife. All the evidence points back to you and Elise. She came up with the idea. She set up the deferrals. She got Stover to buy-in and Reingold and Thompson to ensure the trials went well. As of right now, we all walk with a ton of money. The stock takes a temporary hit and I clean up the story in the quarterly report. Unfortunately, your wife is targeted for the blame but she's dead now. Nothing more can happen. You have everything to lose and nothing to gain."

"Why didn't you bring me into this in the first place?" Alan asked.

"I already said it, you asshole. You're a fucking Boy Scout. Sometimes you need to manipulate the rules if you want the big win. You weren't willing to do that."

"Did you sleep with my wife?" Alan asked again.

"No, Alan, I did not fuck your wife. You happy?"

"Would you have?"

Darryn sighed and waived his hand down at Alan as if he was dismissing him. "Are you asking if I wanted to bang your wife? Absolutely. I would have fucked her all night long, you goddamn asshole." He paused and placed his hands back on the table. "Now, you listen to me and you listen good. I did not want Elise killed. That was all Reed. He called the shots on the murders. He said your wife was a liability, as well as Reingold. He was going to cave to the police. I'm sorry Elise died, but she's our ticket out of this mess. I already talked to our attorney. She said if the evidence is as I promised, she can create doubt. So I ask you now: Do you want to spend the rest of your life in prison, or do you want to walk away free, keep your job, and live a wonderful life for the time you have left? Hell, you can retire and never work again if you want to."

"I could have done that for a long time, you asshole." Alan paused, paced a few steps, and then turned back to him. "What about Thompson? Why him? He was not part of the deferral."

He smiled. "Actually, he deferred on his own and we didn't know it until later. That was just a fluke. We put a contract out on him just like Stover. Thompson found the same thing you found—that we had been falsifying the test samples. He told Reingold at work and then later I heard him tell Stover at your party. However, if you can believe our luck, Thompson was killed by someone else. Freaking crazy. Then when Stover was hit, we thought all were clear. Then Elise started talking to the fucking police. I don't even know what she was doing. It was like she was playing both sides or something. Reingold got hinky and we had to make a few other tough decisions."

"Elise was innocent in all this. She was just getting back at me for my affair. She didn't even know about the fucking false test samples."

Hermann looked down. "Damn, we probably jumped the gun then. I never would have thought her the jealous type." He smiled. "It's too late for her now. I have everything set up. We transferred a bulk of money for the murders from accounts in your name. We can put that on her. You are in the clear. We are all in the clear. Everyone who can say anything to harm us is dead. I'm sorry Elise died, but she is your get-out-of-jail-free card. I suggest you take it."

Alan moved away from the table. "I am not going to jail, Darryn."

"That's my boy. I knew you'd see it my way."

"No, I mean I am not going to jail because I already cut a deal."

"What?" he asked.

"I told them everything. Everything I found at the plant. Everything I know about my affair and your affair. I told them everything. And, I am going to tell them everything you just told me."

"Well, that's all well and good, but they turned off their cameras and my attorney had an agreement with the police that you couldn't testify without corroborating evidence."

"How about a police wire? Is that evidence enough?" Alan unbuttoned his shirt to show a wire taped against his chest.

Staci Lambda's turned beet red and she turned and glared directly into my eyes. "You asshole."

I smiled at her and then turned back through the window in time to see Darryn Hermann swing at Alan. He ducked and returned the punch making contact directly below the nose. Blood exploded from his face and Hermann went down. Franky and Huston rushed into the room and grabbed both men, Franky taking Alan and pinning him to the wall, and Huston bending Hermann across the table, his nose spilling blood across the top. She pulled his arms behind his back and cuffed his hands. "Darryn Hermann, you have the right…"

I looked back to Staci Lambda. "We followed your rules, even though we didn't have to. Your client and those he works with are going away for a long time, but if you want to change that, we need the names of everyone involved and who committed the murders."

"Nobody's in prison yet, Detective O'Malley. I will get that recording and everything else thrown out. Your tactics are not legal, Detective, and that's all I have to say."

"Talk to your client, Staci. We don't want him. We want who he hired to commit murder. That is your client's best option, you know that as well as I do."

She turned to walk out and stopped just short of the door. "I'll talk to him."

•　　•　　•　　•　　•

I sat in Carter's office. With me were Karen, Franky, and Patti. We all looked toward Carter who was on the phone with James Esson, District Attorney James Esson. We could only hear one side of the conversation, but it appeared like it was going the direction we wanted it to. He hung up and looked at the three of us.

"Do we have a deal?" I asked.

"Yes, the DA has agreed to the deal for all three of them," Carter replied.

"Three?" I asked. "I thought it was just Anderson and Hermann?"

"Although he's dead, the records will show Reingold's part as well."

"What about Dr. Grove, Elise, and that pharmacist who also deferred his stock, Dennis Child?" Patti asked.

"Well, according to signed confessions from both Hermann and Anderson, Dennis Child had no idea about the tainted trials. He simply joined the deferment plan through overhearing some discussions. They actually liked having more people involved to take suspicion off of them."

"Makes sense," Patti replied. "But what about Dr. Grove? Did he know?"

"He was their fall guy from the start. Hermann was furious at Alan for starting the affair with Julian Stover's wife. He also had designs on Elise from the start, more than a year ago. In his world, if this ever went south, Dr. Grove would go down for it, which would end the affair with Wilma Stover as well as potentially end Alan and Elise's marriage."

"Are you saying that in the end neither Alan nor Elise did anything illegal?" I asked.

"Elise came right up to some really thin lines on these stock moves, but infidelity is still not a crime, at least from a legal point of view. From a spouse's view, it's probably a high crime." Carter pressed his lips together and nodded. "Someone should let Alan know."

"I can do that," I replied. "I wanted to go by and see him anyway."

"What about the killer?" Franky asked. "What do we know about the one he called Sandman?"

"As you know, we tracked the number he used and it led nowhere," Carter stated. "We don't have any ideas on how he pulled that off. We have both Anderson and Hermann in the Bulls Room now. Mrs. Lambda is there too and—"

I interrupted him. "There's no reason to use the Mrs. title now, she can't hear you."

He smiled. "I know, but I like to stay in practice." He paused a moment. "As I was saying, Ms. Lambda is with both of them. We wanted to interview them together to verify that their individual stories matched when they were in the same room. I had planned on you doing it." He motioned to me. "But if you're going to see Dr. Grove, then..."

I interrupted again. "Halterman can do it. She absolutely smoked the interview with Wilma Stover. She has a way with people."

Carter glanced to Patti and she nodded acceptance, a quick smile and glance to me in the process. "Very well," Carter said. "I'll watch from the observation room."

"Do we have any leads on the whereabouts of this Sandman?" I asked.

"I have every department checking, as well as GiST and the feds. There have been more than thirty-five cases across the United States with white sand left at the scene for no other reason tied to the murder. They were all assassinations and all with no evidence left behind."

"No evidence except the sand," I added.

"They have run the sand through every lab. It's always the same and always untraceable to anything that's been identified at this time." Carter stood and walked around his desk. "To cut to the chase, we have nothing on him. He could walk by us on the street and we wouldn't even know it."

"How many of these murders have been in Chicago?" I asked.

"Including Reingold and Stover, two."

"So, what brought him to Chicago?" I asked.

"And what connected Hermann and Anderson to him?" Patti added. "I'll pursue that when we talk."

Carter looked to Franky and then to me. "Tommy, I know you have the best relationship with Marco Filini, but he's always been a step ahead of us. He knows something about Sandman. Maybe a new run from different players would work. Franky and Huston, you think you can connect with Filini? He knows you." He motioned to Franky.

"I don't know, Sergeant. I know Filini, but he won't talk to me." Franky's voice was questioning.

"It won't hurt to give it a shot, Franky," I said. "It might send a message to Filini that he needs to work with us. The more police that get involved with him, the worse his business will get."

We talked a few more minutes, but we each had a job to do so we quickly went our separate ways. When I walked by the interrogation rooms on the way to my desk, I saw Anderson and Hermann sitting down with Ms. Lambda between them. Our eyes met, and we nodded. I think she smiled. She may not have, but I'm running with the idea that she did. I left the office and happened to reach the elevator at the same time as Franky and Huston.

"Flap Jaws later?" Franky asked.

"Sounds good," I replied.

"Any guidance for where to find Filini?" Franky asked.

"Millennium Park," I answered without hesitation.

"How the hell do you know that?" he asked.

"Because I left a message on his service asking him to meet me there," I replied as I exited the elevator and headed to my car.

Franky and Huston just stared at me. "You asshole. You have his number?"

"See you guys later," I replied.

•   •   •   •   •

Twenty minutes later I walked into the hospital room. "How are you doing, Alan?" I asked.

He raised a finger to his lips. "Ssshhh," he replied whispering. "She's sleeping."

"No, I'm not," Elise answered, her voice muffled through tubes.

"Hey there, Doc, you're awake?" I returned, my pleasure clearly showing in my smile.

She smiled broadly in return. "Alan told me everything you did for us." She coughed slightly. "You saved us."

"I wanted to let you both know that you've been cleared of all wrongdoing involving the stock case and the murders." I noticed they were holding hands. "That doesn't mean you're clear from everything you *are* guilty of, but it looks like you're working on that already."

Alan gripped her hand tighter. "We have talked a lot. We're both guilty of some really bad choices, me more than Elise, but we're both willing to work on it."

Speaking more to Elise, I asked, "Did he tell you all he did to get the confession from Dr. Hermann?"

She nodded. "I heard he had to pretend I was dead."

"We did," I replied.

"It was the hardest part of the plan, but it made me realize I never want to risk losing you again." Alan stared at Elise, and she looked up at him.

They may make it after all, I thought. It was either after that thought or during, I can't be sure, but the sound of the explosion across the city was very clear.

"What was that?" Alan asked.

"A bomb." I said running to the window. As I looked across the cityscape, I saw the smoke.

Elise had tried to sit up but Alan held her down. "Where is it?" she asked.

"Shit!" I stated.

"Where is it?" she asked again.

"The department." I dialed Halterman's phone as I ran out of the room. It went straight to voice mail.

•   •   •   •   •

"Well, here we are," Franky said. "What do we do, just wait?"

Huston pulled out her phone and pointed it at the giant, shiny egg. "Here," she said and pointed it upward. "Smile."

"Jesus, really?"

"Smile," she said more firmly.

Franky leaned in next to her and smiled. She clicked her phone and took the photo. "That will be one for the department calendar, if we had a department calendar," she said smiling.

Just then Franky's phone rang. The number was blocked. He slid his finger across the phone to answer. "Sullivan."

"Why are you here rather than O'Malley?" a male voice asked.

"Tommy got delayed," Franky replied. "He asked me to come. Who is this? I know Marco's voice and this is not him."

"If you want to speak to Marco Filini, you need to come to the address that just arrived to your phone."

"Okay, I wi—" The phone clicked off before Franky could reply. His phone immediately beeped that he had a text.

"That was odd," Franky said.

"Who was that?" Huston asked.

"I don't know, but it was someone who knew we were here to meet Marco Filini and knew it was supposed to be Tommy."

"And they knew your phone number?" she added. "What did they say?"

"He said if we want to see Marco Filini, we have to go to the address in my text message."

"Where is it?" she asked.

Franky clicked the address. "GPS says ten minutes by foot. It doesn't give me the location name."

"You want to walk it?"

"By the time we get back to the car, drive there, and find a place to park, it'll be more than ten minutes. We might as well just walk it."

They left Millennium Park together, walking back toward the city buildings. It was roughly eight total blocks zigzagging around corners. They came to a small storefront that was boarded up. "What do you want to do?" Karen asked.

"Let's break the boards down and see why Marco led us here."

They began pulling at the boards. The first one came off with a great deal of difficulty, but after the first, they were able to get their hands under the lip of the boards better and the next two came off much easier revealing the front door and two adjacent windows. The front door was locked and the building was dark through the small windows they had exposed.

Franky stepped back and kicked the door. He fell and landed on his butt. "Shit, sometimes I really wish Tommy was here." He stepped back up and kicked with all his force. The dead bolt burst and the door flung open. The smell was immediate.

"Jesus," stated Franky. "Call for backup, *now*."

Franky pulled out his flashlight and pointed it inside. It appeared to be an old mom-and-pop Chinese restaurant. There were some tables and a front counter where you would pay, and a swinging door to the back which gave the impression of leading into a kitchen.

His flashlight slowly spanned the eating area as Huston appeared at his side with gun drawn. "Backup is on the way. I called Carter directly."

The light stopped right when he saw it. "Oh my God," Huston stated.

"We have to clear the room," Franky replied.

"Are they dead?"

"We have to clear the room," Franky repeated. "I'll take the back, you clear the front."

"Okay," she replied.

Franky burst through the back swinging door. It was a kitchen in the back. The area was for the most part still intact. There was a walk-in cooler. Franky cleared it and checked the back. The rear exit was boarded up as well from the outside. He heard Karen holler, "Clear."

"Clear," Franky returned.

He turned back to the front of the building and met Karen in front of two hanging bodies. They had been beaten almost beyond recognition. There was a pile of sand beneath them in a pool of blood. Written in the sand was:

Boom, They are all dead.

"What's it mean?" she asked.

"I don't..." Franky stopped in mid-sentence. "What was that?" he said. "It sounded like a bomb."

Huston stepped outside and heard numerous sirens in the direction of the police station. "Franky, what happened?"

Franky was already on his phone. "Carter didn't pick up. It went straight to voice mail."

"We need to get back there," Huston said.

"We have to stay here," Franky replied. "We have our own crime scene that most likely is related to whatever just happened." He turned to her. "Stay on your phone. Call anyone you can get. I'm going to call Tommy."

•　•　•　•　•　•

"Did you hear it, Franky?" I asked when I saw Franky's name on my caller ID.

"We did. What happened?" Franky asked.

"I don't know. I'm on my way back to my car. I'm at the hospital so I am at least fifteen minutes away. Where are you?"

"We're at an abandoned and boarded-up Chinese restaurant about eight blocks from Millennium Park."

"What are you doing there?" I asked.

"Hey, Tommy, I need to tell you something." His voice was slow and weak.

"What is it, Franky?"

"We have two bodies here. They were tortured. Tommy, it's real bad. It's Marco and the guy from the dojo, Andre. I called for medical but I don't think they're alive. The explosion happened before I could check."

"Jesus," I said. "Marco? Who the hell could get to Marco?"

"There's more, Tommy. Written in the sand by the bodies was a statement."

"What did it say?" I asked as I fired up the Camaro.

"Boom, they are all dead," he replied.

"What is going on, Franky?" I asked.

"I don't know, partner. Karen and I, we can't get ahold of anyone."

My phone beeped. "Franky, I have a call from Carter coming in."

"Take it, and let me know—" He was cut off.

"Carter, what happened?" I said as I answered the phone.

There was a great deal of noise in the background—sirens, voices, horns. Carter's voice was loud, like he was fighting to speak over the commotion. "Tommy, it's bad. Get back here, Tommy, as soon as you can."

"I'm on my way, Sergeant," I answered. "What happened?"

"They're all gone, Tommy. The floor blew up. There was a bomb."

"What bomb, Sergeant? What floor?"

Carter's voice calmed slightly. "*Our* floor, Tommy. There was a bomb in the interrogation room. We can't tell the extent of the damage. I had just gotten the call from Huston so I was headed out. I was in the parking lot when it went off. I can only see from the outside. There's a huge hole in the wall where the Bulls Room used to be. Chicago Fire are in looking for survivors."

Just then I connected the dots. "What about Patti?" I asked.

There was a long silence. "I don't know, Tommy. She was in the room with them when I left."

My heart sank. I placed the police light on top of my car and floored the gas. "Find out anything you can. I'll be there in ten minutes." I clicked my phone off. I told Franky I would call him back, but I needed a few minutes. I know he would want to know, but I couldn't talk right now. She had to be okay. It couldn't be like Dixon. I couldn't lose another partner. I stopped my own train of thought when I realized this had nothing to do with Dixon. I could not lose Patti.

I was a few blocks away when I called Franky and filled him in. His words were kind, but I knew that he knew I was scared. I let him know he needed to just hold that crime scene. The clue to finding Sandman may be at that scene. He was a narcissist that wanted everyone to know who he was. Franky agreed. Franky did say one piece of critical information. Andre and Filini were both alive, but he didn't think they would make it. They had been partially skinned alive but medical was there now and working on them.

I pulled down the street of the station and saw all the emergency vehicles. Multiple ambulances and fire trucks. One truck had a ladder reaching up to the fourth floor where a large hole now appeared in the side of our building. Some of the fifth floor had collapsed above where the bomb went off, but the two floors above it seemed to be stable.

Carter was by one of the trucks. I showed my badge and my car was waved through. Carter saw me approach. He met me at my car. "I don't know anything, Tommy. They pulled one body down. It was Hermann. They said there were at least two more dead for sure."

Quickly in my head I counted people. Hermann, Anderson, Lambda, and Halterman, not to mention other detectives that may have been in the area. At least three total dead. "I'm going up."

"They won't let you, Tommy." He paused. "*I* won't let you, Tommy."

"Try and stop me, Sergeant."

"*Tommy*," he shouted.

I was already headed to the building when two officers grabbed me. "You can't go in, Tommy," the larger of the two said. "They have all the help they need up there."

"My partner is up there, Cabot. I'm going in, whether you draw a gun on me or not."

The smaller officer looked to the one who had spoken. They had a brief conversation with their eyes and then Cabot released my arm. "Go on, Tommy, but don't get hurt."

I didn't bother to respond and simply burst through the doors. I knew my way through this building in my sleep, which was good because they had cut all power to avoid electrical fires. The elevator was also shut down so I ran straight to the stairwell. There were a handful of rescue personnel in the lobby area. They did not pay any heed to me and assumed I was cleared to be there. I crashed through the door to the stairwell and proceeded running up the flights. I was skipping one to two steps at a time. I was in training shape, but I was no runner. Today, however, I didn't feel a thing. The adrenaline was pushing me forward.

I busted through the fourth floor stairwell door and instantly felt the cool air from the outside. I could not believe what I walked into. The office area was gone. Our desk area, the walls, everything was wiped away. There was nothing but debris.

There were several emergency teams in place. A helicopter could be heard above the building. The noise from the street and the emergency crews were deafening. One fireman came over to me and had to shout to be heard over the noise. "Who are you? Nobody but essential personnel on this floor."

"I'm Detective O'Malley. I was approved to come up."

"Not approved by me, Detective, which means you were not approved," he replied.

Just then another man shouted, "I have a body over here."

Both our eyes swung over to the area of the voice. He swung back to me. "You need to get out of here."

"I'm not leaving, sir," I stated firmly.

"I don't have time for this. Stay out of our way."

The fireman ran toward where his man had called. I followed. He pushed through a little debris to reach his man. When we got there, I saw a fireman leaning over a body. Who was it, I thought? Was it a woman? The fireman looked up to the one who had stopped me when I entered and shook his head negatively. As he did so, he leaned back and I saw the dead female body of Ms. Staci Lambda. I lowered my head.

Another voice hollered, "I have someone over here. They're alive."

I ran to where the voice came from, actually ahead of the fireman in charge. There she was, my partner.

"I got a pulse," the fireman hollered. "Get me the medics."

The medical team came over immediately. They had oxygen on her in seconds and were checking her vitals. They started shouting out orders and medical information, and I couldn't tell you anything that was said. Within ten minutes, she was being transported out of the area. They moved her to the far stairwell. It was wider and there were emergency teams ready to transport her down the stairs. It was a tricky process that they performed flawlessly. Within a few minutes, she was in the back of an ambulance and headed to the hospital.

Carter stopped me on the way to my car. "What do you want to do, Tommy?"

"I want to find Sandman and kill him, Sergeant," I replied.

"I do too, Tommy, but now you're needed at the hospital. I'll call you when we find out anything."

I was in my car and headed to the hospital when my phone rang. I looked at the screen and saw the name. I thought about not answering but I knew he'd keep calling until he heard for sure. "Hey, Zimm," I said.

"I just heard about Chicago. All states and government offices are being notified. We are rolling into lockdown. I'm thrilled you answered."

"It's pretty bad here, Zimm. I'm on the way to the hospital now."

"Are you injured?" he asked immediately.

"No, but my partner is. She was in the building when the bomb went off." I paused and then anticipating his next question said, "I don't know, but she's pretty beaten up."

"What do you need from me?" he asked.

I almost said nothing, but then I thought about something. "I need everything you can dig up on a murderer known as Sandman. He's behind this. I know he is."

"I can do that," he replied. "But how do you know he's behind it?"

"Because there was sand all over the place."

•   •   •   •   •

I arrived at the hospital right behind the ambulance. They pulled Patti out of the back end and a team from the hospital met them at the door. They were shouting out vitals and other information. I could not hear anything specific other than something about her lungs. I followed her in but I was immediately stopped at the double doors leading into surgery. I tried to break through but it was made clear to me that I would not be allowed in. I pushed the security guard away and reluctantly walked back toward the entryway.

As I arrived there, my phone rang. I knew it was Franky calling to check on me and my partner. I knew he was worried. I looked down to my phone, and saw the screen. Blocked call? Who the hell was this?

"O'Malley."

"Detective O'Malley," the voice said in return. "Or should I call you Tommy, like everyone else does?"

"You can call me anything you like if you tell me who the hell this is," I answered.

"You can call me Sandman." There was a long silence on the phone. "Yes," the voice said, "now I have your attention."

I walked toward the outside electronic doors where they had just brought my partner in. "You have my attention, Sandman. Why are you calling?"

"How's your partner?"

"Fuck you, you bastard. I'll rip your goddamn arms off when I—"

"How's your partner?" he asked again. "She wasn't supposed to be there. It was supposed to be you."

"It should have been me," I replied more softly.

"Ah, always the martyr. Don't worry, it will be you at some point. I don't like loose ends. I don't like people looking for me."

"I won't be looking for you. I'm going to find you."

"I also wanted to let you know that I was sorry for what I had to do to Filini. I know you liked him. It was just business." Sandman's voice was cold and low. It lacked emotion. He sounded white, in his forties, and from the Midwest. I was trying to identify all I could and still remain focused on the words.

"Why are you calling me, Sandman?" I asked.

"Good, no more name-calling and emotion. I hate that," he replied. "I wanted to let you know I am leaving Chicago for a while. Things are getting too hot here for me. I also wanted to let you know if I ever think you're following me, I will kill you and everyone you love. I will start with Alex and Mallory, or maybe your father in Aldersgate Village, or maybe just Patricia Halterman, if she lives." He paused and then right before I could speak, he added, "Or maybe I will shoot you right now, just inside the doors at the hospital in that blue button-up shirt and tie. I could do it to you, right now."

I did not move. "Maybe you should," I replied.

And the phone went dead.

About the Author

Kenneth S. Kappelmann starting writing in 1991 focusing on his first love of fantasy. The success of his *Hidden Magic Trilogy*, starting with *The Return of the Dragons*, built the foundation for allowing him to grow his writing into his true love, twisted murder mysteries and crime dramas. The humor, sarcasm, and nail-biting mystery carried in the award-winning *Tomas O'Malley* series has captured readers of all ages with more books to come with *Never Been in the Sand* being the third book in the series.

Note from the Author

Word-of-mouth is crucial for any author to succeed. If you enjoyed *Never Been in the Sand*, please leave a review online—anywhere you are able. Even if it's just a sentence or two. It would make all the difference and would be very much appreciated.

Thanks!
Kenneth

Thank you so much for reading one of our **Crime Fiction** novels. If you enjoyed the experience, please check out our recommended title for your next great read!

Never Been Found by Kenneth S. Kappelmann

"This was a great murder mystery." –*Smashbomb*

View other Black Rose Writing titles at www.blackrosewriting.com/books and use promo code **PRINT** to receive a **20% discount** when purchasing.